MIND STORM

MIND STORM

K. M. Ruiz

THOMAS DUNNE BOOKS
ST. MARTIN'S PRESS
NEW YORK

THOMAS DUNNE BOOKS.
An imprint of St. Martin's Press.

MIND STORM. Copyright © 2011 by Katrina M. Ruiz. All rights reserved. Printed in the United States of America. For information, address St. Martin's Press, 175 Fifth Avenue, New York, N.Y. 10010.

www.thomasdunnebooks.com
www.stmartins.com

Book design by Jonathan Bennett

Library of Congress Cataloging-in-Publication Data

Ruiz, K. M.
   Mind storm / K.M. Ruiz. — 1st ed.
       p. cm.
   ISBN 978-0-312-67317-8
   1. End of the world—Fiction.   2. Psychic ability—Fiction.   I. Title.
   PS3618.U54M56 2011
   813'.6—dc22

                                                          2010054459

First Edition: May 2011

10   9   8   7   6   5   4   3   2   1

To my father, Michael Ruiz, for everything. And my mother,

Barbara Ruiz, for showing me what real strength is.

[ACKNOWLEDGMENTS]

It takes a lot of time and effort to bring a book to life. A good chunk of that effort belongs to other people. First and foremost, I want to thank my dad, who told me to go play outside as a kid, but never told me to stop writing. Thanks in a huge, huge part goes to my fabulously awesome agent, Jason Yarn, for loving this story as much as I do and taking a chance on me. Big shout-out and thanks to my editor, Brendan Deneen, for wanting this story and helping me to make it so much better.

Thanks to Kelly Weingart for being so patient and supportive. I promised you this story for years and I finally got it right. Thanks to Trudy North for being the best first-reader one could ask for and a really awesome friend. All your help got me here and I couldn't have made it without your lovely and brutal honesty throughout this entire process. Thanks to David Eccles and Tawnie Thiessen for humoring me and answering all my questions. Writing feels like its own different world and sometimes that really is the case. Thanks in large part to Cathy Yu, Demi Ruiz, Noël Sakievich, Melissa Taylor-Salvador, J. P. Salvador, and Daniel Martinez for putting up with my insane habits over the years. I love you guys! If there are any mistakes left in this book, they are (rightfully) my own.

PART ONE
CONTACT

SESSION DATE: 2128.04.19

LOCATION: Institute of Psionics Research

CLEARANCE ID: Dr. Amy Bennett

SUBJECT: 2581

FILE NUMBER: 346

"Lucas wants to know if they're worth it," the girl says as she colors outside the lines. "If what's left of humanity is worth the future I can see."

"And are they?" the woman who sits across the table from her asks, both of them centered in the camera. The room they are in is sterile and white, no color anywhere except on the yellow dress the child wears and the crayons she wields so carelessly.

"He wants the truth, but I don't even really know what that means anymore." The girl looks up and smiles at the doctor, the charm in her tiny child's face an almost alien expression beneath the faint exhaustion. "I'm not lying, Doctor."

The doctor marks something on her notes, shoulders tense. The girl, hooked to half a dozen machines by way of wires and electrodes attached to her skull, spine, arms, and hands, only hums. She is young, four years old, and seems content to stay where she is.

"*Who,* exactly, is this Lucas you are talking about, Aisling?"

"You don't know him," she says, discarding one crayon for another. "He's not born yet."

The EEG and supporting machines spike almost off the grid, the readings nothing like the human baseline they are layered over. The doctor's expression becomes strained.

"Aisling, can you tell me when the war will end?"

"If I tell you, it'll only make things worse." She bites her lip, brow furrowed in concentration as she turns her head, bleached-out violet eyes staring right into the camera. "We're psions. You have to remember that, okay? We can't survive a human lifetime when we die so young. I don't really want to anyway."

3

[ONE]

Ali passengers, please remain seated. For your safety, the protective shutters will be coming down as we pass through Las Vegas. Vidfeed will be available on the train's public stream. All passengers, please remain seated."

The computer repeated its modulated tones over a static-filled comm system. Threnody Corwin cracked open one blue eye and watched as the thick protective shutters slid down the graffiti-covered windows on the outside of the maglev train, locking into place with the soft squeal of hydraulics. The heavy seal blocked out sunlight, her view of the dry, dead land beyond the windows, and the lingering radiation that still covered most of the country.

"Don't even think about opening that vidfeed," her partner said from the seat beside her. "If you've seen one deadzone, you've seen them all, and I want to sleep."

"Then sleep," Threnody said around a yawn. She stretched in the thinly padded seat and shoved straight black hair out of her eyes. In her mid to late twenties, she was built long-legged and lean, which made contorting herself to fit inside the limited travel space difficult. "We've got time before we reach California."

Quinton Martinez merely grunted, brown eyes narrowed down to slits as he scratched at the stubble on his chin. He wore the same type of outfit as Threnody, a black-on-black battle dress uniform, and boots that had walked across three continents. Taller than Threnody, with muscles corded thickly against his bones, Quinton's skin was a deep brown,

5

scarred lightly over the knuckles and the back of his hands from the fire he could control as a Class III pyrokinetic.

Fire wasn't something he could create, not without external help. That's what the thin, malleable biotubes containing compressed natural gas were for. The biotubes were grafted along the metacarpal bones in his hands, radiating up his forearms where skin and muscle biomodifications held them in place. The skin at the tip of each middle finger and thumb had been replaced with razor-thin pieces of metal. Quinton had given up on keeping track of how many times he'd lost his hands and arms to fire. He'd seen the inside of a biotank for regeneration too many times over the years for it to matter anymore.

"The Rockies, then down to the Slums of the Angels," Quinton said, thinking of all that was really left of civilization on the West Coast since the bombs fell, a mirror for the rest of the world. "Chasing a blip on the grid into a goddamn warzone."

Threnody rubbed at her forehead with careful fingers, wishing her skin didn't feel so new. "You didn't have to come, Quin. You're salvageable, according to the psi surgeons. They would have transferred you if you asked."

"And like a good dog I should have asked, right?" The smile Quinton gave her was thin and hard with anger. "You're my partner, Thren. The only family I've got. I go where you go. End of story."

Two failed missions back-to-back: Madrid, and then later Johannesburg, where she had opted to let unregistered humans and potential psions live instead of killing them in the face of threats from higher-Classed enemy psions. Their current mission was simply punishment for past failures.

The Strykers Syndicate contracted out enslaved psion soldiers for high-risk jobs. Death was a known and accepted by-product of those contracts, and the dead needed to be replaced for the company to turn a profit. Those children with psion potential she let go were resources she had no right to touch or lose. Insubordination had only gotten them a stint in medical and a black mark on their records. Quinton could have argued his way out of it. She was the one in charge, after all; it had been her decision, not his. Except they were partners, now and always, and he'd opted to come with her once again. One last mission to prove her loyalty. One last mission to prove she deserved to live.

The government owned her, as they owned every psion. Her independence, according to the ruling World Court, had become a problem.

Never could learn to come to fucking heel, Threnody thought bitterly as she reached over and touched a sensor on the side panel of her seat.

A hologrid snapped into existence before her, projected through the air from overhead, the logo for TransAmerica MagLev Inc. spinning slowly before blending seamlessly into the welcome menu. She dragged her finger over the public-stream option and was treated to a view of the stark, polluted ruins of a lost American city. Just a skeleton of a time abandoned generations ago, of a world no one even remembered. The ruins were similar to all the ones in the many deadzones they had been pushing through since departing from what was left of Buffalo, New York.

She reached out to shift the feed to something different. Only this time, when her fingers touched the hologrid, the data flickered, wavered into colored lines, then sizzled into sparks that shocked her. Whatever pain or irritation Threnody experienced, it was drowned out by the frustration she felt at her lack of control. It wasn't something she could afford.

Quinton yanked her hand away before anyone noticed, reaching over to press the control screen on her seat's arm panel that would shut down the hologrid.

"Don't," he said, mouth pressed close to her ear. "You're not ready. Johannesburg was a mistake and you're still recovering. They shouldn't have discharged you from medical."

Threnody rubbed her fingers against her knee, the shock of the charge nothing more than a tingle beneath her nails when it shouldn't have been even that, not for a Class III electrokinetic. Her power, like that of all electrokinetics, was limited to conduits that she could touch and feed. An involuntary reaction to a machine simply meant Quinton was right. That didn't change a damn thing.

"Can't fight orders, Quin."

"Then we do what we can to work around them. Why do you think I registered our route via train instead of an air shuttle?"

She gave him a sharp look. "Did you even look at shuttles to get us out here?"

"I looked. They didn't interest me." Quinton settled back in his seat, closing his eyes against the dim interior lights of the train. "Go to sleep, Thren. We won't get much of it once we hit the West Coast."

She knew that. She knew the details of this mission better than he did. That didn't make working through it any easier, not when they had to travel across radiation-tainted land to a state that was still being fought over by the government and drug cartels beneath the glitz of seedy glamour. The tension wasn't over the gold California had once been known for—most of the Sierra Nevada had been strip-mined bare decades before the first bomb dropped—but over the government-owned and government-protected towers of SkyFarms Inc. that filled the southern part of the Central Valley. The farming and agricultural company that kept the world fed with its heavily shielded towers of limited produce and animal pens would always be worth dying for.

The world was a different place ever since the first bomb fell in 2124 somewhere in the old Middle East, beginning the worldwide nuclear genocide known as the Border Wars. Five years of bombing hell across nearly all the continents had practically annihilated the human race. The fallout from that time still lingered in a toxic environment, still showed up too many generations later as genetic mutations that caused physical deformities and incurable disease. Since 2129 when the Border Wars finally ended, people hadn't been living, they'd only been surviving.

What cities had managed to survive the Border Wars and rebuild themselves into some semblance of society again were where most of the world's population remained. Linked by way of maglev tracks built as a way to jump-start a broken global economy, or government-built air shuttles designated for the educated rich, countries remade their borders accordingly around deadzones. Travel wasn't promoted or always permitted, but humanity would never give up the urge to explore.

Two hours later the train finally pulled free of the Central Valley, wending its way toward their destination in Southern California. Sunlight burned into Threnody's eyes, burned through sleep, as the protective seal finally lifted well beyond the old state line.

Quinton was already awake, even if his eyes were closed. He felt different to her fine-tuned senses when he was conscious. She knew better than he did the electric song his nerves sang at any given hour. Every person gave off an individual charge. Like the mind, it was as unique as a person's DNA, and DNA was the only thing they had to stand on out here in a place ruled more by street law than judicial opinion. Psion power would always have an edge over guns.

"Time?" Threnody asked.

"Thirty-five and counting."

She nodded, pushed herself up, and made sure her single bag was still stowed securely beneath her seat. They had a forward row in a middle car with enough space to breathe in, but that was about it. Anyone with enough credit to mean anything traveled by air shuttle, and they definitely didn't travel to the West Coast of the United States of America. Elite society held stock and coveted living space in pockets down the East Coast of Canada and America or in Western Europe. The only things left in Australia were deserts and firestorms. What remained of South America was overrun by drug cartels, and most of Asia had turned into a toxic graveyard generations ago, its barrenness rivaled only by the desert Africa had become.

Threnody could feel the maglev train begin to decrease its speed from 320 kilometers an hour to a full stop when they finally pulled into the only platform still servicing the outer edges of the Slums of the Angels. Ceiling lights blinked their arrival as the doors slid open with a crack that shook every car. Quinton helped Threnody to her feet and made a path for them through the Spanish-speaking crowds of people that were pitching themselves off the train, breathing smoggy air for the first time in days. The pollution stung the back of her throat, made her eyes water. What sky they could still see above through the ruins was pale gray from polluted clouds, the wind gritty, and the heat was like a weight against her skin.

It didn't compare to the presence that slid into her mind as they headed for the exit stairwell.

Down on the street, a cautious mental voice with a heavy Scottish accent said. *We've been waiting awhile already. Guess HQ wasn't lying about you guys coming out here. You going to be able to handle this mission?*

Shouldn't that be my question? Threnody asked as Kerr MacDougal pulled her and Quinton into a psi link with his telepathy.

I'm not the one who spent half a month in medical getting their nervous system put back together.

I'm not the one whose shields are slipping.

Touché.

I'm walking. That tell you anything?

That you're a stubborn bitch and your file doesn't do you justice. Over here.

They had reached the ground below the platform, and her gaze zeroed in on two men standing at the taxi zone with heavy-duty bags at their feet. Threnody schooled her expression into one of polite neutrality and swallowed her pride as they approached the team they were assigned to work with. From the top of the list to the very bottom. From being the best to being a problem. It was a strange feeling to know that the standing she and Quinton had fought so hard to attain and keep in the Strykers Syndicate could so easily be wiped away. People only got assigned partnership with this team as punishment. No one liked working with dysfunctional psions, and that's all these two would ever be.

Kerr was a head taller than she was, whipcord thin, and not carrying the weight he should have with his height. The closer they got, the darker the circles beneath Kerr's teal-colored eyes became. His partner, Jason Garret, stood silently beside him, chewing on the filter of a half-smoked cigarette.

Kerr was the Strykers Syndicate's only Class II telepath, with mental shields that never stayed up. Kerr should have been able to make his own, but even the best geneticists hadn't been able to categorize all the quirks that showed up in the DNA and RNA of psions on the human accelerated regions of the human genome. His shields were unstable and his telepathy put him at risk of losing his mind in a maelstrom of the world's thoughts. Riding along behind someone else's shields was a stopgap procedure. It worked for now, but nobody back at headquarters was sure how many years he had left until it stopped.

Jason was Kerr's patch, his temporary fix, a Class V telekinetic that could teleport, making him a dual psion with average reach and strength. He was also the only Stryker in their entire ranks—their entire history— with intact natal shields that had never fallen. Psychically bonded at a young age by a psi surgeon telepath, Jason's shields were Kerr's only saving grace when Kerr's own shields would fail him. The two weren't lovers, despite the bond. They weren't compatible that way. They considered each other family, and while Jason preferred men, Kerr didn't like anyone.

"Threnody," Jason said with a sharp smile, hazel eyes cool in their assessment of her, but warmer when they focused on her partner. "Quinton. Never thought we'd ever get the pleasure of working with you two."

"Apparently you're not doing as good a job as you should be and they sent us to sort you out," Quinton replied with a steady look. "It's amazing you haven't been terminated after so many failures."

Jason only shrugged as if he'd heard that accusation many times before. Threnody resisted the urge to touch the back of her neck where all psions got a neurotracker grafted to their cranial nerves and brain stem the moment they were brought to the Strykers Syndicate. Government control wasn't just lip service, and removing that collar was a death sentence.

"The Strykers need me," Kerr said quietly. "Which means they need Jason. The fact that you two, their favorites, have fallen this far means that they don't need *you*. Not as badly. Maybe you should think about that."

Quinton looked as if he wanted to argue, but Threnody caught his eye and shook her head. "We're all on the same side. We have a job to do and a target to find. If we fail this time, then we'll all be terminated," she reminded them. "Let's just get where we need to be."

Jason stepped away to hail a taxi, the car pulling away from a long line of other service vehicles as he fed credit chips into the pay meter. Down here, credit chips were hacked to be untraceable, and they were all anyone used to purchase things, from transportation to pleasure to murder.

They climbed into the taxi and got settled, bags at their feet and silence among them. Jason told the driver where to go in Spanish. It took an hour to get to their destination, driving down damaged streets in a car that had long ago ruined its shock system. They felt every hole the patched tires rode over in the streets that led to an old expressway, the main artery into the wreckage that existed in the shadows of the environmentally sealed city towers that made up Los Angeles. It was the only part of the city that the American military had managed to save during the Border Wars.

Cars outnumbered the air shuttles that cast quick shadows from above. Threnody stared at the city towers, built high with neon bright adverts scrolling down their sides, until she couldn't see them anymore as they drove into the murky depths of the Slums of the Angels.

Like most of the world, the West Coast of America had once been a thriving, living place. That was before the Border Wars. That was before the deadly radiation and acid storms that filtered over all the continents, before the earthquake of 2167 that devastated the surviving population of the three coastal western states of America. The only pocket of civilization in the West, settled between large swaths of deadzones, to survive the 2167 quake was Los Angeles, but it lost half a dozen city towers when the land shook itself to pieces. The majority of the ruins were never dealt with, couldn't be dealt with. They simply became something different.

What replaced the infamy of Los Angeles and the tech-driven north were South American drug cartels running through the Latin Corridor and Mexico, eager to cater to those who didn't care if their addictions damaged their DNA. The Slums of the Angels became a hole in the world that people with no identities fell into, where a person could buy and sell anything, but the only way out was by death or sheer, mind-boggling luck.

Or power.

Something that the four Strykers had plenty of.

The taxi driver dropped them off a good fifteen kilometers into the Slums, at a corner braced by a building written over with warring gang signs. He seemed glad to leave them behind.

Where are we? Threnody asked as they stood on the crumbling sidewalk.

We need a cover to get us deeper into the Slums, Kerr replied. *Jason and I had orders to build one. This is it what we were able to buy.*

A cartel soldier came out of the building and into the grimy sunlight. He spat between them, military-grade gun held steady in his hands as three more soldiers came out behind him, fanning out on the sidewalk. Their presence had the few people scattered around the street ducking out of sight.

"Ident," he snapped.

Jason spread his hands and offered up a slick smile. "Carlos, you know it's us. We paid good money to get clearance from you."

"*Ident.* You don't get no special treatment just because you got credit."

Jason shrugged and stepped forward, body loose and expression bored as a soldier came close enough to scan his eyes. The portable bioscanner fit neatly in the soldier's hand. The infrared light protruding from the tip scanned the identity of the iris peels Jason had been wearing since he and Kerr were assigned this mission weeks ago.

"Clear," the man said in heavily accented English as he stepped back.

"You got our way in?" Jason demanded.

"I got it." Carlos's gaze swept over the group, skipping over the pair he knew, lingering a little on Quinton, before finally settling on Threnody. His mouth curved into a leer. "She's new. *La gringa* looking for some fun?"

They have orders to kill us, Kerr said through the psi link.

Guess we didn't pay up to scale, Jason said.

Threnody smiled invitingly at the soldier. "Come a little closer and find out."

The soldier's buddies whistled sharply at him as Carlos approached her. Rubbing at his chin, Carlos let his gaze drift up and down her body in an assessing manner, mouth curling up in a hard smile when it became apparent that none of the men with her were going to interfere.

"You'd make more money lying on your back than playing at being a man," Carlos said with another leer as he reached out and squeezed her left breast hard.

"Whores don't keep the money they make down here," Threnody said coolly as she grabbed his wrist and tapped into the bioelectricity that the human body ran on.

Threnody's own nerves sparked as electricity exploded out of her and into him, their bare skin the bridge she needed to work with. Her power coursed through the soldier's body faster than his brain could process and he was dead before he hit the ground; skin blackened, burned and cracked.

Before any of the other three humans could react, Kerr was in their minds and burning them out. A telepathic strike that hard, backed by his phenomenal Class II strength, had them dead in seconds. Humans didn't have the genetic capability to defend against what a psion could do. They weren't built that way. Their minds winked out on the mental grid, that vast psychic plane full of a world's thoughts that all 'path-oriented psions functioned on. Tied into Kerr's mind through the psi link, Threnody could feel through his power the holes those deaths left behind on the mental grid.

"Get our clearance," Threnody ordered as she peeled the dead man's charred skin off her bare fingers.

Quinton rifled through the pockets of the dead for the passes they had paid for. Kerr's telepathy could wipe a person's mind clean of their presence, but he couldn't touch machines, and all checkpoints down in the Slums had extensive security. Quinton found what they needed on the second body, pulling out four thin, transparent pass cards.

"Blanks," he said. "We need someone to program them."

Jason nodded. "Give them to me."

Quinton tossed the pass cards to Jason, who caught them with his telekinesis. Jason dug out a slim datapad from his pocket and jacked the first pass card into the portable computer. He was one of the best hackers in their ranks, one of the reasons why he and Kerr hadn't been terminated yet. The faint gleam in Jason's eyes told Threnody his implanted inspecs were running through the data, connected to it by a wire plugged into the neuroport on his left wrist, as he hacked his way through the pass key's minimal defenses.

Threnody looked at Kerr. "Are we clear?"

The telepath cocked his head to the side, eyes focused on some distant place. "Building is empty inside. Got human peripherals getting curious. I'll take care of them."

"Do it."

She bent down, snagged the collar of the nearest dead soldier, and hauled the body into the dirty office. Kerr followed her lead, pulling one dead man by the arm while Quinton dealt with the last two.

Inside, against the far wall, was a terminal with a single wide vidscreen displaying dozens of security feeds. Threnody glanced at the images as she approached the control console and took a seat in the abandoned chair. She was a brilliant tactician, but a piss-poor hacker. Her body couldn't take most of the biomodifications that a quarter of the remaining population had grafted to their nervous system. All the delicate biowiring that was required to directly uplink with various computer systems wasn't compatible with her body. That didn't mean she was useless.

"Nice of them to leave it accessible," Threnody said as she dragged her fingers over the controls and started pulling up command windows. "Some of it, at least."

Quinton peered over her shoulder. "You going to fry it?"

"Soon as Jason wipes us from the system."

It took her half a minute to find the home feed that showcased the corner right outside the office. She pulled up the log for the past hour, getting all the basic information ready for Jason to parse and do what he did best, outside of flinging things around with his mind. Three minutes later he was there, taking over her spot. He jacked into the system through two neuroports and hacked into the feed, hiding the murders they had committed by wiping the system clean.

"Not even going to bother with a loop. Their server farm is on-site, so the damage needs to go deep, Threnody," Jason said as he pried the wires out of his arms when he finished. "It's all yours."

He shoved the chair back and got out of the way. Threnody leaned over and pressed a hand to the console of the terminal. She took a deep breath, steadied herself for the burn, and pushed her power into the electric heart of the system before her. Not the same as burning it through a human body, but electricity was electricity, and enough of a surge could kill anything, especially a machine.

The system crashed. Circuits melted to slag and the vidscreen went dark. Threnody pulled her hand away and clenched her fingers down tight against the heat that tingled across her palm.

"Are you feeling that?" Quinton asked sharply.

"Some." She couldn't lie to her partner when it might cost them later on.

"I *told* you they should have given you more time. If we had argued, Jael would have allowed it."

"And I told you we had our orders." She looked pointedly at Kerr. "What's our destination?"

Kerr's eyes were closed where he stood in the doorway, hands pressed against the frame, head bowed. Sweat dripped down the skin of his face, falling off the point of his chin. "South. Target's broadcasting twenty klicks away. So far I'm not sensing any Warhounds in the field."

"For once," Jason muttered. "Even if this is their territory."

Threnody ignored him. "We'll use that SUV around the corner to get there. The soldiers won't miss it. Or their uniforms."

Jason nodded at the bags he and Kerr had been carrying. "We've got supplies in there if we need them."

"Good."

They stripped the dead for clothes to create the illusion of cartel coloring over the standard black that should have meant neutral, except no one was neutral in the Slums.

Kerr pulled on a flak jacket, buckling it tight over his chest as he glanced at Threnody. "No Stryker has ever discovered the identity of the target since it showed up on the grid two years ago. Jason and I, we've been tracking it off and on for the past few months and have never gotten close."

"I know," Threnody said as she added extra ammo to her belt pouch for the gun she carried on her hip.

"What are your exact orders?"

"We can't have a high-Classed psion running around unchecked. The government hates when we're not leashed or dead. We've been ordered to find out who it is and bring them in. If retrieval is impossible, we've been ordered to terminate the target."

She didn't bother with the rest of the order, about what would happen if she failed. Everyone in the Strykers Syndicate knew about their demotion, this sanctioned death sentence. Threnody stared at Kerr, daring him to say something, anything, in the face of her situation.

Those strange teal eyes of his searched her face for a few seconds before he said, "You belong to one of the best teams we've got this generation. Why are they wasting your life like this?"

"It's not your business," Quinton said.

Threnody thought otherwise. She didn't experience a traumatic flashback to their last mission. The psi surgeon in charge of putting their minds back together over and over was better than that, but the memory of it was difficult to ignore.

"There was a school," she said, voice steady, even if her thoughts weren't. "An illegal one, run by unregistered humans. There were children. I wouldn't—"

Her nervous system remembered that nightmare better than her head. She could still feel that Warhound's hand around her throat, his electric power cutting past her defenses and into her body. It was pure damn luck that Quinton had reached her when he did to save her.

"Everyone deserves a chance." Threnody swallowed tightly. "Even those without identities."

The Border Wars made this world 250 years ago, and they all survived in the long shadow of that nuclear aftermath. Education was the privilege of the registered elite, not meant for the gene-damaged masses. Population was regulated because there were only so many resources to go around, but laws would always be broken.

Threnody thought about those unregistered children and the handful born with psion potential. She should have killed them to prevent the Warhounds from keeping them, but she was getting old for a psion. She could afford to question their superiors when others would simply obey. She'd lived long enough that the punishment didn't sting as much as it might have if she had more years left to her. Strykers were taught to value human life, or at least the lives of those who belonged to the Registry. The government didn't care about unregistered humans, but Strykers did. She did.

Threnody's body still twitched, even now, from that last remembered electric shock before the Warhounds had disappeared with the children in a teleport.

Kerr pushed the memories aside for her.

They're alive, Kerr said. *If you can't think about the good somewhere in that, then think about the mission.*

It was, after all, what they lived for.

[TWO]

JULY 2379
SLUMS OF THE ANGELS, USA

The Cathedral of Our Lady of the Angels had seen many decades come and go since the ground it stood on was broken and blessed. It survived the upheaval of land and society when so many other structures had not. Perhaps by the grace of God, or so the priests still taught in thinned-out Sunday schools.

While it still stood in all its grimy, gang-marked glory, with its alabaster windows long covered in mold and the bronze on the door stripped and pitted, it had not seen the light of day for over one hundred years. The adobe-colored walls had turned gray over time, marked in layers of ink and grainy pollution that stained the exterior. Generations of gangs had scrawled their call signs on the skeleton of the place even before the city towers were erected over that lonely piece of God's land.

A tiny amount of dim sunlight filtered down through the cracks of metal and the smog-filled air, covering the street just meters beyond the dry expanse of bare earth that once held grass and now only held vagrants. The entrance to the cathedral was located on the south side of the building, overshadowed by a crumbling cement cross that jutted out from the cathedral's wall. The light inside that fifty-foot effigy had burned out before the turn of the century. It had never been relit. Electricity down on the ground was expensive, even back then, and even more so now.

Bishop Michael Santos had spent nearly his entire life in the Slums of the Angels. The only time he had ever left it was when he completed his seminary studies at the Vatican's fortress in the Swiss Alps and earned the right to wear the collar of a priest. The world was in need of men and women who gave their time and effort toward bettering the lives of others. In this secular, technology-filled society driven by desperation and greed, faith burned only in the background, in the cracks, with the forgotten. It wasn't easy living life with faith, but he did it, one breath at a time.

Bishop Santos stared up at the worn and cracked image of Christ on the cross that hung on the wall of the chancel and smiled. *"Otro día, mi Señor."*

No one was in the cathedral except for himself and a handful of Sisters. Mass was only offered on Sundays, confession had to be scheduled in advance, and he was tired of presiding over funerals. Bishop Santos sighed, running a hand through thinning gray hair. He'd been offered other posts over the years, because the pope believed in furthering the education of the faithful, but Bishop Santos didn't believe in neon-colored crosses and biosculpted personalities that preached on vidscreens. Most days of the week he preferred his cracked and dying cathedral to the top of the city towers. But some days he wanted more. Some days he sinned.

It's human nature. Or so it has been said for thousands of years.

Bishop Santos jerked around in response to the voice that echoed in his ears—amused, with a faint English accent—but he didn't see anyone in the vast emptiness of the cathedral.

I never did understand why people would believe in something so limited.

It took Bishop Santos several long moments to realize why that voice seemed so odd as he reached up to touch the side of his head. He wasn't hearing it in his ears, but behind his eyes, in the middle of his brain. Brown eyes darted from side to side, squinting through the sparse brightness that the lights provided.

"Who's there?" he called out, voice rough from years of breathing pollutants.

No one was in the nave. Bishop Santos would have bet his eternal soul on that. Between one blink and the next, a tall young man appeared in the front pew, long legs stretched out in front of him, one elbow propped on the back of the pew so that he could rest his head on his fist. He was dressed all in black, claiming no cartel color when everyone always claimed a side down here on the ground.

Bishop Santos didn't know how the young man had made it into the cathedral without someone discovering his presence. The doors were locked and alarmed for a reason, and he didn't like the faint, mocking smile on the stranger's face.

"The cathedral is closed today," Bishop Santos said. "I don't know how you got in here, but I'm going to have to ask you to leave."

"You can ask all you like. I need to be here."

Bishop Santos bit the underside of his lip, unable to deny that request. Some distant instinct told him he should, but the warning was ignored. "If you've come for confession, you missed the designated day. Tuesday is when the booths are open, and they are booked through the end of summer."

"I have nothing to confess, at least not to you."

"Everyone has something to confess, my son."

That smile got wider. "Your sense of morality is severely misplaced. You're wasting your time trying to convert me. Your God isn't what I believe in. Your God isn't why I am here."

Bishop Santos watched as the young man pushed himself to his feet and brushed past the bishop on his way up to the marble altar and the table that sat in the chancel on the small dais. He stood there, back to the bishop and the empty cathedral, and stared up at the larger-than-life crucifix for a long moment. Then he picked up the metal tin on the table that housed the thin, expensive wafers used in Communion, pulled a few out, and ate them. The shock that Bishop Santos knew he should be feeling never came. The stranger turned around to face him again.

If this is all you have to offer your followers, no wonder they prefer cartel drugs.

Bishop Santos wrestled with the uncomfortable feeling that something wasn't right. Only when his eyes latched onto that smile, to that mouth that had not moved to speak, did he realize that he could still hear the stranger's voice.

I need this place, this last surviving Los Angeles landmark, for something far more important than evening Mass. Dark blue eyes that Bishop Santos *knew* should mean something to him didn't blink and he could not look away. *Just think. You've spent a lifetime praying for your God to send his son to save you.*

The stranger poured all the remaining Communion wafers on the floor and ground them into dust beneath his bootheel. He spread his arms wide.

Here I am.

His mouth didn't move and still he talked. Bishop Santos flinched. He could feel the blood drain out of his face as the stranger's voice filled his mind.

"*Demonio,*" Bishop Santos whispered in a voice that had never shook in the face of countless guns, countless bodies, and countless threats in all his years working in the Slums. But it shook now because understanding wasn't coming to him. He didn't know if this was a test from his Lord or from the devil himself.

Demon? I'm no demon, human.

Bishop Santos blinked, or thought he did. One second the stranger was on the dais, the next he was standing before the bishop, intruding in his tiny bubble of personal space. He tried to run, but found that the only order his body obeyed was one the stranger gave. Bishop Santos watched as the young man raised a hand, palm to the ground, then slowly lowered it again. Bishop Santos's knees bent of their own accord and he slammed down onto the floor in a kneeling position. Crying out in pain, he looked up with panic-stricken eyes.

"Please!" he gasped out. "I don't—"

Understand. Yes, yes, I know you don't. Just like all the children you fucked didn't understand how you could betray their trust. One long-fingered hand reached out to touch the bishop's wrinkled face, tracing over the lines of age. *You are something I will never be, Bishop Santos. You should be thankful for that. I know I am.*

Knowledge finally came to him, too late to mean anything in the face of a disease and a power he had always preached as unholy. "Psion."

They say your life flashes before your eyes when you die. It doesn't, not really. It was only the neurons in Bishop Santos's head forcibly overloading. Just his mind exploding in a novalike burn that rippled across a small pocket in the mental grid, hidden beneath strong telepathic shields.

Maybe he thought about the years he had lived, the people he had led, the God he had served. Maybe he thought about the precious pool of pure, clean water he'd bathed in before being vested with a bishop's robe years ago. Maybe he thought about a lot of things—things that didn't matter any longer—but Lucas Serca made him forget.

Lucas Serca made him die.

Bishop Santos didn't feel a thing when he fell to the steps leading up from the nave to the chancel. Nothing was left of his mind, no life was in those unseeing eyes. His heart still beat and blood still ran through his veins, feeding a body of cells that had nothing to live for anymore.

Lucas stared down at the man lying at his feet. He had never understood the religious, how they prayed for a way out of hell, but couldn't be bothered to find it themselves. The idea of mindless service to a higher power was anathema to his way of thinking—Sercas ruled, they did not serve. Tapping into his power, Lucas finished what he had started.

Telepathy had turned off the bishop's mind; telekinesis stopped his heart.

If there was a heaven, maybe the bishop was there.

[THREE]

JULY 2379
SLUMS OF THE ANGELS, USA

The shuttle came in over the Pacific, cutting across air traffic with priority clearance, dropping down out of vertical. The pilot adjusted the shuttle's vector as it approached the landing docks that stuck out like sharp spokes along the sides of every remaining city tower that made up Los Angeles. With a rush of air, the buzz of gyros and buffers, the shuttle settled firmly into the anchoring arms of a restricted docking cradle at the top of the tallest city tower. It locked in with a shudder and the anchor lights went from green to red.

No one disembarked.

On a midlevel work zone in the tower below, three people appeared in an all-white room, the faint crack of displaced air muffled by soundproofing.

"I hate cleanup duty," the man in the lead said irritably.

Jin Li Zhang was someone who couldn't be ignored. In his early thirties and close to the end of his short life as a Class II electrokinetic, Jin Li was tall, with black hair and brown eyes. He wore black BDUs similar to the style that Strykers used, designed that way to promote confusion between the government-controlled psions and the Warhounds, rogue psions secretly owned by the Serca Syndicate.

Jin Li chewed on the cigarette clamped between his teeth as he walked down the hallway, the cigarette nearly burned down to the filter, smoke blending into the air around him. The first office he found was empty; the second was not. Two people looked up as the door slid open. Recognition came hard and fast, and the one sitting behind the workstation stood up on shaky feet, all the blood leaving his face.

"Sir." The man swallowed. "I wasn't aware you were coming."

Jin Li drew in a lungful of smoke and let it out slowly, wisps of it twisting behind him as he approached the workstation. The man and his assistant, a woman in a neat business suit, scrambled to get out of Jin Li's way.

"You had your orders to keep us appraised of the situation," Jin Li said as he tapped command codes into the system that overrode every security feature present, shutting it down. "You didn't. We don't appreciate failure."

For a moment, the only sound in the room was the businessman's loud, ragged breathing. Finally he said, "It's difficult to track someone in the system who has the ability to hide from bioscanners."

Jin Li's mouth curled up around his cigarette. "I hate excuses. Come here."

It was painfully obvious that the man didn't want to obey. Sweat had broken out all across his face in a bright sheen, pupils dilated wide from fear. Repeatedly licking his bottom lip, the man took a few scuffling steps forward until he was within arm's reach of Jin Li.

Jin Li wrapped his hand around the man's bare wrist and forced him to his knees. Electrokinetic power burned through human nerves with frightening ease. The man screamed, the sound choking off only when Jin Li released him.

"You were supposed to get a lock on the target. You didn't. The Serca Syndicate requires obedience and results from its employees. You're going to have to work on that," Jin Li said, glancing over at the man's assistant.

The woman took a few steps back, face pale and eyes wide. She let out a little shriek when she ran up against someone she hadn't known was there.

"Humans," a disgusted soprano said. "You're really only good for breeding and menial tasks."

Jin Li spared a glance for the person who was leading this mission. The tall, slim teenager standing beside the woman in the middle of the room was dressed in the same streamlined BDUs as he was, her attention focused firmly on her father's best enforcer.

Samantha Serca was eighteen years old, beautiful, and extremely powerful; attributes courtesy of her genes. Her dark blond hair was pulled back away from her face, opaque glasses hiding the dark blue eyes that were the signature trait of the Serca family. No amount of gene splicing could legally re-create this deep, solid shade of blue outside her family. Anyone who followed the founding family of the Serca Syndicate would know who she was by her eyes alone. Which was why for this endeavor she wore the glasses and strips of synthskin lined with translucent bioware over the facial recognition points of her bone structure.

Standing a step behind her, with hands gripping the buckles of his flak jacket and wearing an identical pair of glasses, was another teen with the same distinctive eyes, the same dark blond hair. Twins; but Jin Li had always liked Gideon Serca more than his older sister. Gideon preferred killing over conversation most days of the week, and as a Class II telekinetic, he was very, very good at it.

"When they initiated a bioscan through security checkpoints in the Slums, they found jack shit and gave up," Jin Li reminded Samantha. "We got that report from HQ on the flight over."

She shrugged. "I'm not surprised. Lucas is almost as good as Nathan when it comes to reading as baseline human on the grid. You're not a telepath, you can't scan for him."

Samantha, however, *was* a telepath, a Class II with the genetics and training that made her capable of tracking their current target. Jin Li's lip curled up, but he stood his ground when she closed the distance between them, her attention focused on the man kneeling before the electrokinetic. The arrogance in the way Samantha held herself was impossible to ignore. So was the strength of her power when it slid into a static, human mind that didn't have the capability to handle such a strong telepathic intrusion.

The man's head snapped back, body twitching as Samantha sifted through his memories, looking for the faint scars that would signify psionic interference. She didn't find any in his mind and released him, sliding her power into his assistant's mind instead.

The woman stumbled from the pain, clutching her head and begging for Samantha to stop as the telepath dug deeper. Samantha found what she was looking for at the bottom of the woman's mind, just a faint dip in her thoughts that a lower-Classed psion wouldn't pick up. Samantha almost missed it. The only reason she didn't was because Lucas had meant for her to find it, some hint of what he was doing, but not why.

Piecing the memory back together proved aggravating, not because it wasn't difficult—it was—but because what she finally found only pissed her off.

The woman had been made to forget the memory Samantha pulled out of the recesses of her mind. The thing about memories was that they were fluid. The brain stored them over a person's life, and unlike humans, telepaths spent their entire lives tearing through other people's thoughts. Samantha knew how to find things most people forgot they even knew. She recognized the mocking tenor voice in that memory, recognized the face of the person she had grown up with. His idea of amusement was something she never appreciated.

It's been a while, Sam. Let's see if you have better luck in the Slums than you did back in London. You do remember London, don't you?

Her first failure as a full Warhound at the age of sixteen was something she'd never forget, nor the punishment she received after she failed to keep Lucas from leaving. Samantha flinched away from her own memories. She couldn't, however, escape the woman's memory of her older brother's knowing laughter, or of Lucas walking into this branch however long ago as if he owned it.

I left something behind for you. Find it, and you'll know where to find me. You know I never like to make things easy for you.

Two years on the run, Samantha thought as she wrenched her power out of the woman's mind, not caring about the permanent damage she'd caused. Two years when it was just her to face their father's sadistic wrath outside the glare of press cameras, because Kristen was unregistered and unknown, and Gideon had become the favorite Nathan used now. Gideon wasn't Lucas, despite her twin's sycophantic tendencies. Lucas had a spine, something Gideon still lacked, but Gideon was becoming adept at being cruel.

Samantha was beginning to hate her twin more than was considered healthy by the empaths in her father's Syndicate. She hated Lucas more for putting her in this situation.

"He's in the Slums," Samantha said, ignoring the seizing woman at her feet. "He stopped here first to make sure we would follow him through an implanted message. He left something behind in this branch. I want it found."

"Lucas isn't careless," Gideon said as he shared a look with Jin Li. "We all know that. He hasn't left anything behind in any of the rest of the cities he's run through, so why start now?"

"He's not careless, no. He just likes to play games. In that, he is very much like Nathan." With a crooked, little smile, Samantha toed the dying woman's body. "Have someone clean this mess up. She's bleeding all over my floor."

A puddle of blood was forming around the woman's head as her body still continued to seize. Her boss was only capable of watching her die from his own position on the floor, mouth forming protests he dared not speak, but Samantha heard him anyway.

"How predictable," she said as she turned on her heel and headed for the door. "He wishes he could kill us."

The man flinched when Jin Li dragged his fingers over the back of his neck. Samantha never saw Jin Li move; she felt it when the human died, a sharp white shock against her shields on the mental grid as Jin Li took care of rectifying the man's poor work ethic.

Nathan could get new humans to fill the vacancies in an instant, that wasn't a problem. Neither was covering their tracks. The problem was that she still wasn't sure what Lucas wanted or why he had left the Syndicate in the first place.

The psion in charge of this Syndicate branch was a Class VI psychometrist who went by the name of Jessica Frist. Samantha barely glanced at the screen detailing the woman's company rank—director of this pigsty—before she was palming open the door and walking inside. The spacious office was full of high-grade work terminals overseen by a slim woman. Jessica looked up from the vidscreens that surrounded her, inspecs glowing in her brown eyes, her face the only part of her not covered by a full-body skinsuit.

"Sir," she said, gloved fingers going still against the controls.

"We're cleaning house," Samantha informed her. "You'll get a new set of qualified humans by tomorrow. Their incompetence regarding the job assigned them doesn't excuse yours. The report HQ forwarded us is unacceptable. You had better have something more for me."

"We got a hit within the last thirty minutes in the grid," Jessica said, discomfort and fear making her stutter ever so slightly. "I thought it prudent to stay and monitor the system before I uploaded a second report."

"The humans said you hadn't been able to find Lucas's location."

"This isn't Lucas."

Samantha's mouth curled up viciously. "Strykers."

"Yes."

"This is our territory and they know it. Who's on the grid?" Jessica handed over a small datapad and Samantha took it, studying the information. Shaking her head, Samantha put it down on the desk. "They just don't know when to quit."

"It makes for an amusing way to pass the time," Gideon agreed as he came into the office. "The humans are dead. I teleported their bodies into the Pacific. Someone else needs to deal with the blood on the floor."

"Sir," Jessica said, inclining her head at the order.

Samantha focused on Jessica. "Take us to the servers. Lucas was here and I want to know why. You're scanning that room for any evidence that can give us that information and you're doing it now."

Jessica managed to physically hide her flinch, but Samantha could still feel the recoil in the other woman's thoughts. Jessica disengaged herself from the system, locked it down, and led her superiors to the server room at the back of the moderate-size office. The lights snapped on as the door slid open, revealing two terminals that hummed on standby power.

Samantha eyed Jessica after they stepped inside, not impressed with the other woman's hesitation. "Well? Get on with it."

Jessica moved around Gideon, peeling off her elbow-length gloves. She tucked them into her pockets and steeled herself for what was to come as she pressed both hands to the console, long practice helping her tamp down the fear of the unknown beneath her fingers.

Every psi power in existence affected the brain in ways modern science still couldn't quantify. Afflicted with an incurable disease born out of the ruins of a vicious nuclear war fought 250 years ago, psions were the people that the rest of society feared.

A psychometrist's power worked through tactile contact. Skin was the focal point of their power, and touch activated it. Psychometrists lived with the constant and brutal knowledge that anything and anyone they touched could and would suck them under into memories that weren't their own.

Jessica sank into the flashes of memories that had been imprinted over the years, sliding her hands through hundreds of moments as she ran her fingers over the edges of the workstation. The past sought to carve out space in the present through her Class VI power. It made her head spin as she followed that glittering line to the one bright moment purposefully embedded in the terminal.

One touch to that memory and the trigger Lucas had left behind in Jessica's mind broke her. Or seemed to. She sucked in a ragged breath, yanking her hands off the terminal as if she'd been burned as a hole she never knew was inside her mind filled up.

In her mind, Lucas smiled at her.

She remembered trying to pull away, but he didn't let her go. Hadn't let her go yet.

It won't be enough, you know, Lucas said to her as he turned her head this way and that, his power eating into her thoughts a week ago. *I still expect my sister to try. So let's make this chase interesting, shall we?*

The image of a broken-down, timeworn cathedral filled her mind. It wasn't complete. Pieces of the picture were purposefully missing, and their absence would make teleportation difficult, if not outright impossible.

Here is where I will be. They shouldn't have any trouble finding it. Enjoy your headache when you remember this.

Jessica opened her eyes, breathing raggedly. She tucked her hands close against her body, refusing to touch anything else around her in an instinctive reaction to keep her sanity safe.

"What did you see?" Jin Li demanded from the doorway.

She lifted her head to look at her superiors, hating the words that came out of her mouth. "It's me. He—Lucas left it all in me."

A sick feeling was already in her stomach, pain in her head. Samantha made it all worse as the telepath cut through Jessica's shields, the psychometrist unable to drop them fast enough. Samantha's telepathy, so different from Lucas's cool interference, filled her mind and drove her to her knees. Where a human was incapable of surviving psionic interference if the psion in question wasn't careful, psions themselves were genetically built for it. That didn't mean it was easy to handle, just that they could. The repercussions were still painful.

"I am getting sick to the back of my teeth with the bloody games he plays. He's almost worse than Nathan," Samantha said, biting off the words as she shared the acquired memory with Gideon. "Can you piece that together enough to 'port us there?"

"Maybe. If you get me a clearer picture from someone else's memory," Gideon said after a short pause. "Unless you want to risk being a smear of atoms in the smog?"

"We don't have the time to wait. I'll get you a better memory, you work on getting a stable avenue of teleportation." Samantha tapped the fingers of one hand against the edge of a terminal even as she skimmed her power over the minds of everyone around them until she found what Gideon needed and shared it with him. "You have any ideas on why Lucas would want cartel contacts? It's the only possible reason why he would be here in the Slums, since drugs are really all we handle out of Los Angeles."

Gideon closed his eyes. "He can't possibly hope to cut into the support Nathan's built up over the years. The drug cartels won't switch their loyalty that easily, not until Nathan formally hands over power to Lucas. Which he won't. Now let me work."

"Lucas needs to be killed," Jin Li said, watching as Samantha walked around the two work terminals, running a finger over the console edge on each one.

"That's your opinion. It's not our orders," Samantha said.

Jin Li scowled. "It's going to come down to Nathan. He's the only one with the strength to pull Lucas back into the fold."

"Nathan hasn't lived this long by being stupid, Jin Li." Samantha gave him a sharp look over the top of a vidscreen. "He won't risk himself to hunt Lucas down. He'll risk us. You'll accept our father's orders, or have you suddenly found a way to save yourself from Nathan's attempt at living longer than a human's average lifetime?"

"Fuck you."

"I thought not. Stop hoping for something that won't happen. You're in the same predicament as we are. If we die trying to bring Lucas in, then we die. At least we'll have worn him down."

"Your mother would be so proud of your human sensibilities."

Jin Li was picked up and slammed into the nearest wall, held there by Gideon's telekinesis. The younger twin glared at him. "Don't insult us."

Jin Li just smiled. Gideon let him go after a moment of warning pressure. Once Jin Li had his feet back on the floor, the electrokinetic straightened his uniform. "Lucas is your brother, Samantha. Out of all of us belonging to the Warhounds, you would know best why he decided to leave."

Samantha grimaced. "I've never been deep into Lucas's head. That's Nathan's prerogative, not mine."

"Some prerogative."

It wasn't, not really, not for those who had to live through it. Nathan's and Lucas's arguments had always happened privately and always ended bloodily, but Nathan inevitably won. The only time Lucas came out the winner was two years ago. Lucas had been eighteen when he'd walked away from the Serca Syndicate, from the Warhounds, leaving Nathan to deal with the fallout of his absence right when their father could least afford it. Samantha still didn't know how he had done it.

Samantha turned her attention to where Jessica was still huddled on the floor. "Put your gloves back on and clean this place up."

Jessica nodded, already yanking on her gloves, and stumbled out of the room. Gideon rocked back on his heels, eyes still closed and fingers tapping against his thighs as he concentrated on visualizing the teleport. "I need five more minutes."

"Then hurry the hell up. We have our orders."

Gideon opened his eyes, the light in the room skimming over the irises, turning them black. "Why the rush? Lucas will see us coming."

"Lucas always sees us coming. It doesn't change anything. It never will."

[FOUR]

JULY 2379
SLUMS OF THE ANGELS, USA

They ditched the SUV two kilometers from their destination.

The streets of the Slums were shrouded in darkness, the ruins beneath the city towers like miniature mountains of rubble. People worked their entire lives down hard-cleared alleyways and never left the cartel territory they called home. Electricity was patchwork at best, always expensive and never reliable, even with backup generators.

Kerr's telepathy kept people from looking at them twice as they made their way down the crowded street in a small group. They had already used up the pass cards after a dozen checkpoints, deep enough now in cartel territory that telepathy was the only thing they could rely on. The target pulsed on the mental grid on the other side of a raucous street market teeming with people who moved out of their way with brief mental nudging.

Kerr had everyone shielded beneath his power, so when the psi signature that he recognized from previous missions pinged off the mental grid, he only hoped they hadn't been sensed here on the ground. Even as Kerr began to build up telepathic walls between the Strykers and the Warhound telepath, that mind winked out. Not dead, because Warhounds could drop off bioscanners with a thought and read as human on the mental grid when it mattered. It was a trick no Stryker had yet learned to imitate. A trick they hadn't been *allowed* to learn. Those who tried were terminated. The government liked to keep tabs on their dogs at all times.

"Warhounds," Kerr warned as they shoved their way through a line of people waiting impatiently for their weekly allotment of vitamins and supplements. "This will probably get ugly."

"Hell," Threnody said. She took a sip of distilled water from her water bottle before re-clipping it to her belt, next to the pouch containing her filter-capable skinmask. "We got further than I thought we would. Psi signatures?"

Kerr pulled his mind out of the masses. "I got enough from the initial touch. Class II telepath, female. You know what that means."

Quinton glanced at Threnody and grimaced. "There's only one Class II telepath in the Warhound ranks."

"Brilliant. I always wanted to die at the hands of someone I'll never see coming," Jason said, voice a little garbled as he cupped his hands around a cigarette and lit it. "Never knew this target was such a prize. Two years and the strongest members of the Warhounds still haven't been able to catch it either. Maybe we should just attempt to take *them* out rather than this target."

"We'd have to be able to identify them, which no one has, but they aren't why we're here. It's not our place to question orders, Jason."

"And look where that's got you."

Threnody reached out and grabbed Quinton's arm before her partner could put his fist through Jason's face. "Not the place," she snapped. "I want to know how often you come across Warhounds when tracking this unaffiliated psion."

Jason pocketed his lighter. "Often enough. If not this set of psions, it's some other Warhound. Neither side has gotten close to retrieving the target."

Threnody didn't say anything. She didn't need to be reminded of how impossible this mission was.

"Still think it's worth it?" Kerr asked.

"Guess we'll find out, won't we?" She glanced at him. "How's your mental balance? We're going to need you to hold steady."

Kerr bristled, offended. "Don't worry about me."

"I'm not. I'm worrying about myself."

Conversation died, both physical and mental, as they picked up the pace. The crowd didn't ease up, becoming thicker the farther they walked. Only when they rounded the corner did they figure out why. Between them and a crumbling landmark cathedral was a veritable tenement of ragged tents and lean-tos. The stench of so many people was worse here than in the streets behind them.

"Is it Sunday?" Jason wanted to know.

"Would it matter?" Quinton said as he reached for his gun, pulled it free, and thumbed the safety off.

"Kerr?" Threnody said. "The target?"

A brief pulse of telepathic power and then: "Still on the mental grid." Kerr sounded surprised.

"Let's do this."

The four of them walked through the dirty crowd, Kerr's telepathy clearing them a way to the locked doors of the cathedral. Threnody placed a hand on the control panel just to the left of the doors and used her power to short-circuit the locking mechanism. Jason hauled the doors open telekinetically, just enough for them to slip inside, before closing the doors.

They came into a space that had dirt on the floor, dust in the air, and lights that were only half on. They noticed the emptiness first, the body second. The corpse was sprawled on the steps leading up to the chancel, white and crimson-edged vestments fanned out around it.

Quinton caught Kerr's eye and the two of them approached the body, Jason's telekinesis wrapped firmly around them in a shield. Quinton rested his finger lightly against the trigger guard of his gun as he kept an eye on their surroundings while Kerr knelt down beside the corpse. Kerr lowered a few of his mental shields, reaching out with his telepathy.

There were no physical wounds, no blood, to mark the bishop's passing. It took heavy, extensive trauma to the mind for the wounds to translate to the body. When they did, they showed mostly above the neck. Kerr studied the dead man's twisted face as he withdrew from the edges of the gaping hole that existed where personality had once resided.

"Six hours," he said. "Judging by the echo left behind on the mental grid, his mind was ripped apart from the foundation outwards. Hard telepathic strike."

"I thought we were dealing with a telekinetic, not a telepath?" Quinton said slowly. "One strong enough to teleport. That's the only explanation we were given for how the target has managed to appear and disappear so quickly from one place to the next across continents."

"Sometimes the mental grid can be made to lie."

Quinton stared at Kerr. "That takes a lot of strength and a psionic power that's *not* telekinesis."

"What about the Warhounds who just arrived?" Threnody asked as she and Jason approached.

Kerr shook his head. "This wasn't them. This is—the wound's too deep. A Class II telepath didn't do this. *Couldn't* do this."

Threnody, trained to have a tactician's mind, snapped through all the possibilities in seconds, coming up with the only one that made any sense. It left her cold, breathing too fast, as she turned to face Jason.

"Get us out of here. *Now.*"

Jason didn't bother to second-guess her order, just tapped into his telekinesis, visualized the 'port out of there, and let his mind carry the weight of them all out of the Slums.

Or tried to.

The world shifted in an instant, their kinesthesia stretching past the point of stability for a long millisecond before snapping back into the same reality they were trying to escape. The backlash ricocheted through their minds, the worst of it burning hard and fast through Jason's mental channels as they all hit against a telekinetic wall that he couldn't break through.

Jason doubled over, falling to his knees as a crippling headache nearly blinded him. The rest of them struggled to get their balance back even as a voice filled the silence of the cathedral.

Rude of you to leave so soon when it's taken forever to get you here.

A tall young man, with dark blue eyes and a messy tangle of white-blond hair, appeared on the dais above them. They recognized him instantly. It was who he was, and what he *wasn't* supposed to be, that shocked the Strykers into silence. Four pairs of eyes were riveted on a face many had only seen in news streams over the years, a young boy growing into adulthood with the world at his feet, the poster child for the privileged elite.

Where's a fucking precog when you need one? Threnody thought in some distant, bitter corner of her mind as she tried to struggle, but couldn't, in the Class I telekinetic grip Lucas Serca had her in.

Usually dead, Lucas said telepathically for all of them to hear. *Personally, I consider them a pain in the arse.*

Kerr's telepathic shields slammed up between them and Lucas as he readied for an attack, but it was a useless gesture. Kerr didn't stand a chance against the man who would one day run the Serca Syndicate, he only knew that he had to try.

Lucas's smile stretched wider.

Psions were ranked for a reason, the various mental powers assigned by tenths of strength of conscious Brain Power Used on the Class scale. Class X were straight humans with 10 percent of BPU, and Class IX were those humans who had a fair amount of sixth sense, the sort that let them survive in a harsh world when other humans would merely die. Class VIII through I were psion ranks, and of them all, Class I was the rarest, most powerful rank.

A Class I triad psion was born only once every other generation, if that. They burned bright and fast, dying off young if they constantly used the powers they were born with, a risk every psion took.

This generation there were two.

Lucas, born with telepathy and telekinesis strong enough for teleportation, cut through Kerr's telepathic attack with a brutality that sent Kerr's power snapping back through the Stryker's brain. The backlash sent Kerr's mind almost to the breaking point, his shields skittering against their mental foundations, his control slipping away. Swearing, Kerr struggled to get his telepathy under control through the agony he was feeling.

Lucas ran a hand through his hair as he eyed the four in front of him. "This is not how it's supposed to go."

"You're a Serca and a *psion?*" Jason asked incredulously.

Lucas arched an eyebrow. "Now, really, how else did you think we keep our Warhounds in check?"

All four Strykers flinched at the admission of whom the Warhounds belonged to. The government and Strykers had known the Warhounds were organized; they simply hadn't known they were *owned* by anyone, much less by one of the world's oldest, most prestigious human families. Only not so human, judging by what Lucas could do, by what he really was.

"What do you want?" Quinton asked in a stiff voice.

"Not any of you dead, Stryker. I'm not here to kill you."

"Do you really expect us to believe that?"

"Belief is subjective. I've already had this conversation once today, I'm in no mood to have it again. You're here for me, Stryker. Or did you honestly think that you were targeting an unaffiliated psion?"

Quinton clenched his teeth, muscles standing out in his neck. He turned his head to stare at Threnody, keeping her in view. Threnody kept her attention on Lucas, knowing all she needed was just one touch to take him down; knowing that she would never get that chance.

"I've got a proposition for you," Lucas said. He leaned back against the table and gripped the edge of it with both hands as he looked at Threnody.

"We don't negotiate with Warhounds," Threnody said automatically.

"I bet I can change your mind. I won't even need telepathy to do it." Lucas turned an indulgent smile on her. "Let's even up the odds, shall we? You've got five seconds."

In reality, it was more like two. Threnody blinked and nearly missed the arrival of three Warhounds as they teleported into the middle of the cathedral. Threnody felt Lucas's telekinesis disappear and she moved instantly, the other Strykers doing the same, because to stand still meant certain death, and shock at the revelation of Sercas as psions wasn't enough to cripple their responses.

Jin Li immediately tossed a dozen small, round electric surge anchors in Gideon's direction. The Class II telekinetic caught them with his power and scattered them around the cathedral with a thought, wires linking all of them together. Jin Li twisted the surge anchor in his hands, activating it and all the others. Electricity flowed through the device, powered by Jin Li, a barrier that was a dangerous extension of himself. The surge net took that power and multiplied it ten times over until the entire place burned with it, electricity crawling across the floor and walls and high, arched ceiling, looking for conductors.

Jin Li's power found it in bodies.

Jason struggled to bring up a telekinetic shield, but he was still suffering from being yanked unexpectedly out of a teleport and wasn't quick enough to block the first wave completely. It shocked through him like lightning, curling through his nervous system and brain. His control skipped just out of reach and his shields wavered.

Hands grabbed his arm and shoulder, dragging him behind the precarious safety of a pew. Kerr focused his power on Jason, looking into those bloodshot hazel eyes, and snarled, *"Shields."*

With Kerr's help, Jason wrenched his power back into place, managing to slide his telekinesis around them both. The sudden absence of electric burn left both of them gasping for breath and reaching for their guns. Together, they took aim at Jin Li. Neither of them were surprised when all the bullets missed. A distraction only, and not a threat; both sides had telekinetics to shield against bullets.

Across the aisle Threnody had her hand pressed firmly to the back of

Quinton's neck, her power regulating both their nervous systems against Jin Li's attack. She was still recovering from the last time she had pulled this maneuver in Johannesburg against Jin Li and it was a strain, her power barely able to cope.

"Jason," Threnody said. "Get a shield around Quinton."

She could handle Jin Li's power on her own. Quinton was a drain on her reserves that she couldn't allow. Seconds later, she felt invisible power hardening between her fingers and Quinton's neck, a telekinetic barrier that would let him live. She pulled away, blue ribbons of electricity arcing from fingertip to fingertip, sliding up her arm and through her body. Quinton took aim with his gun at Samantha and fired, the weapon the only thing Jason wasn't shielding. When the gun was wrenched out of his hands, nearly breaking his trigger finger, Quinton realized that Gideon didn't much like people targeting his twin.

Jason looked up, eyes sweeping over the cathedral's interior to visually tag everyone's position. His inspecs were dead in his eyes from the electrical surge, leaving only the human spectrum for him to work with, and eventually even that threatened to shut down as a massive telepathic blow pounded against his mental shields. The surprise that leaked from Samantha into his mind when they didn't break wasn't comforting.

You can't keep those up forever, Samantha said as she began to bear down on his mind.

They keep themselves up, Jason shot back even as he dialed back on the strength of his telekinetic output to focus on the telepathic strike that was carving mental canyons into the outer edges of his mind. Canyons that were then filled by Kerr's power, a burning challenge that Samantha was forced to reckon with.

Get the fuck out of his mind, Kerr said.

The twins had spent their entire life learning how to wield their powers simultaneously in a merge, like the dual psion they resembled, but weren't. Kerr and Jason didn't have the twins' expertise, but that didn't mean they weren't up to the task of protecting themselves against a pair of Class II psions. It just meant they would be the first to falter.

Nearby, Threnody had emptied an entire clip at the Warhounds, the bullets going everywhere except into bodies. Ejecting the empty magazine, she looked over at Quinton and said, "Burn it the fuck down."

He didn't answer her in words. The air down in the Slums was heavy, thick, and hard to breathe at the best of times. It trapped heat and caused the temperature to rise higher than the regulated environment in the city towers of Los Angeles. It was already sticky hot in the cathedral, mere degrees cooler than the suffocating heat that burned outside.

Quinton made it hotter.

He couldn't create fire, but he could control it, use it, make it grow. Quinton clenched his hands into fists, the biomodifications in his limbs releasing the natural gas from biotubes in his arms. He snapped his fingers, the metal tips sparking the gas into fire that crawled through the air and expanded around where he stood. The red-orange flames flickered in the air until it was like an inferno that he sent roaring down the middle aisle of the cathedral toward the Warhounds.

Gideon's telekinesis saved the Warhounds as fire engulfed them. It blinded them from any physical attack even as Gideon reached out with his power and grappled with Jason's to get to Quinton. Quinton's attack still bought them seconds, precious time for Threnody to lunge for the nearest electric surge anchor, get her fingers around it, and slam her power through its electrical field. The surge net broke beneath her power, circuits frying as she overloaded its limited system faster than Jin Li could counteract it, bringing down the barrier separating the two groups.

In retaliation, Jin Li targeted her first, as he had in Johannesburg, electricity sparking across his fist as he aimed for her face. She knocked aside his first attack and dodged an elbow to the throat, Jin Li's blow connecting with her shoulder instead. They fought their way down the aisle toward the back of the cathedral, a pitched battle that was as much fists as it was power. Threnody was fast, but Jin Li was faster, and he caught her in his grip, slamming her up against the wall. His hands were around her throat, just as they had been the last time when he almost killed her. Right now, he meant to rectify that failure.

Threnody planted her hands against his chest, fingers digging into the bare skin near the hollow of his throat, and shoved her power into him before he could off-load into her. She needed to stop his heart if she was going to kill him. She almost did.

Electricity ripped through both of them, frying their nervous systems and pushing their hearts to the breaking point. Their screams mingled over the roar of the fire, over the rush of blood to her head as telepathy that wasn't Kerr's swallowed her mind.

Come with me, Lucas said. *You know you don't have any other choice.*

Threnody gasped for air as her skin got hotter and hotter, her nerves seeking to burn right out of her body. The world bled colors brought on by extreme stress from Jin Li's power, a disconnect caused by a nervous system out of whack, synapses not firing correctly. The neuroplasticity of the brain freezing up, just for a nanosecond.

She didn't answer him.

You can die here or you can die when the government flips the switch to fry your brain through their collar. Or all of you can come with me and live. Make your choice, Threnody Corwin.

What do you want?

The same thing you do—a chance.

Threnody saw bleached-out violet eyes inside his mind, the image of a little girl in some sterile white room frozen in his memory. A cascade of orders, of actions, that couldn't be a hallucination, not when it came from Lucas Serca, of all people.

The shock of that shared memory propelled Threnody to say, *Yes.*

Or maybe it was Jin Li's hands choking the life out of her that made her reach for a way out.

It didn't matter.

They disappeared. Lucas teleported out of that cathedral with four Strykers, leaving behind his siblings and Jin Li to the quiet darkness of a broken place of prayer.

PART TWO
RETRIEVAL

SESSION DATE: **2128.01.15**
LOCATION: **Institute of Psionics Research**
CLEARANCE ID: **Dr. Amy Bennett**
SUBJECT: **2581**
FILE NUMBER: **1**

She sits alone at the table, young and small, with feet that do not touch the floor. Paper drawings are scattered across the tabletop and the floor around her. She has stayed silent for over three hours, the chrono marking time in a corner of the feed, amused by the pad of drawing paper and the crayons provided her. Only now, when she is out of paper, does she go still. The machines she is connected to click and whine like a disharmonic orchestra.

"Don't sulk, Marcheline," Aisling says as she frowns at the camera. "I'm trying to help you."

As if summoned by her voice, the door to the white room slides open and a doctor steps inside. The woman is thin and dark skinned. She ignores the camera.

"Hello, Aisling," the doctor says. "Do you know who I am?"

Aisling tilts her head away from the camera, attention on the woman. "Hello, Dr. Bennett. I saw you months and months ago."

"Did you? Fascinating." The woman sits in an empty seat, places her documents and a deck of white cards in neat piles on the table. "Do you know why you're here, Aisling? You're here because you are a very special little girl."

"Mama thinks I'm sick."

"Your mother is concerned about you. She was right to bring you here."

Aisling shrugs and slouches in her chair, something like resignation settling on her face. "You always say that, Doctor."

Behind her, the high-pitched sound of the EEG machine is louder than that of all the rest, loud enough to force the doctor to cover her ears.

[FIVE]

The crowd of personal aides, lobbyists, military soldiers, and reporters jostled for view of the vidscreens that lined the walls of the International Court of Justice, known in the vernacular as the World Court.

The heavily fortified Peace Palace was an old building residing over the bunkers that had protected the only seat of power to survive the Border Wars. It was the world's premier functioning government, the place that all remaining countries with viable populations looked to for guidance and obeyed in the face of continuous societal decline. Its fifteen justices held office for life, whereas they had once been restricted to term limits. In these trying times, so the saying went, justice needed a long eye.

It still wouldn't be long enough to see the future. Humans didn't have that power. Neither did the woman who strode down the main hall. She had been born a Class V empath, not a precog.

Her face—oval-shaped, with a straight nose above a full mouth and wide brown eyes—was well documented on news streams. It needed to be. As the officer in charge (OIC) of the Strykers Syndicate and one of the few psions that the World Court had allowed to go fully public, Ciari Treiva was not a woman most people were willing to tangle with. At forty-one years of age, she was the de facto leader of the government's psions and had held that position for over a decade. It still left a sour taste in her mouth, even after all these years.

Ciari traveled light, accompanied only by a single aide. Keiko Nishimoto was the Strykers Syndicate's only Class II telekinetic, a slim Japanese woman in her early thirties who was chief operating officer (COO) of the company. As Ciari's direct subordinate, Keiko was just as well-known to the public. Both women wore the standard black-on-black BDUs of Strykers, though they carried no weapons. Ciari's brown hair was pulled back in a slick knot, hands loose at her side as the crowd, immediately aware of her presence, fell away from her.

The government's dogs didn't come to the world capital all that often. Business with the Strykers Syndicate occurred behind locked doors. A stigma was still attached to doing business with someone who possessed unclean DNA.

Ciari had clearance, higher than most, that got her through the public domain of the Peace Palace to the restricted wing without so much as a pat down. She didn't need one. If the current president of the World Court felt that she was a danger, he had the code that would activate the implanted neurotracker in her head and terminate her. Almost every OIC died by that neurotracker. The Strykers Syndicate didn't offer retirement to its permanent employees. It only offered a grave. The threat of death didn't mean that Ciari wasn't incapable of independent thought. It meant she was better at hiding her contempt than most people for the man who effectively ruled the world.

When they arrived at their destination, the executive assistant who guarded the door along with a set of quads knew better than to keep them out and simply announced their presence through an uplink to the man they wanted to see.

"I didn't summon you," Erik Gervais said as he studied the hologrid displayed above his antique wooden desk, inspecs glittering in his brown eyes.

"Consider this visit one of preemption," Ciari said, her soprano voice empty of all emotion as she walked into the office and approached his desk. Keiko remained by the door. "We need to talk, sir."

Erik looked at her through the data on the hologrid before it winked out. The World Court's president justice was a tall, lean man, whose black robes of office were perfectly tailored and only left his shoulders in the privacy of his own home. Like anyone who held a government position, or who could afford the cost in the private sector, his brain was wired with a bioware net that constantly monitored the baseline readings of his mind. Any psionic interference—if any Stryker would be foolish enough to do so—was tagged on the grid and the offending psion killed. If it was a Warhound, then that was another problem entirely, and the Strykers were expected to die for the humans they protected.

Unless legally instructed to, Ciari never directly touched Erik's mind. His emotions, however, didn't just exist on the mental grid. Emotion was physical as well as mental, and she tapped into the physical aspect that afternoon. She could read bodies as well as the emotions of a target, and for all that Erik was a judge well schooled in the art of a neutral expression, he couldn't hide what he felt from a psion. Not completely, no matter the technology he had grafted to his brain. Ciari could read him; she simply didn't have the freedom to twist what he was feeling into something useful to her without dying.

"Your predecessor was never one to give orders," Erik said as he leaned back in the chair made for his specific contours alone, eyeing Ciari speculatively. "Perhaps you should follow in his footsteps."

"I know my place." Ciari's mouth quirked slightly into something that might be called a smile if one was generous. The by-product of being an empath of any Class meant that she was a stone-cold bitch when it mattered and utterly ruthless when it didn't. Emotions were her forte; that didn't mean she had the luxury of succumbing to them.

"Really. Because I don't see you on your knees."

Ciari made a tiny throwing-away gesture with one hand from where she stood. "My loyalty is the same as it has always been."

"Then why are you here?"

"Your docket today encompassed the Serca Syndicate and their proposed Act."

"I don't see how a case that has been pending for the past ten months merits you storming in here."

"You ruled in their favor. That merits a lot of things."

"If I didn't know any better, I'd accuse you of professional jealousy. But then, your professionalism extends only so far as we allow it. You should remember that."

The look in Ciari's eyes was flat. "We Strykers obey the directive of the World Court. That doesn't mean we can afford to go about it blindly. What law you allowed the Sercas to author, and which you legalized, will affect how we do our job."

"Please tell me that you aren't seriously accusing one of the premier companies and families of being dangerous to the government?" Erik arched an eyebrow, the twist to his mouth condescending. "The same family that authored and helped implement the Fifth Generation Act, which set the requirements needed for a person to be accepted into the Registry with clean DNA? The Serca family was one of the first elevated out of the trenches of mutation after the fifth-generation benchmark passed. They continue to work toward the betterment of humankind, and I'll be damned if you'll belittle their accomplishments, so choose your next words carefully, Ciari."

Ciari paid lip service to the order, but the silence lasted only a few seconds. "Allowing them an autonomy you've refused all others in this venture the World Court has spent generations hiding from the public view won't end well. It can't. You have a right to keep your secrets, and it's our duty to guard them, but we can't guard what we aren't allowed to see. We need to know what the Serca Syndicate is working on in order to protect you."

"Trade secrets are granted exceptions from the laws that govern us. The Sercas have more than earned their right over the years to retain the cornerstone of their company. What they intend to pursue is integral to the survival of all of us."

"What about oversight?"

"It will be taken care of." Erik studied her through slightly narrowed eyes, his calm tone belying the annoyance his microexpressions were projecting. "You don't need to concern yourself with the how or the why, just that it will be done."

Ciari's own expression was remote and cold as she said, "By letting the Sercas dictate this human trial for however long it takes won't result in the findings that you think will be uncovered, sir. Genetics, especially since the Border Wars, have never been easily harnessed or explained. I and those like myself are living proof of that."

They were psions, people born with a disease caused by mutated genes that could be traced back to the Border Wars. Humanity had spent over two centuries trying to eradicate that taint in their own genetic groups. Ciari knew it was a wasted effort.

"The Serca Syndicate has the capability to discern who is and isn't worthy to be on the colony lists we are building out of the Registry. Their results are the only thing I and the rest of the World Court care about."

"Then what of us Strykers? Will you give up all our identities to satisfy their scientific hunger? You have to know that if you do that, you're going to strip yourselves of the privacy we've fought to give you. Then what? There will be too many humans fighting to reach a launchpad or gain access to a city tower's collection of air shuttles in order to reach France. Even if you put every Stryker between unregistered humans and those on the colony lists, you still won't be able to stop all of them."

Erik reached for the glass of water that sat near the edge of his desk, ice half-melted in the expensive liquid that had been distilled and filtered to remove any and all pollutants and heavy minerals. Water that clear was hard to come by. He drank half of it before setting the glass aside again.

"What's the worth of unregistered humans compared to those on the Registry lists? I'll tell you what they're worth. Nothing. Absolutely nothing." The smile he gave her was chilling in its intensity. "You forget that *your* place in this world is to protect those of us who have worked long and hard to clean our genetics of nuclear taint. If unregistered humans ever discover what we've built in the Paris Basin, then you and the rest of the Strykers will be on that wall, Ciari. And you will kill whoever attempts to climb it, be they human or psion. Do I make myself clear?"

"Of course, sir."

"You've overstepped your bounds, Ciari. Don't come here again until I call for you. Just because you're the face of the Strykers Syndicate doesn't mean you are exempt from the rules every psion must follow." His fingers stroked over a thin, familiar remote on his desk. "Remember that."

The burn at the back of her skull was a reminder that she didn't really need. Ciari didn't let her discomfort show as she turned to leave, the pain magnifying with every step she took until she couldn't stand anymore. She almost made it to the door before she fell to her knees, fire ripping through her brain.

"Ciari." Cool fingers gripped her neck, a startling counterpoint to the heat beneath her skin. "As much as I appreciate your concern for humanity's continued survival, I think I liked it better when you knew how to hold your tongue. Your place in this world is to serve."

"Sir," she gritted out, feeling blood slide out of her nose and down the rigid line of her mouth.

Over the roaring in her ears, she heard Erik sigh, the cluster of his tangled emotions battering against her shields. Ciari carefully kept her defenses passive until the pain receded to something more manageable as the World Court's president took his finger off the remote and let her live.

"You make an excellent OIC, Ciari," Erik said. "Learn how to be a better dog and I might not be so harsh in my punishments next time."

He wanted a reaction out of her, some hint that what he had put her through was as humiliating as he thought it should be. She could feel that. Except Ciari had spent approximately thirty-five years of her life as a government dog and six years before that surviving in the ruins of New York in America as a child before she was picked up by the Strykers. Psions, no matter the Class rank, held on to their memories longer than humans ever could. Ciari remembered what it took to survive in the sprawling mess of a city that made up Buffalo on the polluted banks of Lake Erie. Much more strength than it took to survive in the glass cages of the government's prison, bound by the collar in her head.

So when Ciari said, "Sir," as if her life depended on it, she meant what she said.

It was her duty as the OIC to take the punishment, after all. She bowed to Erik in order to protect the Strykers beneath her. She always would.

He took his hand away and another helped her up. Keiko held Ciari with a firm grip as she escorted the older woman out of Erik's chambers. The door slid shut behind them and both ignored the armed quad, a group of four soldiers, that still remained in the hallway. The humans always feared for their leaders when psions walked through the seat of government.

"Your orders?" Keiko asked.

Ciari lifted a hand to wipe the blood off her face. She ended up smearing it across her skin in a vivid crimson streak as she let her thoughts expand beyond her mental shields to the edge of her public mind in a pointed request to the person who she knew was telepathically listening in. *We need to talk.*

To Keiko, she said, "Stay calm and walk with me."

Keiko followed where she went. Before they even made it down the hall, the two women were teleported out of the Peace Palace and into a shuttle that had yet to leave the government's private airfield. The man who had initiated the teleport at Ciari's request raised a glass of champagne to them, a cold smile their only welcome.

Nathan Serca was a brand first, a man second, and made no apologies for his family's place in history. At fifty-one, he was as long-lived as psions came, with the physique of someone who had grown up with access to clean water and food that wasn't grown in poisoned ground. He kept his blond hair cut short and his eyes were that signature Serca dark blue. His life as psion masquerading as a human was the ultimate sleight of hand. That the Strykers helped ensure his family's success was something no one in the government could ever know.

"Ladies," Nathan drawled as he took a sip of champagne. "Have a seat."

"No thank you," Ciari said, voice cool, calm. "We won't be staying long."

"Just long enough to congratulate me? You shouldn't have. Really."

Nathan's voice was dry, the smug superiority on his face difficult to ignore. As he was a Class I triad psion with telepathy, telekinesis, and teleportation his to command, Ciari knew it was a superiority she had no hope in matching.

Not often could a human brain handle the BPUs required for the control of two psi powers. One power was *always* a lower-Classed level when they existed together, and the main power was almost always telepathy. The more common dual psions that were a steady, if small, presence in their short history were telepaths and telekinetics on the low end of the Class scale, as well as telepaths and empaths. Telekinetics who were a Class V or higher and capable of teleportation were labeled dual psions as well.

Triad psions were something altogether different. They *should* have been impossible, but the Serca family had proven that wrong. There were theories—there were always theories—on psi powers and the brain that housed them. It was possible for that combination to exist, the Sercas were living proof, but a Class I for all *three* powers? The brain shouldn't be capable of holding that much power, but the Sercas could. They were the only psions ever to be labeled triads.

Ciari supposed Nathan had a right to be smug.

"Your family has illegally recorded the DNA of unregistered humans over the course of generations," Ciari said. "The Genome Privacy Act you won out of the World Court today was granted retroactively and grandfathers in your family's previous work. Why request legality now when the World Court was willing to continue turning a blind eye to your efforts, Nathan?"

"My timetable isn't yours." Nathan set aside his glass and leaned back in the shuttle seat. "I have the information I want. The government knows the Serca Syndicate works fast. I'll have a list for them by the end of summer at the latest and they will have to accept it."

"They will never accept unregistered humans."

"Who said anything about them being unregistered?" Nathan waved his hand disdainfully at her. "My family helped create the Registry in preparation for the fifth generation after the Border Wars. Do you really think I *don't* control that information? I have no intention of giving up the power we've worked toward finally owning. I am in the position to make my own future. You are nothing more than the government's bitch."

Keiko took an angry step forward, but Ciari gestured for her to back down. They would lose in a direct confrontation with Nathan, and a fight wasn't the reason why Ciari had asked for this meeting.

"There isn't enough time for me to give you who you need from the Stryker ranks," Ciari said.

"That's your problem, not mine."

Everyone knew there were rogue psions. The Sercas had never been owned by the government, and most of the Warhounds they took in never had either. Psion children, when discovered, were either retrieved by the Strykers or the Warhounds, whoever managed to track them down first, or they were terminated. Usually the Strykers came out ahead, but whereas the Warhounds' numbers were equal to half the total psions in the Stryker ranks, they had more of the stronger psions. Some within the Warhound ranks, at least a sixth of their fighting force, were Strykers saved from government termination, but only those that the OIC of the Strykers Syndicate deemed worth saving and that the Serca family needed.

The Silence Law was a twofold rule. A small group of top officers in the Strykers Syndicate helped keep the Serca family's secrets, and those same few officers were the only Strykers who made sure that the willful, purposeful setup and escape of Strykers tagged for government termination was never discovered. The Sercas only took the best when they deigned to retrieve Strykers at all. Which was why Ciari had these conversations with Nathan on his terms. The survival of her people was worth the humiliation of begging.

Sometimes it simply wasn't enough.

"Give me a little more time to save my people," Ciari asked.

Nathan looked her straight in the eye. "You and your predecessors have had more than enough since the Border Wars. I am through being generous. Now leave. I've got a schedule to keep."

Ciari turned to look at Keiko. "Take us back to headquarters."

Keiko wrapped her telekinesis around the both of them, visualized the office they had left barely an hour ago, and stretched her power halfway across the planet. A long-distance teleport required more power than one that simply took a person across a city. She was traveling across continents. No one else in the Stryker ranks could bridge that distance in a single teleport, and Keiko only did it when it was necessary.

The world shifted in a way it wasn't meant to as they left Nathan's shuttle under psion power. Keiko's teleport brought them to Toronto, Canada, their sudden arrival in Ciari's spacious executive office met by two Strykers. Keiko sucked in a deep breath once her feet hit the floor, a pinched expression of pain crossing her face briefly. She'd need a few hours of downtime to settle her mind and recover from two straight teleports of such long distances. She didn't really want her brain to start hemorrhaging or her heart to burst anytime soon. Recovery was something all psions needed, it just wasn't something all psions got.

"Keiko?" Ciari asked.

"I'm fine. Just a bit of a headache."

"Looks like Erik had fun with you," Jael Dawson said, hazel eyes assessing their damage with a critical look. "What did you say to him this time?"

"Would it matter?" Ciari asked as she walked behind her desk and activated the biometric log-in. "I was breathing. What do you want?"

The Class III telepath and chief medical officer (CMO) set two thin hyposprays filled with painkillers on the desk as Ciari activated the office's jamming defenses. The government liked to listen in on their conversations, and the Strykers Syndicate officers had long ago learned to work around that intrusion for very short periods.

"One for each of you," Jael said as Keiko reached for the closest hypospray and put it to use. "Though you need something more than medication to fix what I can feel past your shields, Ciari."

Ciari ignored the hypospray for the moment, knowing her mind would eventually compensate for the trauma she had just experienced. "It can wait. The World Court is granting Nathan's request to retain the Serca Syndicate's anonymity, at least when it comes to the newest Act they got the government to pass. Which means no one is going to have any sort of clearance to see just who the hell they're choosing for the colony lists. The government won't share that information with us."

"They still don't know?" Jael's expression was one of disgust. "About the Serca Syndicate?"

"We're just as much to blame for their ignorance as they are. Our Silence Law still holds when it comes to the Warhounds."

"Nathan's as charming as always," Keiko added.

"You saw Nathan?" Jael pointed her finger warningly at Ciari. "You need a scan and psi surgery. No telling what that bastard did to you."

"He didn't do anything," Ciari said as she waved off that demand for the mental procedure that telepaths were uniquely capable of administering on wounded or subverted psions. Psi surgery had grown out of instinct and into a field of medicine that only psions were capable of using.

"You don't *know* that."

"Nathan isn't interested in breaking my mind, Jael. He's got other things to worry about."

"Hell." Jael bowed her head as she squeezed the bridge of her nose, the thin dreads of her black hair swinging to hide her dark face. "Times like this I wish we had a chance at stopping what the Sercas are planning."

"You don't think we do?"

"Being optimistic isn't in my job description. I put minds back together, not lives. That's your job."

"Then tell me we have some information on the target that's been holding steady on the West Coast."

Ciari was looking at the man standing next to Jael when she asked the question. Aidan Turner was the Strykers Syndicate's chief administrative officer (CAO), a Class IV telepath, and the last living member of a three-person team that hadn't made it to the age of thirty on the field. He had got past the bitterness and pain of survivor's guilt only by a severe application of psi surgery. Telepaths were the most numerous psions, but the majority were a Class V or lower. The Strykers Syndicate needed him, and it needed him sane.

It did not need the report he delivered.

"We lost contact with Threnody and Quinton in the field," Aidan said. "Jason and Kerr dropped off the mental grid as well."

Ciari's expression didn't change. "When?"

"There was a spike around the same time you left for The Hague. The psi signatures were that of Nathan's twins." Aidan hesitated a moment before continuing, "The target's psi signature changed into that of Lucas Serca's."

Those three were the best murderers on the planet aside from their father, psions that could read as human on the mental grid and you'd never know they were there until they were killing you. Only the OIC and her top supporting officers knew of the Sercas' true nature, a truth that complicated everything.

"Did you give the Warhounds our Strykers, Ciari?" Jael asked sharply.

"You know I didn't," Ciari said as she looked each of her officers in the eyes. "None of us granted those four a reprieve, and Lucas has never been assigned retrieval duty. He's been missing from the field for two years."

Keiko frowned, rubbing fingers over her left temple. "Which begs the question of why?"

Lucas Serca's absence in the media and by his father's side had been noted. Whatever game Nathan was playing, they were far behind on knowing his goal. There wasn't a chance in hell that Threnody and Quinton could be alive, not after the last two escapes. The third time was never the charm, not in this world. Kerr and Jason might have a chance, with Jason being a telekinetic and able to teleport, but Ciari doubted it.

Was it worth it? Ciari thought. She reflected on the government's decision, at her urging, to cut Threnody loose for a suicide run because the electrokinetic cared more than she should for the humans she had been indoctrinated to protect. Threnody had never been one to swallow propaganda whole without choking on it. All Strykers were like that, most were just better at hiding it.

"Get a team together," Ciari said, her face devoid of all emotion. "Bring back the bodies. The World Court always requires proof when Strykers die. It's so damn difficult to make them believe anything without a corpse."

[SIX]

JULY 2379
LONDON, UNITED KINGDOM

New York City had been a crater since the Border Wars, the remains swallowed by the Atlantic Ocean and worn down by acid rain. The world's financial center had been transplanted perforce to London once the fallout dust settled, because London still stood, thanks to the fanatical service of long-ago RAF pilots. The metal clock hands on Big Ben's face remained stuck at 3:27, a historical testament, a reminder, to the arrogance of the human race.

The main city towers that spanned both sides of the sluggish Thames River cast long shadows over the crowded city below. Downstream, the Thames Barrier stood like a silent sentinel, an engineering feat something that only the educated, registered humans understood and were allowed to operate. The streets themselves teemed with unregistered humans who would never find themselves removed from obscurity and written into the safety of the Registry. Their genetics hadn't passed muster when the time came to prove themselves clean of radiation taint and mutation. At least, not any mutation that was profitable. They would never join the ranks of the educated to better their lives save through illegal schools that would mean their death if found out. The government cracked down hard on those who disobeyed the directives that had separated society into what it was now.

Freedom, with all its various connotations, was one of the first casualties of survival.

Nathan was used to his sort of freedom and getting his way, even if the humans—registered and unregistered alike—weren't exactly aware of how he did it. The problem was that he hadn't been getting his way for two years and it had left him in a foul mood for just as long. Nathan was excellent at hiding his displeasure, though, especially in front of the cameras.

The pressroom of the Serca Syndicate was filled to capacity, everyone jostling for the clearest read on the man whose sheer presence up on the speaking stage was enough to capture everyone's attention. Nathan smiled at his audiences, both the one present and the one beyond the cameras, as he stepped behind the podium, and he meant the expression for what it was—a means to an end.

"Ladies, gentlemen, it's always a pleasure to have something to celebrate," Nathan began, his voice carrying through the room. He cut a striking figure behind the microphones, with the shine of a hologrid at his fingertips. All the reporters leaned forward, eager for what one of the most prominent figures in their society had to say.

"The government, in its righteous duty to further enable the survival of the human race, has a difficult balance to keep when it rules on issues that come before the World Court. My family, as you know, has had a unique relationship with the ruling politicians that seek to keep us alive in a world our ancestors made. Not everyone has or will agree with the Fifth Generation Act my predecessors campaigned and fought for, but it was necessary at the time. It remains necessary today, despite its detractors.

"This year marks the two hundred and fiftieth anniversary since the last bombs fell inside China, ending the Border Wars that held the world prisoner for five long and terrifying years. We nearly annihilated ourselves through shortsightedness and greed. The fallout of that time was so much more than radiation sickness and a ruined planet, so much more that we have had to live with and survive through over the past two and a half centuries.

"In 2179 we set a benchmark year to ensure our survival so that those who could prove five generations' worth of clean DNA would be allowed full rights as registered citizens when the time came. Was it a draconian law at the time? Of course it was, but it was needed. And when, one hundred and fifty years later, we reached that finalization point, there were those of us who had made efforts to keep the integrity of our DNA intact. My family never set down in stone how one should go about achieving that goal, just that one *should*."

Nathan offered up a faint smile, the pride in his family's accomplishments unmistakable. "The Border Wars gave us many and varied problems to deal with, not the least being the psions we seem unable to cleanse from the population. The government, thankfully, has the problem under control. Which is why I went about my proposal to the World Court the way I did. You see, I've come to the conclusion that psions will not be purged from our society anytime soon, if at all. Their genetics are too complex, and we still have yet to discover what the Border Wars changed in *us* to make *them*.

"The Serca Syndicate has pursued the Genome Privacy Act for the past few decades since the first clean generation was granted approval by the government to join the Registry in 2329. Those of us who have been lucky enough to remain free of mutation in any form have a duty to save the less fortunate. We must strive with everything we have to better the lives of those who still suffer from our past failures. To do that, we must first study where we went wrong, and the psions are the most prominent mistake that we have.

"The World Court ruled in favor of the Serca Syndicate today. They gave this company the approval to keep our work private for the sake of the average citizen. We all have our secrets, some more than most, and while we are a people now who uphold truth above all else, sometimes there is a need for secrecy. That is why this Act was granted, to allow those who never got the government's approval to join the Registry an answer to a most pertinent question. What, after all this time, taints their DNA, but not others? It is a question that everyone knows better than to ask, because some things are just too personal for public consumption."

Nathan leaned forward a little, the shine in his dark blue eyes that of reflective camera glare, not inspecs. "What's not personal, and which will be presented once we have solid findings, is our results. It may take ten years, twenty, another generation or even two, before we figure out how the psions are being born and why some people remain immune to the mutations brought about by the Border Wars and others do not. But rest assured, we *will* find out. To spare those the stigma that comes with being unregistered in our society, participation in this project will remain private. It has to if we are to have any chance of getting enough people to help us find the answers we are all looking for. Now, I will take some questions."

"Sir," a tall reporter called out as he stood up. "Where will you be getting the samples? Are you restricting your company to just one or two continents, or all of them?"

"There will be a broad representation of subjects pulled from every continent that carries survivors, both registered and unregistered," Nathan answered. "They won't just be from the livable areas. We'll send excursions into the areas around the deadzones as well."

"Sir," another reporter asked. "Where will the psions factor into this?"

"We're still coordinating with the government on that."

"What about the rumors that your eldest son doesn't approve of the direction you're taking the Serca Syndicate and that you've heavily restricted his access to all your current projects?"

Nathan's expression didn't change as he looked at the reporter who had asked that question, a slim Chinese woman of slight stature. "My family is off-limits."

"Lucas Serca hasn't been seen for two years."

"Contrary to rumor, my eldest is currently helping gather the samples we'll need to perform this research and has been for many months now. His appearance before your cameras is unnecessary. Next question."

The ten agreed-upon questions passed quickly, Nathan's answers memorized rhetoric. Once the last question was asked and answered, Nathan left the podium for the side door, ignoring the clamoring behind him for more of his attention. Coming out into a secured hallway, he was quickly joined by his bodyguards and last two functioning children.

Neither Samantha nor Gideon met his eyes as they fell into step behind Nathan. They had changed out of their BDUs into sharp designer attire for the press conference, even though they hadn't been allowed before the cameras. Appearances were everything, especially in the public domain.

I despise failure, Nathan said into all their minds, the incredible force of his Class I triad strength peeling apart their shields like rotten fruit. *You know better than to return empty-handed.*

Lucas has never been an easy target, Samantha said carefully as they were escorted down the hallway to the private lift. *He knew we were coming.*

I do not tolerate excuses, Samantha.

Sir.

Lucas left the Slums with Strykers, Gideon said as the door to the lift slid open and the group stepped onto the platform.

Nathan's face was impassive as he pressed his hand against the control panel. The computer read his biometrics and granted him access to the tower levels restricted to the Serca family alone and the people they owned. The lift began its ascent.

I'm beginning to think that Lucas doesn't want to live, Nathan said.

It was just the three of them and two Warhounds in the guise of bodyguards on the ride up. One of them was biting on an ever-present cigarette, the smoke curling up toward the ceiling. Areas of Jin Li's skin still carried bruises that looked like burns, imprints from someone else's power his body had barely been able to counteract. He hadn't gone through medical yet because they'd been ordered to attend Nathan immediately upon their arrival back in London.

"Do we finally have a kill order, boss?" Jin Li asked.

The lift came to a stop and Nathan's answer, while without words, was unmistakable. Already in their minds, Nathan drove his power deeper between one heartbeat and the next as he stepped off the lift.

The agony of the intrusion drove all three to the floor, the last bodyguard stepping out of the lift and standing at attention with a distant look on his face that every Warhound learned to master by his or her first year in the ranks. Punishment was handed out indiscriminately. Warhounds learned to ignore it when it happened to the person next to them and suffered through it silently when it was their turn. Protesting was considered a waste of breath. So was screaming.

Samantha felt her head hit the floor, the dull ache of it distant and irrelevant against the immediate presence of Nathan deep in her mind. Instinctively, she tried to gather her power into some semblance of defense, but Nathan broke her control with a single thought. Her mind caved beneath his, as it had so many times before. Samantha could do nothing but stare blankly at the open doors of the lift, feeling the coolness of the metal she was lying on seep into the skin of her face as Nathan took from all of them memories of the events he felt he needed.

She could feel the channels in her mind where her power flowed begin to bleed through where they shouldn't. She took in a shaky breath, tasting blood in the back of her throat. Beside her, writhing just as desperately, Gideon and Jin Li struggled to breathe.

Lucas will learn his place, Nathan said as he walked away. *Unfortunately, I can't be the one to drag him back to his knees. I can't afford the damage it might cause to my health and to our political position. I expected more from all of you. It seems my faith in all my children was misplaced.*

Oddly enough, Samantha felt shame; shame that she hadn't been enough, that she never could be, because she hadn't been born that way. She wasn't what Nathan needed; never would be. Lucas hadn't been his answer either, but he'd been close, and that's why they still hunted for him. Samantha was just an afterthought, and not a good one. She, Gideon, and Kristen still performed their duties because their being alive meant Nathan could delegate. It meant he could live just a little longer. One of these days, if Samantha was lucky, she was going to wake up and he would be gone, dead, mind burned away by his power and body broken. It was how all psions died, she just hoped she lived long enough to see it happen to him.

I see your filial piety is as touching as always, Samantha.

She felt it when Nathan exited her mind, like the shattering of glass. Only she knew she could put the pieces back together, given enough time. Pressing her hand against the side of her skull, she sniffed wetly, sucking up blood through her nasal passages. Carefully, she wiped it away on the sleeve of her crisply pressed gray blouse.

Get up.

They stumbled to their feet, staggering out of the lift and into the private space that belonged to the Serca family. Five levels of residential rooms and offices and five more above that no lift could reach, because those levels were accessible only by stairs.

The Serca family had always been a buffer between the rest of the world and the Warhounds, more so here in that psion group's unofficial headquarters than anywhere else. The Serca Syndicate was a human endeavor, founded and controlled by psions who masqueraded as human in the public eye because that's what everyone expected. A prestigious company owned by a family with a prominent place in history wouldn't dare harbor rogue psions. People who discovered or were offered the truth were simply mindwiped until they were useful, or killed.

Samantha and Gideon collapsed gingerly into the available seats in Nathan's office once they arrived. Jin Li, used to Nathan's lashing out viciously, propped himself up against the credenza. Nathan's desk terminal was keyed to his biometrics alone, and it snapped on at the first touch of his fingers as he sat down behind it. He said nothing, simply brought everything online, images and data drifting across the opaque console attached to ancient wood.

The door to his office slid open and a static, human mind pressed up against Samantha's shields. She swallowed her disgust and it tasted like blood. Samantha had never cared for the humans Nathan showed special interest in, especially the ones he fucked.

"You're late, Dalia," Nathan said.

"Apologies, sir," the brunette woman said as she crossed the office to take the last seat.

Dalia would never be described as pretty, but she was striking given the right identity to inhabit. Right now she was wearing the drab uniform of an Eastern European bond worker, someone who would take any job, so long as it paid. The stretch of surviving countries that once belonged to Russia weren't wanted by Western Europe and were shunned by what remained of their former mother country. Shantytowns outnumbered civilized city towers, and people survived in those places only through the skin trade, be it labor, sex, or the sale of body parts and organs. The deadzones there were nearly as bad as the ones the Middle East had become.

Dalia, however, was not a bond worker.

She met Nathan's gaze unwaveringly when few people could. She was human, a static mind to his vast senses, but what she lacked in mental capacity she more than made up for with her hacking skills and Syndicate loyalty. She was Nathan's pet, yes; a decent fuck on the side; but more important, she was his way into the inner sanctum of the government-controlled scientists. Bioscanners could differentiate between a psion and a human, and no official in the world would knowingly let a psion into government-restricted areas.

Dalia pulled a data chip from the pocket of her uniform and slid it across the desk to Nathan. "We have a problem."

He picked it up telekinetically and loaded it into his terminal with a flick of mental power. The hologrid that snapped into view between them hung heavy with a security feed that showed Lucas, in a bond worker's uniform, infiltrating the plant that Dalia had been sent to six months ago. The plant developed the Serca Syndicate's software and hardware, some of which had been held back from public use not because it wasn't ready, but because the Serca family hadn't been willing to give it all up. Nathan's mother had bargained with the government quite a bit when she'd been alive. Thanks to her persistence, the World Court wanted those computer programs, and Marcheline had made them pay for it. Nathan refused to let his family's success be marred by anything.

In the security feed, Lucas tipped his head back, looked directly into the recording device, and smiled, as if he wanted to be seen, before disappearing in a teleport. A visual *fuck you* that wouldn't go over well with the public if that feed got out.

Nathan stared hard at the image of his son, letting the feed replay three times before he finally leaned back in his chair. "When was this taken?"

"Last week," Dalia said. "I've deleted the file from every available hard drive and from the servers supporting that particular security grid."

Nathan's gaze settled heavily on his other children. "This is exactly why I want him brought back."

Samantha willed herself not to look away from her father's gaze. "It's been two years and your Warhounds have employed every known method to retrieve him. We are *trying*. Sir."

"Then apparently you need to open up that mind of yours and try harder. Lucas is planning something and he's spent at least two years laying down the groundwork for it." Nathan gestured at the vidfeed. "This isn't the first time he's infiltrated our satellite branches and stolen data. I am getting *tired* of waiting for Lucas to show his hand when *our* goal is to cut off his head. We can't afford interference, not when we're so close to the launch date."

"What would you have us do?" Gideon asked.

Nathan was silent as he watched the vidfeed one last time. "Two years of teleporting around the planet, interacting with Warhounds and Strykers alike, and only now he takes hostages? The Strykers didn't give up those psions, whoever they were. Ciari didn't request a retrieval. I want to know which Strykers Lucas took and I want that information as soon as it's been confirmed, along with an updated report on everything Lucas has taken from this company. Gideon, that is your task. Dalia, we're going to stage two of our plan. I want the agents you've been working with terminated. You can find new ones."

Dalia inclined her head in silent acknowledgment of that order.

Nathan's heavy gaze settled on Samantha. "I'm sending you to Spain for the oil transfer that the government has scheduled. You're taking Kristen as backup."

Kristen, his youngest child, was sixteen, a Class III empath, unregistered and insane. She was a mistake that Nathan kept around because she was still useful. Crazy, vicious, and difficult to control, but useful.

"She needs to feed."

Samantha knew better than to argue and merely nodded, careful to keep her thoughts as neutral and settled behind her cracked and damaged shields as she could.

"Jin Li," Nathan continued. "We leave for Japan shortly. Prep the shuttle. I have to maintain the *illusion* of living as a human. Dismissed."

The four of them got to their feet and left Nathan to the task of spinning this latest victory for the Serca Syndicate. Once out of sight, Gideon teleported away immediately. Samantha didn't bother to hide the disgust on her face at her twin's eagerness to please. The remaining three took a lift four levels up to the last public level of the Serca Syndicate. Getting farther than that required passing through a host of biometric security features before they could take the stairs to the first restricted level of the Warhounds' headquarters. Samantha left Jin Li and Dalia once they arrived in that brightly lit place.

The top of the city tower that the Serca Syndicate was located in had been built with no real windows to look out and see the polluted sky. Instead, hologrids flowed over every outer wall, detailing scenes of blue skies that no one had actually seen in the past few generations. Samantha didn't notice them as she worked her way to the top floor of the tower, passing through a few security checks on the way up. The last door she walked through led into a short sterilization corridor. Every possible speck of contaminant was stripped from her body in the time it took her to cross that short space in four strides.

Samantha came out into a level that was all white, bright lights shining down on everyone. The medical level was geared solely to psions, and she made her way to the special room assigned to her younger sister. Samantha ignored everyone she passed, just as she ignored the headache that was pounding out a rhythm against her skull. Faint traces of blood had dried around her nose and chin. She scraped them off with one hand, pressing the other against the control panel to a heavily secured door.

It took biometric measures to open that medical room, and only six people in the entire Warhound ranks had access to the person who lived behind that door. Samantha was one of them by right of blood. The door slid open and Samantha shored up her shields as well as she could before stepping inside.

"Been a while, Sammy-girl," a rough, amused voice said from the corner.

At sixteen, Kristen Serca didn't weigh much more than forty kilos, and the specialized skinsuit that she wore was as much her prison as her clothing. With built-in bioware that could monitor her status at all times, it acted as a leash for those with the controls. The skinsuit had the ability to short-circuit Kristen's nervous system and keep her in check when sanity slipped from her, which was often enough for the dysfunctional Class III empath to be a problem for everyone else.

"Hello, Kristen," Samantha said, her voice leached of all emotion.

The girl lifted her head, face full of sharp angles and that ever-present smile, which was her default expression, a rictus grin of happiness. Lank, straight blond hair barely touched her shoulders. A sick silver sheen radiated outward from her pupils and dark blue irises, giving her a vacant, almost dead gaze that most people believed meant she was incapable of paying attention to the world around her. Samantha knew otherwise.

She couldn't ever recall a point in her life where Kristen didn't need the death of another person to keep her mind from falling apart. Maybe it had something to do with all the genetic altering Nathan had done to each of his children, trying to make them into something that none of them were. Kristen hadn't been born this way, mentally unbalanced and always looking for a little bit of sanity. She had Nathan to thank for her predicament, for her need to model her shields and her thought processes on another person's mind in order to try to stabilize her own. It never stuck long.

When she managed some semblance of sanity, the empath knew exactly what she was doing. Outside of those moments, it was anyone's guess what was going on in Kristen's mind.

Samantha eyed the deep scratches on Kristen's face, which were covered with the distinctive shine of a quick-heal patch. Kristen tore herself up just as often as she tore up everyone else. She didn't register the pain for what it was; her empathy didn't let her. Pain was both physical and mental, and while Kristen understood that her body and mind were connected, that understanding got lost in the ravages of her power. She could feel nothing, produce no emotion of her own except a twisted, maniacal glee when given someone to kill. The emotions of other people, however, were easy enough for her to tamper with. There was something to be said for instinct, after all.

"Hungry?" Samantha asked, staying exactly where she was.

The brightness in her sister's eyes matched the spike on the mental grid. Kristen pushed herself up on surprisingly steady feet and approached Samantha with grasping hands and a needy mind. Samantha, still reeling from Nathan's punishment, didn't bother to be gentle when she sent a driving telepathic spike straight into Kristen's mind. The empath grunted, falling to her knees, but she was still smiling as a faint trickle of blood slid out of her nose. She licked it off her lips.

"You taste good," Kristen slurred.

Samantha turned on her heels and left. "We've got a briefing to attend. Keep your mind to yourself, Kristen. Or I'll stick you back in that cell of yours."

The soft laughter that followed Samantha down the hall was cheerful. The gaping, raw need for the kill tainting the mental grid was too dangerous to ignore, and Samantha kept her shields up high and tight as Kristen closed the distance between them.

[SEVEN]

Y ou're sure?" Ciari said, staring at the face on the vidscreen. The connection wasn't the best coming out of the Slums, but it had still been picked up by a communications officer. "You didn't find anything?"

"Not a single body," the Stryker in the field said, her voice thick with a Portuguese accent. "Emilio and I searched a wide area once we teleported in from Brasília. The cathedral is a mess, but we found no remains."

"Thank you, Imenja. I appreciate your efforts."

"We can extend the search if that's what you want. Move into a different cartel area. I don't know if it will make a difference, though. We've spent twenty-four hours here already."

"That won't be necessary. Return to your posts in Brazil."

"Sir."

The connection was cut, leaving silence behind in Ciari's office. She hesitated a long moment before tapping out a request for an uplink. It took ten minutes for it to go through, for her code to be screened by two separate communications officers in two cities, before Erik's face appeared before her on the vidscreen.

"Ciari," Erik said. "I'm heading into session within the hour. You have five minutes."

"Preliminary reports from the team in the field confirm that the four Strykers we sent into the Slums are missing, sir."

"Can you confirm that they're dead?" Erik asked, gaze cool.

"Negative. We've found no bodies."

"Then we're going to presume they're somehow still alive and MIA."

"Did you want to initiate a hunt or kill order?"

"You know the law as well as I do. There are enough rogue psions in the world as it is. We can't afford to add more to the mess we're still fighting."

"That's a Class II telepath you want to terminate, sir. I realize you don't much care about the rest of them, but—"

"That's a *dysfunctional* Class II telepath I'm telling you to terminate," Erik interrupted sharply. "There's a difference between a psion that is worth something to me and one that hasn't proven useful in all the years we've let him live."

"Permission to speak freely, sir."

"If you're going to try arguing for their lives, then no. Terminate them."

The screen went blank, Erik having cut the connection on his end. Ciari rubbed a hand over her face, mouth twisting slightly before the expression smoothed away. She hated this part of her job.

Getting to her feet, Ciari left her office for the lift beyond her doors, taking it down to the busy command level. It was a maze of hallways, offices, and command rooms, full of humans and Strykers alike monitoring Strykers out in the field on contract and those within their headquarters. All Strykers showed up on the government's security grid through bioscans from the signal that their implanted neurotrackers transmitted, a precaution that was law. If they dropped off the grid, they were either dead or attempting an escape, the latter of which resulted in the former.

There was no way out of the Strykers Syndicate except by death. Everyone knew that.

Ciari made her way silently to a room where a Stryker and a human were still struggling to locate four missing Strykers and having no luck. When she entered, the Stryker stood as a sign of respect. The human remained seated. Ciari didn't take it as an insult.

"Contact Jael," Ciari said. "Tell her to report here for a termination."

The Stryker bit back whatever protest he wanted to voice and did as Ciari ordered. He was a telepath, as was Jael, so in seconds Ciari felt the other woman's mind pressing against her mental shields.

You can't be serious, Jael protested. *That's one of our strongest teams and our strongest telepath you want to terminate.*

It's the order Erik gave. I need you as a witness and to sign off on their deaths.

For all that the World Court owned the Strykers and had control of their lives, their capacity for justice paled in the face of their cruelty. That wasn't a popular opinion, but most people weren't psions, beholden to a tangle of delicate, devastating bioware in the back of their head capable of killing them. Rarely did the World Court terminate Strykers themselves. They gave the order to do so.

The OIC initiated the punishment at the World Court's command in situations like this. The act was a punishment in and of itself. A reminder of who was really in control.

Jael arrived some minutes later, her white scrubs spattered here and there with blood. She'd been doing rounds when Ciari had summoned her. Ciari knew the other woman would prefer to be there and not here, but they both knew how to do their job, as distasteful as it was sometimes.

"Ciari," Jael said, her voice flatly neutral.

"Dismissed," Ciari said to the pair of handlers. The Stryker and the human left in silence. Ciari knew word of this termination would spread through the ranks within the hour.

Hate, when projected by several hundred people directly at her, always gave Ciari a migraine, despite her shields.

The door slid shut, leaving her and Jael alone in their personal hell. Jael stepped forward, her eyes flickering over the data on the hologrid before them, a map of what was left of the world prominently displayed.

"I hate this part," Jael said through clenched teeth.

"Me, too," Ciari said quietly before raising her voice. "Computer, mission override. Authorization code Sigma Two Seven One Zeta. Request termination sequence."

"Voice identification confirmed. Ciari Treiva, Officer in Charge," the computer's voice announced in a gratingly pleasant tone so at odds with what they were doing. "Initiating termination sequence."

Jael let out an explosive sigh. "Chief Medical Officer Jael Dawson present as witness."

"Medical authority present, witness acknowledged," the computer responded. "Request Stryker files."

"Pull entire files of the following Strykers," Ciari said, her voice curiously calm. "Threnody Corwin, Quinton Martinez, Kerr MacDougal, and Jason Garret."

"Acknowledged. Files found."

Four dossiers opened, laid atop the world map on the hologrid. Four faces frozen in holopics stared out at them. Four lives were written out in reports of strengths and weaknesses, missions accomplished and missions failed. Numbers, words, that didn't fully encompass the lives Ciari was being forced to cut short. They never did.

"Location of targets?" Ciari asked.

"Location unknown."

Ciari's gaze never wavered as she pressed her hand down on the biometric scanner. The computer read her print in an instant. She formed the word reluctantly. "Terminate."

Their network was fully integrated into the government's security grid that spanned the world, enabling them to track Strykers anywhere on earth. With these four Strykers, Ciari was hoping it wouldn't work, but recklessly hidden or not, neurotrackers would always respond to their programming, even if the person was already dead.

Four sharp spikes on the bioscanners that monitored baseline readings erupted somewhere on the east coast of Russia. The computer magnified the area five times, satellite feed finally pinpointing an area in Magadan, Magadan Oblast, as the final resting place of *someone*. They just weren't Strykers.

The baselines terminated by those neurotrackers were human.

Jael took a step forward, surprise filtering through her voice. "Ciari?"

"Acknowledge the results, Jael," Ciari said, never taking her eyes away from the hologrid.

Jael swallowed tightly before saying, "It is my assessment as the Strykers Syndicate's CMO that the four baselines on record do not match the ones which were terminated."

"Confirmed," the computer said, recording Jael's report for the record.

"This doesn't make any sense," Jael said.

Ciari tilted her head to the side. "No, it doesn't."

They stared at each other, both of them reading between the lines of what they were saying and what was showing up on the grid.

"Computer, save files and shut down," Ciari said.

It took less than a minute for the computer to obey Ciari's command. Only when the terminal went dark did Ciari turn to look at Jael, easily reading the uncertainty in Jael's troubled expression.

"Contact Keiko," Ciari said. "Tell her to report to my office in twenty minutes."

Ciari left Jael behind and returned to her office with determined strides, where she followed protocol and contacted Erik once again. She sent the request red-lined as priority, and he answered more quickly than she thought he would.

"We have a problem, sir," Ciari said when the connection was made.

"It hasn't even been half an hour, Ciari. It takes less than a minute to fry a psion's brain. What could *possibly* be the problem?" Erik said.

"The neurotrackers were activated. The kill results are inconclusive. They spiked as human on the grid."

Erik stared at her. "That's impossible. A psion's baseline is nowhere close to a human's."

"Those are the results, sir."

"I want the results changed. Immediately."

"Of course, sir."

It was just like him to want the impossible.

The connection cut off and Ciari leaned back against her chair. She let out a long sigh, thinking about everything that had gone wrong just now and what had gone right.

Keiko walked into her office ten minutes later, expression neutral, even if her tone of voice wasn't. "Jael told me what happened. Your orders?"

"I'm sending you to Russia. The World Court wants answers."

"I'll see what I can find."

PART THREE
NEGOTIATION

SESSION DATE: **2128.06.02**
LOCATION: **Institute of Psionics Research**
CLEARANCE ID: **Dr. Amy Bennett**
SUBJECT: **2581**
FILE NUMBER: **514**

A nurse holds her arm gently, carefully extracting yet another vial's worth of blood as the doctor looks on. When the nurse is finished, she leaves with what she came for, and it is only the two of them again. Aisling carefully touches the small bandage that covers the hole in her skin.

"You won't find what you're looking for," Aisling says, glancing up at the doctor. "You think you can stop the wars by trying to make me better, but you can't."

"I think you need to share with us exactly what you know," the older woman says as she taps her fingers against the table in a steady rhythm. "It's been months, Aisling. The bombs are still dropping."

"They've been dropping for years."

"You can stop it."

"It doesn't stop here." Aisling kicks her feet and sighs, sulking. "You're like her, you know that? Threnody thinks I know everything, too."

"Again with this Threnody," the doctor says in exasperation. "You've mentioned her exactly twenty-three separate times now."

"She's my favorite imaginary friend."

"Aisling," the doctor says as she crouches down beside the girl's chair. "You know what you see isn't imaginary."

"I know," Aisling whispers, sounding scared as she curiously tilts her head to the side, wires brushing her face. "I almost wish it was, though. I just don't want to worry you."

[EIGHT]

Jason came awake to a roaring, screaming pain in his head that made it impossible to think. For once, the pain wasn't caused by his power, just his actual *skull*, and that was enough to drive the unconsciousness away.

Blinking slowly down at the dirty gray floor stained liberally with blood, Jason realized that he could see clearly in all the human visual spectrum, along with the overlay of data in his eyes. His inspecs were back online, which was impossible without surgery, and this sure as hell wasn't the medical level back at headquarters.

He tried to move and became immediately aware that was impossible. The power clamped down on him was familiar, a telekinetic strength that he recognized and couldn't break. Bent forward, spine arched, Jason could sense someone behind him, even if he couldn't see the person. He couldn't feel a damn thing at the back of his skull, but the rest of his head was feeding him pain. He could feel the blood that was trickling down his back. He could smell it, too.

"Interesting dilemma, you know," that vaguely familiar tenor said through the hum of a sterility field, and thank fuck for that, because this place didn't look clean at all. "Your natal shields never fell. You're going to feel this more than the rest of your team since I can't get very far into your mind to block the pain. First time *that's* ever happened."

A pair of scuffed, all-terrain black boots stepped into his sight, but even when he rolled his eyes upward, Jason couldn't see the person's face. Not that he needed to. Even doped up on drugs, it was difficult to forget the shock he had felt when they'd learned that a Serca was a high-Classed psion. Difficult to forget those eyes. Made him wonder about the rest of that famous family and if Lucas was merely an anomaly or *normal* for the Sercas.

"What have you done with them?" Jason managed to get out through clenched teeth. He didn't bother to correct Lucas's assumption that the four of them were a team. At the moment, he really only cared about Kerr, but he could worry about Threnody and Quinton. Especially Quinton. He kind of liked the way the other man looked.

Lucas's tone was amused. "They're recovering, even if everyone's pissed that they can't use their powers. I have them blocked. The doctor's almost finished with you."

"What?"

More blood trickled down his back and Jason squeezed his eyes shut. He didn't know what was going on behind him, not until something clattered on the floor an indeterminable amount of time later. He opened his eyes and stared at the tiny, oval-shaped device with six short spikes and six long filaments of bioware wet with his blood that had been tossed near his feet.

Jason didn't need to ask what it was. He knew, just as every Stryker knew, about the neurotracker one was implanted with upon joining the Stryker ranks. He also knew that removing it should have instantly killed him. Any tampering sent out an immediate signal to the government as a red alert. Standard operating procedure was to terminate. At the very least, the Strykers would know—*should* know—that he wasn't wearing it anymore. Which meant—

Jason laughed, the sound desperate. "I thought you said you didn't want to kill us, because you just did."

The neurotracker lifted off the floor and was drawn upward by invisible telekinetic power, settling into Lucas's hand. He crouched down in front of Jason, focusing on him. No apologies were to be found in his gaze.

"Its programming is active. The signal, while blocked right now, still functions. When the time comes, it will send through the government's security grid, even if it's no longer in your head," Lucas said. "They'll be implanted into some desperate bond worker attached to the skin trade. This procedure is one that my side has done before."

Jason swallowed drily. "And when the government flips the switch, your chosen little carriers will be dead instead. Do *they* know that?"

"Of course not. They just think they were paid for a body transfer over international lines. You should really be happy about being taken off your leash, Jason. Most of you Strykers are when we pull you off the field before you're terminated."

Jason squinted up at him. "What the fuck are you talking about?"

"Nothing that matters at the moment, since I'm no longer a War-hound. I haven't been for many years."

"I doubt that."

"Lucky for both of us I don't care what you think, just what you can do."

Lucas stood up and walked away. Jason had no other choice but to stay where he was, listening to a strange, rough voice mutter behind him as this doctor, whoever he was, grafted pieces of his skull back together and closed his skin inside the safety of the makeshift sterility field. Whatever drugs he'd been given were beginning to wear off quickly, and Jason could feel *exactly* what had been done to him. He squeezed his eyes shut and tried to breathe through it all.

Eventually it was over. The operation complete, Lucas lifted the telekinetic hold he had on Jason. Able to move, Jason straightened up in the seat and immediately regretted it. Nausea came, swift and brutal, and he puked stomach acid onto the floor while Lucas kept him from falling over with a hand on his shoulder.

Jason lifted one hand to the back of his skull, feeling the small area of shaved hair there, the sealed skin, and the hardness of a quick-heal patch. His bones ached.

"I can give you more drugs," Lucas said. "Except you know as well as I do that a psion's metabolism will burn through them in less than thirty minutes. Still want them?"

"I'll manage," Jason rasped as he spat bile-coated saliva onto the floor.

"Better than most, I suspect. Come on. Your team captain seems to think I'm torturing you, even though I already proved that I wasn't after putting Quinton and Kerr through the same procedure. She got to go first."

"We aren't a team. She's not my captain."

"I know. But it irritates her to be called that."

Lucas hauled Jason to his feet, watching critically as the Stryker struggled to stay upright. The doctor shuffled around the operating area, and Jason nearly lost control of his stomach again after getting a good first look at the man's face.

The doctor had no eyes and half his skull had been replaced by metal plating. In place of organic material was bioware designed to process images to the brain in microscopic layers that traditional human eyesight could never hope to attain. Glittering wires frayed out of the man's eye sockets around tiny optics, twining back inside his body through his temples, feeding into his brain. Everything about the doctor's appearance was illegal, and Jason felt contaminated just looking at him.

"Korman is one of the finest transplant surgeons on the black market," Lucas said, sounding almost cheerful as he steered Jason out of the room. "The best part is that he did all of this for free."

"Only because you altered his mind," Threnody said as they stepped out into a cluttered living space, if one could call the mess livable. Her voice, Jason noticed, was slurred just a little.

"You say that like it's a bad thing."

The faint sound of displaced air came from the makeshift operating room. Jason glanced over his shoulder, seeing that the doctor had disappeared. "Warhound?"

"No," Lucas said calmly. "Mine. I teleported him somewhere else to finish the transfer."

The three Strykers were sitting around a rickety table in various stages of recovery. Jason's eyes settled on Kerr, and the telekinetic moved over to his partner as quickly as he could, sitting down heavily on the bench there.

"You're bleeding through your shields," Jason said, studying the familiar pain lines on Kerr's face that weren't all just because of the surgery. "Get behind mine."

Kerr's face twisted just a little. "Jays, you just got out of *brain* surgery. I can't—"

"That wasn't a goddamn request, Kerr. Just do it."

Jason pretended that Lucas wasn't watching them, that he didn't have his telepathy anchored tightly in their thoughts, allowing what needed to be done only after Jason glared at him. Kerr burrowed through the bond that linked him to Jason, transferring as much of his power behind the thick natal shields that stood out in stark relief against Jason's mind as he could. The pressure in Kerr's own mind eased, leveled off, as Jason's shields took up the task of protection that he was incapable of providing himself.

"Interesting." Jason glanced over at Lucas, not liking the calculating look in those dark blue eyes. Lucas just smiled, the expression remote as he crossed his arms over his chest. "I'm sure all of you have questions."

"You think?" Threnody's voice was caustic. "You condemned us to rogue status."

"I saved you," Lucas corrected. "And if you want to know why, you'll follow me outside."

"Here's not good enough?"

"These walls have eyes and ears that I don't trust. Camden Market is safer."

It wasn't, not really, but Strykers thought differently from Warhounds. Threnody stared at Lucas, details clicking into place about what they now knew of the Serca Syndicate, and what they knew of the Warhounds. Camden Market was in London, and London was dominated by the Serca Syndicate as much as it was by the government.

"You brought us to the Warhounds' home turf and you think this is *safe*?" she demanded.

"What better place to hide you than here in plain sight?" Lucas reached up and tapped the side of his head before sliding a pair of dark glasses over his eyes. "I've got you all off the mental grid under my power. You read as human, just like I do, and I can make all of you disappear completely if I need to."

"How?" Kerr asked.

"Today's not the day you learn that trick. Now let's go."

They left the back-alley surgery room for the pipe dreams and broken promises of Camden Market because they had no choice. Quinton kept a hand on Threnody and both eyes on Lucas, while Kerr helped Jason up the rickety stairs to the street. The silent looks the four shared were mirrored by the thoughts in their heads. If there was even a slim possibility at escape, could they take it?

You won't get further than the thought of it, Lucas promised. *So don't bother trying.*

Threnody stumbled on the way up, swearing as Quinton caught her before she hit the crumbling cement steps. Her arms and legs were shaking ever so slightly, and it wasn't just because of the operation.

"Can you feel?" Quinton asked her as he took more of her weight.

"I'm not paralyzed," Threnody said.

"That's not what I asked."

"There's some numbness." Threnody bit her bottom lip and struggled the rest of the way up. "I've lost some muscle control."

"We need a real medical center with a biotank and nanites. The disconnect you're experiencing is going to be lethal in another day or two if we don't get you fixed up all the way."

"I know."

It was more than just knowing that she was dying from the inside out. Jin Li's power had short-circuited her body just as it had in Johannesburg. Only back then, she'd been at her best. This time, she'd been patched. Her nervous system was breaking down, a slow, uncontrollable death that would eventually trickle down from the voluntary functions to the *in*voluntary functions of her body. Quinton didn't want to watch her drown with air in her lungs.

You'll be all right, Lucas said into her mind alone as they reached a heavily secured door. He opened it telekinetically. *Korman fixed what he could after pulling out the neurotracker. He's done the same sort of operation on other Strykers over the years. Your power will do the rest on its own. Aisling said today isn't your time to die. Neither is tomorrow. You'll recover.*

Who the hell is Aisling?

You'll find out soon enough.

His promise wasn't one Threnody would ever trust. Lucas just laughed off her fear as they stepped outside.

Camden Market shone with the glitter of hologrids against the evening sky, neon light edging their faces as they joined a crowd looking for an escape that would never be found in the gutters. Not here, not in the place that was the world's entertainment and pleasure center, built on the back of the skin trade.

The streets teemed with people looking to sell, looking to buy, looking to forget, areas of London carved into territories by gangs who would never live longer than their next adrenaline rush if they were lucky. Whores sold themselves with a look, on their knees no matter their gender so long as the price was right. Addicts looked for their next fix, hands curved into the signs of their individual requests, begging for the next possible high. And all through the miscreants roamed the gray-uniformed quads of military soldiers, their pulse-rifles set to kill, never to stun. They were the only law down here, but it was anyone's guess on who lined their pockets this hour—the government or those on the streets.

Lucas led the Strykers with telepathic and telekinetic chains that replaced the collars the eyeless doctor had cut away. His power guided them to an outside pub that was all counter and nothing else. Aside from the watered-down beer—the vidscreens behind the barkeep advertised a dozen different drafts, but only two ever poured out at any given time—the place also doled out protein meals. Plastic bowls full of GMO rice and cubes of colorless protein that had no flavor would never be their first choice, but it was calories, and they needed that almost as badly as they needed answers.

The Strykers practically fell on the bowls Lucas passed out to them at the far end of the long bar, space provided to them by a subtle telepathic nudge. The beer was stale and warm, but it was distilled enough that it didn't taste too acidic. Lucas watched them eat over his own bowl, dark blue eyes still hidden behind his glasses.

"Does your entire family consist of psions?" Threnody asked around a mouthful of food, ignoring how much it hurt to chew while she watched a heavily armed quad walk past their position. She hunched her shoulders a little and turned her face away from the four soldiers.

"We can trace our lineage back to the Border Wars" was all Lucas said.

"Fuck," Kerr muttered. "I'm going to take that as a yes."

"Why didn't you kill us?" Threnody wanted to know.

"I needed you alive," Lucas said. "A rebellion can't consist of just one person if everything is going to get accomplished."

He was looking at Threnody when he said it, the twist of his lips almost a smile. A flash of bleached-out violet eyes flickered through her mind again. The memory wasn't hers and it hurt after the operation she had just gone through. She reached up to press one hand against the side of her already aching head, as if she could press the pain way by sheer will alone.

"Stop it," Threnody said.

"Thren?" Quinton said, glancing between her and Lucas. When Lucas ignored him, Quinton reached out and gripped his partner's shoulder. "What's wrong?"

"I'm making a point," Lucas said.

Quinton glared at him. "Get out of her head."

Threnody grabbed hold of Quinton and kept him in his seat by digging her fingernails into his skin. Quinton didn't move. Lucas stayed in her mind.

"Aisling makes it difficult to believe in her." Lucas took another bite. *Always has, though the results are worth the effort.*

His telepathy flared up in their minds, reminding them that he was, and would remain, there in the back of their thoughts until he chose to let them go. If he ever did.

"Who?" Kerr finally asked for all of them.

"Not who," Lucas corrected. "What. She's the reason why I'm doing this. She's the reason why I need all of you."

Kerr frowned. "When do we meet her?"

"You don't."

"So, if you're not going to kill us, and we don't get to meet some girl, when are you going to mindwipe us?" Jason said, mouth twisting with disgust. "Or have you done it already?"

"As of right now, I need you all with minds and personalities intact. Though I'll have to find time to fix what your side never bothered to diagnose. You Strykers never cease to astound me with your stupidity. Two wrongly Classified psions active and in the field. You were both accidents waiting to happen."

"What are you talking about?" Threnody said. "And can you do it more quietly? Someone will hear you."

"Everyone's ignoring us because I'm telling them to. They won't remember a thing. What I'm talking about is the mess that are those two." Lucas took another bite of food, chewed, swallowed it, then pointed his fork at Jason and Kerr. "Or didn't you know both are dual psions and that Jason hasn't reached his full potential yet?"

Jason and Kerr stared at Lucas as if he were absolutely crazy. "You don't know what you're talking about," Kerr said flatly.

"Fuck you," Lucas said with a bark of laughter. "I'm a Class I triad psion. I know the human and not-so-human mind better than any Stryker ever will. I know what you are, Kerr, and I know what Jason should be."

"I'm a Class II telepath."

"Also a Class IX empath, something your side apparently missed when giving you your Class rank."

The look in Kerr's eyes was glacial. His tone was just as cold. "That's impossible. A Class IX is a baseline human ranking and I think I *know* my own mind."

"A Class IX still has traces of psion power. It's the gradient Class, the one where people are either mostly human or mostly not," Lucas explained in a tone one reserved for a small child. "Your telepathic strength overshadowed your secondary power by a huge margin, and there's no one Classed higher than you in the Strykers Syndicate to ferret out that channel of empathic power. *You* might not have known your empathy was there, but your *mind* did. Over the years, it tried to compensate for it. The result is that you're a fucking mess and your shields always fall because you can't gear mental shields solely toward one power when you've got two."

Lucas looked at Jason. "And you. A Class V telekinetic with natal shields that have never fallen. Didn't it *ever* occur to anyone in your Syndicate that our first shields need to fall in order to release our powers, or haven't you ever wondered about what your mind is still holding back?"

Jason recoiled from Lucas as if he'd been burned.

"Scientists can reverse engineer pretty much any technological equipment on the planet given enough approval from the government," Lucas said. "I can reverse engineer the process of the human mind. You need access to all your power, Jason. I just need to figure out how to make that happen."

"That's impossible," Jason said. "My shields won't break. People have tried."

"Not hard enough. If the government can rebuild space shuttles for a launch into space, then I sure as hell can find a way to break your shields."

"What are you talking about?" Threnody said sharply. "What launch?"

Lucas signaled the barkeep for another bowl of food. He had hardly touched his beer. "I suppose if I said that I wanted all of you to trust me, you wouldn't believe me."

"We're Strykers," Quinton said. "We don't trust anyone."

"Then you'll have to believe in ulterior motives, and not just my own." The barkeep placed the requested bowl in front of Lucas without really seeing him. Lucas mixed the food all together before starting in on it. "How good is your history?"

"Regarding what?" Kerr said.

"Everything. Specifically, what started the Border Wars."

"A launch command" was Quinton's sardonic answer as he took a swallow of his beer. "Several thousand of them."

Lucas smiled humorlessly. "Yes, but over what?"

"Who knows? Resources, probably. Everyone back then was fighting over what their neighbors had, same as they are right now."

"Depends on the neighbors. Countries blew each other up because no one could launch a nuke to Mars and hope it would hit the colony there."

All four Strykers gave Lucas their undivided attention at that announcement, staring at him with a mixture of disbelief and confusion in their eyes.

"What are you talking about?" Threnody asked slowly.

"It's not common knowledge. The government didn't want it to be." Lucas shrugged his opinion on that. "They couldn't wipe out the fact that the Border Wars happened because we're living with the aftermath still, but they were able to make people forget the reason *why* it all started. Everyone wanted an escape to Mars from a dying Earth, and in the end, no one got it. The world population was small enough after the war happened, and people were desperate enough, to accept the dictates of the World Court as the new government so long as they were saved. Funny how things haven't really changed."

"That's crazy," Jason said. "A colony on Mars? Our ancestors practically destroyed Earth over *Mars*?"

"Mars was in the process of being terraformed. The colony there was half a generation old already, according to the reports I've been able to find, and it was growing. They already had an energy source from giant solar panels in geosynchronous orbit around the planet and at two Lagrangian points between the sun and Mars. They were working on getting a viable atmosphere when the Border Wars happened. Communication died after that. So did supply runs by the ship that's still cold-docked on the other side of the moon."

"A ship," Quinton echoed.

"A *colony* ship, to be precise. The government calls it the Ark." Lucas glanced up at the night sky, which could just be seen past the tops of the buildings that surrounded them. "Bloody thing still has a functioning system, even after all these years. The government got it completely back online about twenty-five years ago. *That* was the mission of the World Court's first manned space launch."

"We lost the capability for space flight after the Border Wars. It killed off most of the population and nearly all the scientists and engineers," Threnody said. "The closest vehicle we've got to a space-faring one are atmospheric shuttles, and they've got limits. They're still earthbound and only registered humans have the right to use them."

Lucas cocked his head to the side as he stared at her. "Humans hate limits and the government hates the limits of this planet even more. The *government* never forgot what the Border Wars were fought over. The *government* never forgot about Mars and the colony there. Neither did my family. Why do you think the Serca Syndicate pushed for the Fifth Generation Act and the Registry? Not everyone can leave Earth for Mars, and not everyone will. The government is going to make sure of that. They're going to leave behind everyone who's not on the Registry, and I've got it on good authority that not everyone in the Registry is going to make it into space either."

The four Strykers were silent in the face of that confession, staring at Lucas and each other as they struggled to swallow a history that made too much sense for it not to be the truth.

"The government thinks Mars is the answer, a new beginning for the human race. *Just* the human race," Lucas said. "Psions aren't human, according to their laws. You Strykers are all going to be dead come the final launch date. Termination is scheduled for the week the space shuttles launch, and Ciari knows it. There's nothing she can do about it."

"They wouldn't kill all of us," Jason protested. "They need us."

Lucas gave him a pitying look. "The World Court isn't going to allow psions on Mars, which is ironic, considering the Serca Syndicate has had berths reserved since before the Fifth Generation Act was passed. And as you all know now, even if the government doesn't, the Warhounds belong to the Serca Syndicate."

Lucas's words tumbled through Threnody's mind as she struggled to make sense of what he was telling them. "Does Ciari know about you Sercas?" she asked.

"Every OIC does."

The betrayal was like a sucker punch to the gut. Threnody stared at Lucas, a bleakness in her eyes that hadn't been there seconds ago. "Then why doesn't she report what she knows to the World Court?"

"I would think you'd be happy that your former masters are going to get a rather bloody comeuppance."

"You're going to kill them." Threnody clenched her hands into fists.

"Everyone who gets on those space shuttles—if there even *are* space shuttles—your family and your Warhounds are going to kill them."

"Oh, there are space shuttles. Platforms of them above the wastewater in the Paris Basin. All those explosions in that area over the years? It hasn't been leftover unstable nukes going off like the government warns in the press. It's not space debris falling from the junk orbiting Earth. And, no, my family doesn't want to kill the humans. My family wants to rule them in the same fashion that the government has owned you Strykers."

"Is that supposed to make us happy?" Quinton asked. "Some half-assed attempt at revenge?"

Lucas leaned forward, staring at the Strykers over the rims of his dark glasses. "It's misguided, not revenge. The Border Wars created psions out of the mutated population left behind. All the humans in the Registry are clean of mutation and disease. No mutation means no psions, not the higher Classes at least. We can breed, but we breed low on the scale. Every psion a Class IV and higher has come straight from the unregistered human population. We go to Mars, we psions die as a people."

"Good riddance," Threnody said around numb lips. "It'll just be you Warhounds."

"You're forgetting the fact that you Strykers will be dead. We fucked up this planet, we've got an obligation to fix it if we want to own it. It's difficult, but not entirely impossible." Lucas pushed aside his empty bowl and half-finished beer. "The means of doing so is standing right there."

He was pointing at Jason as he spoke, focus sharp and unwavering. Jason just shook his head in denial. "You're crazy. Yeah, maybe parts of what you've said make sense, but we still don't know who fed you this information, and I don't know what you want with us. There are other Class V telekinetics out there, not just me."

"When I break your shields, you won't be a Class V," Lucas told him. "You're going to be a Class I if you're lucky, more likely a Class 0."

"Jason isn't a precog," Kerr said, standing a little straighter and putting himself between Lucas and his bonded partner. "Precogs are the only ones who get labeled a Class 0, and there hasn't been one on either your side or ours for over a hundred years. They're the rarities, not telekinetics."

"Microtelekinetic," Lucas corrected. "Power enough to work on the atomic level. And you're right. There haven't been all that many precogs because the use of their power burns out their brains after only a few years of living. I'm offering you a guaranteed way out of hell, it just comes with a price. Question is, are you willing to pay it this time in order to save everyone and not just the registered elite?"

Threnody opened her mouth to answer him when she felt the hard edge of a gun barrel press against her spine. "Running away, dog?" a man's voice growled. She glanced over her shoulder and caught a glimpse of the quad that had passed them earlier, their faces obscured by protective helmets.

Three other weapons were aimed in their direction, and the people at the bar scattered, leaving a swath of empty space around the group. Threnody focused her attention on Lucas.

"I thought you said they couldn't find us," she said.

Lucas waved a hand at the soldiers. "Those are quads, not Warhounds, which means it's the government who located you. Human effort, not psionic. Facial-recognition software is embedded in the security feeds around here and I can't affect machines with my power."

Threnody glared at him. "You knew they'd find us."

"I'm making a point, Threnody. Honestly, did you really think the government was just going to let you *go*?"

None of them got a chance to answer as the quad pulled the triggers on their guns, the bright flare of energy darts striking against Lucas's telekinetic shield, not flesh. The blasts flared dangerously wide and ricocheted backward to hit the soldiers and whoever was still stupid enough to be sticking around, knocking them to the ground. Everyone who had been hit screamed, their voices mingling with the sudden sound of alarm. One of the quad members had tripped the security system for reinforcements.

Casting about for a distraction, Lucas poured his power into the minds of the people around them, starting a riot. Then he telekinetically tossed the members of the quad directly into the path of the suddenly rampaging crowd.

His attention, for the most part, was still focused on the former Strykers.

Lucas pulled the glasses off his face, dark blue eyes bright and fierce with something that might be madness. "This is your one and only chance."

"A bit of an extremist, aren't you?" Threnody said as she shoved away from the side of the bar.

"More of an opportunist." Lucas smiled again, showing all his teeth. "Yes or no?"

She thought about what Lucas had said, they all did. For a vital few seconds, they weighed the words of a Warhound against the edicts of their government, and all of them came away with the same realization.

None of them wanted to die a slave.

"Get us out of here," Kerr said as the noise of people fighting, of people dying, mingled with the shrill alarm of unrest that echoed up and down the street, summoning quad reinforcement.

Lucas teleported out of London, pulling them along with his vast telekinetic strength into the unknown.

[NINE]

AUGUST 2379
TORONTO, CANADA

News of the termination spread quickly through the Stryker ranks. Three days since the two Stryker teams had gone missing, and the World Court hadn't thought anything about giving the kill order. The OIC of the Strykers Syndicate had no choice but to obey. That Ciari became the focus of everyone's fear and hatred was nothing new. That she let herself feel it? *That* was new.

"It's terribly illegal, I know, to want to murder him," Ciari said tiredly, thinking about Erik. "But it would make me feel better."

"You don't like to feel," Jael said as she looked at where Ciari stood in front of a wall filled with vidscreens all streaming different programs in the OIC's office. "You prove that fact over and over again. Why are you choosing today to keep your shields down?"

Jael was angry. It was in the burr of her voice, pressing against the power of Ciari's mind, difficult to ignore. She had every right to be, Ciari thought as her eyes tracked over the dozen or so news streams before her. Every right, and then some. It still didn't mean anything to her despite her empathetic power.

"I knew he would ask for their deaths," Ciari said. "Threnody made too many mistakes during the last few missions. She was on the watch list after Madrid and the botched transfer."

"She and the other teams working with her still got back the stolen crude oil, got it off the trucks, back onto the train, and on its way back to the processing plant in Andorra."

"They lost half of it."

"They still salvaged the rest."

"Doesn't matter. It was still enough of a commotion that the press got wind of it and the government had to do some heavy spin duty to make them look the other way. Propaganda is all well and good, but the government doesn't control *every* news stream."

Jael shook her head, disgust making her voice sharper than usual. "You set Threnody up for failure with this current mission. That blip on the grid turned out to be a Class I triad psion—a rarity—and there's no one in our ranks capable of handling someone like that; not and actually survive the encounter intact."

"The target never previously read as a Class I in all the time we tracked it. It never read as Lucas Serca."

"That's a piss-fucking-poor excuse if I've ever heard one and I've heard many. You *knew* the target had to be dangerous if none of us could pin it down."

Ciari finally turned to face her subordinate, gaze cool. "Everyone in this world is dangerous to someone, Jael. We needed what Threnody could possibly get us, suicide mission or not."

"And what would that be other than two dead teams?"

"A chance. Keiko brought back human bodies from Russia carrying neurotrackers assigned to the missing four."

"I know. I did the autopsies, remember? Best-case scenario is that our Strykers were killed elsewhere, which is better than being tortured. Worst-case scenario is that they're hostages of a rogue Class I triad psion, either being tortured or reprogrammed. You pick."

Over the decades, the Sercas had mastered the skill of hiding their presence on bioscanners and the mental grid, able to project themselves as something they weren't when they had to, which meant their ability to murder unsuspecting Strykers made them formidable enemies. They had passed on that skill to every psion that joined their ranks as a War-hound who had the power to uphold the charade. Ciari had no way of knowing if Lucas Serca was still within the Slums of the Angels or even in Russia. She had no way to confirm if her Strykers were truly dead. The Strykers in the field were still searching in America and Russia for answers, as well as scouring London as discreetly as they could since the government had contacted them about the riot. It was anyone's guess if they would ever know the truth.

"Why let this happen, Ciari?" Jael asked quietly from behind her. "You have the means to work around problems like this. If we had coordinated with Nathan before this happened—"

"No." Ciari cut her off. "We had no other choice."

"I think you're lying."

Ciari let out a low, tired chuckle and carefully raised her shields. "You think?"

"All right, I *know* you're lying." Jael stepped up beside Ciari and looked at her instead of the vidscreens. "You usually appeal every kill order handed down to you, just to have it on record, and it takes a while. It doesn't change a thing—it never has and never will—but it's a sick tradition every OIC has kept. You didn't with these four. Why change the way you do things now?"

Ciari kept quiet long enough that Jael knew she wouldn't get an answer. Letting out a frustrated sigh, Jael turned away from the other woman and headed for the door.

"I'll add their names to our list of the dead," Jael said.

"Don't." Ciari glanced over her shoulder. "Not yet."

"They deserve that much, if not more."

"I know. I'm not saying they don't, but if you put their names on that list, we close out their lives. We can't do that until we've got something to report to the World Court."

"Give us our fucking right to *grieve*, Ciari."

"You only get that right when we've got bodies to burn, and even then only with the government's say-so. They're alive, Jael, and we need to find them. Until we do, they will be listed as rogue status in our records and that won't change. It *can't* change, do you understand me?"

"Perfectly," Jael bit out.

"Good."

Jael strode out of the office, leaving Ciari alone with her thoughts and the twenty-four-hour news stream. Rubbing at the back of her neck, she sighed and turned away from the vidscreens. Retreating to her desk, Ciari dug through the data chips that cluttered one corner, finally finding the one she needed for her next meeting. In her searching, one fell off the desk, and she bent to retrieve it.

Holding it between two fingers, Ciari peered at each side of the data chip. It wasn't shaped like the government chips that they normally used. Clear, with no file number of any sort written on the outside, it was unusual in its blankness. She was never sure when these particular data chips would appear on her desk, but she never questioned their arrival. She'd been getting these data chips at intermittent intervals over the last five years. They always made for a better read than any orders the government sent her.

She put it in her pocket.

Hours later, when she found the time to read the information it held, on a datapad that wasn't synced to any system or acknowledged by the grid, the heavily encrypted message would only be two sentences long: *You know that chance I took? It's paying off.*

The encrypted reply she saved to it was even shorter: *Good.*

In the morning, the data chip was gone from her desk. Ciari didn't question that, either.

[TEN]

There was a phrase in this country's language for what Nathan was doing: *nemawashi*. Formally confirming what had informally been proposed, even if it was still all under the table until the press report went out. Corporate mergers never really came as a surprise to the public. The reason behind every single one was always neatly detailed for anyone to read, though it was the oral agreements that really mattered. Those were the deals that were never recorded. Every businessman and woman seated around the long conference table had come for just such a promise. Nathan Serca's word was better than that of most. His family had spent decades making sure that they were indispensable to the world's needs. This was no different.

Jin Li stepped into the windowless conference room, wearing a severe business suit that wouldn't hamper his movements at all, and a single gun on his hip. Casing the room with a glance over the top of his dark glasses, he pulled a small gray sphere out of his pocket and walked over to the only empty seat at the long table. He pressed two buttons on the side of the sphere, activating it. A green light blinked on and the jamming sequence cut off all vidfeed coming from the security points built into the wall and all recording devices scattered around the table.

"We said no records," Jin Li said, voice flat and dangerous as Nathan finally stepped into the conference room.

"Apologies," said Sydney Athe, the venerable old man rising to his feet with the use of a heavy, ornate cane. "This room is set automatically for recording every time it's in use. I did not think to check that it had been deactivated."

Nathan offered the head of the Athe Syndicate a polite smile as the man's grandson and successor, Elion Athe, stood to help his grandfather sit back down.

The Athe Syndicate was much like the Serca Syndicate in its survival of the Border Wars to become what it was today. The family had been trapped in Sapporo on a business trip during that horrific time, and of all the islands that belonged to Japan, only Hokkaidō had managed to survive partly intact. The Athe family had made themselves indispensable to the survivors of the country and learned to thrive. Elion's father, Travis, was a member of the World Court, and for that alone they would have been allowed into the Registry. Additionally, their genetics were clean, which was a bonus, and their success in aeronautics and space science was worth the delicate dance the Serca family had done with the Athe Syndicate for the past four generations.

"Ladies, gentlemen," Nathan began as he took his seat at the head of the conference table. "Mistakes happen. Just be aware that I do not tolerate them more than once. Our business tonight is far too important to allow our final decisions to fall into outside hands. None of us desires the spotlight for this little addendum of our merger."

Sydney nodded agreement. "The announcement is set to hit the news in the morning. The Athe Syndicate will become a subsidiary of the Serca Syndicate, but I will retain the position as CEO with the understanding that all final decisions will be left up to you, as we agreed."

"As it should be, for what we've offered you," Nathan said. "The additional berths on the Ark we've agreed to sell you means that when the time comes, you will support us on Mars."

"Of course," Sydney said, looking Nathan straight in the eye when no one else would. It wasn't the Japanese way to get straight to the point, but Sydney still retained some of the mannerisms of his Western ancestors. "A deal is a deal, Nathan. My family will be whatever you need us to be, so long as you take us with you."

It was funny how desperation could make anyone willing to sell his soul. Nathan spread his hands over the datapad he had brought with him, keying in his biometrics to open it. Files appeared beneath his fingertips and he tapped at the only one he needed. The executed merger agreement filled his screen, and Nathan perused all the signatures that had brought him here.

"There will be a meeting for all the subsidiaries of the Serca Syndicate at the beginning of September. Keep your calendars clear. I will send you the confirmed date once I've met again with the World Court." Nathan looked up, his gaze sweeping across the table, capturing everyone's eyes. "I expect the transfer to run smoothly."

"Do you anticipate any difficulties?" Elion asked, his green eyes startlingly odd in a face whose features were predominantly Japanese.

"I plan for all possible avenues, which means you will be ready. If you are not, you forfeit the seats you asked for and I will sell them to someone else. Whoever you hope to bring with you will be left behind. As you know, there are only so many seats available, and my Syndicate is in control of at least half. Not every registered human is going to be on those ships."

"But enough will," Sydney said. "And you are more than capable of keeping everyone in line."

Nathan's smile was indulgent. "Always."

Sydney banged his cane down once on the floor, nodding at those who worked for him. "Leave us. You have your assurances."

All the men and women around the table except Elion got to their feet and bowed, first to Sydney, then to Nathan, before filing out past Jin Li. None of them bothered to hide their disgust for Nathan's bodyguard, and it had little to do with his slouching against the wall.

During the Border Wars, China had fared worse than most countries outside of Africa and the Middle East. Already saddled with a near impossible population density living off hugely strained natural resources and with a toxicity level that was already dangerous before the first bomb fell, China spiraled into devastation faster than most other countries. Like the rest of the world, it wasn't the radiation poisoning that killed off most of the population. That would be the starvation, the disease, and the mass deaths in the countryside that surrounded the craters most major cities had become.

The survivors had no choice but to relocate, and the Chinese numbered more than their neighbors, even after the last bomb fell. Southeastern

Asia still had pockets of ethnic minorities from the countries they had once been, but they were ruled by the Chinese now. Japan had patrolled the East China Sea for over 150 years, refusing any and all refugees looking for port that came out of what China had become. No love was lost between the two countries and Jin Li knew it.

Jin Li smiled at every person who walked out the door, then spat on the floor behind the heels of the last woman out. The door slid shut before any of them could voice their anger.

"Your children have better manners than your guard," Elion said coolly as he eyed Jin Li from where he sat.

"Jin Li has his uses, or don't you remember the last time we came calling?" Nathan arched one pale eyebrow. Elion swallowed his anger with appropriate swiftness as he recalled the businessman whom Jin Li had summarily executed after Nathan discovered his treachery. Corporate spies were annoying, and that one hadn't been worth the effort of reprogramming.

"I see that you do," Nathan said. "It's always refreshing to deal with people who know when to keep their mouths shut."

"What more do you require from us?" Sydney said slowly.

Nathan leaned back in his chair and touched the screen of his datapad with one finger. Another list, this one detailing every known city and company Lucas had hit in the past two years. The Athe Syndicate numbered high on that list, beneath all the Serca-owned branches his son had gone to.

"Your Syndicate built the satellites that the World Court sent out fifty years ago to Mars," Nathan said. "I want you to go through your security records for the past two years and do a facial recognition search. You will be looking for Lucas."

Sydney frowned. "For what reason?"

"Because we psions cannot hide from machines and I want to know what he was searching for."

"Why would your son have broken into our Syndicate?" Elion asked.

"Lucas is no longer my son."

This telling response caused Elion and Sydney to share a brief, sharp glance. Nathan knew what they were thinking, and he allowed them to think it. This was a calculated dispersal of information, seeds that needed to be sown. Nathan's own mother had disclosed the Serca family's true nature to the heads of the Athe family years and years ago to make them think that the Sercas needed them. Sometimes secrets were the best bargaining chips when used appropriately.

"Two years of security feed," Sydney said. "Give us a week to do a thorough review of all our holdings. I will send Elion in person to London with the results once we have them."

"That is acceptable." Nathan pushed himself to his feet. "The launch date may be moved up, depending on certain timetables that the World Court is relying on. If it does, you and your family will personally be brought to London. I can promise you that."

"I thank you."

"I don't do it out of need or some sense of generosity." Nathan offered Sydney a mocking smile. "I do it because I can. Your family is useful. Continue to be useful and maybe you will survive another generation."

The men Nathan left behind were smart enough to heed this warning. Their ability to bend was part of the reason why Nathan had chosen to bring them under Serca control through this merger and why Nathan kept them there. The Athes had always been useful to someone.

Jin Li followed Nathan out of the conference room and down the ornately decorated hallway of the Athe Syndicate's executive suite. A security guard bowed as they stepped into a lift that went to the roof, where their shuttle sat on the landing platform, engines on standby and guarded by Gideon.

"You're not supposed to be here," Nathan said pointedly to his son after Nathan and Jin Li climbed into the shuttle beneath the morning sunlight.

"No one saw me arrive when I teleported into your shuttle," Gideon assured him. "And this needed to be reported in person."

"I take it you finally have what I told you to find?" Nathan shook his head as he sat down in his seat and buckled on the harness. "Three days late."

"I wanted to be sure." Gideon took a seat opposite Nathan and hooked himself into the harness there. "I found something of interest."

Nathan narrowed his eyes. "Get to the point."

"You asked about the Strykers that Lucas picked up out of the Slums." Gideon pulled a data chip from his shirt pocket and passed it over to Nathan telekinetically. "Jin Li fought two of them in Johannesburg thirty-four days prior to the skirmish in the Slums. Threnody Corwin is a Class III electrokinetic. Her partner, Quinton Martinez, is a Class III pyrokinetic."

"That's not unusual."

"She ordered her partner and the teams she commanded in Johannesburg not to pursue Jin Li when he escaped with the children we had targeted at the school there."

"Occasionally Strykers *do* think, Gideon," Nathan said as he uploaded the data chip on his datapad. "They were outmatched in that venture and they knew it."

"Maybe. Those two joined up with a second team for the mission in the Slums. You'll see on that data chip that our records for the Strykers Syndicate's only Class II telepath, Kerr MacDougal, aren't very informative."

"He's dysfunctional. We discovered that when he was first put in the field."

"His partner, Jason Garret, is an anomaly."

"A Class V telekinetic is nothing out of the ordinary."

"Samantha fought him, sir. It was the first time she's faced off against those two. She said the telekinetic had mental shields that were impervious to her strongest telepathic strike."

Nathan looked up from the information on his screen. "Samantha is capable of getting through most shielding. I taught her myself. A Class V of any kind of psion should have been relatively easy."

Gideon shrugged, having to raise his voice over the sound of the engines starting up in order to be heard. "I asked her about it. She said his shields wouldn't even crack. She bruised his mind, but she couldn't break his defenses. And there was something else. The shields? They weren't like any that Samantha's ever felt before."

Nathan scrolled through the brief file they had on Jason Garret before casting his telepathy outward across the world for his daughter's mind.

Her psi signature sparked brightly above all the rest of the humans on the mental grid, and he sank into her thoughts with ease.

This telekinetic you fought in the Slums, he said. *What was so different about his shields?*

Samantha didn't hesitate in answering. *They were anchored in a way I've never seen before. They went deeper than I thought shields could ever go.*

Show me.

Samantha opened up her memories to his perusal, letting him dig again through those moments in the Slums where she had attempted to break into the telekinetic's mind. This time he took more than just her memories, he took her thoughts, her reasoning at the time of the fight. Nathan drew back after a few seconds, faint surprise coloring his thoughts.

Nathan's reaction was enough for Samantha to say, *Sir?*

That doesn't make any sense.

What doesn't?

Those shields you tried to break. They're natal shields.

Samantha's confusion matched his own, but Nathan didn't let her sense it. *That's impossible. How can he access his power if his natal shields are still standing?*

How indeed?

Nathan dropped the psi link, pulling back into his own mind. He opened his eyes, meeting his son's gaze. Gideon was waiting patiently for whatever order would come his way. Gideon waited, when Lucas would already have been suggesting action. Nathan wished Gideon's ability to know and obey his betters had bred true in Lucas.

Nathan had raised his children under the personal bylaws that governed the Serca family, following a long tradition of grooming the next generation for the fight for power. Psions never lived all that long, and the Serca Syndicate's goals needed to be maintained over generations. Nathan had survived longer than most psions only because he'd never used his power enough for it to kill him—yet. Nathan's decision to use his children first before he used his own powers had come at the direct order of his mother, Marcheline, when she had ordered him to risk the next generation for a reason she had never explained. His mother had been a singularly manipulative woman who died in her forties. No love had been lost between Nathan and his mother. Only hate was left between himself and his children.

"I want Lucas found," Nathan said. "I want him brought back to me before autumn, as well as the Strykers he took, if they're still with him and alive."

"Why the Strykers?"

"Lucas wanted them. I want whatever Lucas has."

The shuttle had reached that high cruising altitude where the sky was dark with the edge of space above and the clouds were ugly wisps below them. Nathan undid the straps of his harness and got to his feet.

"Return to London without me," he said, before teleporting away.

[ELEVEN]

AUGUST 2379

THE HAGUE, THE NETHERLANDS

You're late."

The aggravated tone of Sharra Gervais's voice floated down the hallway of their bunker suite. Erik looked up from where he stood in the foyer, shrugging out of his robes of office. His wife walked toward him with a glass of expensive wine in her hand, the stiletto heels of her shoes sinking into the plush carpeting that lay atop the hard metal floor of their home. Sharra was tall, blond, and blue-eyed, a Nordic beauty with her name in the Registry and a ring on her finger given to her by one of the most powerful men in the world. Any man in his right mind would have loved her.

"It can't be helped," Erik said as hung his robes in the wide closet by the front blast doors. The small bunker city carved below the rubble above was still more lived-in than any other building aboveground. By law, the members of the World Court had to reside in the safety of these underground hallways and homes.

"You say that every time. Pick another excuse." Sharra glared at him over the rim of her wineglass. Lipstick had transferred a perfect imprint of her mouth to the delicate, clear glass. The color looked like waxy crayon, which meant this was not her first, second, or even third glass of wine.

Erik stepped closer to kiss Sharra on the cheek. He hated the taste of her drunk on his tongue.

"I take it Lillian has already gone to bed?" he said.

"It's midnight. Even the bunker guards have gone to bed except for a skeleton crew." Sharra spun on her heels and left him where he stood for the mess the dining room had become.

When Erik finally joined her there, he saw that the ribbons and balloons from the party were still up, the half-eaten cake still fresh beneath the preservation cover, and the wrappings from all the presents scattered across the floor. Sharra sat her wineglass down on the table and leaned her weight against the wooden edge of it.

"I asked for one thing from you, Erik," she said in a low voice. "Just one."

"I give what I can. You know that." Erik looked around at the remains of his daughter's birthday party and felt no regret for missing it. He'd had other matters to attend to. "Lillian is young. She'll hardly remember I wasn't here."

"Lillian is *five,* you son of a bitch," Sharra snarled. "She'll remember that her father wasn't here, just like you weren't there for the other four."

"She's a *child,* Sharra." The irritation in Erik's voice was thick after a sixteen-hour workday. "I have no use for children until they're old enough to understand what it is I expect from them."

The laughter that came out of his wife's mouth was strained. "The sad thing is that she has use for *you,* Erik. You're her father. At least one day this year, couldn't you have bothered to *act* like it?"

The headache that had been pounding through his skull since before noon became worse at the shrill tone in his wife's voice.

"I'm not doing this," Erik told her as he walked out of the room. "I've had a full schedule today and it's only going to be worse tomorrow as we run down the clock to the launch. You're impossible to reason with when you're like this."

He left her standing alone in the dining room, with its bright lights and carefully chosen decorations; with the mess on the floor and the mess in her head and tears of frustration in her eyes. She was forty-three years old with the face and body of someone half her age. She should have been *enough,* Sharra thought as she picked up her wineglass and drained it in two quick, long swallows. She should have been more than enough to hold his attention.

Sharra knew Erik wasn't cheating on her. The press would have a field day with that story, but more than the threat of social humiliation for Erik, she *knew* he didn't have the desire to cheat on her with another woman. She'd paid enough for that promise; she just hadn't seen all those years ago that politics was a bed her husband would wallow in more than her own.

"Mama?"

Sharra set the wineglass down and carefully wiped at her eyes with a fingertip. She blinked back the tears, steadied herself despite the alcohol in her system, and turned to face her daughter, pasting a smile on her face that not even the best politician could have seen through for the lie it truly was.

Lillian was a tiny slip of a thing, with her mother's wide blue eyes and her father's dark hair. Wrapped up in her favorite blanket, with her small feet peeking out beneath her nightgown, she was hopeful in the way that only children could be in this world, before they learned their history. The ones who had their names in the Registry since birth, clean air, clean water, and a future paid in full.

"Sweetie, you should be asleep," Sharra said as she carefully bent down to pick up her daughter. "It's very late and the party has been over for hours."

"I thought I heard Daddy."

The taste of wine on Sharra's tongue turned rancid as she looked into her daughter's hopeful eyes. Cradling her close, Sharra walked on surprisingly steady feet through the hallways of their large living quarters, carrying her daughter back to her bedroom.

"Your daddy's still at work," Sharra lied. "I'll send him in to say goodnight when he finally gets home."

"Oh."

The sound of disappointment was thick in the little girl's voice, and Sharra gave her an extrahard hug before tucking Lillian back into the soft bed, which was still warm from when she'd crawled out of it. Sitting beside her, Sharra smoothed her daughter's hair out of her eyes and smiled down at the little girl.

"In the morning, I'll make you breakfast. But only if you go to sleep."

"Pancakes?" the girl asked, knowing she usually got her way.

"Pancakes. With chocolate chips." An expensive dish, about as expensive as the wine Sharra drank. Cacao plants were grown in only one Sky-Farms cluster somewhere in Brazil. Only the very rich in the Registry had ever tasted chocolate. Lillian had a terrible sweet tooth.

Lillian smiled up at her mother, her small teeth shiny and white in the light coming from the hallway. Then the girl squeezed her eyes shut and flopped on her side, pretend snores coming out of her mouth. Sharra leaned down and pressed a kiss to her daughter's cheek, careful not to breathe. She didn't want her daughter knowing what a drunkard her mother was, not yet at least.

She left Lillian's room, but didn't immediately retreat to the one she shared with Erik. Half a bottle of wine left in the kitchen still needed to be finished. Waste wasn't tolerated, even in the households of registered humans. When she finally made it to the kitchen, she found the wine being poured down the sink.

Sharra jerked to a shaky halt on her high heels as she glared at the man standing in the kitchen. In her drunken state, he could have been a hallucination, but even when she was sober, he'd always been real, even when she wished he weren't.

"*What* are you doing here?" she demanded in a low, frantic voice.

"Erik won't wake up," Nathan said as he set aside the empty wine bottle and turned to look at her. "He never does when I'm here."

"You don't *know* that."

"When I put someone under, they *stay* under, Sharra." Nathan came over to her and wrapped a hand around her upper arm, guiding her with learned politeness to the nearest seat. Stiff with panic and fear, Sharra followed like a wooden puppet and sank into the chair. "You need something a little stronger than wine."

A small crystal tumbler appeared on the table in front of her. An eyeblink later and a bottle of aged Scotch joined it. Sharra stared at both as if they were bombs.

She swallowed back bile. "What do you want?"

"I got what I wanted from you years ago." Nathan smiled at her, the expression as cold as his voice. "Right now, I'm more interested in what Lucas wants from you, if he wants anything at all."

"I don't speak to your children, Nathan."

"They're half yours, or don't you remember what it cost to get where you are today?"

Sharra closed her eyes, the wine in her stomach souring into something that wanted to crawl up her throat. A woman of her stature, with a life lived on a mountain of lies. A woman with her name in the Registry, a ring on her finger, and five children to her name. She didn't care about Nathan's. She only cared about her daughter.

That didn't mean her children wouldn't come looking for her, and Nathan knew it.

"He hasn't been here," Sharra said, opening her eyes. "Why would he? I've nothing he could possibly want."

They had their father's eyes, but her straight nose, shades of their blond hair. The rest was all a mixture of DNA—hers and Nathan's, and whatever was in her human genome that could make Nathan's psionic attributes breed true. She was useful, and Sharra knew from personal, painful experience that being useful was the only way to survive. Her current position—her marriage, her *human daughter*—were the results of producing four embryos for the Serca family. In return, she'd been promised certain survival.

Nathan stared at her from where he stood, tall and perfect in his business suit, with power at his fingertips that Erik could never hope to harness. Psion power that no one ever saw because Nathan was a master at being just human enough that no one looked beyond the veneer.

"I've kept your secrets," Sharra whispered bitterly.

"Because you can't speak a word of them to anyone. We made sure of that," Nathan said. "You will notify me if Lucas comes calling. I will know if you don't."

Sharra reached up instinctively to touch the side of her head, thinking of the bioware net that spanned the entirety of her brain and how fucking *useless* it was in the face of psionic power.

Nathan's smile was slow and dangerous as he noticed the motion of her hand. "When has that ever stopped me before?"

It hadn't, and the systems that monitored the bioware nets for those on or related to those on the World Court never showed psionic interference. Nathan and his Warhounds were amazingly adept at circumventing human technology when they needed to.

"Why don't you simply kill us all?" Sharra asked, the alcohol in her system making her braver than she could ever be sober.

Nathan let his fingers stroke through her hair and Sharra drew in a strangled breath.

"Humans live long enough to be useful" was Nathan's calm answer. "Our one evolutionary shortcoming is your gain."

"You've lived nearly two lifetimes, Nathan."

"Yes. Only because I'm killing our children in order to do so, but that isn't a guaranteed cure. If I used my power even half as much as I order them to use theirs, I would be dead. And, oh, you would enjoy that, wouldn't you, Sharra?" Nathan's hands settled heavily on her shoulders, a weight that always pulled at her. "I will live long enough to see Mars Colony. I will live long enough to rule there in the open instead of here behind closed doors. I want that new world, not this mess our ancestors left us. I deserve better than that."

Sharra closed her eyes and breathed through her nose. "I hope to God you die out in space."

Nathan laughed, the sound low and amused, his breath blowing over the shell of her ear. "I want the latest launch information by the end of the week."

"I don't know if I can get that for you."

"Then I suggest you find a way, as you've done all the times before, or your daughter will grow up without a mother. Or perhaps you will grow old without her." He squeezed her shoulders. It felt as if he squeezed the life out of her. "When I tampered with Erik's mind all those years ago to make sure he saw you and only you as a possibility for his wife, you knew the cost of that deal."

She didn't say, *Erik doesn't love me*. She didn't need to. Nathan picked the thought straight out of her mind with an ease that still frightened her, even after all these years of him doing it.

"I never promised you something as useless as love. You got safety. I get information. You have a week." He pulled his hands away from her and she could breathe again. "Good-bye, Sharra."

He disappeared in that disturbingly alien way that teleportation encompassed. Sharra shivered, suddenly cold, and hunched over in her seat. Pressing hands that shook to her mouth, she breathed slowly, trying desperately not to get sick there on her kitchen floor.

In the end, she chose Scotch over sleep, Nathan over her husband, because for all the vows they'd spoken at their wedding, she owed Nathan everything and Erik only the appearance of fidelity.

[TWELVE]

AUGUST 2379

TARRAGONA, SPAIN

Spain was a wasteland cut apart by deadzones and desertification that had swallowed half the country over a century ago. Madrid was a crater, bombed over and over again during the Border Wars, like most of the major and not so major European cities. Barcelona, east of Tarragona on the Iberian Peninsula, was nothing more than a wide bay of water, the newest coastline addition to the Mediterranean Sea.

Tarragona was half-underground to escape the radiation taint that fallout had spread across the country during the Border Wars. Nuclear winter had lowered the planet's overall temperature, but only for a short time. Warmth eventually returned, and with it, massive, deadly storms that swept periodically over the world: hurricanes and tornadoes, sandstorms and derechos, monsoons and whiteout blizzards. Pollution was still a problem, climate change had altered the region even before society nearly blew itself up, and Tarragona had no city towers for registered humans, only segregated bunkers.

The military-grade shuttle flew just above the low-hanging cloud cover in the night sky, lights off, stealth mode up and running. The engines were barely a hum in Samantha's bones as she peered over the pilot's shoulder through the flight-deck windshields. A hologrid shone in the air between the pilot and the navigator, a ground map with precise details of the maglev train gunning toward Spain's largest surviving city. With a population around 146,000, Tarragona was second only to London in population in Western Europe.

"Speed?" Samantha said.

"Two hundred twenty and decreasing," the pilot said as he lightly adjusted his grip on the stick. "Your orders?"

Samantha pushed away from the seat. "Descend. We'll take it from here."

The pilot nodded, attention already focused on the route his navigator was building. Samantha walked back into the cargo bay of the shuttle, letting the hatch close and seal shut behind her. She steadied herself as she felt the shuttle beginning to change its angle of flight for the descent, feeling a telekinetic touch brace her body and give her additional support. She nodded her thanks to the Warhound who had reached out to her.

"We're descending," she told everyone in the cargo bay. "Telekinetics, be ready for assault. Telepaths, you're with me in merge."

"How many Strykers do you think are down there?" Genevieve asked as she checked the clip in her assault rifle and slung the strap across her shoulder, bracing the weapon against her bent legs. The twenty-five-year-old

Class III telekinetic was the best train hijacker in the Warhound ranks. Samantha still wished she had her twin by her side.

"Several teams, at the very least." Samantha dragged herself back to her assigned seat and strapped into her harness. "Fuel transport trains always have heavy defenses."

"Hungry," Kristen said from beside her. The empath was strapped into her harness, fingers tapping out a soft rhythm against the armrests of her seat.

"Not yet." Samantha pressed her power against her sister's mind, skimming it over those jagged broken shields. "You feed on my say-so."

"Sure, Sammy-girl." Kristen's smile got so wide that the corners of her mouth cracked and bled. "On your say-so."

Which, in Kristen's demented way of thinking, could be whenever Samantha opened her mouth or 'pathed out an order. Samantha offered her sister a sharp look and a warning telepathic probe before sliding out of Kristen's mind.

It had taken five days to track the oil shipments coming through the Suez Canal to the Mediterranean Sea and up to Europe's southern shores. Previous generations had nearly depleted the Middle East oil supplies, but the regional governments in control at the time had placed trade restrictions on exports to save some of the fossil fuel for their own people. What the World Court had slowly been siphoning out of the surviving storage bunkers wasn't headed anywhere except to the Paris Basin, to be transported to Mars, or so they thought.

Samantha clenched her hands into fists until her knuckles popped. Warhounds had stolen a quarter of those shipments over the past thirty years, ransoming it back to the government at ridiculously high prices. Her grandmother—may Marcheline's sadistic soul never rest—had begun the credit buildup that the Warhounds would need for their bottom line once they got off-planet, and Nathan was continuing that effort. They would need that monetary leverage when all the functioning parts of society were transplanted to someplace better. Humanity, what they would allow of it into space, was worth its weight in gold.

The shuttle picked up speed as it descended. Samantha pushed those thoughts aside and focused on the scene around her. Genevieve and her telekinetics were out of their seats, held stable in the shuttle's unsteady course by their own power as they pulled on the oxygen helmets attached to the small tanks buckled to their backs. They didn't need safety lines, not when they had the option of teleportation and the anchoring grasp of telekinesis. The six telekinetics ranged from a Class V to a Class III. More than enough telekinetic power to grab those fuel tanks off the back of the train and 'port them out of human reach.

The only problem with that plan, Samantha mused as the shuttle took evasive maneuvers against ground-to-air missiles, was that the humans employed Strykers.

Open the cargo doors, Samantha ordered.

Wind whipped through the interior of the shuttle as hydraulics opened the rear cargo doors, the cabin pressure falling. The telekinetics were lined up in pairs at the very edge, gravity and air pulling at their limbs. Genevieve didn't wait for Samantha's order; she had more experience than Samantha at leading these kinds of missions. The telekinetics wrapped themselves in their power and jumped out of the shuttle, dropping in a controlled fall toward the speeding train below.

Samantha closed her eyes, struggling to breathe; easier to concentrate in darkness than the brightness of the shuttle. The roaring of the wind faded as the cargo doors closed back up, the pressure equalizing again. Samantha dropped her shields, slid her power into the minds of her fellow Warhounds, and started to build the merge.

This was something that the Strykers still didn't know how to duplicate, or simply weren't allowed to learn. The layered strength that came with three telepathic minds coming together meant that they had that much more power to draw from. Samantha took up the apex position in the merge and sent their minds skimming over the mental grid toward the bright spots that burned like fire.

"Leaving me out in the cold," Kristen murmured from beside her.

Samantha felt her sister's bitten-down nails dig into the skin of her left wrist. She ignored the pain that skittered up her arm, the majority of it empathically created.

Ready to break, Samantha said into Genevieve's mind, her mental voice echoed by the other three in the merge.

Genevieve's answer was calm. *Missiles are diverted.*

Samantha couldn't hear the explosions on the ground below; didn't need to. She could hear the panic in the human thoughts of the workers that rode the train as clearly as if she were standing in the cars with them. Samantha felt her mouth curve into a smile, but it was a distant expression.

The merge spread like a net across the mental grid where they fought, telepathic power pressing down like a heavy load onto the Stryker and human minds below. Only when the Warhounds had their positions set did Samantha drop most of her shields, letting her telepathy ram into the minds they had surrounded.

The government had opted for a full squad of Strykers, eight teams, at a pair apiece. Sixteen Strykers of varied types, varied Classes, but none of them could counter a merge backed by her Class II strength. They didn't have the resources available to them, just their orders, and those would get them killed tonight. They would still go down fighting.

Shit, Samantha said, tapping into Genevieve's thoughts. *They're going to blow the train.*

Getting desperate, Genevieve replied. *That's a fucking waste of perfectly good oil. We're working on getting a grip on the weight. We need a few more minutes.*

She was asking Samantha to buy them time.

Samantha did one better.

She reached with the strength of the merge for Kristen's mind, her sister greedily reaching back. The jagged, deep holes in the empath's power bit into Samantha's mind with a viciousness that made her physically flinch. Kristen's mind was a starved thing, twisted into swollen knots as her empathic power fed on itself in a continuous state of desperate survival. Samantha shunted Kristen's mind through the merge, beneath their shields, the other telepaths helping her to control Kristen's descent, as they forced the girl to obey their chosen course of action.

The merged telepathic strike, braced by Kristen's malignant empathic power, broke through the Strykers' defenses with a ferocity that left two Strykers dying immediately of critical psi shock. The rest didn't have the ability to defend against Kristen's need to feed, and the teen had never discriminated between the minds of registered and unregistered humans, nor the distinctive burn of psions who weren't fast enough to escape. They all tasted the same to her.

The mental grid got darker, minds winking out as Kristen's empathy fed on the emotions and thoughts around her. Her power simply ate through the defenses thrown in her way, transferring the foundations of her victims' sanity into her own. Her sanity was makeshift, nothing more, and everything she stole would disintegrate within days, leaving behind yet another hole in her mind.

Samantha left Kristen to her fun, but kept fingers of her power at the edge of her sister's mind even as she checked in with Genevieve.

Forgot how she wrecks everyone's concentration, Genevieve said tightly. *We need some shields, Samantha. These tankers are heavier than the last shipment we stole.*

Can you 'port them? Samantha wanted to know even as she erected a telepathic shield between Kristen's swath of mental devastation and the knot of concentration that was the Warhound telekinetics.

It's a matter of distance and weight. Genevieve's mind dipped heavily against Samantha's, power burning through the psi link they shared as she tapped into her telekinetic strength. *We'll get it done before the train crashes.*

We still need the maglev platform to remain intact.

Train still has to crash. Trust me. I know what the fuck I'm doing.

Samantha didn't have any doubt. Looking through Genevieve's eyes from where the telekinetic was crouched on top of the train's engine car, all she could see was progress. The line of tankers following behind were slowly disappearing.

"Military jets are scrambling," the pilot said over the comm system, splitting Samantha's concentration. "ETA five minutes."

Break away, Samantha ordered. *We're finished here. Genevieve, you've got five minutes before the government's fighter jets are on you.*

We can finish in two.

The shuttle banked hard, throwing Samantha against the straps of her harness and the seat with bruising force. She felt metal bite into the meat of her shoulders, the edge of her cheek. She could feel the shuttle pick up speed as the pilot sought to put distance between them and the jets that appeared on their radar.

Pulling out of Genevieve's mind, Samantha blinked open her eyes, staring hard at the gray wall of the shuttle's interior to ground herself as she untangled her mind from the merge. Something warm slid down her wrist, and she looked down to see that Kristen's nails had cut into her skin, leaving crimson crescent-moon marks across the ridge of her tendon. She flexed her hand, watching the play of muscle beneath her skin.

"I'm not your anchor," Samantha said as she wiped the blood away on her uniform.

"Of course not," Kristen replied calmly, sanity creeping into the tone of her voice, cutting through the gleam of her eyes. They both knew this was a temporary state. "Mine left."

"Lucas isn't coming back."

Kristen's smile tempered itself into a smirk as she lifted bloody fingers to wipe them over Samantha's throat before the older girl could stop her.

"So little faith, Sammy-girl."

Samantha reached out and slammed her sister's head against the cradle of her seat. "Keep your hands and mind to yourself."

Kristen laughed low in her throat. "Never gonna happen. Can't happen. *Won't.*"

Samantha's mouth curled up in disgust as she pulled back. "I don't know why Nathan hasn't killed you yet."

"For reasons exactly like this." Kristen licked her lips and shrugged one shoulder. "He still needs me. Same as he needs you."

"Maybe I'll get lucky and he'll leave you behind when we ship out to Mars."

A cheerful "Maybe" was Kristen's opinion on that as her mind evened out some. With the death of all those humans and Strykers on the ground, Kristen was gaining back some shred of mental balance.

In the depths of Kristen's twisted mind, at the bottom where her damaged power stemmed from, the psi link that Lucas had buried in her insanity years ago when she was just a toddler switched on at the barest trace of sanity.

Hello, Kris. Lucas's telepathic power flowed through the swirling madness that was, for a brief moment, dimmed. Controlled. *How was dinner?*

Kristen stared at her sister until Samantha looked away, the contempt between them an emotion that Kristen didn't bother to brush aside.

Delicious.

Why don't you tell me all about it?

On the flight back to London, high in the atmosphere, Kristen did exactly that.

PART FOUR
ALLIANCE

SESSION DATE: **2128.09.22**
LOCATION: **Institute of Psionics Research**
CLEARANCE ID: **Dr. Amy Bennett**
SUBJECT: **2581**
FILE NUMBER: **879**

"I want to go home," the girl says, sounding tired and hoarse, sitting slumped in the same seat as before. She is thinner than she was at the beginning, drawn brittle by time that is running out.

"You know you can leave if you just tell us what we want to know," the doctor says.

"You want a second chance on Mars." The girl wrinkles her small nose at the doctor and shakes her head. "But you should want Earth."

"I think you should tell us how to stop this war."

Aisling blinks at her slowly, bleached-out violet eyes set in a hollow face. "I'm tired. I want to sleep."

"Do you know," the doctor says, voice gone ragged and harsh, "how many countries have been lost to this madness?"

"Yes," Aisling says softly as she picks at the electrodes on the back of one hand, the machines spiking on a high-pitched whine. "I saw them all die. But don't worry, Threnody. It's going to be okay in the end."

[THIRTEEN]

AUGUST 2379
BUFFALO, USA

Buffalo was where the survivors fled during and after the Border Wars. It was where their descendants remained, locked into underground bunkers and sealed city towers.

In the local parlance, it was a sprawl as opposed to a slum, but it had its borders, it had its limits. Pocketed between the deadzones of the Midwest and the inner areas of the East Coast, with a little slice of toxic water named Lake Erie on one side, Buffalo was sanctuary and hell all in one.

City towers stabbed into the sky in the northeast, a shrewdly built wall between the masses and the closely guarded SkyFarms. A detoxification plant hugged the shores of Lake Erie, the make of it different from that of the combo-detox plants that were built into ocean waters. No desalination was needed here, but the price of clean water, which was worth dying for some days, was still high.

Overhead, shuttles winged through the sky to lock in on anchor docks jutting away from the city towers, never settling to the ground. Maglev train platforms spiked away from Buffalo in half a dozen different directions, turning the city into a distorted fat insect when seen from above. The ancient train tracks made of iron and wood from before the Border Wars were no good anymore. They were either completely broken or ran straight through deadzones with radiation levels still high enough that no amount of shielding attached to the maglev trains could block it.

In the sprawl of Buffalo, people got around by foot more than by car or bus, using underground tunnels before risking the open air. The electrical grid that powered everyone's lives only had so much to spare for the ground vehicles that kept humanity lurching forward from one day to the next. Acid storms tended to eat through even the best-protected wires, and the salvaged steel homes of unregistered humans got lower priority than transportation. First priority went to the SkyFarms, second to the city towers of the registered humans. The government controlled the hierarchy in Buffalo, but people still fell through the cracks, just as they did everywhere else in the world.

It was into one of those cracks that Lucas teleported them.

The small warehouse at the city limits was empty when they arrived. The teleport sent all but Lucas sprawling to the ground, the Strykers still shaky on their legs after illegal brain surgery. Lucas was used to the pain that came from a teleport, which bridged the distance between continents. That didn't mean pushing himself like this was a good thing. Sniffing up blood, ignoring the throbbing pain right behind his eyes, Lucas squinted through the dust that drifted in and out of sunbeams pouring through a line of windows on one side of the warehouse. It was like an oven inside these four walls, the environmental systems off and the air almost too thick to breathe.

"Security feed?" Threnody gasped out as she shoved herself to her hands and knees.

"Not here," Lucas said as sweat dripped down his face, soaking into the collar of his shirt. "The scavengers I deal with don't like the government watching their every move. This place is off the government's grid, but the scavengers will know we've arrived."

"Scavengers," Quinton said, the only one who seemed unbothered by the heat in the warehouse. "Those crazy bastards who dig around in the deadzones without protection? Tell me you're joking."

"I don't joke. About anything."

Lucas moved away from the Strykers, who were picking themselves off the ground. He activated the control panel by the warehouse door, tapping out a code that didn't require biometrics for input. With a heavy grinding sound the door unlocked and a long line of light appeared at its bottom. The door jacked itself up slowly, the sound grating on their ears. It stopped at head height for Lucas. A breeze rolled into the warehouse, hot and heavy, clearing out the stagnant air.

Walking into the afternoon sunlight, Lucas spun around in a slow circle, taking in any changes since his last visit. He still had his dark glasses on, his black clothes soaking up the sunlight uncomfortably. More sweat beaded on his skin, streaking through dirt as it slid down his face and arms. He lifted a hand and offered up a mock salute at the nearest security feed monitoring the area.

You coming? he sent across the mental grid, skirting down the psi link he'd implanted in that obnoxious woman's mind years ago, knowing she was keeping a lookout for them.

Your scrawny ass needs more weight on its bones, that raw voice sent back.

You going to put it there?

The laugh echoed down to him; amused, revolted. *You psions are too expensive to feed. Who're the riders?*

Needed. Just get down here.

He broke contact, turning to watch the Strykers stumble out of the warehouse. They still had that shocky look to them, a fear at the back of their eyes that came from being unleashed from the government. The freedom might have been a lie, but it was heady.

Except they weren't free of Lucas. He still had his power threaded through their minds. He'd know their intentions before they even thought them all the way through, and their powers were his until he decided otherwise.

"Where are we?" Threnody said.

"Buffalo," Lucas replied. "New York."

In sync, all four Strykers looked north toward the city that they couldn't see, not behind jagged teeth of buildings and towers and hazy pollution. Toronto was too far away to be anything but a dream, and they were too smart to believe in something so out of reach.

Jason grimaced and reached up to touch the back of his neck where the quick-heal patch had yet to dissolve. "Why?"

"We made a bargain, remember? You help me do what needs to be done and you'll have your freedom." Lucas tucked his hands into his back pockets and bent backward some. His spine cracked softly as he stretched. "You can have Aisling's word on it, since none of you trust mine."

"You're going to have to introduce us to that girl someday," Kerr said in exasperation.

Lucas pointedly ignored them as he wandered back over to the side of the warehouse, sitting down on the dirty and cracked ground with his back against the building. "We've got a while to wait. Get comfortable."

Three of them would have argued, except Threnody obeyed Lucas's order with a faint shrug, sitting down on the ground with at least a meter's space between the two. Quinton joined her after a moment, with Kerr and Jason following their lead. Kerr helped Jason sit down, the telekinetic still pale in the face. The initial drugs that the doctor had pumped into him for surgery had long ago worn off, and Jason's shields prevented Lucas from manipulating the pain. It hurt Jason to move his head and neck, hurt to walk. He needed more than a quick-heal patch over sealant, and Kerr knew it, could feel it through their bond.

Lucas, Kerr said. *Let me help him.*

He was surprised, to say the least, when he felt the shift of that formidable telepathic strength in his mind, opening up one of Kerr's channels for use. Telepathy flooded through his mind, a rush that Kerr tried desperately not to crave as he sent his power down the bond he shared with Jason. It took a little more effort than he would have liked, but Kerr tricked Jason's mind into ignoring some of the pain. Jason didn't say thank you, just squeezed Kerr's arm. It meant the same thing.

Lucas blocked Kerr's power again.

"Back in London with the quads," Threnody said after the silence became too much, "we all know how they found us. The government has that same facial recognition software here. You can keep us off the mental grid, but they'll still be able to find us if you don't give us what keeps you hidden as well."

Lucas smiled a little at the accusatory tone in her voice. "Smart woman. Still not smart enough to realize that I needed that little scene at Camden Market."

"You like pissing Nathan off that much?" Quinton asked, voice hard. "Use someone else next time you want to get his attention."

"I've got you four. I don't need anyone else just yet." Lucas stretched out his long legs and tilted his head back. "The scavengers will bring the supplies that I need."

He was right.

They heard the cars before they saw them, the harsh growl of engines a distant buzz that grew. The Strykers were the only ones to get to their feet, reaching for weapons they no longer had and powers that were no longer readily available to them. Lucas remained where he was as two rusted and dented SUVs rounded a nearby building, patched tires kicking up dust as they braked to a halt. The handful of men and women who got out were heavily armed. The last person out ordered everyone to remain by the SUVs while she approached the psions.

The middle-aged black woman had short, graying hair and wore her street armor like a second skin. Illegal cybernetics showed in the lines of her hands where sharp metal cut through synthskin provided for other's sensibilities, not her own. She carried a military-grade rifle on one shoulder like an extension of her arm, the weapon clean and well cared for; illegal in civilian hands, but scavengers didn't care about laws.

"Hangman comin' down from the gallows," she said in a rough voice around an unfriendly smile. "Give me one reason why I shouldn't shoot your ass."

"Because I always make you miss," Lucas said as he finally got to his feet. "Matron."

"Lucas." Her dark eyes settled pointedly on the other four. "They ain't unregistered. I don't like surprises."

"How is this a surprise when I told you five years ago what was going to happen?" Lucas offered up a slick smile. "Trust me, Matron. When have I ever not come through?"

"You want that answer in bullet points?"

Lucas laughed as he reached out to clasp her hand, an easy greeting between the two that was still tempered by wariness on Matron's part. The woman wasn't stupid. She hadn't lived this long by ignoring threats, despite Lucas's promises. She knew exactly who and what Lucas was, even if almost no one else in her scavenger group did. Telepathy could work wonders on the human mind.

"I've got kits in the vehicles," Matron said, looking past Lucas at the four he'd brought with him. "Let's get you people hidden."

The Strykers remained where they stood, in a line behind Lucas shoulder to shoulder. One of Matron's scavengers pulled a bag out of the nearest SUV and dropped it at her feet. She knelt down and dug through it, coming up with two different traveling cases. The first one had tiny containers full of iris peels loaded with false identities. She picked four at random and handed them over to Lucas, who flicked them out of her hand telekinetically and slapped them into the Strykers' palms. Threnody and Kerr looked at each other before prying open the cases and inserting the iris peels into their eyes. Following their lead, Quinton and Jason did the same.

The second box had thin strips of clear synthskin woven through with translucent bioware. Matron peeled the first few strips out of the cool gel that kept them active. She walked over to the Strykers and adhered the strips to their faces, making sure to hit as many main recognition points over their bone structure as she could. The government's security grid would read them as someone else long enough to get them past the security checks.

"Do this often?" Jason asked as Matron none too gently pressed a strip over his forehead, aggravating his headache.

She grinned at him, revealing metal teeth. "It ain't none of your business."

She walked away, packed up the bag, and shoved it toward her people with a kick from one dusty boot. Lucas was already heading for the nearest SUV, climbing into the backseat. It was telling that no one tried to stop him.

"You trust him?" Threnody asked Matron as the woman made a quick hand gesture at her people, sending one person to lock the warehouse and the rest back into the vehicles.

"I'm alive because of him."

"You didn't answer my question."

"Get in the fucking car, Stryker."

Matron said it low-voiced, more breath than sound, her eyes on her people and her distance from them rather than the four beside her.

Threnody twitched, just a faint jerk of her shoulders, but it was enough of a reaction that Matron saw it out the corner of her eye.

"Did he tell you what we are?" Threnody said, her voice soft and careful.

"Lucas didn't tell me he was bringing you people into my territory. I know government lapdogs when I see them. I don't appreciate it, but I'm not going to fight him on it. Now *move*."

Threnody and Quinton got in the SUV with Lucas while Jason and Kerr climbed into the one behind. They buckled up as the doors were shut. The noise the engines made as they started up was almost too loud to talk over.

Lucas leaned forward on the middle bench, grabbing on to the front passenger seat where Matron sat for balance. He raised his voice so that he could be heard over the engine. "Are we on schedule?"

"Close enough," Matron said, voice just as loud as she passed back a handful of ration bars that Lucas split between himself, Threnody, and Quinton. "We need to charge the engines, do a few diagnostics runs. The last set of codes you brought us got the hive connection online, but it still needs some work. We can hack the grid to get us over the arctic circle, so long as we've got someone jacked in. We still need to do a test flight."

"The arctic circle is a no-fly zone," Threnody said loudly from the back of the SUV. They had all the windows down despite the dust, making the engine sound even louder. The air-conditioning didn't work and it was too hot without the gritty breeze from outside.

"Ever wonder why?" Lucas asked over his shoulder, leaning back against the seat he shared with another of Matron's scavengers, chewing on his food.

"Wasn't our business."

"It is now."

They drove away from the outskirts of Buffalo, heading southeast along the outside ring of tenement-housing blocks, many just entrances to the tunnels and bunkers below. The skyline of Buffalo was low and knobby until it got to the city towers in the distant north. Haze sat heavy and thick close to the ground, a hot blanket between them and the clouds that moved sluggishly through the sky. They were putting distance between them and what passed for society, and Threnody didn't much care for the kilometers that ran out behind them.

How did you meet Matron? Threnody asked Lucas, wondering if anyone else could hear her through the psi link.

Like I met everyone else. Through Aisling, Lucas said.

Threnody was quiet for half a minute. *I find it difficult to believe you defected from your family and your Syndicate on the whims of some child.*

And yet, you followed me when I offered you a way out. We are very much alike in the ways that matter, Threnody.

You were never a slave. Don't fucking patronize me.

You never lived my life, Lucas said, quiet menace seeping through his words. *It's not as easy or as glamorous as you think.*

Come cry to me after you've had a neurotracker implanted and used on you for the first time.

What makes you think I haven't? Threnody gave him a sharp look from where she sat. He didn't turn around to look at her. *Nathan has always been creative in his punishments.*

That's just sick.

And you wonder why I listen to some child. Lucas's thoughts shifted against hers, but he shared no memories with her again. *Aisling has a way of making people do her dirty work for her.*

Like you?

Not like what she asks for is any different than what I did for Nathan. The killing, at least. The lies. The scope is a hell of a lot bigger.

Threnody couldn't hide the surprise that colored her thoughts. *Nathan doesn't know about her?*

No, Nathan doesn't know about Aisling. His generation wasn't one she talked to.

But she talked to others in your family? Threnody asked with dawning horror at the thought of what they were throwing their support into.

Aisling talks about *a lot of people. She only talks* to *specific individuals. Guess which group you belong to?*

Threnody pulled her thoughts together, trying to make sense of something that was out of her control. *I find it hard to believe Nathan never knew what you were doing.*

Marcheline took care of that after Aisling spoke to her. I'm alive because of the actions both of them took. Nathan can't find what he doesn't know how to look for, or what he can't comprehend or see.

Threnody jerked in her seat so hard that Quinton reached out to steady her. She nodded her thanks, closing her eyes to hide her shock. *A mindwipe? On* Nathan?

Or something. Nathan doesn't know half the things I've done on Aisling orders, Lucas said. *I never took to his form of mindwiping, Aisling made sure of it. What I learned about survival—the important parts—I learned from her.*

From a child?

She died that young. Doesn't mean she lived that briefly.

It was such a simple explanation. Such an easy admission that choked the very breath out of her lungs.

Don't worry, Threnody. You'll still get to meet her.

She got a flash of his memories that her mind balked about believing. Precognitives never lived long, but they lived long enough to be useful.

Threnody sat there, in the back of that SUV on a road somewhere in Buffalo, with her whole world going to pieces.

She realized she could do nothing but let it break.

[FOURTEEN]

AUGUST 2379

TARRAGONA, SPAIN

The wreckage of the maglev train was scattered over the surrounding area, tossed aside like the pieces of a child's broken toy. Oil was a slick sheen on the ground where it wasn't fuel for the fire burning through the remains of the train. The engine car was crumpled where it had been flung far from the rest of the cars, broken into pieces. The air was thick with smoke, making it hard to breathe.

There were no bodies to retrieve, no closure. A fire like that wouldn't even give up ashes at the end.

Ciari frowned behind the skinmask she wore, the filters sucking in near her mouth. Standing beside the intact maglev platform, she gazed at the mess and wondered how much this was going to cost them, in money and in blood.

"No one's going to be happy about this," Keiko said from where the telekinetic stood beside her, hands gripping the buckles of her flak jacket. Around them, working diligently to try to contain the fire and salvage what they could, were government soldiers grouped in quads and first responders from Tarragona. All of them gave the two Strykers a wide berth.

"Of course not," Ciari said calmly. "We had a contract. We failed in meeting the terms."

"Eleven Strykers are dead. Seven barely managed to teleport out, coming back with mental burnout. Jael had a mess on her hands in medical, dealing with all of them. You really think the World Court will ask for their termination?"

"Erik isn't that wasteful. He'll want compensation, but I don't think he'll kill them."

Keiko swore softly behind her skinmask. "We did what we could against Warhound interference. The humans have an unregistered shuttle on record out here for the hijack. Our surviving Strykers gave testimony as to who was on that shuttle."

Ciari gave Keiko a warning look. "Warhounds. Rogue psions."

Keiko's expression didn't change. "Of course."

They all—Strykers and Warhounds alike—still abided by the Silence Law, even after the past few centuries of slavery of psions by the human race. Incalculable damage could be done to society if word got out that some of the most powerful, free people in their history since the Border Wars were, in actuality, psions. Some secrets were meant to be kept at all costs, and it was the OIC's job to ensure that happened.

The World Court had enslaved psions since their initial discovery and trained them over their short generations to believe that humans were the only thing in the world worth worshipping, worth saving. That harsh indoctrination resulted in soldiers that the government loaned out for anything from protection to murder. Strykers turned a pretty profit when they weren't dying for humanity.

"No, I want answers!" a disgusted voice shouted in Spanish from behind them. "This train was supposed to make it to the transfer point. It *didn't,* and I want to know why. Rogue psions aren't a good enough fucking excuse. Not for *this.*"

Telepathic implants for language translation allowed both Ciari and Keiko to understand what was being said and the ability to communicate. The two women shared a brief look before they turned to face the man who had just arrived. The shuttle that had ferried him out of Tarragona was powering down to standby mode while the man himself was a flurry of emotion. Fear and anger, yes; possibly something else. Ciari didn't actively try to read his emotions. He had a bioware net attached to his brain, as all high-ranking politicians did, but the mental grid surrounding his mind was saturated with his emotions and those she could read.

The president of Spain—a position monitored by the World Court to ensure its laws were enforced—was a short, stocky man with dark hair, dark eyes, and light brown skin that didn't see the sun all that often. Alfonso Rodriguez's lips were pulled back from his teeth in a furious scowl behind the clear skinmask that he wore. He wasn't thinking straight; Ciari could feel that through her empathy. When he lifted a hand to strike her, she wasn't surprised at all, nor was she surprised at Keiko's reaction.

Keiko slammed a telekinetic shield down between Alfonso and Ciari. The president walked straight into it and nearly fell to the ground. Only the quick actions of the quad assigned him saved him from making a total fool of himself.

"You have *no right* to attack," Alfonso said, the words coming out harshly.

Ciari just stared at him, the cold blankness on her face and in her eyes difficult for any of the humans to look at for long. "Mr. President, that wasn't an attack. It was simply a defensive reaction by my subordinate," Ciari said in the same language.

"Call her off."

"I think not, Mr. President."

"Your contract is with *me,* psion. You will do as I demand and pay for your failure."

"The contract you bought was negotiated through the World Court," Ciari reminded him. "If you have a problem with my Strykers dying for your shipment, then lodge a complaint with the government."

Keiko didn't drop her shield as the quad surrounding Alfonso reached for their guns. Neither did she ask for permission to interfere. She merely reached out with her power to keep their handguns firmly anchored in their hip holsters, finding it slightly amusing how long the soldiers struggled to remove their weapons before they realized what was going on.

"Get your fucking power off us," the man in charge of the quad demanded as he took a step toward them.

Keiko anchored the man's feet to the ground. "We don't take orders from you."

"Then *you* will take them from *me,*" Alfonso said.

"Our orders come from the World Court," Ciari said. "They have already been informed of what happened here. What punishment, if any, is up to the judges."

"They will hear of this, psion." Alfonso spat between them. "If you dogs can't accomplish what you are paid to do, then you should be punished accordingly."

"Then ask to pull the trigger. That *is* the entire reason why you flew out here, isn't it?" Ciari gazed at him unblinkingly, brown eyes flat and cold. "To demand satisfaction?"

Alfonso went white, then red in the face. "Get out of my head."

"I'm not in it."

"Then tell the bitch beside you to get out of my head."

"It's a wonder that you people never take the time to figure out what you buy when you sign contracts with the Strykers Syndicate." Ciari reached up to tap the side of her head. "Empathic, Mr. President. I don't read thoughts, I read emotions. Keiko here is a telekinetic. She doesn't read minds at all. Check your baseline readings when you return to Tarragona. You'll find no interference."

"Fuck you."

Ciari's smile was pure politeness, her tone sweetly acid. "We don't contract out for sexual exploits, Mr. President. Please remember that."

The space between them was filled by the invisible strength of Keiko's telekinetic shield. Even without it, Alfonso and his people wouldn't have crossed that line to strike at them. Strykers were government property, despite their segregation, and an attack on them was an attack on the World Court itself.

Ciari turned her head so she could see the ongoing cleanup and not the furious expression of a man who wasn't as powerful as he thought he was.

"We'll need your records from the military base on the attack," Ciari said.

"No."

"That order comes directly from the World Court, Mr. President. If you do not give them to us, then you can make your excuses to the judges yourself. We'll gladly teleport you before the bench to save you the cost of a shuttle flight to The Hague."

The silence between them was heavy with hatred. Finally, Alfonso snapped out an order to one of the soldiers, who peeled away from the quad and headed back to the shuttle at a quick jog.

"We'll deliver the records to you," Alfonso said. "Encrypted."

Ciari shrugged her ambivalence to that petty decision and said nothing. Keiko kept her undivided attention on the group in front of them, keeping up a light telekinetic shield around herself and Ciari. Only after the soldier had returned with the data chip and handed it over did the group move away to confer with those in charge of the cleanup. Ciari rolled the tiny data chip between her fingers as she stared at the fire in the distance.

"Should we send for a psychometrist?" Keiko asked softly a few minutes later.

"No," Ciari said. "Anything that would have held any shred of memory is burning."

"We could try the tracks. Desperation and fear are strong enough emotions to embed in the maglev platform."

"Not worth the effort, Keiko."

The telekinetic sighed and reached up to knuckle one eye. "That's six tankers stolen, Ciari. Two burned. The Warhounds are no doubt going to ransom the oil back to the government."

"Typical."

"We still don't know why." Keiko pitched her voice lower, the expression on her face never changing. "They can't be planning a secondary launch with extra supplies. Can they?"

"No." Ciari blinked rapidly as the wind changed direction, blowing smoke and dust into their faces. She turned her head to the side to escape most of the grit. "They won't do that. It's not conducive to their plans. Nathan hasn't once gone after the shuttle fuel stored in Paris, which means he isn't interested in tampering with what will get them to Mars. He's more interested in what he can use on the colony once they arrive, hence the oil."

"Can you be sure?"

Ciari pressed a hand to her stomach, knowing that what she did now might not be enough to save what she carried. "Yes."

She wondered, when the time came, if anyone would ever forgive her.

"Should we report back?" Keiko said. "The military looks like they have this well under control, and no one has asked for Stryker assistance."

Ciari blinked and turned her attention back to Keiko. "At this point, they wouldn't. They'll blame us for this fiasco and the insurance company will cover their loss. Our job right now is to figure out what can be used in our favor to grovel appropriately before the World Court."

Keiko gnashed her teeth. "I hate begging."

"It keeps us breathing." Ciari pocketed the data chip. "Take us back to Toronto."

In the blink of an eye, they were gone. No one save the quad noticed the departure. The military was beginning to regroup, preparing to leave. They couldn't do anything more than they already had.

The fire would burn itself out, just like all the ones before.

[FIFTEEN]

AUGUST 2379
BUFFALO, USA

The first thing Quinton did when they made it to the tenement that Matron's scavengers called home, past the outskirts of Buffalo, was to shave.

He stripped, disposing of the filthy clothing he'd been wearing since the Slums and used the tiny bit of grudgingly rationed water to clean up. They didn't have razors here, but he had a knife, and the sharp scrape of the blade over his face and jaw was comforting. He bled a little, and the water stung in the cuts, but he didn't care.

He would have given anything for a shower, but he wasn't going to get one. He wasn't a Stryker anymore, he didn't have the government picking up his bill. Staring at himself in the small cracked mirror of his borrowed room, Quinton wondered why he didn't look different, feel different, without the collar still wired to his brain.

"Well, this looks less rat-infested than the room Kerr got," Jason said as he came inside without knocking and dropped his bag on the floor by the bed that had Quinton's gear spread out all over it. "Guess I'm taking the floor."

Quinton turned around. "What do you think you're doing?"

"There's not enough space in this building for everyone. People were doubled up before we got here. Lucas said he needs to work on Kerr's mind, so they're sharing a room." Jason's expression was viciously annoyed. "I didn't even get a say in that and Kerr's my partner. Fuck that shit. Matron gave Threnody a room to herself and told me to find you. We're sharing."

"I'll bunk with Threnody."

"Your partner has a room half this size. Two won't fit in that closet. Just don't step on me when you wake up."

Quinton watched through narrowed eyes as Jason stretched out on the floor by the bed, using the thin blanket roll he'd been given as a pillow. The telekinetic was lying on his side, hazel eyes closed, pain lines drawn tight over the skin of his face.

"You need any medication?" Quinton asked after a moment.

Jason wriggled his fingers in Quinton's direction. He didn't open his eyes. "You're cute when you pretend to be worried."

"Just about my own skin. I trust Strykers, not scavengers."

"We're not Strykers anymore, Quinton."

"I've been a Stryker for most of my life. That mentality isn't going to change just because we've gone rogue."

"Something tells me Lucas expects it to."

Quinton reached for his shirt and pulled it back on, not caring that it wasn't clean. He just wanted to get out of there. "I don't give a fuck what Lucas wants."

Jason huffed out a tired little laugh that held no humor. "Now you're just lying to yourself."

Quinton left the room without responding to that pointed remark. Letting the door close behind him, he went in search of Threnody. A scavenger sent him in the right direction and he knocked on the door to her room, waiting for her okay to enter.

"It's open."

The doors in this place were old, manual, with knobs that needed to be turned. Jason had been right, Quinton decided. The room Matron had given Threnody wasn't even big enough for the door to open all the way. He slid inside carefully, eyes focused on where Threnody lay on the small bed that was more a pallet than anything else. She didn't seem to care. He noticed, almost immediately, the way her arms and legs twitched, little spasms that rolled through the lines of the muscles he could see.

"Is it getting any better?" Quinton asked as he settled on the floor beside her. Reaching out with one hand, he smoothed her hair off her forehead, tucking it behind one ear.

Threnody barely stirred. "Getting there. Lucas was right. That doctor did enough that the rest of my system is building off of the surgery. The reboot kind of sucks, to be honest."

"Still think you need a biotank."

"Won't find one here. Can't go to where we know they are." She sighed softly. "It'll keep."

Quinton wrapped his hand around hers where it was tucked beneath her chin. She was lying on her side, curled up around whatever pain she was feeling, but she still gave his hand a squeeze back.

"You're not allowed to die on me, Thren. I can deal with Jason's attitude, but I don't want to deal with Kerr's breakdowns. I don't have the patience for that shit."

"They're all we've got to rely on. Them and Lucas."

"Yeah, about that." Quinton leaned his head back until it hit the wall. He closed his eyes. "What were you and Lucas talking about on the drive here?"

"What makes you think we were having a conversation?"

"Don't pull that shit with me," Quinton growled. "I'm your partner. *Family,* Thren. I deserve better than that."

"You do," Threnody said after a brief pause. "I'm sorry. That was wrong of me. I don't even know why I said it."

"Yeah, you do."

"Can you fault me for wanting to protect you?"

They'd been partnered when he was nine and she was eight, almost two decades' worth of training and fighting, bleeding and surviving together on the field. So many years where he followed where she led, building up a reputation that kept them both safe from the threat of termination, only to see them lose that safety in the face of someone else's interference. Quinton knew that survival now meant hiding from Warhounds *and* Strykers as much as it meant relying on Nathan Serca's oldest son.

"Shut up and get some rest, Thren. I've got this watch."

She didn't argue, just settled into a restless doze beside him. Quinton wasn't sure how many hours passed before the door to the room was opened, but he knew it wasn't long enough to make a difference to their exhaustion.

"If you want to eat, better get down to the cafeteria," Lucas said as he leaned into the room. "Meals are offered only twice a day in this place."

"Are they that short on supplies?" Threnody asked as she rolled onto her back and stretched out her legs, hissing as blood rushed back into stiff muscles.

"They're unregistered and they're scavengers. They're always short on everything." Lucas disappeared, but they could still hear him talking. "I did a brief run into the city while you slept. I brought back enough supplies for us that we won't eat too badly into their allotment. Matron wouldn't appreciate that."

"Help me up, Quin," Threnody said, reaching for him.

It took both of them to get her to her feet. She leaned heavily on him for a moment, hands clenched tightly on his shoulders, breath coming raggedly. Her nerves burned off and on, hot and cold, numb and full of feeling as her system struggled to readjust through the damage she'd inflicted on it. She sighed, momentarily resting her head on his shoulder.

Quinton gave her a brief hug. "How long do you think until you're fully stabilized?"

"Maybe another day or two. Possibly longer," she said. "I wouldn't mind a painkiller right now, though. One that actually *works*."

"Come on," Quinton said, helping her out of the room. "I don't know about medication, but let's get some calories into you."

Psions had a higher metabolism and burned through energy faster than a normal human ever would. The government was the only one who employed psions because only the government could afford their upkeep.

The tenement the scavengers occupied was three levels tall, practically ancient, with few upgrades and only those that would keep the building standing. The cafeteria and kitchens took up half the second floor, one long, open room full of tables and chairs. Quinton and Threnody queued up with the others waiting for their dinner, and neither complained when the cooks filled their plates with GMO rice, strips of dried vegetable substitution, and cubes of protein. The last serving cook in the line deposited two ration bars on their trays when no one else got extra. Threnody and Quinton didn't question being singled out; they just took a beer from the drink area and joined the long table where Lucas, Kerr, Jason, and Matron were already sitting.

"My second," Matron said, jerking her head at the blond man beside her. "Everett."

He had as much illegal cybernetics as Matron did in his hands and arms, with a glitter in the back of both brown eyes that weren't inspecs, but cybernetic ocular nerves. The wiring done to his eyes was top-notch, none of it showing outside his body. Threnody wondered how he'd been able to afford it.

"Psions," Everett said, his tone revealing that he knew what they really were outside of the obvious.

"Got a problem?" Kerr asked, voice cool.

"Nah. Lucas always pulls through when it matters, even if it does take months." Everett shoveled a bite of food into his mouth. "In this case, years."

"Years," Jason echoed, looking down the table at Lucas.

Lucas methodically demolished a plate holding twice the food of any-one else's. "You don't really think I was in the Slums by chance, do you?"

"Lucas has a way of getting people to do what he wants," Matron said, sounding only vaguely bitter.

"Willingly?" Quinton wanted to know.

"Most of the time." Matron's dark eyes were focused on Lucas. "He means well."

"Choke on your words, Matron," Lucas said. "Finish up. We've got places to be."

It was telling, Threnody decided, that Matron did as Lucas ordered without argument. So did Everett. Threnody took another bite of food, forcing herself to finish what she had been served, even as her stomach kept twisting into knots.

They finished their food before anyone else. Matron got to her feet and left her tray on the table. Lucas followed her lead, but he was the first one out of the room. They took the stairs at the end of the hallway down one floor. Matron led them to a back room, the only place in the tenement with modern security. It was locked, but Matron's biometrics opened it. The entrance that room protected was also locked and physically guarded.

The second door was set in the middle of the floor, braced by steel and concrete, anchored into the very foundation of the building. It was an old design, a holdover from when the threat of nuclear attack was always imminent and people had needed a place to go to ground.

Two scavengers sat at a single terminal, monitoring a dozen different security feeds. Threnody spared them a glance only when Matron pointed at her and said warningly, "You don't touch shit in this place without my say-so."

Threnody shrugged minutely, unapologetic for the ability she had been born with.

"Open her up," Matron ordered.

The scavengers entered a set of codes into the computer, unlocking the blast doors in the floor. The doors opened smoothly, almost silently, revealing sturdy-looking stairs that led into pitch-blackness.

"What, no lights down there?" Jason asked as Matron and Everett handed out flashlights.

"We're off the electrical grid on the best of days," Matron explained. "We've got generators we use on a strictly rationed basis. When the time comes, we'll have to hack into the government's electrical grid."

Kerr knelt by the entrance, letting his hand rest against the side of one of the blast doors. "How'd you find this place?"

"You really think we're going to tell you everything?" Everett said.

"We always have this argument, Everett," Lucas said as he spared the scavenger a brief, annoyed look. "You always lose."

Everett spat between them as he tossed Lucas a flashlight. "I don't like giving up our secrets to people like you."

"It's the people like me who made sure you and yours didn't die from radiation poisoning." Lucas pressed his thumb over the sensor on the slim metal flashlight, activating it. The light coming from the tip was sharp and painfully bright. "Or don't you remember that I was the one who 'ported you to a doctor that replaced your arms?"

"Don't ask me to thank you."

"I could just force it out of you. Now shut up and let's go."

The seven of them descended two flights of stairs into cool darkness. Their footsteps echoed against metal.

"Smells like clean air," Jason said as they walked through a tunnel that could fit three people across.

"First thing we did when my ma claimed this territory as hers," Matron said without looking back at them. "Fixed up the environmental system in this place. Cost a fortune on the black market for the material and even more for government agents to look the other way."

"How long did they stay off your back?"

"Until we killed them."

"Typical."

"You say that like someone who's always had access to the best that the government offers."

"You think walking around with a death switch in our heads is fun?" Threnody asked sharply.

"It ain't there anymore." Matron glanced over her shoulder, the shadows cast by their light source unable to hide the contempt in her eyes. "Quit your bitching, girl."

Threnody clenched her hands into fists, telling herself it wasn't anger, but to prevent the next little wave of tremors that rolled through her arms.

"Here," Quinton said as he passed over a ration bar to her. "Eat this. It should help."

"I'm fine," Threnody said, but she took the little packet anyway, tearing it open with her teeth. She was still hungry, even after the previous meal.

Quinton tucked one hand beneath her elbow, letting her lean on him just enough to give her support. Jason and Kerr were between them and the other three, so no one else saw that brief moment of weakness. Threnody's body wasn't fully healed yet, wouldn't be for a while, not unless Lucas could pull a high-tech biotank and medical support system out of his pocket somehow.

She'll live, Lucas said into Quinton's mind. *I need her alive.*

I don't put much faith in what you say.

That would be hysterical if you hadn't already done exactly that.

I followed Threnody here, not you.

Lucas's laughter was low and tired-sounding in Quinton's head. *You'll have to come to terms with what's going on someday. Might as well be today.*

Let us access our powers and maybe I'll start listening. You're as bad as the collars we used to wear.

Really? Pain spiked heavy and sharp through Quinton's brain, causing him to miss a step and stumble a little. Threnody glanced at him worriedly, but he didn't acknowledge her. *If it comes down to me killing you, at least you'll know why. That's more than the government ever gave you.*

Lucas pulled out of Quinton's mind, the psi link cutting off. Quinton doubted that he had been left completely alone. Lucas had a way with mental monitoring that not even the best Stryker psi surgeons were capable of matching. Quinton chewed on the inside of his lip, keeping the flashlight in his hand trained on the ground. Even with a kind of freedom, it was proving difficult to give up the culture he had come from. His hatred for the Warhounds, even for one who had saved them, hadn't abated.

It was a full kilometer to Matron's destination, a metal tunnel set with half a dozen blast doors between their destination and the questionable sanctuary behind them. Walking through the last set of blast doors, they came into an underground hangar, lights snapping on as the control panel embedded in the wall read Matron's biometrics.

"You're early," a rough voice said. A figure stood up from a work terminal a few meters away. "Next check-in was supposed to be three days from now."

"Novak," Matron said by way of introduction. "He's the best hacker we've got."

"I'm the only hacker left that ain't had his brain fried yet, is what you mean."

Novak was stocky and scarred, body carrying illegal cybernetics like the rest of Matron's scavenger group. He was dark-skinned, with inspecs in his eyes and wires cutting through his temples. His head was shaved, revealing black lines of tattoos inked over his skull. All around the neuroports in his wrists were burns, stretching over his knuckles and palms. He was as makeshift as they came, but makeshift had gotten Matron's scavengers pretty damn far.

How far they'd come was sitting on the launchpad, systems off and metal cold.

"This isn't a shuttle class I've ever seen before," Threnody said as she walked closer to the first of three large shuttles that the hangar housed, each shuttle modified for stealth.

"Course not," Matron said as Novak handed over a datapad. "These were salvaged from deadzones."

Threnody came to a hard halt. "Have they been sterilized?"

"Had to be. Lucas here wants these babies for a specific flight. There's no trace of radiation in those shuttles or this space."

"Did you lose your skin in deadzones?" Jason asked, eyeing the trio from where he stood by Kerr.

Matron raised one hand to show him her middle finger, metal gleaming through the synthskin. "I don't question your physiology and disease, psion. Don't fucking question mine."

"Like father, like son," Threnody said as Lucas walked over to her. "Not willing to do all the dirty work yourself? You just had to get other people to do it for you, didn't you?"

"The people who make up scavenger groups in any settlement were never going to have clean enough DNA when the fifth generation finally came upon us." Lucas slanted her a look. "Just because they're unregistered doesn't mean they're useless. They're good at what they do, even if it kills them quicker than most."

"Are they the only ones you've saved?"

"I save who Aisling wants me to save."

"And how many do you have left before she's satisfied?"

His answer was for her alone when he said, *Everyone.*

Lucas approached the nearest shuttle where it was propped up on its landing gear, walking a wide berth around the wings and attached thrusters.

"The shuttles are in better condition than the last time I saw them," Lucas said, raising his voice.

"Yeah, because they're not all in *pieces*," Matron retorted. "I told you it was going to take time."

Lucas ignored her as he walked around the shuttle to check out the other side. "How are the cold-storage units holding up?"

"They're holding. There's more space for cargo than there is for crew."

"Cold-storage units?" Kerr asked. "What are you guys hoping to transport?"

"We," Lucas corrected as he stepped back into view. "What are *we* going to transport. This is a heavy pickup mission when we finally go wheels up. We're dealing in tonnage, not kilos."

"Just what the hell are we transporting?"

Lucas didn't answer, either vocally or telepathically, as he walked back to the group. His attention was on Jason, who watched his approach warily.

"You were one of the best hackers in the Stryker ranks," Lucas said. "Which means you're the best hacker we've got now. I'm going to need you to get familiar with the hive connection that we've installed in the shuttles."

"Thought you had everything all set up."

"Novak is the only hacker who survived the job. He helped start the process, but his code is lacking. We need something less fragile, and you know how to write government code quicker and better than he does. Your shift starts now."

"And everyone else?"

Lucas let his dark blue eyes slide sideways, his gaze catching Kerr's. "Your partner and I have some reconstructive psi surgery to begin."

"Hell no," Jason said, stepping into Lucas's personal space. Lucas was taller than he was, but that didn't matter. "Whatever you're going to do to him, I want to know."

"You're a telekinetic, Jason. You can't do shit for him."

"I'm his *partner*."

"Yes, and I can't help but wonder if that permanent link has caused more damage than benefit. Hiding behind your shields, strong as they are, hasn't helped his mind deal with the problem of his shields collapsing. You're his crutch."

As Jason opened his mouth to argue, a heavy telekinetic hold picked him up and slammed him to the floor. Gasping for breath, Jason stared up at Lucas with anger and not a little bit of fear. Lucas knelt down and grabbed a fistful of Jason's hair, jerking him to a semi-sitting position.

"You're forgetting your place, psion," Lucas said, annoyance twisting lightly through the tone of his voice. "Aisling needs you alive, but there are many definitions of *alive*. We need the power locked up inside your head. That doesn't necessarily mean we need *you*."

Jason felt his heartbeat kick up, but he chose to ignore the adrenaline pumping into his veins. "We'd all be useless to you if you mindwiped us."

"Your idea of a mindwipe is so limited. I'm used to dealing with insanity. We need your power, not your personality."

Lucas let Jason go, and the telekinetic fell back to the floor with a hard thump. Lucas straightened up and looked over at the other Strykers and scavengers. "Anyone else want to argue?"

No one said a word.

Lucas curled his fingers at Kerr as he walked toward the doors they'd come through. "We're going."

Kerr helped Jason to his feet first, giving his partner's shoulder a brief squeeze. "Keep your mouth shut," Kerr said quietly. "I still need you."

"Yeah," Jason muttered as Kerr turned to follow Lucas out of the hangar.

"You really are stupid, aren't you, boy?" Matron said, looking and sounding unimpressed. "If me and mine can trust Lucas with certain things, you Strykers can as well."

"He's a Warhound," Threnody said. "Why do you trust him when it's his family that's helped segregate the world's population? And don't give me that crap about how he saved your lives. He saved ours as well, but it hasn't helped us any."

"See, now, that's where you're wrong." Matron dug into her back pocket and pulled out a pack of cigarettes. She stuck one in her mouth and lit it up. "What Lucas has planned? It's gonna save everyone."

"I find it hard to believe he's shared his plans with a mere human."

"And I find it hard to believe he brought you narrow-minded Strykers into the mix." Matron spat between them. "If *we* believe in what he's try-ing to do, then you people can."

"Why should we?"

Matron blew smoke out of her nose and smiled, showing her metal teeth. "Other than the fact that he's got his power so far deep in your brains that you can't piss without his say-so? Tell me, what do you know about the arctic Svalbard archipelago?"

"The what?"

"Exactly."

[SIXTEEN]

AUGUST 2379
BUFFALO, USA

Can you be," Kerr asked, struggling for politeness, "a little more careful with him?"

Lucas didn't open his eyes from where he lay on the other bed. "You actually sound like you care."

"He's my partner."

"Shut up and lie down, or you're going to hit the floor with your face when I break open your mind."

Kerr stared at the other man for a few more seconds before carefully lying down on the bed that had been assigned to him. Stretching out, he put an arm over his eyes to block out the room, even if he couldn't block out the relentless presence of Lucas in his mind.

I'm touched you think so highly of me, Lucas said. *Drop your shields.*

Kerr went against everything inside him that was saying no and did as he was ordered. Lucas's power filtered down through the layers of Kerr's mind, his own shields wrapping around the both of them on the mental grid with such strength that they burned like beacons in Kerr's thoughts.

Just like you Strykers to make a mess of things.

I've survived.

I'm still not sure how.

That was the last thing Kerr remembered. The mental grid dipped under the sudden disappearance of Kerr's presence, Lucas holding the other man's mind in his power.

Sometimes I wonder about what you ask of me, Aisling, Lucas thought to himself as he decided where to begin.

The first thing Lucas needed to do was permanently destroy Kerr's shields. The Class II telepath had gone twenty-five years without acknowledging the empathy he carried in his mind. All of Kerr's deeply ingrained thought processes weren't going to be reversed in a single night, but they had to be factored in for this psi surgery.

There was no point in trying to keep up a shield geared solely toward telepathy when empathy kept undermining the process. There had to be acknowledgment of that secondary power, and Kerr had to weave both into the framework of his shielding. There was no getting around that, unless he wanted his shields to continue falling apart.

What had been clear-cut and obvious to Lucas upon a single dip into that mind had apparently been unintelligible to the Stryker psi surgeons. Even a lower-Classed psion had ways to diagnose problems in the minds of those ranked higher. This whole mess could possibly have been avoided, except this was what Aisling wanted. Collusion between previous Stryker OICs and Serca CEOs had only helped along the inevitable.

Digging his telepathy deep into the crevices and canyons of Kerr's mind, Lucas let himself be lost in the problem, allowing his power to bleed carefully into Kerr's. Lucas hadn't been lying, back in London. Scientists could reverse engineer pretty much any technological equipment on the planet with government permission. Lucas could reverse engineer the processes of the human mind only because he'd had his own torn to pieces over and over since his birth by Nathan.

Lucas didn't want anyone else to have that skill. Not that he wouldn't wish that pain on anyone—because there were many people that he *would*—but he wasn't willing to let anyone else have the knowledge that came with it. Marcheline, under orders from Aisling, had helped him gain control, but he'd been the one to build his mind into the weapon that Nathan had thought was his. Lucas hoped it had come as a shock to his father when he walked away from the Serca Syndicate two years ago.

This was the purpose Lucas had worked toward for all of his life: all the different people, all the different pieces, all the various powers that could come out of human DNA. It was hope for a different world that Aisling had instilled in him for the two decades she had seen him grow up. It was the belief in her promise that he was meant for so much more than the prison of his life, for however long he had left.

Ambition was what drove members of the Serca family to attempt the impossible, among other things.

Lucas let himself be lost in the processes of the human mind and felt, vaguely, at ease. When he opened his eyes hours later, he wasn't at all surprised to find Threnody sitting on the floor between the two beds.

"How is he?" Threnody asked, her face turned toward Kerr's unconscious body.

"He's not your partner," Lucas said.

"He's a Stryker."

"We've gone over this, Threnody."

"Getting the collar taken off me doesn't make me any less a Stryker. It never will." She turned her head to look at Lucas. "What have you done to us?"

He sat up slowly. His senses shifted with the migraine-strength headache he was suffering from after performing a long and complicated psi surgery on Kerr, not to mention everything else he'd been orchestrating to get to this point. The physical and mental toll on his body wasn't something he could escape. Growing old wasn't in his genes.

"I actually thought it would be Kerr who would ask that question," Lucas said as he rubbed at his face with both hands. "Him being the telepath and all."

"Before or after you screwed with his head some more?"

Lucas let out a harsh little laugh. "Oh. I like you, Threnody. You actually *think*."

"Can't say I feel the same about you."

"I figured as much." Lucas moved to put his feet on the floor, leaning forward as he studied Threnody. He wiggled his fingers at his head.

"You're wondering why everyone's not as pissed off as they should be. Why everyone is just going along with what I want when all of you should be fighting me tooth and nail."

"Something like that."

"Mental suggestion. I implanted it when all of you were under during your brain surgery back in London. I needed you four to trust me."

"Trust isn't something you *suggest*. It's something you *earn*."

"Since when have rank-and-file Strykers ever trusted Warhounds outside of an ordered suicide mission?"

"What do you mean?"

"Ah." Lucas nodded to himself. "So you *weren't* scheduled for retrieval. Even better, because it means Nathan doesn't know about any of you."

"What the hell are you talking about?"

"Sometimes I think your OIC keeps more secrets than my family does." Lucas lifted a hand to rub at the back of his neck, fingers digging into the knotted muscles there. "We're the ones you rogue psions run to when the government wants you terminated and the Strykers still need you alive. Your OIC asks and we retrieve. I've always thought the Silence Law was more favorable to my side. We've been doing things with psion powers that none of you have even been allowed to *think* about, for fear that the government will lose control of its favorite dogs. It's a bargain, if you will. Your silence for my family's freedom."

Threnody recoiled sharply from him, disbelief thick in her voice. "You and your Warhounds aren't something I would ever willingly run to."

"Lucky for us, those Strykers we're sent to retrieve never get a choice in the matter, either during the transfer or after, when we mindwipe them for loyalty. Technically, I suppose that doesn't apply here. I'm not a Warhound the same way you're no longer a Stryker. Keep your title, if you want. If it makes you feel in control. Just know that you're not. That you never will be."

"Neither are you."

"I know what my sacrifices will gain me," Lucas said as a thin trickle of bright red blood slid down out of his nose. "I know *exactly* what I will get at the end, if we pull it all off this time. And I will do absolutely everything and anything to achieve what Aisling promised my family. What she promised *me*."

Threnody's gaze followed that slow-moving line of blood until it dripped off the edge of Lucas's jaw and fell to the floor. "Even if it kills you before you turn thirty?"

"Try twenty-three."

Threnody met Lucas's gaze without blinking, a slight tick twitching at her jaw. Nerves, but not the emotional sort. Synapses that still weren't healed, but better than they had been. Lucas leaned forward, using his telekinesis to keep her still while he curved his hand over her chin. He tilted her head from side to side, ignoring the fury that came into her blue eyes.

"You need to understand something," Lucas said, voice quiet, tired, the set of his shoulders tense. "We're what the future turns on, you and I. We're the ones who have to do what Aisling says if any of us are going to survive humanity's belabored attempt to reclaim Mars. Everything changes, Threnody. Without mercy, without exception, without pause. The best we can do is change the future into something better. If psions are ruling on Mars or ruling here, what does it matter? We'll all still be alive as a people."

"Don't touch me."

Lucas released her, lifting a hand to his own face to wipe at the blood there. Threnody watched as he studied the red smear on his fingertips, mouth pulled slightly off-center in a dissatisfied frown.

"What's in the Arctic?" Threnody said.

Lucas sighed. "Matron doesn't know when to keep her mouth shut."

"That free will you let some of these scavengers keep, kind of annoying, isn't it? Why didn't you just mindwipe them?"

"Because that's not always the answer."

Threnody shrugged dismissively. "The Arctic. What's so important about it?"

"There's a Norwegian island in that archipelago. Spitsbergen. Pretty much everyone except those on the World Court and my family have forgotten it exists." Lucas pushed himself to his feet and stretched until his bones cracked. "A lot of people died during the bombing years of the

Border Wars. The majority of the world population died afterward, from disease and starvation and environmental change. Every country that exported food to the masses was targeted and destroyed. Agriculture as we knew it back then became impossible on radiation-tainted soils. That's where the deadzones came from."

"I know that. Everyone does."

"Then ask yourself how the SkyFarms came to be. Clean soil? A decent selection of foods and farm animals that could feed the remaining population that the World Court just *happened* to have at their fingertips? Please."

Threnody opened her mouth to argue, but paused, thinking hard. After a long moment, she said, "If the world was so polluted and damaged from nuclear war back then, where did uncontaminated food supplies come from? That's what you're asking, isn't it?"

"Glad to see that the government didn't fry all the synapses in your head every time they flipped that switch of theirs."

Threnody waved off his insult, brow furrowed in thought. "You said we left terraforming machines on Mars. Did we have any here before the Border Wars for our own use?"

"Terraforming machines were expensive. Governments couldn't agree on where to begin here on Earth, which is why they focused on Mars."

"You didn't answer my question." She looked up at him, understanding dawning on her face seconds later. "The SkyFarms. They were built with terraforming machines, weren't they?"

Lucas just smiled.

Threnody dug her fingers into the durable synthfabric of her black BDUs. "What's on that island, Lucas?"

"Machines," Lucas answered after a moment. "Machines and the Svalbard Global Seed and Gene Bank. You don't really think the government is willing to leave without the supplies that feed us, do you?"

Threnody could feel her heart beating against her ribs, the blood rushing in her ears.

"Aisling wants us to save the world, Threnody. It's a little more complicated than simply inciting rebellion."

"I—" Threnody swallowed thickly, her mouth gone suddenly dry. "I'm beginning to understand that."

"Reasoning. Better than a mindwipe any day of the week." Lucas headed for the door. "I'm done with Kerr. His shields will stay up now."

"And Jason? Are you going to work on him?"

"I've been in his head and tested his shields."

"Meaning?"

"I'm going to need a little help breaking them open and Kerr isn't going to be enough."

"So who's going to help you?" Threnody said, suspicion creeping into her voice.

Lucas didn't answer, and then he was gone. Threnody wasn't surprised at his silence. Sighing, she turned her attention back to Kerr's unconscious form, half her thoughts on Lucas's words.

PART FIVE
SUB ROSA

SESSION DATE: **2128.03.15**
LOCATION: **Institute of Psionics Research**
CLEARANCE ID: **Dr. Amy Bennett**
SUBJECT: **2581**
FILE NUMBER: **249**

"She thinks there's another way," Aisling says as she peers into the camera, her image larger than usual due to her proximity to the camera. The glue that keeps the electrodes attached to her skull has left her skin red and raw in places. "There are, you know. Lots of them. They just don't work."

Aisling pushes away from the camera and wanders back to her seat and sits down. She is alone in the room, a bright spot of yellow in the whiteness. The machines she is connected to hum with results that are off every reliable scale. The fingers of one hand curve over one knobby knee and tap out a rhythm that matches the pulse of her heartbeat.

"It's so hard to find the right one." Aisling tangles one small hand in her hair and the wires there, gently yanking at both. She squeezes her eyes shut. "You wanted a better half-life. You wanted a better future for everyone."

Aisling tilts her head to the side as if she is listening to something no one else can hear. "You always say that. Every time you get this far and fail, you blame me."

The little girl sighs and opens her eyes. She stares at the camera and peels an electrode off her forehead. "What's wrong, Ciari? Don't you like your present?"

[SEVENTEEN]

AUGUST 2379

THE HAGUE, THE NETHERLANDS

The old doors to the Deliberation Room closed with a quiet click, the jamming technology that was activated at the start of each session coming online. The fifteen robed men and women surrounding the long, rectangular conference table knew their privacy was assured. Those whose job it was to man those programs knew if they failed at their position, death would be a hoped-for punishment, not necessarily one they would ultimately receive.

"I call this Court into session," Erik said as he struck the gavel he held in one hand on a small tablet of old, lacquered wood. The antiquated gesture had been repeated thousands upon thousands of times before this. He would give it up if he could, but it was tradition. Some things even the World Court couldn't be rid of. "We have work to do, Justices."

The fourteen other men and women nodded, their voices ringing from deep bass to high soprano as they stated agreement. They were different in age and nationality and gender; the one solid thing they had in common was clean DNA.

"The launch date has been moved up to the end of September. We're beginning to prep registered citizens for swift transfer to the Paris Basin. Where do we stand on those totals?" Erik said.

Travis Athe, in his late fifties, tapped decisively at the screen of his datapad. "We have solid readiness from the United Kingdom, the European Union, the East Coast of America, the Canadian Territories, the South American Coalition, Japan, China, and the Southeastern Asian Territories. The numbers are sufficient so far."

"Registered dissidents?" Anchali asked, looking down the table at the president. The elderly woman who was Thai in name only and culturally Chinese was the oldest serving member of the World Court. She was also Erik's strongest conservative supporter as the vice president. That didn't mean they always saw eye to eye.

Erik gestured expansively with one hand. "We've quietly tagged those we believe to be a problem through the security grid. Quads are monitoring their movements. They will be rounded up at the slightest hint of defiance and contained well before the launch date."

"What of the hijacking in Spain?" Cherise Molyneux said. "Those tankers were en route to the Paris Basin when they were stolen and the rest destroyed."

"While we don't know where those rogue psions retreated to, we have enough oil to supply our endeavors once we arrive at the colony. They've never targeted the shuttle fuel transports, and the shuttles on the launchpads remain fully operational. That shipment was simply a precaution."

"I'm more worried about rogue psions knowing our plans." Cherise leaned forward, the beautiful Frenchwoman glaring at Erik. She was the youngest judge on the World Court, with aspirations that would get her killed, sooner or later, if she continued antagonizing him. Erik rather hoped she did. Her dissenting opinions over the past few years had been quite annoying.

Erik leaned back in his cushioned leather chair and stared at Cherise. "Are you questioning our position, Justice? I can assure you that this has been decades in the making and we have been vigilant in keeping it secret. Unless you doubt your own work?"

A faint hint of red stained Cherise's face, but faded in moments. She lifted her chin slightly in defiance. "I don't doubt our accomplishments, Erik. I'm stating a fact that *all* of us here worry about. The Strykers and these Warhounds have been fighting for what seems like forever. The rogue psions are not leashed as they should be. What if they *know*?"

"Do you doubt the protection that our dogs provide us?" Erik said, brown eyes steady as he looked at her.

"Through what constitutes slavery," Travis said from down the table. "Which is never a guarantee."

"Since when has that bothered you and yours?" Erik arched an eyebrow. "When our ancestors hunted down psions after the Border Wars, we saw their uses and hobbled the threat. They obey us because they know little else, we make sure of that. For every generation we humans live through, psions go through two. If they reach thirty or beyond, it's a miracle. Genetics play as much a role in keeping them in check as we do. In the grand scheme of things, psions are useful up to a point, but they're an evolutionary dead end."

"The fact that they are slaves doesn't bother me," Travis said slowly. "What concerns me is that they are more dangerous than the average slave, and for all that we control the Strykers, we don't control *all* the psions in the world."

"Would you rather have all of them free to use their powers against us rather than just some? The Strykers Syndicate was created for a reason. The Strykers live to obey and serve humanity. They have their orders. These Warhounds will not have access to the Paris Basin, nor to the shuttles that wait there. No psion will follow us into space. That directive still stands, and the OIC knows to keep that fact classified until it's time to inform the rank-and-file Strykers about the launch."

"For how long?" Travis gestured sharply at nothing. "If we kill them all before we launch, we lose our protection against the Warhounds. If the Strykers live right up to the launch, we risk them realizing that they have no seats on those shuttles, no berth waiting for them in the colony ship. Their retaliation might be quick enough to damage enough of the shuttles that they will not launch and too many of the needed gene pool will die."

"We need the Strykers," Erik agreed. "We need them to continue to believe that they need us. They are the wall that will stand between us and everyone else when we launch. The OIC will inform the rest of the Strykers when the time arrives for them to do their duty. If only half are alive to do it? It's a shame, but they'll still get the job done."

"And the Warhounds?" Anchali asked coolly. "Surely they won't take our leaving so easily."

Erik's smile pulled thinly at his mouth. "We integrate loyalty into the training of our dogs, and their loyalty is tied to us. The Strykers will be more than enough to hold back the Warhounds when we launch. The Warhounds number less than the Strykers after all. A great many less."

"You sound certain of that fact."

"You don't."

Anchali shook her graying head and reached for her water glass. "I have never trusted in the people whose leashes we hold. They are not *human,* Erik. They do not think the same way we do, they do not feel as we do. Their loyalty is a fabrication built up through indoctrination. Such programming can be undone. There have been instances in the past of Strykers escaping termination to join with the Warhounds. Where do you think the Warhounds came from?"

"We have become adept at putting down rabid dogs."

"Being proficient in killing psions is beside the point. I think it's fair to question if the Warhounds know."

Faint nods of agreement came from around half of the table, an admission that irritated Erik. He didn't let it show on his face or in his voice. "If we stayed rooted in the fear of the unknown and refused to take a chance, then this launch wouldn't be happening. We will be gone from this planet in a month's time. The preparation team is already on the Ark, working to bring the colony ship fully online. We are in the final hours of this countdown after decades of waiting. We shouldn't be looking at the past. We need to be focusing on the future."

"Considering that our past begot this future, I think it's imperative we remember how we arrived here," Cherise argued. "Too many cultures, too many nations, are nothing but deadzones because of our ancestors' actions during the Border Wars. We are effectively doing the same to this world by leaving it behind. We are responsible for the survival of the human race. How can we know for certain that the psions will remain on Earth?"

"The same way that we knew the Fifth Generation Act would work. If we apply the rules to everyone, then no one can claim favoritism. The psions are a product of the Border Wars. Their mutation is a direct block to them being registered. Their *duty* is to serve and protect. Their final act of loyalty will be to die. Who here does not approve of that?"

Erik's gaze swept the length of the table, meeting every set of eyes looking his way. One by one, the judges dropped their gazes in silent agreement to the president's demand. Fifteen strong personalities, each with his or her own set of people to protect, meant that disagreement was a way of life. Compromise was what they fought for.

The World Court collectively owned the Strykers Syndicate in equal shares, but the president alone had the right to give the Strykers their orders. That right only came from unanimous agreement. Killing them only took a single vote.

"I believe we are in agreement," Anchali finally said in her rough voice.

Erik reached for his gavel. "All in favor of continuing on this present course of action?"

"Aye," fourteen voices said without hesitation.

Erik hit the wooden tablet with his gavel once again. "It is so ordered."

Chairs pushed back from the table and everyone stood, gathering up datapads. The judges left in groups of twos or threes, with only Travis and Erik remaining behind.

"A word, Erik," Travis asked, as the doors clicked shut.

Erik gestured with one hand, studying several new messages on his datapad. "Yes, what is it?"

"The Warhounds won't be left behind so easily." Travis paused, studying Erik's profile. "Will the Strykers really be enough?"

"They've been enough since we collared the first one. They will be enough until we kill the last." Erik glanced up at the other man. "You've used them before, you know what they're capable of."

"I know. That doesn't stop me from worrying."

Erik shrugged as he locked his datapad and tucked it into the inner pocket of his dress robes. "It's a little late for you and your Syndicate to second-guess your actions."

Travis frowned. "My family made this possible for everyone. I trust in the science that we rebuilt. I simply don't trust psions."

"No one in their right mind does." Erik offered him a slight smile as he guided Travis out. "Walk with me. I need to give these court minutes to my assistant before we can break for lunch."

They left and the technicians responsible for monitoring the judges turned off the jamming sequence in the Deliberation Room, breathing soft sighs of relief. For all the machines that were built to protect the World Court's privacy, there was no blocking the signal that the bioware nets gave off.

All the judges' baseline readings never deviated, even with Nathan listening in through Travis's mind.

When he managed to extract himself from the delicate, incredibly light psi link that was implanted in Travis's mind, Nathan lifted his head and blinked his office in The Hague back into sight. Even for a Class I triad psion, it took effort to work through a human's mind beneath the bioware net without damaging the human or triggering an alert on the baseline readings. It was complicated enough, and the risks were high enough, that Nathan rarely initiated such a link. Nathan was determined, he simply wasn't stupid, which was one of the reasons he had lived so long.

"Sir?" Dalia said from where she sat in front of his desk, the human woman wearing the identity of an executive assistant this time instead of a bond worker. It suited her better.

Nathan focused his gaze on her. "What is it?"

"We're nearly finished rounding up the bond workers you ordered to be terminated. We're keeping the scientists alive, unless you want them killed as well. Gideon thought you might want to keep them. He thinks they might be useful for the next step, but that's up to you."

"When I said get rid of them, I meant it." Nathan offered her an irritated look. "Gideon's suggestions are useless for my timetable. There are government scientists on our payroll who know how to use what we've created. I want everyone else dead. I hate repeating myself, Dalia."

The human flinched against the threatening presence of Nathan in her mind. "My apologies, sir," she said quickly. "I was only thinking of what might help you."

"I don't pay you to think." Nathan pointed at the door to his office. "Get out."

Dalia got to her feet and left, quick strides taking her out of his office. The door slid shut behind her and Nathan grimaced. Finding good help was getting harder and harder. It was getting to the point where he couldn't even rely on his own family, which was unacceptable. He might not love his children, but they were extremely useful at helping him stay alive by doing nearly all the needed psionic work.

Perhaps that was why Lucas had fled. Dying for other people wasn't nearly as satisfying as dying for oneself.

[EIGHTEEN]

AUGUST 2379
BUFFALO, USA

Lucas knew the location of every Serca Syndicate branch, every Warhound hideout in the world. He knew how personnel were rotated through, how unregistered humans were recruited. He knew how his father operated everything because the company would have been his one day.

Funny how the demands of a single child could change so much.

Lucas walked through the front doors of a manufacturing warehouse in Buffalo with his face bare of synthskin and bioware, no iris peels in his dark blue eyes, and no dark glasses to filter out the security grid's probing identity searches. Lucas went in as himself and that was enough to incite war.

Fifteen unregistered humans died in the first three seconds, collateral damage to the telepathic strike Lucas sent out to deflect the attack coming from a Class IV telepath. The Warhound died instantly, mind fried from the burning strength Lucas carried with such ease.

An alarm sounded as Lucas dropped some of his shields, allowing his presence to register on the mental grid. The workers at the plant knew never to question the sharp sound that pierced their eardrums. Instinct had them racing for the exits, fleeing the warehouse in droves. Lucas let them live. He had more important things to deal with than escaping humans who would come back first thing in the morning for their next shift. A little unscheduled murder wouldn't be enough to make them give up their paychecks.

Lucas walked across the warehouse floor, his worn and scuffed boots taking him past the work area and packing machines. This warehouse only dealt in parts, not the finished product. The environ filters were finished only by registered humans in the city towers.

He focused his telepathy on the mental grid, counted out five, eight, ten Warhounds Classed from IV to III, a mix of 'path-oriented and 'kinetic-oriented psions. They weren't teleporting out. Lucas smiled as he confirmed that, the expression caught by a multitude of security-feed sensors embedded in the walls around him as he took the metal stairs up to the second level. He wasn't in a hurry, which didn't bode well for anyone's survival.

We have orders to kill you, one of the remaining Warhound telepaths said.

Oh, please try. I need the workout, Lucas replied on a wide public 'path.

Warhounds knew never to disobey the ruling Serca. That Lucas had, at one point, been their superior didn't stop the ten from trying to kill him. They knew the odds; dying by Lucas's hands would be quick. Nathan would kill them slowly, if he killed them at all.

The fire that exploded around Lucas's layered telekinetic shields was hot enough to suck out all the moisture in the air. Feeling sweat evaporate off his skin, Lucas teleported out of reach of that burning bubble. Appearing elsewhere, Lucas lashed out with his telekinetic strength, breaking the spine of the attacking pyrokinetic. The fire left behind began to expand, burning out of control.

The telepaths gathered in a merge, striking out at Lucas's mind. Telekinetic pressure bore down on his shields. Defending on two fronts took strength, which Lucas had but couldn't afford to deplete.

Lucas's shields—both telepathic and telekinetic—were solid walls that the Warhounds could not breach, smooth and without the chinks found in lower-Classed psions. The telepaths didn't have a chance, even with their power swelled by three minds. Lucas had been taught by his father, descended from a family who had produced more Class I triad psions in their short history than any other.

The telepaths survived the bright, novalike burnout Lucas inflicted on them. They did not survive sane.

The pair of telekinetics found their minds bent beneath the strength of Lucas's power until they broke, their control shattering to pieces.

If you're finished with this whole pathetic mess, I've got a message for you, Lucas telepathically sent to every remaining Warhound in the building.

You'll kill us, the psychometrist said.

I need some of you alive. You can be that percentage. Choose now.

The surviving telekinetic agreed first, followed by the remaining Warhounds. Lucas watched as they slowly came out of their positions, military-grade guns in the hands of the psychometrist and electrokinetics, the others with their powers held sharply at the ready in their minds.

Lucas rocked back slightly on his heels and smiled at them, the expression malicious and cold. "At least some of you are intelligent."

"We've got standing kill orders," the psychometrist said, her voice flat. "Start talking."

Lucas raised a finger and slammed her into the wall with his telekinesis. He stripped off her gloves with a thought, pressed her bare hands to that old metal structure, and broke her shields. He took away her control and left her with everything that her power could feel in the memories left behind in the warehouse. Her screams echoed long and loud as the memories in that wall overloaded her power in seconds, choking out a mind stripped of all defenses.

"I give the orders here," Lucas reminded them. "Anyone want to argue that?"

The Warhounds stayed silent and stayed where they were, long accustomed to obeying a Serca, no matter which one it was.

Lucas nodded his approval and let the psychometrist fall to the ground. She curled into the fetal position and pressed her hands to her chest, fingers digging into her body as her mind shut down, becoming catatonic.

"Your kill orders are useless without the right people," Lucas finally said, his eyes roving from face to face. "If Nathan wants me, he can come himself."

"You know he never will," an electrokinetic said with careful respect.

"I'm counting on it." Lucas sounded almost cheerful. "Tell my siblings I'll be waiting for them here in Buffalo. Three against one sounds like fair odds, don't you think? I'd even settle for two."

The Warhounds were silent in the face of his mockery, but their thoughts were crystal clear. He picked through their minds with ease, deducing their hierarchy of rank now that he'd killed a third of the integrated teams. With a thought, Lucas teleported into the personal space of the electrokinetic who hadn't yet spoken, the only Class III in the group. She was young, nineteen or so, reaching what psions considered middle age, and smart enough to show fear even as she held her ground.

Lucas let her live for that compliment.

"They have two days," Lucas said, searching her brown eyes with his own dark blue as he implanted the challenge and memory straight into her mind. She doubled over in pain from the transfer. "They won't pass it up."

The electrokinetic nodded, wiping at the blood that was leaking from her nose. "I'll report," she gasped out. "Sir."

Lucas let her go. "You do that."

He teleported out, arriving back in the place he'd left barely twenty minutes ago. It was a small, one-room building thirty kilometers outside Buffalo, built right up against a tall, derelict signal tower. The government had abandoned it years ago; scavengers took the leftovers.

Matron was sitting in front of the building's only control terminal, feet propped on the console, a knife in her hand carefully cutting a small green apple into pieces. She didn't look up at his arrival. "You finish whatever you needed to get done?"

"I wouldn't be here if I hadn't."

"Good. I'd hate to think you failed. I like your bribes too much." Matron popped a section of the expensive fruit into her mouth. The look of bliss that settled over her face stemmed from genuine pleasure. "This is why I believe in God. Or what passes for that negligent asshole."

Lucas huffed out a small laugh as he sprawled in the only other chair in the small control room of what Matron considered to be her property. She had built it up five years ago on Lucas's orders, piggy-backing off the government's official signals to retrieve weather data. It was rarely used by her scavengers, so its sporadic resurgence was never picked up by anyone in Buffalo. The government had other things to worry about than a broken weather station.

Lucas rested his head against the back of the chair and closed his eyes. A headache was creeping across the breadth of his skull, a warning he acknowledged, but couldn't heed. Finishing the mission came before his own health.

"Two days," he said. "If that."

Matron continued to eat her apple. "You're taking a risk, running everything up against that acid storm. Its spine is a derecho. It's gonna be the worst weather Buffalo has seen in a decade. Maybe two."

"This is how it goes."

Matron hummed her agreement; maybe her dissatisfaction. It was impossible to tell. "I have been all things unholy," she whispered as she licked the bright green peel and tasted the sweet tartness of dreams. "'And yea though I walk through the valley of the shadow of death, I will fear no evil; for thou art with me.'"

"Why is it you humans always look outside yourselves for answers?"

"Why is it you psions can't believe in anything but yourselves?"

Lucas stretched out his fingers, filled the space between them with his power until it was difficult for the both of them to breathe. Matron didn't flinch.

"We are your gods," Lucas reminded her. "You made us to save you."

"I didn't make shit." Matron looked up at the faint warning beep coming from the computer as the weather Doppler-radar grid shifted, moving from green to red somewhere over the Midwest. The projections that the computer spit out weren't pretty, bow echos and rain across the vidscreen, across the country; a radar line of storm clouds. "Do I call you Noah now?"

Lucas turned his head and opened his eyes to look at her, this woman he had saved years ago. "Two by fucking two, Matron. Two by fucking two."

Matron bit down on the core of her apple and chewed slowly. She spit the seeds out into her hand and tucked them into her pocket for safekeeping. Things like that should never be wasted.

Somewhere in the far distance, several states to the west, a storm was brewing, moving quickly in their direction. They watched it fill the screen, the only sound in the small weather station their quiet breathing and the crunch of an apple between Matron's metal teeth.

[NINETEEN]

AUGUST 2379
LONDON, UNITED KINGDOM

Nathan was in the Netherlands, securing his political relationships over the latest Act he had pushed through the World Court. Which meant it fell to Samantha to extract the memory from the electrokinetic who had been stationed in Buffalo.

Lucas never failed to piss her off.

Standing in her office, arms crossed over her chest, she glared furiously at the electrokinetic crouched at her feet, letting her older brother's challenge tumble over and over through her mind.

"We shouldn't give him what he wants," Gideon said from where he sat behind Samantha's desk.

"Of course not," Samantha spat out. "The only question is what the fuck does he *really* want? Us there or not there? It's a fifty-fifty chance, and no matter what we choose, you can fucking *bet* Lucas will compensate for it."

"He always asks for you." Gideon gestured at the Warhound on the floor, teleporting her out with the casual use of power that came as naturally as breathing. "Perhaps you should stay behind."

"You wouldn't be able to find him." Samantha shook her head. "I want him *dead,* Gideon."

"So does Nathan." Her twin shrugged. "Unless Nathan goes after Lucas, we'll never be able to bring him back. You know that, every Warhound knows that. It's death to believe otherwise. Nathan doesn't because he *can't.* Not and risk everything we're working toward."

"Then what the bloody hell are we *doing?*"

Gideon gave her a level look. "Obeying."

Samantha ground her teeth, tongue pressed hard against the roof of her mouth. Bending her head, she closed her eyes and easily drew her brother into a psi link that she sent skimming over a sea and a continent to where their father was.

Sir, they said together on the outskirts of Nathan's mind.

After a moment, Nathan dropped his shields and allowed them into his mind. His attention, while solid, was focused elsewhere. That didn't mean his power couldn't hurt them. Samantha steeled herself and dropped the report directly into Nathan's mind. His anger seeped through their thoughts.

An ultimatum? Nathan asked slowly. *Does he never learn?*

It's a trap, Gideon said. *He wants us there.*

Nathan's disgust was thick enough that it translated into an actual taste on Samantha's tongue. *Of course he does. Lucas can't bargain without witnesses.*

Your orders?

Nathan was silent for a long moment. *We're too close to the launch date. We can't afford any interference.*

Sir? Samantha this time; alone. Gideon was a silent presence in her mind that she resented with everything she had.

I want him dead, Nathan said, echoing his daughter's desire. *I don't care about the cost. Our mission is Mars Colony. Lucas is a distraction that needs to be stopped. Do what needs to be done, Samantha. I'll leave the decision of how to go about killing him in your hands. I trust I won't have to tell you what will happen if you fail.*

Samantha buried her anger deep, because it wouldn't help her here—only obedience would. Gideon was right. *Sir.*

Nathan pulled away, cutting the connection, needing all his attention on manipulating the humans. Samantha opened her eyes, raised her head, and found herself staring into her twin's face. Gideon's expression was calm, almost triumphant, as if this were all he'd ever been waiting for, this chance to prove himself to the few who mattered. Samantha was pretty damn certain that she didn't matter, not for this.

"I'll go," Gideon said. "You should stay here."

"No," Samantha said as she clenched her hands into fists.

"You failed to stop Lucas when he left London." Gideon reached out and wrapped his hand around her wrist, the look in his eyes disapproving. "You've failed all the times since when ordered after him."

She tried to twist out of his grip, but she couldn't break free of his telekinesis. "So did you, Gideon."

"I'm not the one who consistently comes up short. That's you." He gave her a little shake, some shred of emotion filtering across his face. It wasn't real, even if he believed it was. "Let me do this for you. For us. You know I can do this for us."

They were twins, born mere minutes apart, she with telepathy and he with telekinesis that was strong enough to incorporate teleportation. Neither of them were a triad psion that Nathan had hoped to control. Hell, they weren't even close to being what he really wanted. They were simply and only functional mistakes that he pitted against each other again and again because it *amused* him. Samantha didn't want the post that Nathan was making them fight for now that Lucas was gone. She didn't want what Gideon would bleed and scream and kill for, though neither her twin nor her father would ever truly believe her, even with her thoughts as proof, not after Lucas's escape.

She didn't want the Serca Syndicate.

She wanted Lucas.

Dead or alive, she wanted her older brother to pay.

"No," Samantha said, backing up her words with her telepathic strength. "Kristen and I will go. You're a telekinetic, Gideon. You'd need a dozen telepaths to help you find Lucas. I can find him by myself."

"Only if he lets you, which is something you can't count on," Gideon said. "When you find him, what will you do? How will you save yourself?"

"Kristen."

Gideon's contempt filtered through to her as he let her go. It was his arrogance, however, that annoyed her. Samantha peeled apart her shields, let her telepathy drag him into the psi link they'd shared since they were born.

You want what Nathan promised Lucas, she said, her mental tone dripping with false comfort. *I don't.*

She let him see how much she simply *did not care* for what Nathan had to offer. Oh, she was a Serca to her core and always would be. She had never understood how Lucas managed to walk away from everything he knew, as if he'd had the opportunity in his restricted existence to learn something different. Samantha's loyalty was carved with blood into her father's Syndicate and it always would be. This was her life, this dual existence of psion and human that she led. She understood that. She knew she had been born to serve, like all Warhounds.

You want it more than I do, Samantha said. *You always have. Lucas would have killed you the second he took that post and you know it. I will always be loyal.*

Her twin's thoughts were bright and hot in her mind, the psi link like scar tissue somewhere deep inside her. Gideon let who he was twist into what Samantha knew she only pretended to be. They were twins. They would always be bound to each other by genetics and Syndicate loyalty, but she was losing faith in that connection. She was losing faith in him.

If you ever betray me, I will kill you, Gideon promised her.

Samantha never doubted it. Just as she had never doubted Lucas when he said, *I will be waiting for you,* two years ago as he left the Serca Syndicate and the Warhound ranks.

She had never told anyone about his promise and forgot it more often than she remembered it. Samantha didn't know where that rebellion stemmed from, where it went when Nathan was searching for betrayal, just that it was a part of her for that one instant. Gideon missed it, because he wasn't a 'path-oriented psi. Samantha broke their merge with a gasp, panting heavily against the back of her hand as she tried not to be sick.

"Nathan doesn't believe you are completely loyal," Gideon said after a long moment as he looked at her. "I know differently. I've *fought* for you, Samantha. Doesn't that count for something, anything at all?"

No. No, it didn't. His subconscious spoke to her more clearly than he did. She knew the truth.

"I need to do this," she said, not answering his question.

"If you fail this time, you'll die. There is no coming back here without Lucas's body. That is the only result Nathan will accept."

"Then I won't fail." Samantha flashed him a wicked, proud smile as she pulled away. It felt like a lie.

Their bond was something that could be broken, but Nathan had never severed it. He called their psi link useful. Samantha thought it was limiting.

Maybe that's why Lucas always worked through Kristen.

The empath understood all the pieces of the puzzle that made up her older sister's carefully broken and reassembled mind better than Samantha herself. Hours later, when Samantha opened up the door to her medical cell, Kristen just *grinned* at her with that same vicious smile she gave everyone.

"Feeling all right, Sammy-girl?" Kristen asked as she pushed herself to her feet. She used the walls to steady herself in the corner she had been curled up against, the skinsuit she wore lining the bones of her body.

Samantha stared at her crazy, empathic little sister and said, "You will follow my orders, Kristen."

"Last chance for you, eh? Always wanted to see what was on the other side," Kristen drawled as she skipped out of her cell, tripped over her own feet, and crashed into the human nurse standing next to Samantha.

When Kristen's power started to eat through the human's mind, Samantha didn't try to stop her. She simply waited while the woman screamed and doctors walked by with hurried steps, pretending not to see the woman dying on the floor.

The mental grid dipped beneath the ferocious strength of Kristen's damaged empathic power, pulling clarity out of the dying woman's mind for Kristen to use. It tasted like memories, like life, a breath that Kristen held in her lungs until her vision grew dark with bright black spots.

Sanity was such a delicate, tentative state of being.

Samantha reached down and curled her hand over Kristen's chin, jerking her head up so she could look her sister in the eye. Kristen's smile eased to something almost sane, the nurse dead beneath the younger girl's white-knuckled grip.

"We have a job to do," Samantha informed her.

"I know," Kristen said cheerfully. "You only bring me along when it's time for a killing spree, Sammy-girl. I get so *hungry* waiting for those moments."

Samantha dragged Kristen to her feet by her neck, pulling the girl down the hallway. In Samantha's mind, through their bond, Gideon was saying, *You really want her instead of me?*

Nathan said it was my decision. He would approve.

Nathan wants you dead. He just hasn't found a reason for killing you yet.

The same could be said of her twin. The day he came to terms with that was the day she'd never see him coming. *Eventually, Gideon. Eventually.*

Samantha pressed her mouth into a hard line as she stepped into the lift at the end of that long hallway, Kristen by her side. The younger girl wrapped her spindly arms around Samantha's waist and pressed her forehead against Samantha's shoulder. She licked sweat off her upper lip and let the salty taste of it spread through her mouth.

"It'll be all right," Kristen muttered against the synthfabric of Samantha's uniform, her smile bleeding onto the material. "This isn't the end, you know?"

Samantha didn't.

She would find out soon enough.

[TWENTY]

AUGUST 2379

THE HAGUE, THE NETHERLANDS

Elion Athe was admitted into the office that Nathan kept at The Hague by way of Jin Li, who didn't offer him anything more than an unimpressed look. Elion spared the man a single glance before walking to Nathan's desk and taking a seat in one of the chairs there.

"You're late," Nathan said, not looking away from the hologrid that flickered images and data between them. "I hope you have something of use."

"Of course," Elion promised as he placed a data chip on Nathan's desk.

He thought it odd that Nathan actually reached over and picked it up with his fingers instead of using his telekinesis, but only for a moment. This was humanity's seat of power. There could be no hint of psionic interference in this ancient building atop an underground city.

Nathan jacked the data chip into his computer and navigated its files with faint motions of his fingers. The information that the Athe family had gathered for Nathan's perusal nearly filled the data chip.

"Interesting," Nathan said after ten minutes of studying the overview report. "My son does seem to get around. Jin Li? Send in Victoria. We'll need a bit of privacy. See to it."

Jin Li set his hand against the control panel by the door before he left, activating security measures that were patently illegal in The Hague, but standard by Nathan's way of thinking. The jamming frequency would ride under the frequency that The Hague used and couldn't be picked up by the government at all. Nathan's office would only show an extremely detailed loop in the system, an interference that would take an expert hacker to detect, and only if the hacker knew what to look for. Elion knew how Nathan conducted business and so relaxed minutely in his chair.

"My father said to tell you that if you require more proof of our endeavors, he would gladly give you our billable hours," Elion said.

Nathan waved aside the suggestion. "That isn't necessary. This is what I was expecting."

"What will you do with the information?"

"It's none of your concern."

Elion bit back on the automatic retort that rose to his lips. He was used to being the one in power, not the subordinate, but was smart enough to realize when to keep his mouth shut. Nathan seemed to appreciate Elion's control and closed down the hologrid to focus on him.

"I have it on good authority that the World Court is beginning to initiate the transfer preparations of its selected people to the pickup points in the major surviving cities," Nathan said.

"I haven't heard."

Nathan's smile was condescending. Elion told himself not to be insulted by it. "Of course not. They wouldn't advertise something they've been keeping secret for generations."

Elion managed not to clench his hands into fists. "We'll be told soon, I presume?"

"Within the week or so. Your family still has the seats promised you."

"We bled enough for them, in blood *and* money."

"Don't be so dramatic, Elion." Nathan gestured at nothing in particular. "Your family enabled our escape off this planet. Even if you had no money left, your reputation would be enough to pay its way onto the colony ship."

"We will do what you require of us."

Nathan's expression didn't change. "I'm so glad to hear that."

Elion wondered if this was what his father felt like, small and unimportant in the face of this man's dangerous attention. Meeting and holding Nathan's gaze took strength. Elion knew what resided in that mind. He knew this was the only course of action.

Aren't you glad your family chose the right side all those years ago? Nathan asked, his mouth not moving one centimeter. *Come now, Elion. You're going to live. Indentured servitude is a small price to pay for your own survival.*

At any other time, Elion would have said yes. Sitting here in Nathan's domain, staring into that man's face and knowing Nathan would be the one that humanity owed their survival to, Elion could only think about what would happen if they stayed on Earth instead.

The office door slid open, allowing Jin Li to reenter. He was followed by a slightly built redhead carrying a heavy black case. At twenty-eight years old, Victoria Montoya had survived well past the median age of a psion and was on a steady trek toward dying. She was the Warhounds' CMO, a Class III telepath who was exceptional at her job, whether it was putting psion minds back together or taking human ones apart.

"Victoria," Nathan said, leaning back in his chair. "I presume you brought everything we need?"

"Of course, sir," Victoria replied as she approached his desk and set the case she was carrying down on the empty chair beside Elion.

Elion watched as she opened it up and pulled out sealed and sterilized operating tools, as well as a portable sterility field device. That last item caused Elion to rise to his feet in alarm, eyes snapping from Victoria to Nathan.

"What is the meaning of this?" Elion demanded, pointing at the medical tools.

Nathan just offered up a smile as he lifted one hand. "I'm covering all my bases, Elion. You don't think you're the first of your family to undergo this procedure, do you? Your father doesn't remember when my mother performed it on him. You won't remember this either."

Nathan clenched his hand into a fist, his telekinetic power immobilizing Elion. All Elion could do was breathe as Victoria worked around him, setting up an operating space on Nathan's desk.

"If you could position him, sir?" Victoria asked, nodding at where she had the sterility field up and running, the quiet hum of the medical machine destroying any and all contaminants within its designated area.

Nathan moved Elion's body like a puppet, forcing the man to sit back down in the chair, then to lean forward with his head resting on the desk within the sterility field. Elion's eyes were blinking rapidly, vocal cords frozen in terror, as Victoria slid an operating cover across his shoulders and around his neck. The last thing he saw was the hypospray that she stabbed against his throat, shooting him full of sedatives. The drugs pulled him under.

Victoria picked up her laser scalpel. Holding it at an angle over Elion's left temple, she cut into his skin and peeled back his scalp, continuing into muscle and bone. He bled down his face and neck as she worked at opening a tiny hole in his skull to reach a viable point of access in the bioware net. Brain surgery was never easy, but this was more a wetware hack than an extraction.

She took her time while Nathan focused on his work. He trusted Victoria to make sure that the wire jacked into Nathan's personal work terminal was connected with precision and with no interference to the bioware net in Elion's brain. When she had the connection, Victoria pulled her hands away from her patient.

"Is HQ uplinked?" she asked.

Nathan glanced at the vidscreen. "Uplinked and hacking. You're clear, Victoria."

She took a step back. "Then he's all yours when they finish."

Bioware nets were a unique form of technology that the Sercas had invented, sold to the World Court generations ago, and subsequently learned to work around over the years. The device was the sole reason why no Serca had ever risked joining the World Court. Too many people had too much access to the servers and networks that monitored the baselines that the bioware nets produced. Better to work outside of that system than to risk it all collapsing due to recorded psionic interference.

Getting around the security system of a bioware net required a strong uplink, a back door in the system, hackers at an off-site location—and the human. Transferring the bioware net signal into Nathan's computer, where the hackers embedded it and kept the signal alive, took less than an hour. Making sure Elion's new baseline readings would copy over the old ones took a little more time, as it involved hacking the Registry through a separate back door that the Serca Syndicate had built into that particular system. The Registry was just one of their many creations, and they never completely gave up what they believed to be rightfully theirs.

Only when they had confirmation that the signal was set in the system did Nathan put aside his datapad and lean back in his chair. Closing his eyes, Nathan reached out with his telepathy for the static human mind before him. He wrapped his power through those muted, limited thoughts and twisted Elion into what Nathan needed. Mindwipes, at least ones that didn't leave humans obviously damaged, were always such a delicate, devious psi surgery.

Elion had walked into Nathan's office with a mind of his own and the ability to choose his own future, as limited as his choices were. Hours later, when he left The Hague—cleaned up and in one piece—he left under Nathan's control, the changes in his personality and mind so subtle that no one would ever notice. His changed opinions, however, would suit Nathan's needs now and forever. With his baseline readings globally replaced in the Registry and through all viable systems that humans used, Elion's conversion was complete.

It left Nathan with a throbbing headache and an ache in his chest, by his heart, small reminders that he was well past the age that a psion was supposed to die.

Nathan turned his attention to the information at his fingertips, gathering up a half dozen datapads from across his desk. Victoria was already long gone and on her way back to London, the mess she had made cleaned up.

"Is my shuttle ready, Jin Li?"

"Ready and waiting, sir."

"Good." Nathan stood up. "I've a schedule to keep."

Jin Li nodded as he followed Nathan to the door. "What have you got planned for the cartels?"

"Nothing they're expecting."

[TWENTY-ONE]

AUGUST 2379

BUFFALO, USA

Jason didn't know what the plan was, all he knew was that it *sucked*.

"If I had a functioning uplink, this might work," he argued with Novak. "If I had a working jack-in system, we might get further than *Canada*. This? This will crash us into the Great Lakes if we're *lucky*."

Novak chewed on his bit of tobacco and just grinned. "Luck ain't got nothing to do with it, Stryker. I did what I could, on top of everyone else finishing what *they* could before dying. Quit your bitching and figure out where we start."

Jason glared at Novak from where he sat in the pilot's seat of the largest shuttle in the underground hangar. "We might need better code than what we've got in this system to support the electronic countermeasures if we're going anywhere near government airspace and not detouring through deadzones."

"So write it."

"I can't go in and rewrite code for every separate program in this damn shuttle. We've been working on upgrading the firmware for the hive connection for days already and we're running out of *time*." Jason leaned forward and stabbed his finger at the hologrid stretched over the wide flight-deck windshield, showing new data that had been down-loaded just that morning. "See that? That fucking storm is going to eat us *alive* and you're crazy if you think we can launch through it safely."

Novak spit black saliva onto the metal flight deck of the shuttle, pieces of synthetic tobacco stuck in his teeth. "Lucas says we will."

Jason groaned loudly and pressed his hands over his eyes, hard. "Fucking *hell*. We're taking orders from a man who listens to a god-damn *child*. We're all going to die."

"Shut up, Jason," Lucas said as he stepped into the flight deck of the shuttle, sounding annoyed. He looked paler than usual, with bruises pressed heavily beneath his dark blue eyes. "Tell me the hive connection is ready?"

"I want to say yes." Jason dropped his hands away from his face and leaned forward. "I do. If I had a system up to the grade I'm used to deal-ing with, possibly. If I had another week, I could be absolutely sure."

"You have two days to finalize everything."

"Two—" Jason choked on his next words and simply resorted to swearing. Novak seemed impressed with his repertoire.

"Two days," Lucas repeated. "More than likely less, so see about doing it in one. The Warhounds are going to start arriving here in Buffalo in force, which will definitely bring in the Strykers. They'll make a nice distraction. The storm is going to hit anywhere between twenty-eight and thirty-six hours from now. Depending on the winds, it could hit earlier."

"You want these shuttles ready for stealth against military jets in *one day*?" Jason shook his head. "That's impossible. You're going to get us all killed if we don't have time to do a dry run on everything."

Lucas walked up to Jason, wrapped his hand around the telekinetic's throat and slammed him face-first down against the flight-control panel. Lucas held him there more by the strength in his arm than by the power in his head.

"Would you fucking be careful with that?" Novak shouted, pointing at the panel. "You break it, we don't got extra!"

"Listen to me, you annoying piece of shit," Lucas said as he leaned in low to whisper into Jason's ear. "The only reason why I haven't broken open your mind yet is because I need a little more power than I've got available. That doesn't mean I'm not figuring out the most painful way to turn you into someone else. We need these shuttles to be flight-ready. Everything about them is solid except the hive connection. Your job is to fix that."

"With three shuttles? I need more *time*," Jason spit out, still trying to breathe.

"Try three dozen." Lucas's grip didn't lessen any as he leaned his weight against the other man. "This isn't the only underground hangar with long-haul shuttles. I'm not stupid enough to pin everything on such a low number. The hive connection will be installed into all the others once you're done here. Novak should have told you that by now."

Jason's gaze cut over to the human hacker. "He hasn't told me shit."

There was the sound of a body hitting a bulkhead and the harsh gasps of someone choking on his own blood. "Novak," Lucas said easily enough. "You know what's at stake. Remember that I can replace you. If you want to keep breathing, play by my rules, or I will feed you to the Warhounds when they arrive. I'm expecting them soon."

Jason glared up at Lucas from where he was pinned to the control console, face pressed against the sensors. "You fucking bastard. You led them here on purpose, didn't you? I thought you wanted to get the fuck out of here unnoticed?"

Lucas tilted his head, dark blue eyes expressionless. "Try to understand something, Jason. This mission isn't just to piss off your side *or* my side. It's about saving everyone the World Court wants to leave behind. That should be easy for you to understand as a former Stryker. Now get the job *done*."

Lucas let him go with a hard shove and stepped back. Jason, gasping for air, reached up to touch his throat. His skin was hot and bruised where Lucas's fingers had held him.

"You only showed us three shuttles," Jason rasped. "What the hell am I supposed to think if you keep lying to us?"

Lucas crossed his arms over his chest, watching impassively as Jason got to his feet. "What you perfect here will be applied to the rest, which is why I need you to finish this sooner rather than later. We're minimizing the risk by containing it to the first three shuttles."

"You just made my fucking job *harder*."

The telekinetic didn't seem to care that he was pissing off one of the most powerful men in the world as he got in Lucas's face. His anger was driving his reactions quicker and faster than logic. Lucas wondered if he had the time to spare to change that.

"Stop it. Both of you."

Jason's gaze jerked away from Lucas in an instant, some of the anger leaving his face as he caught sight of the figure stepping over Novak's unconscious body and coming into the flight deck. Kerr looked as if he'd been dealing with psi shock for the better part of a month, not the handful of days he'd been lying unconscious in that borrowed room. It wasn't a good look for him.

Jason shoved past Lucas, reaching Kerr and putting his shoulder beneath the other man's arm. Kerr nodded his thanks for the support, even as he leaned most of his weight against the bulkhead. As bad as Kerr looked, his mind was stable. His shields were a solid barrier that weren't going to skid out from under his control anytime soon. Lucas eyed him, satisfied to see that the trick he had taught Kerr in reading as human on the mental grid was working.

"You're finally awake," Lucas said.

"I puked on the floor between our beds," Kerr said evenly. "Matron said you get to clean it up."

With Kerr's shields solidly raised, Lucas couldn't tell if he was lying. It was progress. "Your mess, your problem. I'll take another room. Not like we'll be here long enough for me to need it."

Kerr wasn't impressed. "I think it's time you give us a full briefing, Lucas. You owe us that much."

"I owe you nothing."

"Please."

Jason heard the need in Kerr's voice and didn't like it, his mouth twisting in anger. But he kept quiet. It would be years before Jason stopped thinking of Kerr as the one in charge of their two-person team, if he ever did.

"Get the others," Lucas finally said as he reached out and nudged Novak into solid wakefulness with his boot and his telepathy. "Matron is in the weapons room. Bring her here. She hates when I 'port her around without warning."

"Do it yourself," Novak groaned. "You're the damn psion."

Lucas simply stared at him until the other man quickly looked away. It took two tries for Novak to get to his feet, but the hacker finally managed it. He stumbled out of the shuttle on shaky legs, Jason watching him go while Kerr focused on some distant point that only he could see as he tapped into his telepathy.

"They're coming," Kerr announced, blinking solid awareness back into his eyes.

"Good," Lucas said as he walked past them, telekinetically stealing a few cigarettes and the lighter from Jason's pocket. He left the shuttle with quick strides, going to sit on the open cargo ramp beneath the bright lights of the underground hangar.

Above him, the launch silo was dark. It wouldn't come online, the blast doors wouldn't open, until they were ready to fly the hell out of here. Lucas figured that time couldn't come soon enough.

Thirty minutes later, everyone started to trickle into the hangar. He was almost done with his second cigarette when Matron, Everett, and Novak finally got there, the last to arrive. They made a ragtag little group, these five psions and three humans, every single one with a part to play. Lucas wondered, yet again, what Marcheline was thinking years ago before she died when she had convinced him to go along with this craziness. Her expectations had been impossible to ignore. So were Aisling's orders.

"Your boy here," Matron said as she pointed at Quinton, "I like the way he shoots."

"He's a crack shot," Lucas said as he stubbed out his cigarette on the cargo ramp he was sitting on. "Of course you would."

"I need a replacement for the one you got killed."

"You can't have me," Quinton said irritably.

"Stop arguing," Threnody said, giving Quinton a sharp glance and a silent warning not to start a fight. "What do you want, Lucas?"

"It's not what he wants." Jason gestured among them all. "It's what we need to know. Did he tell you that these aren't the only shuttles?"

Quinton's expression became stony. Threnody didn't look surprised, and Jason narrowed his eyes at her. "Did you know?"

"I guessed." Threnody shrugged. "We had a talk the other day after he was finished working on Kerr. I needed confirmation on something Matron had told us."

"You've been keeping secrets an awful lot lately," Quinton said, unable to keep anger out of his voice.

"I'm sorry." Only she wasn't. Lucas could read that in her mind, if not in her face, in her voice. Threnody stared at him. "Jason's right, though. We need to know the full extent of your plans, Lucas. We need access to our powers again if you want us to actually help you."

"Four against one," Jason muttered.

"It wouldn't be enough," Kerr said. "And I won't fight him."

Jason's expression was one of betrayed surprise. *"What?"*

"Neither will I," Threnody agreed quietly.

Quinton stared at her, a tight, wounded expression on his face. Jason caught his eye when he looked away. "You and I, Quinton. We're the only sane people in this group."

Threnody rolled her eyes. "It's not about sanity, Jason. It never was. It's about doing what's right."

"How is joining forces with Lucas Serca, *right*?" Quinton demanded.

"Because he's the only one willing to save the human race. Mars isn't the answer. We can't just pick up and leave like none of this ever happened, like we didn't ruin this planet. Maybe everyone who launched the bombs all those years ago knew that as well." Threnody lifted her chin a little, squaring her shoulders like the soldier she wasn't supposed to be anymore. "Tell them what's in the Arctic, Lucas. Tell them what you told me."

Lucas looked at the expectant faces of the Strykers, the bored stances of Matron, Everett, and Novak. Getting to his feet, Lucas stepped off the cargo ramp and onto the launchpad.

"Threnody's right about the shuttles. Don't blame her because she's smarter than all of you combined," Lucas said. "There's an island in the Arctic that holds a seed bank that survived the Border Wars. The World Court knows of it—hell, they've *used* it. How do you think we got the Sky-Farms to feed everyone after the fact? The world was too polluted, too *dead,* to grow anything in the aftermath of the Border Wars. The World Court is going to take all of that with them when they leave Earth— every last seed, every last frozen embryo of all the species we drove to extinction over the centuries, and all the ones we lost in the Border Wars. They'll take it with them and leave us with *nothing.*

"They're only taking registered humans to try and stop the spread of psions. They're taking with them everything that lets us survive on this planet and leaving us behind to die." Lucas shook his head, his accustomed expression of sarcastic amusement and disdain slipping away. "What they want isn't going to fix their lives how they think it will. We destroyed the future we should have had with the Border Wars. This is the one we have to survive in. This is *all we've got.* We owe it to the next generation to build a better world."

"Thought that was supposed to be Mars," Novak said.

Everett smacked him upside the head. "Shut up."

"If Mars was meant to be livable, it would have stayed habitable," Lucas said. "It died out long before humans walked on this planet."

"That doesn't explain the Warhounds," Jason said in a frustrated voice. "Or why you're purposefully bringing them here."

"They've got someone in their ranks who can break through your shields. We need what's in your head, Jason. More than you realize."

"You can't do it yourself?" Jason's mouth curled into a sneer. "I thought triad psions were capable of anything."

"Just because I'm a Class I doesn't mean I'm always going to be the right person for the job or that I will have the required strength. Why do you think I brought all of you together? I had to wait for the Strykers to demote Threnody and Quinton, had to wait for them to be paired up with you. It's going to take all of us to make sure those left behind survive."

"Wait," Quinton said. "You mean you *don't* want to stop the launch? I thought that was the whole point of us working with you?"

"Let them go to Mars. We'll keep Earth. We just need half of what they're going to take with them. Half the seeds. Half the embryos. Half the people. Half the psions, once we ensure the Strykers' survival. We can build something new with all of that."

Lucas was staring at Threnody as he said it, seeing steely agreement in her eyes.

"The government is gonna fry all your brains before they launch into space," Matron said. "Even *I* know that."

"There's a way to reprogram the neurotrackers," Lucas said. "How do you think the Warhounds managed to keep all the defected Strykers alive long enough to remove the bioware?"

"There's twelve hundred of us in the Strykers Syndicate," Kerr said. "How are you going to stop the kill sequence for that many psions?"

Again, Lucas looked at Jason. The telekinetic just frowned. "I'm not *that* good of a hacker."

Lucas shook his head. "It's not your hacking skills we'll need."

"Fucking great. Why do I have to be your crux?"

"Not the crux. The linchpin." Lucas walked over to where Jason and Kerr were standing, then reached out and pressed a finger to Jason's forehead. Jason knocked his hand away and took a step back. "I said it before. You were misdiagnosed, Jason. You're not an average telekinetic. All that power inside your head means you're something more. Our natal shields *always* break. They have to if we're at all able to access our powers. But your shields are still up and you can still use your telekinesis to a certain degree. You're strong enough to teleport."

Jason gave a derisive little snort. "So, what, you're saying that just because my shields never broke, I'm a Class 0?"

"Yes."

"Bullshit. The only psions who reach that rank are precognitives. I don't see the future. I'm not whatever it is you think I'm supposed to be."

"Microtelekinetic," Lucas said as he brushed past him. "You are what Nathan failed to produce in me, Jason. The Strykers got lucky when they picked you up. So did the world."

Lucas twisted his telepathy through their minds. He broke the mental blocks he had erected around the areas in their brains that bridged the synaptic distances between conscious thought and the powers they had been born with. Control came back in a heady instant, making the four light-headed.

We're either not human enough to leave, or we're too human to stay, Lucas said into all their minds. *It can't be about who is more deserving anymore. That's what got us here in the first place.*

They watched him walk away, none of them saying a word. What broke the silence was the faint hiss of gas, the scrape of metal on metal, and the crackle of fire as Quinton let tiny flickers of flame twist around his fingers. Clenching his hand around the fire, he put it out with a thought, skin hot to the touch.

"I'm in," he said, glancing over at Threnody and giving her a nod. He watched as some of the tension drained from her shoulders, loosening the rigid way she held herself.

Jason threw his arms up in the air as he went back into the shuttle. "You're all fucking crazy. Now leave me the hell alone so I can work in peace."

[TWENTY-TWO]

AUGUST 2379
TALLINN, ESTONIA

They threw the bodies into the toxic burn pits.

Dug deep into the limestone cliff that ran through the remnants of the capital city, kilometers from the Gulf of Finland, the burn pits were mostly full, but they still smoldered.

Dalia panted through the filter of her skinmask, believing that she could taste the dead on her tongue. She couldn't, not really. Didn't stop her brain from trying to tell her nose that she *should* be smelling the dead. Perception was so easily messed with.

"Is this the last of them?" the telepath beside her asked.

Dalia looked at the small group of bond workers and scientists that were huddled together as if that solidarity could save them. They were dressed in worn-out work uniforms or lab clothes, faces full of terror, unable to run. Transferred here from farther inland, these were the people that had been assigned to her warehouse for a job that couldn't be on record. Which meant they could not be on record.

"Yes," Dalia said as she reflexively touched her front pocket, feeling the multitude of data chips safe in her possession. Schematics enough to liberate them all. "Nathan wants no witnesses."

A telepath to turn off their minds.

A telekinetic to toss them into the burn pits.

Dalia licked her lips and tasted nothing but her own sweat. She had long ago gotten over the guilt for being a murderer. The government wouldn't miss their stolen data, just as they wouldn't miss the dead. Nathan, she knew, would be pleased that his orders had been so perfectly executed, here and in all the other places across the world like this. Those who weren't wanted would be left behind and forgotten.

There was no place in the stars for the useless.

PART SIX
CONVECTION

SESSION DATE: **2128.02.27**

LOCATION: **Institute of Psionics Research**

CLEARANCE ID: **Dr. Amy Bennett**

SUBJECT: **2581**

FILE NUMBER: **196**

"Where's Matthew, Mama?"

"Your brother's not here, sweetheart," a dark-haired woman says as she crouches down beside the table, peering beneath it at the girl hiding in the only darkness that exists in the room. "He made it out of the country, remember? But he's watching over you. Just like you wanted."

"Good, good," the girl mutters, picking at the lace on her white socks as she glances at the camera. "I miss him."

"I know you do, but if you're really good—"

"Maybe I'll get to see him," Aisling interrupts, the frustration in her young voice impossible to miss. "You always say that."

The woman goes still. "No, I don't."

Aisling raps her knuckles on the floor so hard the skin splits. "Here. You always say it *here*."

"Stop it." The woman reaches out and pulls the girl into her arms, several wires pulling free because of the sudden movement. An alarm sounds, coming from one of the machines. "Stop hurting yourself."

"What if I'm wrong? Mama, what if I got it wrong?"

The woman slides her fingers through her daughter's dark hair, touching more wires than anything else. She hesitates only a moment before she grips a handful and yanks them off the girl's head, setting off a multitude of alarms.

"I should never have brought you to this place," she whispers as the door slides open and a nurse comes in. "You're not God, baby girl. You can't save us, no matter what they say."

"I know, Mama." Aisling wraps her small arms around her mother's neck and holds on tightly. "I can't save you here. I'm sorry."

[TWENTY-THREE]

M iss me?"

Ciari didn't bother to look away from the hologrid above her desk displaying all the recently gathered data from field Strykers. "You shouldn't be here, Lucas."

"You always say that. Notice how I never listen."

This time Ciari did look up, watching the person who sat across from her through the colorful sharpness of the hologrid. The smile on Lucas's face hadn't changed a bit in the five years she'd known him. It was still as challenging as ever.

"One of these days they'll find out."

"Yes," he agreed. "Sooner than you or I would like, but that's the cost of success."

"*Are* we succeeding?"

He looked away from her to stare at the ceiling. "*Success* is such a dangerous word. Everyone's definition of it is different."

"I'm only interested in yours."

"You aren't the only one." Lucas glanced back at her, the smile on his face twisting into something unreadable as he rose to his feet. "There won't be time after today for us. Not for a while yet."

"There's never been time for us," Ciari reminded him as he came around her desk and stopped behind her chair. "You showed me that when you revealed those old files showing Aisling and what she wanted. Disagreeing never got me anywhere."

"What have I told you?" He leaned down to whisper the words into her ear even as one hand curled over her chin to turn her head toward him, the other settling over her stomach. "You can argue about what Aisling wants all you like, it's not going to change a damn thing."

"It could."

"Oh, Ciari." He pressed his mouth against hers, the pressure just a ripple in her mind. "There's a reason why she told me to include you. I've lived my entire life trusting in the veracity of details. Aisling is the devil in all of them. You can't fight her, so stop trying."

Lucas.

"Ciari?"

The space behind her was empty, her mind just as barren. Just a memory, of some moment before this. Sucking in a soft breath, Ciari turned her head to acknowledge the pair of Strykers that had entered her office. "What is it?"

Aidan and Jael shared a brief look before both telepaths focused on their OIC. Aidan stepped forward to set a data chip on Ciari's desk. "We've got incoming reports from Buffalo of Warhound arrivals on the mental grid. Some of their shields slipped a little and we got confirmation of two psi signatures that match Samantha and Kristen Serca."

Ciari gave them both a surprised look. "Kristen? Are you sure?"

Aidan nodded. "It's her."

"She hasn't been seen in years. I thought Nathan had her put down." Ciari shook her head. "Kristen being alive complicates things."

"We'll warn the Strykers that a dysfunctional psion has entered the fight." Aidan shrugged. "I'm not sure if that warning will do any good, though. Everyone who's ever gone after Kristen has always ended up dead."

Ciari minimized the hologrid with a wave of her hand. "It doesn't matter. If those two are in the field, then that means Lucas has to be as well. Did the scans find any evidence of our missing Strykers?"

"No. That's not to say they aren't with him, if he is there."

"Or dead," Jael added.

"It's been a while since we lost the four in the Slums." Ciari frowned. "If Samantha is leading the Warhounds in Buffalo, then most likely that is where Lucas is."

"We still don't know if Lucas is aligned with them or not," Aidan said.

"I vote not," Jael said sharply. "Two years on the run, being hunted by Strykers *and* Warhounds? Looking back at the information we've accumulated on that outlier blip that we now *know* is Lucas Serca, there's not much evidence to the contrary. He was integral to the Serca Syndicate's image while growing up as Nathan's successor. Now it's the twins. Lucas is no longer with the Serca Syndicate, nor the Warhounds. I think it's time we let the Strykers Syndicate know that blip is still alive."

"And have everyone worry that we've got a *third* psion group coming into play?" Ciari grimaced as she pushed her chair back and got to her feet. "The World Court would blame us for allowing that to happen. The punishment would be severe. Not to mention the Silence Law is still in effect."

"They're just going to kill us all anyway," Jael argued. "What's a few weeks early?"

"Jael," Aidan said, giving the CMO an admonishing look. "Remember who you're speaking to."

"I do." The petite black woman lifted her chin and glared stubbornly at Ciari. "The one person who has the power to argue our existence to the World Court. How's that going, Ciari?"

Ciari's expression didn't change. If she was angry at Jael's accusation, at her bitterness, she didn't show a single shred of it. "I'm not the one who's going to save us. That's someone else's task."

"Really." It was hard to ignore the ugly hatred in Jael's tone. "Care to explain what you mean by that?"

"I'm not obligated to explain anything." Ciari shrugged. "But I'm a Stryker, Jael. No matter what happens, my goal is our continued survival. Give me some credit. I'm too close to the World Court to be able to effectively do everything that needs to get done. Every OIC has always relied on others for the more delicate work we do. You know that."

"Then who's your scapegoat if you're ours?"

"You'll know soon enough." Ciari turned her attention to Aidan. "I'll review what you gave me within the hour. Begin a callback of Stryker teams that we can afford to remove from the field for an immediate emergency transfer."

"What are you planning?" Aidan said.

"What needs to be done. You have two hours to get me a list of teams that we can ship into Buffalo."

"What's our limit?"

"This is a Class I triad psion we're going up against. You don't have a limit."

Aidan nodded and turned to leave the office. Jael remained behind. Leaning against her desk, Ciari gazed at her CMO and offered up a half-smile.

"Do you even know what you're doing?" Jael asked, reeling in some of her anger.

"I know what needs to be done."

"That doesn't answer my question or ease my worry at all, Ciari." Jael came around Ciari's desk to stand by the other woman, looking out through the window wall that lined half of Ciari's office. Jael could see the horizon, where Lake Ontario was still and placid in the summer heat beneath the haze of lingering pollution. "Unlike almost everyone else in our ranks, I've got full access to Stryker records. It may take me a while, but eventually I realize when something doesn't add up."

Ciari didn't bother to correct Jael's misunderstanding of her own knowledge. She'd let the telepath believe what she wanted if it would keep the peace for just a few more weeks. "Aidan doesn't question me. Perhaps you still have something to learn from him."

"Aidan doesn't see the wounded, the dying, and the dead on a daily basis" was Jael's flat response. "I do. We Strykers in command positions know about the launch date. Some of us just know, same as you do, that we won't be on those ships when the engines trip over into full burn."

"No, we won't."

Frustration bled out through Jael's shields, thick enough for Ciari to almost taste it. "Then why aren't we fighting to free ourselves? We have a right to *live,* Ciari."

"The World Court doesn't think so. Luckily"—Ciari held up one hand to forestall Jael's instant argument—"I've never believed that. I know what I'm doing, Jael. I know what's at stake. So I'm asking you— *asking,* not ordering—to give me a little more time."

It was ironic, Ciari thought, that she was asking for the one thing that none of them had if she didn't play this game *just right*. Jael meant well, but her desire to save people just made Ciari's own job harder. Just as the World Court had decided that not everyone could have a seat on those shuttles, a berth on that colony ship, Ciari knew that not all of her Strykers would survive. It was just the way this particular world worked.

That was the way it *had* to work.

Jael shifted her gaze away from the skyline, turning her head to stare at Ciari. "You haven't looked as hard as you could have for Threnody's and Kerr's teams. Is this why?"

Ciari managed to give the other woman an actual, genuine smile that made Jael's skin crawl. Real emotion never looked right when empaths used it for themselves, but it was all the answer that Ciari gave her.

That, and "Trust me."

Looking at her right then, Jael thought that not even the gods some humans still believed in would trust Ciari. Jael supposed it was a good thing she wasn't human.

"It's not like I've got a choice," Jael said, hazel eyes narrowing ever so slightly in her dark face. "You're all we've got standing between us and the World Court."

No, I'm not, Ciari thought. "Go coordinate with Aidan on the teams. I want them transferred as soon as possible once we have that list."

"How do you hope to explain this to the World Court?"

"That's not for you to worry about."

Hearing the dismissal in Ciari's words, Jael left.

"Computer, initiate lockdown," Ciari said as she sat in her chair, hearing the chime signaling that her verbal order had been obeyed. Sighing, Ciari reached for the data chip that Aidan had delivered, unsurprised to find a second one resting beside it, clear, with no markings whatsoever to show whom it had come from or even where it had been manufactured.

Ciari scooped them both up, holding the tiny squares in the palm of her hand, trying not to think about everything else that she couldn't hold on to.

[TWENTY-FOUR]

The hypospray hissed softly against his throat as Jason jammed his thumb against the release button. Adrenaline shot through his veins, sharpening his senses to an almost dangerous degree. He pulled the thin cylinder away from his body with a ragged gasp.

"That's your sixth injection in the past twenty-one hours," Quinton said from the hatch behind him, almost sounding worried. "You're going to burst your heart if you use any more."

"Can't be helped," Jason rasped as he tossed the empty hypospray onto the floor of the flight deck. "I have to be able to think."

"Why not get one of the telepaths to keep you awake? Turn your mind permanently on for a few hours, or however much longer this will take."

"Doesn't work on me." Jason craned his head around to give Quinton a strained smile. "My shields don't allow for very much psionic interference. Always wondered why, before Lucas said I'm supposed to be something other than a regular old Class V telekinetic. Anyway, I burn through this stuff so quick that I have to keep it in my veins with continuous injections. You know how it is."

Quinton stepped into the flight deck and watched as the younger man sat himself down in the pilot's seat. Jason's hands skimmed over the control terminal, prying hardwires out of the console and connecting them to the neuroports in his arms. Hologrids sparked into existence all around him, the light turning his skin a sickly gray.

"Kerr can't do anything for you?"

"Kerr can only go so deep in my head, even with the bond," Jason explained as he dragged his fingers through the readout, most of his attention on the program. "He needs to focus on his own mind right now. I'll be fine. Something tells me Lucas won't let me die before I finish this hive connection. The hackers they used didn't know government code as well as I do."

Quinton grunted soft agreement.

"Why are you still here, Quinton?"

"Threnody was worried about your limits. I'll tell her you've got none."

It drew a strained laugh out of Jason, making him glance over his shoulder at Quinton. The inspecs in his eyes were bright spots in his pupils. "Oh, I've got limits, but Lucas doesn't care about them. I'm all out of hyposprays. Bring me another one in three hours. I'm going to need it."

Quinton shook his head as he turned to leave. "Just don't get dead, Jason. We still need you."

Quinton walked through the cargo bay and down the open ramp of the cargo door to the launchpad. The area, which had been empty when he'd gone into the shuttle, was now filled with large metal supply trunks, courtesy of Lucas, who was looking a lot worse for wear. After ten straight hours of constant teleportation between underground hangars, ferrying supplies, Quinton figured anyone would.

"What's in these?" Quinton asked.

"Insulated skinsuits," Lucas said as he kicked one of the trunks with his boot. "We're going to need them when we hit the Arctic. It might be summer, but it's still cold as fuck."

"Where do you want them?"

"Cargo hold. Three in each. I'll leave you to it."

He teleported out and Quinton swore tiredly. Just a fucking stevedore, that's all he was right now. Quinton retrieved the hoverlift that was sitting idle past the launchpad and dragged the trunks one at a time into the shuttles, because more than just skinsuits were in those huge containers. The weight had carefully been calculated by Matron, things that they would need for and after the Arctic. Lucas hadn't said as much, but everyone knew they weren't going to stay on Spitsbergen. They couldn't. The World Court would wage a quick and dirty war with them if they tried to, and the psions would lose.

The thing was, Quinton thought as he guided the second set of trunks into the next shuttle, Lucas was damned good at keeping them all in the dark. Whether it was psionic interference or just a slick mindwipe, Lucas only gave out enough details to get the results he wanted. Didn't matter how many lives he took or ruined, the only thing that he cared about was a final goal he shared with no one.

"Where's Jason?"

Quinton glanced up as he finished anchoring the latest supply trunk beside one of the massive cold storage units bolted to the deck of the shuttle. Threnody stood at the bottom of the open cargo ramp, a tense expression on her face.

"In the other shuttle," he said.

"Kerr just informed me that he picked up Warhound and Stryker psi signatures on the mental grid."

Quinton grimaced. "They're early."

"Or they're right on time." Threnody climbed up into the shuttle, peeling open a ration bar. She had two in her hands and offered the unopened one to Quinton. "Depends which schedule we're running on. That's not all of it. Matron said the acid storm out west caught the polar jet stream. It's going to hit here sooner rather than later. We don't have much time left."

"How soon?"

Threnody chewed hard on the bite of ration bar she'd taken before saying, "Three, maybe four hours. We can predict the weather, but we can't control it."

Quinton took in a careful breath. "Guess that's why Lucas just teleported out."

"We've got sixteen underground hangars to prep for launch in less time than we thought we'd get. That's what I need to tell Jason. He needs to get these shuttles online *now*."

Quinton finished securing the last trunk before following Threnody to the shuttle Jason was working in. The telekinetic was hunched over the console, wires streaming out of both arms and inspecs running at high capacity as they parsed out the downloads that were coming through the bioware in his brain.

"Jason," Threnody said.

"Busy" was his absent-sounding answer.

"Not as much as you're going to be." Threnody leaned over his chair and put a hand over his eyes, forcing a physical connection he had to deal with instead of the hologrids in the air around him and the data being downloaded into his brain. "That storm is going to hit within the next few hours. We've got Strykers and Warhounds on the ground in Buffalo. We need these shuttles flight-worthy."

Jason swore, finished what he was working on with a few quick commands, and started the compiler. Then he pulled her hand off his face and twisted his head to stare at her.

"Are you *kidding*?" Jason asked, voice dry. "How long?"

"You've got two hours to finish this, Jason. That's it."

"Or we're all dead, I *know*. You're lucky I've already installed all the firmware on the rest of the shuttles." He refocused his attention on the data before him. "You did your duty by me, now start warning everyone else."

Quinton and Threnody left the shuttle side by side, hurrying back to the tenement where Matron had kicked her scavengers into high gear hours ago. There were fewer scavengers than when they'd first arrived in Buffalo. Matron had been sending them out in small groups to the other hangars over the last few days.

"This is it people, we're at the endgame," Matron shouted over the buzz of conversation as a multitude of bodies worked around her. "You know your places. I want you all there before that acid storm hits. Keep your head down, stay off the grid, and stay the hell away from the quads."

Matron saw the Strykers approaching and nodded in their direction. When they got close enough, Threnody said, "Jason knows. He's going to have the hive connection fully up and running in two hours."

"You sure about that?"

"He was one of the best hackers the Strykers Syndicate had. He'll get it done."

Matron grunted as she continued to separate out weapons on the table she was standing at. "Novak's at his assigned hangar with Everett. I've got reports in from half my crew, the ones that are already at the other hangars or on their way. They're worried about being discovered by you psions."

"Lucas and I have their minds shielded," Kerr announced as he slipped through the crowd to plant himself next to Matron. "Don't worry about them."

"Yeah, the last time Lucas said that, I ended up with a third of my crew dead." Matron scowled, lips pulled back over her metal teeth. "How many is he going to let die this time?"

"You'll survive." Kerr shrugged as he reached for a gun and hooked the weapon to his belt. "Isn't that the only thing you're worried about?"

"Stay the fuck out of my head."

"I'm not in your mind."

Kerr nodded at Threnody and Quinton before disappearing back into the crowd with his own set of orders to follow.

"Fucking psions," Matron muttered as she loaded yet another gun and set it aside for someone else to claim.

Quinton joined her at the table, sorting through the stash of weapons with familiar ease. Threnody positioned herself on the other side of the room, helping a trio of scavengers destroy the accumulated data the tenement held, which meant burning out everything electrical they handed her until it was just slag.

Based on Matron's orders and the way she was giving them, Threnody knew that Matron wasn't going to return to Buffalo anytime soon, if ever again. She was covering her tracks in a methodical, almost brutal, way, stripping the tenement down to its bones. Threnody had a feeling that the other sites around Buffalo the scavengers owned were going through the same strip-and-burn scenario.

"What about the hangars?" Threnody asked as she placed her hand on yet another hard drive and sent her power through it. "You're not going to leave them for the government to dig through, right?"

"That's why we've got the C-4," Matron said. "Don't worry your pretty little head, girl. I've been doing this for longer than you've been alive."

The tenements that Matron's scavengers used as their base of operations were off the electrical grid most of the time, but not for this mission. Matron was savvy, in the way most survivalists were. She didn't have a permanent hard connection to the rest of Buffalo, but her restricted system could still uplink through a secondary one. It ran under the connections that the government used, but Matron considered information and secrecy more important than credit and following the law. Always had; it's what enabled her to survive. Right now, they needed to be connected to the government's grid.

The vidscreens in the building switched on all at once, the emergency stream that appeared flickering red around the edges. A reporter for Buffalo, a pretty brunette press anchor set up high somewhere in the city towers, smiled at the masses.

"People of New York. Please do not be alarmed. Curfew has been enacted for your personal safety. It has come to the government's attention that rogue psions have infiltrated Buffalo. The government advises everyone to remain in their towers or in their bunkers. Strykers are on the ground for your protection against the rogue psions. Adhere to the curfew or face a heavy fine."

The average citizen didn't know that rogue psions were a well-organized group, just that they were a dangerous enough threat to make people think twice about venturing outside the bunkers and the sealed city towers. The government didn't want their problem spun any which way but dead, which was why they mentioned the Strykers.

The broadcast repeated itself a second time before the stream went to standby mode. Like all emergency streams, it would be repeated every few minutes. Matron turned her head to look at Threnody.

"How's that notoriety feel?" the woman asked.

Threnody clenched her hand around the latest hard drive she was holding, electric lines of power crackling from her fingers to the small machine in her hand as it became nothing more than slag.

"They aren't revealing our identities," Threnody said. "Which means the government doesn't want the world to know that Strykers have gone rogue."

"Most rogue psions are Strykers who defect."

"That's not common knowledge outside of highly classified reports." Something Threnody had only recently learned. "And *most* is a little too high a count."

Matron's mouth curled up in disgust. "Fucking sheep."

Threnody chose not to feel insulted. Matron's disgust only lasted for a few seconds, or as long it took for the lights in the tenement to flicker and die out, only some coming back online with the whine of generators a few seconds later when they were *supposed* to be tapped into the main electrical grid.

Matron's teeth clacked together loudly in the sudden silence. "That ain't good."

Threnody followed her gaze to the nearest dark tracts of lighting. "I thought we were already running off the generators?"

"We normally are, but how do you think we're going to open fifteen launch silos?" Matron shook her head. "One would drain all my genera-tors. Fifteen isn't possible. We've been tied into the government's electri-cal grid since Jason started his hack."

"And now?"

"Now we're fucking *not*." Matron spun around. "Someone get me an uplink! I want to know what the fuck just happened here!"

She rushed off, barking out orders as she went. Threnody was still needed for a few more minutes of disposal work, so she jerked her head at Quinton in a silent order. Weaving his way through the crowd of scav-engers who were busy gathering up what they would need to get them to the other launch sites, Quinton kept doggedly on Matron's heels.

The two ended up back in the room that guarded the blast doors to the underground hangar. Matron was leaning over the chair in front of the control terminal, fingers stabbing at the hologrid that hovered in front of the vidscreen. A map of the Buffalo sprawl was sketched out in the air, rapidly expanding and decreasing, depending on Matron's order. It was feeding her data through the neuroports in her cybernetic limb, a wireless feed that wasn't as stable as a wired connection.

"Coincidence?" one of the scavengers in the room asked, sounding hopeful.

Lucas teleported in, saying, "*Coincidence* is a word used only by liars and fools."

"You would know," Matron snapped. "Come look at this."

Lucas paced forward and watched as Matron zoomed out from the street view of Buffalo to the citywide view, bright blue dots pulsing where their launch silos were and an overlay of green from the electrical grid that was steadily blacking out over the entire city.

"What about the main bunkers?" Quinton asked tightly.

"They have environmental systems that run on backup generators located all over the city," Lucas said. "For a lockdown like this, people can last a day, maybe two, with the environmental systems running at full before emergency restrictions would have to be enacted."

"You don't think it'll take that long, do you?" Threnody said as she came into the room.

"I think a lot of people are going to die under a government-sanctioned power outage with an acid storm riding a derecho spine about to hit." Dark blue eyes flicked her way. "The storms always do damage, that's expected. The government never shuts off the power just because the weather's bad. They're doing it this time to find us. Warhounds are spreading out through the city, so are Strykers, and they're all hunting for us. Kerr and I have already deflected search scans through human minds. We're linked to every scavenger, but that's a network that can be found more easily than a single mind, despite the precautions we've taken."

"So what are you saying?"

"I'm saying that we need the power plants to be turned back on—at least one of them."

"Can't you mindwipe those workers to change it for you?" Quinton demanded, not liking where this conversation was going.

"No," Lucas said, voice firm. "The second I start altering minds, my sister will pick up on it. Samantha's on the ground here and she was trained by Nathan, just like me. She knows the same tricks I do. If she finds out what I'm doing, she'll want to know *why* we want the generators on when

I could just as easily teleport everyone out of this place. It won't take her very long to figure it out."

Threnody's gaze was steady when she looked at him. "You need us to turn the electrical grid back on for you."

"I need *you* to turn it on." Lucas turned his head and reached out for the map, dragging his fingers over the hologrid to zero in on one of the two power plants that kept the city running. "You're a Class III electrokinetic. You can override whatever lockdown they've got on the power plants and jump-start the grid."

"That much power in those places will fry her nervous system," Quinton said, voice hard. "That's suicide."

"Not necessarily. It'll take time for her to make her way to power plant two, and by then, the storm will have hit."

"The other power plant is closer."

"The other one feeds only into the city towers. We need the one for everyone else." Lucas pushed away from the chair he was leaning on to face the Strykers. "If you want to go with her, then fine. Take Kerr along as well. You'll need the coverage a telepath can provide."

"What about you?" Threnody asked. "And Jason?"

"Jason's working on the shuttles. He's not going anywhere until we launch. As for me? I'm going to be the bait." The smile Lucas gave them was tired, but every bit as dangerous as the ones he'd offered up before. "The Warhounds are looking for me because I called them here. The Strykers are just an additional bonus. I'll draw their fire and let them take each other out."

"And if you die?"

"This isn't where I die. I'll be there at the end to pick you up, as long as you get the job done."

"What if we don't?"

"Then Aisling was wrong."

Threnody pressed her mouth into a hard line. She swallowed and said, "I'd rather she wasn't."

"Kerr's getting a vehicle ready right now." Lucas nodded at the door. "Get your gear and get out of here. That curfew is already in effect and quads are going to be on the street."

"You'll want to hit the underground entrance about six kilometers north of here," Matron said as she hurriedly downloaded the city map into a data chip. "You'll need to travel underground half of the way to the power plant on the maglev trains, if they're still running. If not, take a pedestrian tunnel. The rest of the way in, when you get closer to the power plant, it's gonna be all aboveground travel. The government likes to see people coming."

"I'm guessing the security grid is still up and running through the backup generators," Quinton said.

Matron gave a hollow little laugh as she tossed the loaded data chip and a datapad to Quinton. "You'd guess right. Get the fuck out of here. You've only got so much time."

Quinton and Threnody left without arguing. Threnody was hell-bent on this mission and Quinton knew better than to try to change her mind. It was too late to back out now.

"Hope you know what you're doing," Quinton said as they finally made it to the garage, the doors winched wide-open and wind rushing inside. "You're still not fully recovered."

"Then you better hope that Lucas packed some decent medical supplies in those trunks you were loading onto the shuttles," Threnody said as they wove their way to where Kerr was checking over the SUV that would get them back to the city.

Kerr tossed a bag at each of them. "Our old uniforms," he explained. "I figured they might get us a little further than civilian attire if we alter them enough."

He was already wearing his, the black-on-black BDUs overlaid with bits and pieces of protective armor. Threnody and Quinton stripped right there in the garage, everyone ignoring them. The uniform felt strange after so many days wearing borrowed clothing. This wasn't who they were anymore, not completely, and Threnody couldn't help but wonder if the changes would show up on a feed.

They still had the strips of bioware on their faces, iris peels coating their eyes. False identities that might get them into the city without being detected, but if the security grid was running on full, Threnody had a feeling the precautions wouldn't get them far enough. They were the hunted this time, not the hunters, but they knew how Strykers thought. Maybe that would help.

Then again, maybe not.

Quinton packed extra ammunition into a case hooked to his belt before slinging a military-grade rifle over one shoulder. A separate hard pack that hung securely from his belt was a match for the one that Threnody wore as well: a field med-kit, specifically decked out to deal with loss of limbs. Quinton tended to lose parts of himself in the field while using his power if the fighting got bad enough.

"We good to go?" Kerr asked as he climbed into the driver's seat and started the engine.

The other two Strykers got into the SUV, Threnody in the back and Quinton riding shotgun. The side windows were all long-since broken and the windshield was cracked. It didn't seem to bother Kerr and it wouldn't impede Quinton's cover fire.

"Let's get the hell out of here," Threnody said. "Quinton, you got our way in?"

Quinton held up the datapad Matron had given him. "Just start driving. I'll navigate."

"Fine." Kerr revved the engine and shifted the SUV out of park and into drive, gunning it forward.

They drove out onto the dusty, barren road for Buffalo. They'd been inside for so long that they hadn't seen the change in the weather. They couldn't see the sun where they knew it was positioned in the western sky. Dark thunderclouds stretched from the city they were driving to all the way to the black line on the horizon that was steadily sweeping over the earth.

The wind picked up, sending dirt flying through the open windows of the SUV. Threnody blinked grit out of her eyes and reached up to tie back her hair as the first tiny drops of acid rain began to fall.

[TWENTY-FIVE]

AUGUST 2379
BUFFALO, USA

The landscape of Buffalo reminded Samantha of broken teeth—worn down, jagged, badly cared for—when they teleported into an empty street of the city. The wind seemed to find every open point of her uniform and blow through it to chill her skin with the damp. As they ran for the blast doors that led to the underground bunkers most of the unregistered humans called home, Samantha looked up at the world that surrounded them.

Broken buildings, broken lives, broken promises. It was the only thing every surviving city had in common.

The acid rain was coming down in sheets, soaking her in seconds as she dragged Kristen after her into the relative dryness of the small receiving building. Samantha swiped at her eyes beneath the dark glasses she wore, ignoring the burn. She tugged Kristen out of the way of the entrance to the far wall.

This entry point was minimally guarded, not meant to handle a huge influx of people going into the bunkers. The quads who had manned this post were already dead, bodies stacked against the other wall. A Warhound electrokinetic in the first wave had fried the security feed, and a hacker was busy writing it back into the main system on a different signal. They needed a place to act as their ground base for communications. The warehouse wasn't viable, not anymore. Lucas had already hit it once; he'd hit it again given half the chance. This would have to do.

"Tastes like fire," Kristen muttered as she licked at her wet lips, watching through half-lidded eyes as the other Warhounds in their squadron came hurrying inside.

"Shut up," Samantha said.

Kristen hummed against her side, and while she didn't open her mouth again, Samantha highly doubted that her order would be obeyed for long.

A tall figure broke free from the crowd and jogged over to them. Jin Li offered Samantha a casual two-fingered salute and a sharp smile. "Every other team's in position. We're the last. Ready to move out?"

"Been ready," Samantha said. "Let's go."

Jin Li gave her a sarcastic little bow. "Lead the way."

The blast doors rolled shut after the last Warhound came through. A skeleton team would remain behind to cover for them. This entry point wasn't going to be accessible to anyone but Warhounds from here on out. The humans still rushing around outside after curfew in this section of the city were going to have one hell of a hard time getting below before the quads discovered their presence.

The long stairs leading down were new, replaced every decade or so after countless feet had trod upon them until they cracked. The stairs led deep into the ground, to a metal tunnel that was big enough to house a maglev train, except it didn't. A quarter of the space that made up Buffalo were tunnels for straight foot traffic, or ground vehicles where it was viable. Another quarter were tunnels for the maglev trains that serviced only a handful of spots in the city, both below- and aboveground. The other half wasn't tunnels at all, but huge bunkers carved deep into the ground, the heart and soul of a city that had died centuries ago.

That's where they were heading, into Bunker East, along with hundreds of humans who had finally heeded the curfew call in the face of an approaching acid storm, late though they were getting down below. The storm above was just the leading front, a supercell that churned above them, a mere precursor for the derecho spine that hadn't yet hit.

Samantha tucked a wet piece of hair behind her ear as she stretched out her telepathy to sink into the human minds all around them. She let the humans believe that the people in the black uniforms were just as human as they were, strangers with faces they would never remember.

Are we hacked into the security feed yet? Samantha wanted to know.

We've got hackers working on it from the city towers, Jin Li said. *They're coordinating with the ones in the field. We won't be recognized by the government, if that's what you're worried about.*

That's only if the Strykers don't interfere.

Here's hoping they do.

Jin Li would want a challenge. Samantha only wanted this mission to be over.

The lights that lined the tunnels were at half-power, the dimness difficult to see through with her glasses on. She didn't have the option of taking them off. Samantha risked being identified without them, and Kristen wasn't even *in* the Registry, but only a blind person would miss the color of her eyes and not know what family she belonged to. They couldn't be made because that would break all of Nathan's carefully laid plans more thoroughly than anything the Strykers could come up with.

Warhounds peeled away at every cross-tunnel intersection they came to, telepaths pairing up with various other psions as they spread out for the hunt. Samantha, Kristen and Jin Li continued on through the main tunnel, followed by two telekinetics. Samantha didn't have Gideon with her down here, and they needed psions with telekinesis to counter what Lucas could throw at them.

Glancing down at the bioscanner in her hand, she couldn't find Lucas on it, but she could place the Strykers if she narrowed down the search. Strykers were incapable of hiding completely on the mental grid, and the government always had them tagged into the system. Government dogs needed to be watched over in case they turned rabid.

It took them an hour to circumvent the Strykers, all the while marching through the tunnels for Bunker East. Just because Lucas wasn't showing up on the bioscanner didn't mean he wasn't flickering on the mental grid. He wanted to be found, Samantha could read that in the way he stayed in one place. Whatever trap he was building, it wasn't going to be pretty, not for him, not for the Warhounds, and certainly not for the Strykers drawn to his mental presence.

Lucas was definitely Nathan's son, and Nathan never did anything by halves.

The Warhounds came out of the main tunnel into a wide underground space that was like a minicity, all steel-gray metal and walled-off habitation, the whine of generators cutting through the sounds of human life. Straight down the center of that huge space, the size of an old stadium, was an empty maglev platform, the line of it lit brighter than anywhere else.

The unregistered humans with the most corrupted genetics called Bunker East home. It was closest to the deadzone that took up half of New York State. Even with shielding against radiation, the people here were never going to scrape their DNA clean. They were never going to escape what their ancestors had left for them.

Kristen moved away from Samantha to the railing that separated the crowd from a short fall to certain death on the maglev tracks below. She leaned over that point of separation to look down at the maglev platform, the tracks and the humans waiting there for a train that wasn't going to arrive anytime soon.

"Bet they'd all taste so good," she said around her smile.

Jin Li clamped a hand on her shoulder and pulled her back into the group. "Start walking, girl. You've got a bigger target to find."

The bioware that lined her skinsuit flickered a warning, which she ignored. Kristen didn't care about the prison she wore, just about her chance at survival that she could taste beyond her shields.

Samantha curled her fingers around the back of Kristen's neck and squeezed down warningly. "We're not here for them."

"Of *course* not, Sammy-girl," Kristen drawled as she reached up and squeezed Samantha's fingers tighter around her own throat.

Even down here, the world wasn't much different from the one above: still a mess of people, of poverty, of the dying looking to forget. Hologrids rolled adverts over every conceivable surface, interrupted here and there by the government's curfew reminder. They weren't enough of a distraction.

Samantha felt it when Kristen started to engage her empathy, Kristen's power bleeding through her shields. It weighed down the mental grid in a way few other powers could, because a mental dysfunction was hard to correct and even harder to hide. Samantha had her own shields wrapped around Kristen's mind, forcing the other girl to work beneath a veneer of human static, but the shields just barely held and their cover didn't last.

They made it to one of the lower levels of Bunker East at the same moment as the Strykers. It didn't really matter to Samantha how they were found out as a telekinetic blow leveled everyone flat between the Warhounds and the team of Strykers coming at them, just that they were.

The attack hit hard against the telekinetic shield that surrounded the Warhounds, and Samantha reached out to pull Kristen up against the wall, trying to make them less of a target. Grabbing her gun, Samantha fired on the Strykers, the two Warhound telekinetics letting her attack get through. The bullets never hit their target. She didn't expect them to.

Kristen, go, Samantha ordered even as she dropped her shields.

A hole opened up on the mental grid, pulling everyone into the manic swirl of insanity that was Kristen. The mental grid buckled beneath the Class III strength made all the more dangerous by her insanity. It washed over human and psion minds alike. The only reason that her power didn't begin to eat through everyone immediately was the solid telepathic shield that slid between Kristen and her next meal.

"Not *fair*," Kristen spat out, dragging herself to her feet to glare at her oldest brother, where he leaned up against the railing, standing between them and the Strykers and the quickly scattering humans.

The security feed, Samantha sent out on a broad 'path. *Shut it down!*

Whether or not their hackers obeyed her in time, she would never know. Lucas wasn't bothering to hide his identity. She could have killed him for that callous thoughtlessness.

"I hear you've been looking for me," Lucas said, his voice barely audible above the screaming and the sharp, shrill sound of the alarm as people ran for a safety that couldn't be guaranteed.

Tension snaked through everyone on both sides of the fight, Lucas the line no one could cross. He knew it, they knew it, and the smile he gave his sisters was both condescending and cruel.

Kristen offered her own in return as she slid her power up against his shields. "Oh, I've missed your games. Nathan's not happy, but come play with me anyway."

"What else is new?" Lucas said as he raised a hand at the Strykers.

The Strykers amassing behind him were bowled over by a line of telekinesis that cut through their defenses hard enough to break bones. Lucas wasn't there for the Strykers. He was there for the Warhounds, for his sisters. The Strykers were just a complication he had dragged here because he needed the distraction. He'd had two years to perfect how to play the role of bait, and getting people to follow him had never been difficult. Digging into three of the Strykers' minds, he broke their shielding and altered their way of thinking, a quick and dirty mindwipe that would leave them unable to differentiate between their teammates and the enemy.

Then he let them go, let them attack humans and psions alike, because even Lucas needed backup sometimes. The results were bloody, but he couldn't regret the deaths of civilians down here, not when the rest of the world needed saving.

Samantha fell into merge with the two telekinetics, their strength together enough to counteract most of what Lucas could possibly throw at them. Maybe. She briefly regretted leaving Gideon behind, so used to her twin fighting alongside her.

The roar of energy darts rained down from above with sudden brutality, smashing into telekinetic shields and ricocheting every which way without finding a single target. Quads, military soldiers. They'd drawn the attention of the government, and that was never a good thing.

Don't worry, Lucas said into her mind. *The humans here won't remember us at all.*

Liar, Samantha said.

His laughter echoed in her mind, the psi link thin enough and precise enough that she knew they were the only two tied together in it. *I never lied about saving you.*

The world shifted, crumbling at the edges of her vision as Lucas's telepathy roared through the mental grid, slicing through everyone's thoughts with a ferocity Samantha could barely counter. She dug in with her own telepathy, slamming her shields up high and tight around her mind, around Jin Li's, around the two telekinetics who lashed out with their combined power at where Lucas stood. She left Kristen alone. Kristen was more than capable of taking care of herself.

The railing Lucas was leaning on cracked, the metal shearing off in large chunks. He lurched backward, catching himself before the spot he'd been resting against fell off onto the maglev platform below.

Fire exploded in the air around him, around the Warhounds, an inferno that scorched the area they were standing in. A Stryker pyrokinetic, because they didn't have a Warhound with that particular power in their current group. Samantha grabbed Kristen by the collar of her skinsuit and dragged her in close when she would have run forward. The girl never did care about her own skin. The telekinetics strengthened their shields and stood their ground. Jin Li took a few steps forward, eyeing Lucas with a feral look on his face.

"Nathan wants you dead," Jin Li said.

Lucas spread his arms wide; offered up a slick smile. "Go ahead. Try. I'll even let you get close enough to touch me."

Jin Li wasn't stupid enough to agree to something like that, at least, not alone. Linked to the telekinetics by Samantha's telepathy, Jin Li was teleported within striking range of Lucas, shielded down tight except for his hands as he reached for Lucas's throat. Lucas reacted like any well-trained Warhound would—with exponential force.

The ground he was standing on *cracked,* the air burned as his telekinetic blow slammed Jin Li into and *through* the support wall of the building they were fighting next to. Jin Li survived only because the Warhound telekinetics with them were well-trained in their power. They managed to cushion Jin Li's landing as best they could. Jin Li fell to the ground across from Kristen, half-conscious and bleeding from his nose and mouth, but mostly whole and alive.

Kristen turned her face in Lucas's direction, the smile she gave him stretched to its limits. "Try," she echoed, then wrapped her power around his mind in ways that not even Nathan could achieve.

The solid, mentally corrosive barrier she erected around her brother skewered his attention for only a few seconds, long enough for Samantha to dig her telepathy into his shields, to scorch her power over his. It was followed, incongruously enough, by two telepathic strikes from the Strykers.

It wasn't a merge. The Strykers didn't know *how* to merge, and

Samantha was alone in her attack because no one merged with Kristen and walked away alive. But a Class I, for all his or her strength, still had *limits*. Every psion did. Lucas, forced to battle on three separate fronts, remembered that when his top shield cracked beneath the onslaught, crumbling away.

He could sense Kristen's glee, Samantha's determination, and the Strykers' desire to see them all dead. He could also sense the minds clustered in the maglev train that was kilometers away and getting closer, running on the last dregs of power that could safely be siphoned off the generators as it struggled to make a stop on its schedule. He reached for the Stryker telepath he had altered, giving her a different set of orders this time, letting the woman target the soldiers in that approaching maglev train and the quads already here for him now that most of the Strykers nearby were either dead or incapacitated. The effort of fighting against his orders would probably break her mind. Lucas didn't care, so long as the Stryker had a target that wasn't him.

With a wrench that left his ears ringing, Lucas slid his mind away from the psions who wanted so badly to break him and teleported down to the maglev platform. Quads were rapidly surrounding the area, having long since shoved their way through the fleeing crowd for a better position from which to shoot and kill the enemy. They lined the second platform with only one intent, but Lucas knocked the group of soldiers down and out with a telepathic blow that left half of them catatonic and the other half bleeding their brains out their ears and noses.

Left behind on the walkway, Samantha holstered her gun and shoved herself to her feet. *Cover me,* she snarled at the pair of telekinetics, even as she launched herself over the railing.

It was a three-story drop to the platform below; she landed with telekinetic help. Still shielded, her movements jerky from running in step with someone else's power, Samantha raced toward her brother where he waited on the maglev platform.

Why now? she sent at him, layering her shields as Nathan had taught her when she was a child, creating a canyon between herself and her older brother on the mental grid. It wouldn't be enough, but she still had to try. *Why ruin everything when we're so close to being free of this place?*

What if I said this was all just meant to be? Lucas told her from where he stood, tense and waiting before her. *That it was inevitable?*

Nothing's inevitable, you know that. Samantha skidded to a halt, breathing heavily, feeling the telekinesis forced away.

The alarm was still sounding in Bunker East, the lights still dim along the walls and ceiling and floor. The hologrids were dark, any and all extra energy diverted to the maglev tracks, which were beginning to hum. This far underground, the storm couldn't reach them, but they were building their own where the humans had lived for generations.

What if it is?

Samantha felt the mental grid stretch itself thin and tight against her mind, Lucas's power reaching for something inside her that she never knew she carried. Consciousness. Awareness.

Memories.

Hers and not hers.

No. She threw up more and more mental shields, but he tore them all down.

I can't do this alone, Lucas told her, sounding tired. Old. As if he'd lived too long and hadn't died young enough before the bitterness overtook his life when he was only twenty years old.

She didn't feel herself hit the ground, just knew that her skull hit first, then her shoulders. The world spun in a sickening lurch that she felt in her gut, and Samantha choked on her breath the way people choked on water when they drowned. Warm hands pressed the side of her face against the stained metal of the platform that too many feet had walked over, dragging the dirt of the world down to a place where people bled out hope.

"You know what they said when the bombs fell?" Lucas pinned Samantha down against the maglev platform with his physical strength alone, his mind busy tearing hers apart. "Don't fear the end of the world. Fear what comes next."

She fought him with everything she had, but it wasn't enough. It had never been enough. As the maglev train roared into Bunker East, sliding with a hard, telekinetically anchored *stop* against the platform, Lucas leaned down and whispered into his sister's ear, "*We* are what came next, Sam. And I am so much better than what you could ever hope to be."

"I'm not—scared of you," Samantha gasped out as his telepathy curled through her mind and ruined what Nathan had built her into.

She broke; pieces of who she was shearing off, all the scar tissue that she had accumulated over the years just—ripped away.

Breathe. I still need you.

"You should be." Lucas rested his forehead against hers for a moment, just a moment, before he got to his feet and walked onto that train, leaving her a panting, bleeding wreck on the platform. "You really should be."

Panicked humans were struggling to get off the train, those that weren't already dead or dying, brains fried by the telepathic attack that the altered Stryker had aimed in their direction mere moments ago. Just bodies lying one on top of the other, on the floor, on the benches, the stink of bodily fluids filling the air. Death, when it came, always smelled human.

Lucas lifted himself above the mess with his telekinesis as the doors slid shut, looking through the clear plasglass at Samantha as she picked herself up off the ground with shaky effort.

Come after me, he said into her fractured mind. *I'll be waiting.*

Footsteps raced over the platform as the maglev train lurched forward with a hum of power. The lights all through Bunker East flickered dangerously low as the train drew nearly all of the remaining electricity out of the generators that kept everyone breathing down below.

Jin Li reached Samantha's side, dragged her all the way to a standing position, then got her the hell out of there. "That train's going to Bunker North," he said. "By the city towers. We'll get another telekinetic to 'port us there."

"Everyone else?" Samantha asked in a ragged breath as he pulled her into a waiting area on the platform with an overhang, where Kristen had her hand against the temple of the telekinetic that had survived Lucas's show of power. Blood was pouring out of the man's ears, pumping through her fingers. His partner had a halo of red around her head on the floor beside him, life already gone from her body.

The Sercas were the best assassins the Warhounds had. They needed to remember that.

"Dead and dying," Kristen reported cheerfully.

Samantha leaned down, letting Jin Li support her as she pressed her hand over the telekinetic's forehead.

Get us out of here, she said into the Warhound's mind, holding on to his thoughts and power, cognizant that she could barely hold herself together.

She kept him alive long enough for him to teleport them all to the surface.

Kristen devoured his mind as he died, smearing her fingers through the blood and acid rain that greeted them when they arrived in the middle of the storm that had been centuries in the making.

[TWENTY-SIX]

AUGUST 2379
BUFFALO, USA

The lights in the tunnels, already a dim emergency blue, flickered ominously. Some went out, others came back on a little brighter than before. No one still making their way toward Bunker West from Bunker South thought that was a good thing.

They'd made it into Buffalo from the outskirts, then been forced belowground, just as Matron had said. It was a good thing none of them were claustrophobic. Threnody slowed to a stop, pressing up against the curve of the tunnel as a straggling group of humans passed them by. Quinton was right beside her, cradling his rifle, watching their back. Kerr was barely an arm's length away on point, his telepathic shields wrapped tight around their minds, projecting them as human on the mental grid with an ease that he'd never before had. Even Threnody, who was not a 'path-oriented psion, could feel the difference against her own shields.

She peered past the brim of her stolen cap, pulled low over her eyes to shadow her face, as the humans continued straight ahead to the cross-tunnel intersection fifteen meters from where they stood.

"Quinton?" she asked softly.

He checked the datapad in his hand, thumb swiping over the screen to get a new readout. "If we follow them, there's no quick way out of the tunnels for another three, four kilometers. We've got to go aboveground if we're going to reach our target. No way around that now."

"Right or left?"

"Right. That tunnel will spit us out northeast of where we need to be, but closer than the last one."

"And with more problems." Kerr was squinting up at the ceiling. "The lights? That was Lucas being our distraction. He's on a maglev train heading to Bunker North."

"Why?" Threnody asked as they started forward again.

"He didn't say and I didn't ask. The good thing is that the Strykers are beginning to focus their attention on him instead of us."

"Were they getting close?"

"Close enough."

It took less than a minute to reach the latest intersection in the maze of tunnels. They turned right, carefully averting their faces from the security feed that they couldn't completely hide from. The tunnels weren't lined with hologrids, not as the bunkers were. Instead, at intervals every quarter of a kilometer or so the gray metal gave way to an opaque hologrid that could become anything it was programmed to be.

Crimson lines sparked across the hologrid, projecting outward to form a mirror image of themselves. Three dark figures running where they shouldn't, the bioware on their faces and in their eyes difficult for the computer to work around. It still got something, coming up not with their false identities, nor their real ones. Just trouble.

"You are in a restricted area," an automated voice said as they stared at themselves reflected in the hologrid stretched between the walls, facial-recognition software still looking for points to build off of. "All citizens are to obey curfew and return to their domicile in bunkers, tenements aboveground, or city towers. You are in a restricted area."

Threnody reached out with her hand, fingers sliding through the holo, until her skin touched the smoothness of the grid. Electricity danced around her wrist, curling from red into electric blue as she tapped into her power and burnt out the hologrid with a controlled shock. Electricity crawled over it, arcing high around her to the other side with a single thought as she fried the localized system that the hologrid ran on.

"You know that whoever is monitoring the security feeds probably got that on record," Kerr said. "Strykers will start coming down into the tunnels where we are instead of where we aren't."

"We won't be in the tunnels long enough for them to find us." Threnody clenched her hands into fists, the electric spark of her power fading away. She took off her stolen cap and tossed it to the floor. "Let's move."

They ran for it, gear and guns secured tight to their bodies. The tunnels were getting darker the farther away from the bunker they ran, the air hotter. A constant clicking sound that they couldn't locate echoed in the guts of the tunnels.

"We're losing oxygen," Quinton said as they turned at another cross-tunnel intersection. "CO_2 scrubbers aren't working right. That's what we're hearing, according to the computer. I've got a warning feed on the bottom of my screen."

"No shit?" Kerr shook his head as they ran. "I couldn't tell at all, the way my lungs are burning."

"The government is taking a risk," Threnody panted out.

Kerr snorted his opinion on that. "The government enforces policy. Everyone else takes risks."

They kept running, the tunnel snaking out in front of them and on the screen of the datapad in Quinton's hand. They made it to the exit point ten minutes later, breathing harshly as they slowed to a stop.

Strykers aboveground, Kerr said through the psi link.

Do they know we're down here? Threnody said.

We're human on the mental grid, but I've had us blocked completely since you slagged the computer back there.

Threnody looked up at the dark ceiling, dim blue light creating long shadows over her features from the emergency shine a ways behind them. *So they're waiting for us.*

This was the most logical exit route for us to take. Yeah, I'd say they're waiting for us.

Can you tell what we're dealing with? Quinton asked.

Kerr closed his eyes, brow furrowing in the darkness. *Two telepaths, one telekinetic, two pyrokinetics.*

Class?

Class IV and lower.

All less powerful than they were. Threnody shared a look with Quinton. *I've got the pyrokinetics,* Quinton said, pocketing the datapad.

I'll deal with the telekinetic and telepaths, Kerr said. *Threnody, you've got to knock them all out. I don't trust myself not to kill them. My control isn't good enough yet.*

The government had a kill order out on them, they knew that. Defection resulted only in a grave if the escaped Stryker was caught. That was never going to change, but they weren't here to kill their fellow Strykers. That wasn't their goal. Their objective was the electrical grid, the power plants it ran off of, and whatever else Lucas needed.

Threnody snapped her fingers together, creating bright electric sparks that lined her nails. *You sure about this, Kerr? Your head's only just been worked on.*

Lucas does excellent work. Grudging respect was in Kerr's mental voice. *I trust what he rebuilt. I kind of have to because I've got to live with it.*

Good enough for me.

They didn't have a telekinetic for offense; Jason was back at Matron's base, frantically working to get the shuttles online. Lucas was elsewhere, pulling Warhounds and Strykers alike to him. That didn't mean they were at a disadvantage.

They took the stairs up to the surface two at a time, minds sharpening into battle focus as the roar of the storm filtered slowly down to their ears. The closer they got to the top, the slicker the steps became, acid water flowing where gravity led. The air became thick and warm and hideously saturated. Side by side, the three reached the surface, coming up into a small storage warehouse, all the windows broken and the blast doors wrenched wide apart.

They stood there for a moment, listening to the wind howling outside the building, catching flashes of lightning sparking through the sky, feeling thunder rattling the ground.

Now, Threnody thought over the psi link even as she raced out of the building, Kerr's mind a heavy presence in her own.

Quinton stayed by Kerr's side, gas and fire lighting up the air around him as he focused his power, draining a tube in each arm to get the fire big enough, hot enough, to burn through the storm that raged beyond the four fragile walls. Pressure existed beyond his mental shields, the unmistakable biting strength of telepaths going to war on the mental grid. Then his attention was divided, the fire he had built suddenly being carved into pieces by other pyrokinetics hoping to steal what he controlled.

Quinton's dark eyes narrowed. Over his dead fucking body. He grabbed Kerr by the arm and dragged them out of the burning building, through the smoke and fire, into the storm.

Acid rain soaked them in seconds, wind whistling in their ears. Quinton blinked the stinging wet out of his eyes, desperately looking for his partner. He gave up after a few seconds, needing to save his own skin, knowing Threnody could survive on her own. He got off a few shots with his rifle before the weapon was telekinetically torn out of his hands and tossed away. Quinton didn't bother running after it.

He thrust out an arm toward the pair of Stryker pyrokinetics, twisting the fire bigger, hotter, forcing it to burn when the storm wanted to put it out. Fuel came from nearby buildings, the flames crawling up their sides with a furious roar. Quinton struggled to maintain control of the inferno and keep the other pyrokinetics at bay.

Silhouetted against that bright orange glow was Threnody, her lean form moving with lethal intent as she fought to get within touching range of her target. The telepaths were between her and the telekinetic, whom Kerr had brought to his knees, but not before taking his gun. Landing a solid punch to a telepath whose mind was mostly tied up in defending against Kerr's powerful attack, Threnody held on to the Stryker as she bore the other woman's body to the ground. Pressing one hand to the telepath's face, she shocked the Stryker's nervous system as hard as she could.

Electricity crawled over the telepath, the woman seizing for a few long seconds before she went limp on the ground. She was still breathing, but was totally and completely *out* as Threnody moved on to her next target. With one less mind to deal with, Kerr was able to sharpen his focus on the remaining four Strykers.

Two, Threnody thought with hard satisfaction as she brought down the second telepath with a punch to the solar plexus and her hand around his throat.

It was easier because Kerr was in his mind, tearing through it with a telepathic strike that the Stryker couldn't counter, not against a Class II. Threnody's power burned into him with instant, shocking results. He screamed, his voice drowned out beneath the sound of the storm as he fell to the ground.

The telekinetic was still in the game. Threnody discovered that the hard way when she was picked up and tossed across the street to land on the crumbling sidewalk there. Landing hard on her side, Threnody rolled with a pained yell, coming to a stop up against a building that wasn't burning. She spat out a mouthful of mud and blood—she'd bitten through her lip—before shoving herself back to her feet. The world spun sickeningly for a few seconds before her inner ear found balance again.

Blinking burning water out of her eyes, Threnody unclipped her gun and took aim at the approaching telekinetic. Before she could fire her gun, it was wrenched out of her hands. Her body slammed back against the building, invisible pressure nearly crushing her.

Kerr, Threnody said. *I need you to take care of this one.*

On it, Kerr said.

It was simpler, now that the telepaths were out of the fight. Threnody didn't know what Kerr did, but the telekinetic fell to the ground between one step and the next, out cold. The pyrokinetics were next, the fire that all three of them had been fighting over expanding dangerously for a few seconds before Quinton got control over the flame. It was easy to let the fire die, to let the rain wash through it and extinguish the inferno.

The street was suddenly dark, but not silent. Thunder still pounded through the sky above them, but a secondary roar was filling the air now. Like the sound of a steam-engine train, in ancient movies saved to vids long after the fact, the increasing rumble couldn't be ignored.

They couldn't see the derecho hit, but they heard it. They felt it.

There on the street, the three Strykers felt the spine of that long windstorm slam into them, through them, knocking them to the ground with sideway winds and stabbing acid rain. It screamed over Buffalo, a heavy wall of nature come out of the west; power that humans couldn't fully predict, that psions couldn't control.

Threnody pushed herself up against the weight of the storm, arms shaking and barely able to hold steady in the face of the wind.

The tunnels? Kerr sent into their minds.

No. Threnody stumbled toward where she'd last seen Quinton, the lightning up above not nearly enough to show where her partner was. *We've got to stay aboveground.*

There's a car near my position, Quinton informed them. *It functions, according to the computer.*

Driving through this storm is liable to get us killed.

So's walking. At least this way we'll be a little drier.

Good point.

Kerr showed Threnody where Quinton was on the mental grid. She worked her way to where Quinton had broken into the vehicle and overrode the controls, headlights barely distinguishable in the heavy storm. She pried open the door and fell into the backseat.

Kerr was struggling to get into the front passenger seat, Quinton already behind the wheel. Kerr was barely able to pull the door shut behind him against the strength of the wind. For a moment, the three sat there in the car, the engine running, and the storm the only sound as the wind battered the vehicle.

"Lucas is crazy if he thinks we can fly out through this," Threnody finally said, surprised at how dry her throat was, how rough her voice came out.

"Crazy, yeah, but it might work," Kerr said as Quinton took the car out of park and pressed his foot to the gas pedal. "I don't think we'd have gotten this far if he didn't believe we could make it all the way."

It was funny, Threnody thought as Quinton drove into the storm, just how much faith all of them were putting in someone who was supposed to be their enemy.

PART SEVEN
APERTURE

SESSION DATE: **2128.05.26**

LOCATION: **Institute of Psionics Research**

CLEARANCE ID: **Dr. Amy Bennett**

SUBJECT: **2581**

FILE NUMBER: **487**

"We can't go aboveground anymore," the doctor says as she sits rigidly in her seat. "Too much fallout in the air is killing us and the towers aren't sealed yet. I haven't seen the sun for almost three years."

"Don't worry. It's still there."

"Aisling."

She is coloring again, rubbing her crayons to small nubs. "Shh, be quiet. He's talking."

"Aisling."

The girl looks up and frowns at the camera as the machines behind her whine. "I could never promise you *the* world, Lucas. Simply *a* world."

The doctor leans forward. "We need answers, Aisling. Not these disjointed reports of people we can't locate."

"You want what he wants." Aisling sounds frustrated as she slowly slides her crayon off the paper and onto the table, forcibly staining the room with color. "He wants what I want, but they aren't the same thing."

"We need to know when the next bomb will fall."

"Lima, Peru," she says, the tip of her crayon breaking off. "Five, four, three, too late. Can I have another box of crayons, Doctor?"

[TWENTY-SEVEN]

AUGUST 2379
BUFFALO, USA

The maglev train slid slowly into Bunker North, but no one was expecting anyone on it to still be breathing. Neither were the Strykers lining the platform expecting enemy psions to still be present in any of the cars as they worked their way through the stinking mess left behind.

Shielded tight on the mental grid, wrapped in a telekinetic shield to stave off the soaking wetness of the storm, Lucas was aboveground. Standing beneath a metal overhang of a building that did nothing to keep out the wind and the rain, Lucas ducked his head against the storm and reached through the psi link for Jason.

Tell me you're close to being done, Lucas said.

It's makeshift, but it should hold. Long enough to get us out of here, at least, Jason replied. *I don't know about this storm. You trust Matron's scavengers to be able to pilot through this?*

Enough of them will make it.

What do you mean enough?

Lucas ignored that question. *Get those shuttles prepped for launch, Jason. As soon as Threnody gets the electrical grid back online, those launch silos will activate.*

You better not fucking leave them behind.

I still need them.

It wasn't really a promise. Lucas cut the connection with a thought, the psi link going dormant. Where he was standing, the world was nothing but darkness and sound. Unlike in the tunnels, no emergency lights were shining to show the way on the streets. Closing his eyes didn't really change his situation, but it let him concentrate that much harder as he expanded his power through the mental grid for that one shining mind he would know anywhere. Through the other person's eyes, he got a glimpse of an office in a city tower, wide, familiar. Empty.

He teleported with that visualization firmly in his mind, arriving beside the woman he had first met when he was a child, and later, at the age of fifteen, when he realized he needed her help to change everything.

"Security feed is being blocked," Ciari said as she stared out the plasglass window at the storm that was hitting Toronto the same as it was hitting Buffalo, with only slightly less force. "My Strykers here are busy and the World Court is dealing with the media. They won't interrupt us."

Water slid off the telekinetic shield Lucas still had up, then fell in spatters when he dropped his defenses. "I can't stay long."

"You never do." Ciari turned her head a little, just enough to look at him. "Did you get what you needed from the Strykers you took?"

"More than. They'll be enough in the end, I think." Lucas frowned. "She hasn't been wrong yet."

"Yet," Ciari echoed.

"You gave me the best you had," Lucas reminded her.

"If I could have kept them from you, I would have."

He reached for her, let his fingers curl around hers for a second or two, no longer. "Maybe in some other future you did. We wouldn't be here today if you had."

"I like to think my choices are my own."

"You're not stupid, Ciari. Your life has never been your own and you know it."

Lucas stepped in front of her, blocking her view of the storm and everything they had made together. He was taller than she was, younger, more powerful; everything she hadn't been in years, but she still reached for what he offered. Ciari liked to think that maybe whatever was between them was real, or had been at one point. They used each other to save their own lives, and the taste of his mouth now was so different from the memory in her head.

His hands were cold against her face, grip painful as he explored her mouth with a ferocity that would have spoken of quiet desperation in anyone else. But this was Lucas, and he didn't do desperation. He only took and never gave.

"She told me you'll be carrying a girl," Lucas whispered against her mouth before he pulled back, a faint, mocking smile on his own.

Ciari closed her eyes, refusing to flinch away from his touch. "I shouldn't be carrying anything, much less a child."

It was just a bunch of cells right now, no more than five weeks old, dividing and multiplying along human DNA with incredible psion potential. She was determined to see the baby born free, outside of the collars the government issued and away from the human veneer Lucas had been forced to wrap around his entire existence.

Aisling had promised her that much, at the least, in exchange for the world. Some new future to survive in. Pipe dreams were something Ciari never normally believed in. Maybe it was the hormones.

Trust me, Lucas said into her mind before he disappeared, teleporting out beneath everyone's searching thoughts on the mental grid.

She didn't. She never would.

Opening her eyes to her empty office, Ciari thought maybe that was the reason why Lucas kept coming back to her. She was the product of a way of life that kept his side of this fight free to do what needed to be done. That didn't necessarily mean that each side was in the right, just that they believed in one simple truth.

No salvation was to be found in anything except escape. Maybe their ancestors had it right all those years ago, when countries fought each other for the chance to leave this world behind.

Ciari liked to think otherwise.

[TWENTY-EIGHT]

ucas's mental order left a distracting ringing sound in Jason's ears, or maybe it was just the way his own mind acknowledged the tension and worry that was holding his body stiffly hostage. Days of working with too little sleep and too much stress had resulted in the completion and installation of the hive connection among thirty-six shuttles. The program that the scavengers had started, and which Jason had finished, would slave the systems together so the shuttles would hopefully read as a single entity on any scan that might hit them if it got past the jamming technology. In the event that they were captured or shot down, every shuttle's black box could instantly be wiped clean with a single command.

With no time to test the code he had written, Jason needed to believe that it would hold up. He'd hacked through enough pirated and government-sanctioned defenses in his time to know what worked and what didn't when it came to security. He wished that they'd had time to do a dry run on everything, but that wasn't possible. Right now, all that was left was to input their destination coordinates, but that upload wouldn't happen until the electrical grid was back up and running. Lucas had been adamant on not plugging in their route until they were in the air, so at the moment all Jason had left to do was wait.

He hated waiting.

"Did you finish?" Matron said tiredly as she came through the hatch into the flight deck, looking worn-out.

"Yeah," Jason said as he rubbed at his burning eyes, the neuroports up and down both arms swollen and red from overuse. "The hack is good. I told Lucas it should hold."

"Guess he was right to bring you people in on this," Matron said as she squeezed his shoulder. "Now get out of my seat. You ain't piloting this shuttle."

"I'm your anchor," Jason shot back as he got up. "How else do you think you're going to be able to fly through this storm without telekinetic help?"

"Go check on my demolitions, Jason. And lock the blast doors open to take the explosion while you're at it. I'll worry about our flight plan."

Matron promptly ignored him, used to instant obedience. She knew what needed to be done, and Jason had been buried beneath code for the better part of the week. He'd trust her judgment, for now at least.

The air in the hangar was a little too warm, the generators working overtime to keep them breathing. It was still barely enough power, stretched thin from hard use. They needed the government's electrical grid to come back online if they were going to get off the ground.

The three shuttles on the launchpad were slowly powering up to standby mode in preparation for flight, Matron and two other scavengers the pilots for this launch. Matron had handpicked every assignment because she knew her people better than Lucas did, despite all his psionic interference. She was as good as her word, not leaving any of her people behind, but only because Lucas actually did need them all. If that hadn't been the case, Jason knew there'd be more dead bodies than live people, and Matron wouldn't have mourned their passing for even a second.

Jason made sure he still had his comm unit with him, hooked to his belt. It was tuned to Matron's frequency, and the soft hum of the connection followed him out of the hangar, back down the tunnel to the empty tenement, a thin beam of light from his flashlight shining the way.

All were already at their posts, had been for hours, and the building was dark. Every available hertz of electricity was being funneled into the hangars. Every block of C-4, every wireless receiver, was set to green, ready to receive the detonation signal. Once they were in the air and they tripped the detonation codes, this place would blow itself up into debris the size of his hand. The tunnels would buckle and collapse beneath the blast, the hangar following suit, which was Matron's intent. Leave nothing behind. They were cleaning house and Jason was making sure no one had cut any corners.

He climbed out of the tunnel sometime later, the blast doors open flat against the floor of that heavily fortified room. A block of C-4 was encased in stabilizing plastic by the entrance to the room across from him, a lead of the stuff stretching out in one long, uninterrupted line that surrounded the tenement. Every level had the same setup. Jason followed the plastic-coated wiring with his light, checking every receiver he came across and making sure nothing critical had been left behind.

Threnody had slagged every computer in the place. All weapons had been distributed equally among the scavengers, any and all personal effects taken along or otherwise destroyed. For all intents and purposes, the tenement had been abandoned.

The people who knocked down the front door to get inside didn't know that.

Jason cut the light immediately, ducking into the nearest room on the first floor and raising a personal telekinetic shield around himself. He hadn't felt a telepathic probe, which didn't mean an attack wasn't pending. One of the many annoying things about being a telekinetic was that telekinetics were always targeted first. They had the only physically destructive, long-reaching psion power in existence. They could do a hell of a lot more damage to property and fragile human bodies than any other psion, and they were numerous enough to be a problem.

The people coming down the hallway found that out the hard way.

Jason couldn't be sure no psions were in the tenement. He didn't want to break cover, but he had no choice. He was the first line of defense and that meant going in for the kill. Stepping out of the room with a heavy telekinetic shield between himself and the intruders, Jason peered past the light coming from scopes mounted on the guns to see just who the hell he was dealing with.

Humans, Lucas's voice said suddenly into his mind. *Quads. I've got them.*

No, Jason said. *Your telepathy might ping off the mental grid during the attack.*

238

You're kidding, right?

You've got a lot to handle already, so let me deal with them.

Their conversation lasted no more than a second or two, long enough for the quads to notice Jason. They took aim and fired, the flare of energy darts streaking down the hallway. Jason averted his eyes as the attack hit his telekinetic shield. Tapping into his telekinesis, Jason yanked the weapons out of their hands, wrapped his power around their skulls, and viciously twisted each head. The sound of bone cracking mimicked the thunder that still rolled outside. When their bodies hit the floor, it was with a familiar, distinctive sound.

Is that all of them? Jason asked through the psi link, taking a careful step forward. When Lucas didn't immediately answer, Jason strengthened his thoughts beneath the other man's telepathic shields that turned him human on the mental grid. *Lucas!*

I hear you, I hear you. No need to fucking yell, Lucas said a few seconds later. *Those were it for this section. The only problem now is their check-in times.*

Pretty sure they've got voice-recognition software on their comm units.

Yeah, so don't even bother trying to use them. Their superiors will just hone in on their last known location, which isn't here, but close enough to be a problem.

You think reinforcements will come after them in a city this big?

I think we're running out of time. Hide the bodies, then get below, Lucas said, mental voice distant.

What's going on?

Those aren't the only quads I have to deal with. The place rigged to blow yet?

I'm just checking Matron's work.

That woman never fucks up her bombs. Just get back to the shuttles.

Jason left his position, telekinesis still a strong barrier between himself and the rest of the world. He used it to teleport the two sets of quads out of the hallway and into an abandoned room on the top floor, stacking the bodies against the wall behind a pile of scavenged junk. Out of sight, out of mind.

The lock had been shot off the front door, leaving a hole that acid rain blew through. Jason telekinetically shoved a table in front of the door to keep it shut before retreating back to the tunnel. He checked the position of the blast doors on his way back down, telekinetically holding the flashlight in the air to help him see as he made sure the two main doors in that room wouldn't close. Only then did Jason take the stairs two at a time back down to the tunnel.

We're finished with the hive connection, Jason reported, leaving his thoughts open for Lucas to retrieve.

Good. I'm pretty sure we're only going to have a narrow window of time to get all the shuttles airborne. Lucas sounded tense, power bleeding against Jason's shields. The lack of control was startling.

Lucas, what's wrong?

We haven't been found out, not yet, Lucas said, ignoring Jason's concern. *The quads are pushing through the typical boundaries. They're hitting up the outskirts.*

Jason swore. *The other hangars?*

No one's been discovered yet, but I've got other problems to deal with.

How far along are Threnody and the others on getting the electrical grid back up and running?

Not far enough.

Jason didn't know what to say in response, so he kept his mouth shut and his thoughts to himself as he worked his way back to the hangar. He double-checked that the blast doors were secured in their retractable casings. When he reached the underground hangar, the cargo doors of the Alpha shuttle were the only ones open. He clambered back inside, the doors closing behind him as he made his way back to the flight deck.

Matron was there, busily running through diagnostics of the shuttle. She didn't look at him. "We good?"

"Yeah," Jason said as he sat down in the navigator's seat, staring out into the darkness of the hangar. "For now."

Matron grunted, whispering something under her breath. He had to strain to hear her, but he managed to make out a few words, just enough to realize she was praying.

"That ever work?" Jason felt compelled to ask.

"Does what work?"

"Whatever you just asked your God for."

Matron offered him a sharp look. "Boy, you leave me and my prayers in peace. If I'm gonna get through this sane, I'm gonna need a little bit of guidance of the sort your government never programmed into you. When you find God, then we'll talk."

He didn't bother to tell her that the Strykers already had, in some way, that it wasn't a god they worshipped, but humanity itself. It was why he was still here, still working with Lucas instead of fighting him, because this course of action made more sense than the one the government was determined to take.

Matron rolled her shoulders, trying to ease some of the tension in her muscles. "Make yourself useful and go check what medical supplies we've got back there. I've got a feeling we're gonna need them."

Jason obeyed. Maybe it would keep his mind occupied instead of thinking and worrying about his fellow Strykers in the field.

It didn't.

[TWENTY-NINE]

AUGUST 2379
BUFFALO, USA

She fell.

Telepaths' minds were layers of control and power, memory from birth to now, perfect recall, and a silent plea that the space in their head remained theirs for just a little longer; that their thoughts and who they were remained *them* and not *other*. Control meant keeping that separation intact. Power meant being able to live through the aftermath of when control wasn't enough and everything in their head just broke down.

Pieces of who she was, who she had been, cut into her thoughts.

Samantha swallowed blood and snot, wiping at her nose. It felt as if her brain were leaking out of her nostrils. Just her mind playing tricks on her, she decided as she studied her bloodstained fingers. Just everything and nothing, because this wasn't what she was supposed to be.

She'd lived nearly her entire life broken. Eighteen years of a *very* slow mindwipe.

How had she missed that?

Arms wrapped around her waist, and Samantha looked down at her sister, Kristen's thin face turned upward. Her gleaming dark blue eyes were hooded, knowing, mouth curved hard in that gleeful smile of hers.

"Shh," Kristen whispered through the noise of the crowd around them in Bunker North. "It always hurts the first time. When you learn to think for yourself."

Samantha dug her nails into her sister's shoulder, held on, because the world was moving without her. Clarity. It was such a fucking bitch.

"I've always thought for myself," Samantha ground out, pitching her voice low, because she couldn't focus enough to *think,* much less use her telepathy.

"No. Nathan thought for you."

Truth never tasted so bitter, so bad. Samantha swallowed against the bile that was crawling up her throat, stomach clenching from pain, nausea making her a little weak. Kristen held her up as they followed Jin Li away from the maglev platform, a few new Warhounds surrounding them as they continued the hunt for Lucas. More telekinetics and two telepaths, because she couldn't fully perform her duties anymore.

Do I want to? she thought somewhere inside the mess of her head, shields barely strung together. Too many minds pressed against her own. It was difficult to remember why they were here, what they had been ordered to accomplish. It was difficult to care.

The hardest thoughts to ignore were her sister's. Kristen was a pulsing, sick presence on the mental grid, a deep well of borrowed emotion and little sanity, despite all the minds she had eaten through that night. The strange thing was that she wasn't intruding, wasn't trying to pull apart Samantha's weakness. The empath never gave up an opportunity to eat her way through someone else's mind; this should have been no different from all the times before. Only it was and Kristen's distance wasn't comforting at all.

"We need to get aboveground," Jin Li said, looking over his shoulder at Nathan's children. "Lucas isn't down here."

"I'm searching through the human minds around us," one of the telepaths said. "I'm not sensing any hidden pockets that he's carved for himself. Just—"

She broke off with a frown, dark head turned in the direction of a set of quads behind them who were ignoring the Warhounds through psionic interference.

"What is it?" Samantha felt compelled to ask.

"They're getting a report from their command central. Something about a break-in at the power plant."

Jin Li rocked to a hard halt, ignoring the humans flowing around him as if he weren't even there. "The power plant? Which one? And what the hell is Lucas doing there?"

"Are you sure it's even him?" Samantha said. "Of the three Strykers he took, one's an electrokinetic. The only reason why they could possibly be there would be because they want to turn it back on."

"Want to? Or need to?" Kristen corrected as she chewed on a fingernail until it bled.

Samantha rubbed a hand over her face. They'd lost their identity-protective glasses a while ago, but the bioware was still attached to their skin. They had their hackers working through the security grid to circumvent the feed, all of them knowing that the Strykers were most likely doing the same. She didn't think it would be enough in the long run.

Jin Li focused his attention on the other telepaths in the group. "Can we get a fix on whoever it is?"

They all looked away in order to concentrate, closing their eyes and merging their powers together. The whole group was stretched out in the crowd, pressed close against the side of the bunker's wall on the second level, unnoticed only by way of psionic interference and hackers in the system. Samantha took in a careful, shallow breath and felt another layer inside her head shear off.

Kristen's power seeped into her mind, sliding past her shields with jagged edges. Emotions weren't something that Samantha had the luxury of feeling; Kristen lived them, day in and day out. It hurt, drawing her sister into a link, as if her mind were being torn to pieces all over again.

And again.

Listen. Kristen's thoughts, soft, modulated, backed by a coherence that Samantha had never before felt in that tangled, ruined mess of a mind.

Samantha had spent all of her life learning when to bend so that she wouldn't break. All Warhounds learned that skill early. The Serca children of any generation learned it earlier than most. Samantha raised a shield between herself and her sister, forcing Kristen out of her mind. It left her with an almost debilitating headache, but she'd lived through worse over the years. Compartmentalizing the pain was easy. Ignoring her sister was not.

Kristen leaned up to press her mouth against Samantha's ear, her voice barely distinguishable from the noise of the crowd.

"You're going about this all wrong, Sam."

Kristen's voice, but not her words. Only one person had ever called her Sam.

She would have pushed Kristen away, except the younger girl was holding on to her so tightly that it was impossible to shake her off completely.

Traitor, Samantha thought, shoving the word straight into Kristen's mind, ignoring how it made her own bleed psionic pain.

The empath smiled at her, her psi signature overlaid with Lucas's presence. *Tell me, Sam,* Lucas said through Kristen's mind. *How am I the traitor when I was the one who pieced your mind back together over and over again? You've got those memories back now. Aren't you grateful?*

Not to you.

Still so sullen. We're going to have to work on that. Lucas stretched his power through Kristen's mind, the empath's insanity a barrier between him and the scans that the Warhound telepaths were doing. *You know what Nathan wants. I want something different.*

I'm not on your side.

Remember when I said I would save you? I never said it would be easy. Trust me, Sam. I'm all you've got left. Do you think you can go back to Nathan with your mind the way it is now?

She couldn't. She knew that it would be impossible to return to London, present herself to their father, and leave his presence alive. Nathan would take her changed state of mind as betrayal, and only one punishment fit that crime in the Warhound ranks.

He'll kill you messy and he'll kill you slow, Lucas told her as he drifted away through the cracks in Kristen's mind. *I need you alive. What's it going to be, Sam?*

Kristen sagged against her, done being her oldest brother's conduit. Her head rolled against Samantha's shoulder, the smile on her face unchanging.

"Strykers," one of the telepaths announced, breaking Samantha's precarious concentration. "That's not Lucas in power plant two. It's Strykers."

"Any of them the ones he took with him out of the Slums?" Jin Li said.

"No. Several teams' worth, though."

Jin Li shook his head as he made his way back to where Samantha and Kristen were standing. More like leaning, Samantha thought, curiously removed from everything as she felt the wall at her back. Jin Li stood before her, eyes narrowed into slits.

"I don't give a fuck what you previously decided with Gideon," he said in a low voice. "But he's a Class II telekinetic and we need his ass in the field. Contact him, give him a visual, and tell him to get here. Now."

Samantha glared at Jin Li. "He stayed behind for a reason. One of us needs to be available to Nathan."

"Bullshit." Jin Li tangled his hand into her hair and yanked her closer to him, his fingers brushing over her bare scalp, over her nerves. "The little one-upmanship game you two are playing isn't helping us here and—"

He broke off with a strangled curse, shoving himself away from Samantha as Kristen slammed her empathy through his mind. Much as Jin Li's power could disrupt a person's nervous system, Kristen's disrupted downright everything. He got his mental shields up before she went too deep, but the first layer was already gone, peeled off by Kristen's insatiable hunger.

She bared her teeth at him, smile fixed and threatening as she put herself between Jin Li and her sister. "Naughty boy," Kristen rasped. "We own you, remember?"

Jin Li raised his fist, pride demanding that he retaliate. Except these two were Nathan's children, his blood, Sercas to their very DNA. Even if Kristen would never be acknowledged, even if Samantha would never take control of the Serca Syndicate after Nathan, they still ranked higher than Jin Li did in the grand scheme of things. Much as Jin Li wanted to tear Kristen apart, he didn't dare touch her. He'd crossed a line with Samantha just now. He couldn't afford to do it again.

"Keep your mind to yourself," he snarled. "And you, Samantha, get Gideon down here. We need a functioning Serca."

Jin Li retreated because he had no other choice. He wasn't 'path-oriented, and no way in hell was he going to fight Kristen unless ordered to by Nathan.

"Do it," Kristen said, laughing through the words. "Oh, bring our brother down here, Sammy-girl."

Samantha would have given anything not to, but if they were going to face a contingent of Strykers in the middle of a powerful acid storm, then they would need whatever strength they could get. With Samantha's telepathy pretty much broken, her mind bleeding through psi shock, she didn't have a choice in the matter. Jin Li was right. They needed a functioning Serca.

She closed her eyes against the chaos of the bunker, against the pain in her head. Stripped as she was of everything even remotely resembling control, the only way she could reach her twin was through the psi link that was still intact between them. She shielded as best she could, but Gideon would still know something was wrong.

Gideon, she sent at him, mental voice strained, the psi link between them shaky. *Gideon, we need you on the field.*

What happened? He didn't sound concerned, just curious, and Samantha swallowed her bitterness until she couldn't taste it anymore.

What do you think? She managed a tight, angry little laugh. *I've hit burnout, pushing into psi shock. We need you to lead.*

You wanted me to stay behind.

Now I want your arse here. Samantha opened her eyes, sharing the space she was in with him, the dimness and crowdedness of the bunker. The way it smelled of old metal and human perspiration, the stench of too many years lived beneath the ground. *Do you have it?*

She felt him like a vise inside her skull, in what little area of her power she could spare, the world gone blurry as another pair of eyes looked through hers. *Yes.*

Suddenly, her twin was standing before her, a little smile on his face that was for her alone. It wasn't supposed to be reassuring.

"I told you it should have been me," Gideon said.

Samantha pushed herself off the wall, let Kristen continue to hang off her because her sister's mind was a better barrier than anything she herself could come up with at the moment. "You really think Lucas will let you find him?"

"One wonders why he let you."

They stared each other down, but Samantha couldn't afford to be the one who looked away first. Kristen solved the problem for them, shoving at Gideon with one hand, or at least trying to. Gideon held her in place with his telekinesis, her hand splayed against an invisible shield millimeters above his chest.

"Don't," Gideon warned. "Or I'll break your arm."

Kristen licked her dry, cracked lips and winked at him. She was shoved back against Samantha, Gideon leaving the pair of them behind whole and intact because they needed everyone they could get to take Lucas down. Samantha sucked in a breath and started walking after her twin, Kristen keeping pace with her. The Warhounds with them were grouping together—she counted sixteen of them, herself and siblings included—everyone except Gideon wearing a field uniform. He didn't need one, nor the armor it came with, not with his power wrapped like a second skin around his body.

"Report," Gideon said, now the center of attention, taking control of the mission away from Samantha.

Clenching her hand into a fist, Samantha looked down at her white knuckles, the blood drying on her fingers, and listened as the War-hounds who had obeyed her for the majority of this mission switched their focus and loyalty to her twin.

Kristen wrapped her arms around Samantha's waist, pressed her forehead against Samantha's spine. "What's it going to be, Sam?"

Kristen's voice, Lucas's words.

Samantha didn't answer. Not here in the bunker, not when they arrived in the middle of the acid storm ninety seconds later, teleported within me-ters of the power plant in question, where Strykers were hunting some of their own. The wind nearly threw them both to the ground. Kristen dug in her heels and kept them upright through sheer will as thunder and lightning crashed above them, the clouds so low, it gave the illusion that if they lifted their arms to the sky, they could touch the storm.

What's it going to be?

A memory. A promise. Lucas seeding rebellion throughout the ranks, throughout her mind.

Trust me.

[THIRTY]

AUGUST 2379
BUFFALO, USA

Threnody couldn't hear anything over the sound of the storm, not even her own ragged breathing as she crouched behind the thick security wall of the power plant, next to the guard building. Quin-ton and Kerr were directly across from her, on the other side of the front blast doors.

To get past the quads who guarded the area, Kerr had altered their minds and convinced a human to walk with the three of them, in the illu-sion of a quad, through the power-plant gates to get inside. Once there, Kerr had knocked out every single human. Humans were always easy to control. Dealing with the Strykers who had arrived soon after was something else entirely.

Quinton's power was useless now that the storm had picked up. So were their guns because shooting bullets through wind that was blowing at 320 kilometers an hour was just asking to die. They had Kerr's telepathy and Threnody's electrokinesis, two powers against ten times that on the other side of the doors. Quinton had managed to close them again, but the doors were steadily being peeled apart despite Kerr's psionic interference that blocked 'path-oriented strikes and teleportation. Not good odds.

The one thing they had in their favor was that the Strykers couldn't find them on the mental grid. Lucas's trick of hiding a psi signature until the person in question seemed only human, or not present at all, was keeping them alive. She didn't know how much longer their luck would last. They *needed* to get inside the power plant. Running right now would leave them easy targets without a telekinetic to watch their backs, and the only way inside that power plant was through the front doors. A lot of open space was between them and those doors.

We should have brought Jason, Threnody said in a tense voice through the psi link Kerr had strung between their minds.

Kerr didn't answer her. Someone else did.

He was needed elsewhere. You'll have your chance to make a break for it in thirty seconds, Lucas said as he appeared beside her, stumbling out of his teleport and needing the wall to support his weight for a few seconds. He'd startled her; blue lines of electricity sparked over her hands out of instinct. She pulled her power back in only after she realized who it was.

Threnody glared up at Lucas through the rain, rapidly blinking the stinging wet out of her eyes. *What did you do?*

Twenty seconds. Be ready.

When the Warhounds teleported in, arriving between where they were cornered and where the Strykers were waiting, Threnody felt her stomach clench. Lucas waved a hand at her, the features of his face sharply lit by the brightness of the security lights that burned hotly through the storm on the walls around the power plant.

Now, Lucas told her, head turned toward the doors that had been torn to the ground under telekinetic pressure. *Both of you, run.*

Threnody was already running toward the entrance of the power plant, slipping through the sheet of mud that overlay the cement pathway, bent nearly double against the wind and the rain. Quinton was running in her direction, both of them highlighted by the lights and the storm, presenting perfect targets to everyone behind them.

Except they would have to get through Lucas first.

Kerr, Lucas said, drawing him into a merge. *I'll need your support.*

Kerr didn't understand what was happening, having never had his mind merged into another's before. He didn't try to fight it, as he hadn't fought Lucas when the other man had fixed his mind, knowing that this was the only way they were going to survive. Lucas needed his strength, he could feel that now, because for all that Lucas was a Class I triad psion, the younger man had been pushing himself hard since well before the Slums. Alone, Lucas didn't have the reach he needed to fight nearly fifty-odd Strykers and Warhounds.

The limits of Kerr's mind expanded, his power pushing through someone else's strength and laying down anchor points across their area of the mental grid. A merged Class I and Class II mental wall was built up along the edge of a chasm that cut so deep and so wide it would take everything all the psions outside the power plant had and more to break through their shields. A breach was still a possibility.

It was similar to how Kerr had worked most of his life with Jason, except this partnership went deeper. Kerr could feel the channels of Lucas's telekinesis more clearly than he'd ever felt Jason's. Kerr let Lucas take whatever he needed, their minds weaving together seamlessly, thoughts paralleling as Lucas became the apex of a two-mind merge.

On the mental grid, pockets deepened with individual powers from the Strykers and the clumping knots of power that signified Warhound merges. None of them even remotely approached the strength that Lucas and Kerr wielded.

Telekinesis wrapped around their bodies; a shield also bubbling over Threnody and Quinton as they made it to the rusted blast doors of the power plant. Lucas and Kerr planted themselves on one side of those torn-down doors, clothes soaking wet and skin chilled beneath the sudden barrier against the storm. Two men who were neither Stryker nor Warhound, just human enough to believe in doing the right thing.

Traitor, Gideon said on a narrow psi link between himself and Lucas, riding a Warhound's telepathic power to make the connection.

Lucas didn't sense Samantha in any of the Warhound merges at all, nor did he feel the devastating pull of Kristen's deadly need. A slow smile cut across his face, Kerr the only witness to it.

You seem to think that because I want to survive, I'm a traitor, Lucas said as he readied his and Kerr's shared power behind their shields. *You can have what Nathan's offering. I found something better.*

Lucas's and Kerr's telepathic strike ripped through everyone's mind like an explosion, burning through the shields of anyone who was a Class V and lower, shattering concentrations. People fell to the ground, Warhounds and Strykers alike, minds whiting out in pain. The backlash of that much power caused Lucas's control of the merge to waver, just a little.

Don't kill them, Kerr said, guilt and a lifetime of commitment to the Strykers asking for a reprieve.

Beg elsewhere, Lucas said as he raised their shields and felt the dip on the mental grid that signified an attack from the Strykers, because they had never learned what the Sercas had imparted to the Warhounds about merging.

Telekinetic strength exploded around them as if a bomb had gone off, cracking the ground and the walls, sending debris spinning off into the storm for the wind to catch. Lucas was ready for it, mind braced to deflect the attack. He grunted, rocking back on his heels from the mental strain, muscles drawn tight over bone as he stubbornly held his ground.

Kerr fed him more strength and Lucas absorbed it greedily, fortifying his telekinesis right before they were hit. Lucas's training and knowledge of how Gideon worked on the field was the only thing that let him anticipate his younger brother's attack. The Class II telekinetic had merged seven other telekinetics with his power. Lucas could feel the difference between his brother and the Strykers like a sharp divide. Gideon had been trained by Nathan. His attack was quick, powerful—expected in this instance in the wake of the kill order. The Warhounds had dropped off the mental grid, covered by telepaths in merge, and this time the telekinetic attack happened both outside and inside Lucas's shields.

The power Gideon wielded would have crushed Lucas and Kerr if Lucas's defenses had been even a sliver less than what they were. His shields weren't a single barrier; he layered them at intervals around their bodies and mind. What Gideon's merge broke down was only half of Lucas's defenses, but the damage was more extensive than that. Power broke apart in Lucas's mind, synapses overloading somewhere in his brain at the backlash. Lucas's mind dealt with the damage instinctually, compensating for a bridge that was lost, the merge shifting just enough to steady both minds.

I'll take the telepaths, Kerr said. *You deal with the telekinetics.*

It was the logical choice, and Kerr was used to being a backboard for telekinetic strength. Lucas didn't hesitate to switch his concentration to the telekinetics, holding up his shields while Kerr used his own Class II telepathic strength in an attack that left holes in all lesser-Classed psion minds. Not as deep as Lucas could go, but deep enough to cause damage.

Not even a month ago, Kerr wouldn't have been able to stand his ground in a battle like this. His shields wouldn't have withstood the follow-up attacks. Here, now, his power had a new depth, strength once used fighting his empathy now relegated to controlling it, twisting his secondary power into an attack that affected everyone's emotions.

He had no formal training for his empathy. What Kerr knew now had been imparted through Lucas from the psi surgery, and what Lucas didn't know about the human and not-so-human mind wasn't worth the knowing. Kerr had control of his minute amount of empathy, just enough to push *fear* against the minds that he slammed through until they choked on it.

A Class IX power wasn't really much of anything to be worried about. Kerr didn't think it would make a huge difference, but it left damage in its wake. People forgot, sometimes, why the higher Classes were rare and why most psions never broke past a Class V. The human mind didn't need a lot of power to do a lot of damage. It just needed enough to leave a scar. A reminder.

Kristen understood that better than anyone else because she lived with it day in and day out. Her mind was just scar tissue built on top of scar tissue, layers of damage that would never be fixed because she'd been broken too young and too many times, and no one had bothered to put her back together again. When she dropped her shields, called by the taste of fear Kerr had projected, her presence shook through everyone's mind.

Lucas cut her off at the pass, sliding between Kerr and his sister with a skill that spoke of long practice. Kristen was only a distraction, though, just a threat that they couldn't ignore and had to face down first even as Gideon dropped out of the merge he led, his place filled by a different telekinetic. Lucas couldn't react fast enough and stop them, not and risk letting Kristen find a crack in his own two-person merge and exploit it.

Lucas, Kristen called to him, laughter in her thoughts. *Come play with me!*

In the midst of all that fighting, only one person stood apart from it all, mind bleeding into her bones as she felt Gideon teleport beyond Lucas's defenses with Jin Li by his side. Samantha spat out a mouthful of blood and saliva as the wind howled in her ears. Kristen was a heaviness between herself and Lucas on the mental grid, a barrier that was steadily eating through the thoughts that swirled all around them.

Samantha's shields were paper-thin and full of holes. Her defenses were no better than a human's, which was all the difference that mattered.

For the first time in her entire life, Samantha could *think.*

She used it—that decadent, giddy sense of freedom—to fight.

THIRTY-ONE

AUGUST 2379
BUFFALO, USA

Threnody fried the control panel to the blast doors until its necessary parts melted beneath her power. The blast doors unlocked, but they didn't open.

Lucas, the doors, Threnody said through the psi link.

Focused as he was on not letting them die, Lucas still managed to telekinetically open the blast doors for them. The two slipped inside the power plant, where the lights were running on half-power.

Power plant two, built in the middle of Buffalo, ran on fossil fuels, like the majority of the power plants left in the world. Nuclear power plants were a thing of the past, humanity's absolute fear of nuclear power etched into the backbone of the remnants of society. Renewable energy plants were few and far between, and America's East Coast had relied on fossil fuel power plants for centuries before the Border Wars. The tradition continued through to the present.

This one burned coal, supplies scavenged from cities all along the coast, stored by the ton in tall steel silos that supplied the plant's six pulverizers by way of conveyer belts. Those belts weren't running, stilled in the face of the acid storm and the government's order. The hum that should have filled the power plant had been replaced by the screaming wind and Threnody's and Quinton's own harsh breathing.

The skeleton crew assigned to monitor the power plant was dead. Only when Threnody tripped over a body did they discover that. They stared at the corpse's face twisted in an expression of permanent pain, a puddle of blood outlining the head. The lack of physical wounds had her thinking it was a mental attack. Lucas's doing, or possibly the Warhounds'. Ei-

ther way, with the scientists dead, anyone who could have helped them
bring the power plant back up to full readiness was dead.

"Well, shit," Threnody said as she knelt down to rifle through the
dead man's pockets until she found a security card.

Quinton glanced at her. "I figure they'll have biometrics throughout
this place."

They looked at the body on the ground. Without a word, Quinton
called up fire from some of the remaining natural gas left in the biotubes in his arms, snapping his fingers to light it. The fire burned bright
and hot, shrinking down to a thin blue line of the hottest heat he could
produce. He focused it on the dead man's right hand, just below the
wrist, and the fire burned through flesh easily. The stench was foul,
something they ignored, having smelled the dead many times before.
Only when they started to smell metal did Quinton stop to bend down
and pick up the severed hand. It was cool to the touch, the wrist area
cauterized.

"Let's go," Threnody said.

She and Quinton hurried down the hall, bypassing the doors that led
to the boiler steam drum and the high-powered steam turbines, all ab-
normally silent. They ran, leaving a trail of wet footprints for anyone to
follow. Working their way to the control room, they found it behind layers of protective shielding and fire-resistant paneling. Threnody swiped
the card over the security reader as Quinton pressed the severed hand
against the screen. The computer read the print, as well as the security
card, and the doors slid open. Quinton dropped the severed hand on
the floor; Threnody kept the security card.

Inside were more bodies, and they hauled two corpses out of the
chairs they had died in. The terminals were still on, access to the power
plant's computer network available. Threnody and Quinton slid into seats
on opposite sides of the control room, the wide, clear windows providing
them with a near 360-degree view of the massive, internal guts of the
power plant.

"You ever wish they taught this in a simulator?" Quinton asked as he
brought window after window up on the vidscreen, furiously looking for
any prompt that would get them further than the public areas of the

system. They couldn't get far without viable codes or passwords, not with the entire network so tightly locked down.

"You're a better hacker than I am," Threnody reminded him.

"I'm not that good, Thren. Maybe it should have been Jason after all."

Threnody didn't say anything to that, just continued to demand answers from a computer that was reluctant to give them up, security card or no. She swore after the fifth failed attempt, slamming her hand down in frustration on the terminal.

"Careful," Quinton barked.

"I *know*."

Frying the main system that controlled this place wasn't in anyone's best interest. There had to be a different way.

Lucas, we need a little help here, Threnody said. *Can you link us to Jason?*

No answer. From the way Lucas and Kerr had been fighting outside, she wasn't surprised. Swearing, she brought up a map of the power plant on the screen and stared critically at every last section of the place. Her gaze lingered longest on the transmission lines and transformers built into the ground outside, some distance away from the cooling tower and the building they were in.

"Think a jump start might work?" Threnody asked as she swiveled her chair around to face Quinton.

Quinton turned his head to look at her, a tight expression on his face. "It'll kill you."

She shrugged, grimacing. "Better here than under the government's control."

"Threnody—"

"*Quinton.*"

She got to her feet and crossed the distance between them in a few quick strides. A bittersweet, ruined smile curved across her mouth. She hid it against the top of Quinton's skull; a brief caress, a thank-you, for all his years of loyalty.

"I'll come back if I can," Threnody said, promising no more than that.

Quinton pressed his hand to the small of her back, pulled her into an embrace that lasted only a second. "Go," he said, voice low and gravelly. "I'll keep trying to contact Lucas or Kerr."

She left the control room and didn't look back. Quinton didn't watch her go. This was how they worked, how all Strykers learned to work with their partner or their team. You did what had to be done for the good of everyone else, for the mission. Personal desires were never, ever allowed.

Quinton put all his focus on the terminal before him and calling out through the psi links for their only telepaths. Distracted, he missed Gideon and Jin Li's arrival. He didn't miss their presence when he was telekinetically slammed face-first into the wall.

His nose broke; so did a few of his teeth. Quinton spat out blood and shattered enamel, the front of his face feeling as if it were on fire.

"Jin Li, go after the other one," Gideon ordered as he flipped Quinton around onto his back against the wall.

Quinton wrenched his eyes open at that command, blinking through the swollen heat that encompassed his face in time to see Jin Li leave the control room.

Lucas! he shouted through the psi link. *Kerr!*

Silence, the psi link empty of any support. Held immobile against the wall by that strong Class II telekinetic grip, Quinton could only stare as Nathan's third child approached the terminal he had been working on, studying all the open command windows on the vidscreen he'd been struggling to break through.

"You're not a hacker," Gideon stated. "Not a good one. I don't know why Lucas allied himself with you Strykers if you don't have the proper skills to get the job done."

Quinton didn't say a word. Gideon was a telekinetic, not a telepath, which meant unless he brought in a Warhound telepath, he wasn't going to be able to pry a damn thing out of Quinton. Mentally, at least, and Strykers had died for less.

Gideon glanced up at him, the intent in his dark blue eyes different from the pair Quinton had been staring at for the past few weeks or so. "Why do you want the power plant turned back on?"

Quinton kept his mouth shut. Gideon was unsurprised at this silence. His gaze settled on Quinton's bare arms and the shadow of biotubes beneath his skin. "Pyrokinetic. You can make this easy on yourself if you open your mouth and start talking."

Quinton couldn't risk a fire here, not in a place that they needed. It didn't matter anyway, not when he couldn't create the very thing his power controlled. Gideon had him held fast, the weight of his telekinesis slowly crushing Quinton up against the wall.

Gideon started with Quinton's fingers first, breaking every bone from nails to knuckle with each refusal to answer his question. Eventually, Gideon moved up to the bones and biomodifications that spanned Quinton's palms and the carefully placed tubing there. Quinton didn't scream, just squeezed his eyes shut and ground his broken teeth together, trying to breathe through the agony of the slow torture as Gideon telekinetically tore his body apart.

"I'm sorry," a new voice said an indeterminate time later through the pain he was feeling, sounding raw and broken and so, so determined.

The power holding Quinton prisoner abruptly disappeared. He fell to the ground, gasping for air around the blood in his mouth, vomiting when his shattered hands touched the floor. This time he screamed, unable to choke it back, the sound mingling with the high tone of Gideon's own voice.

Lying on the floor of the control room, Quinton stared in disbelief at the sight before him. Samantha Serca had both her hands pressed against Gideon's temples, eyes narrowed in concentration, lips pulled back in a snarl as she focused all her telepathic strength on frying her twin brother's mind. The effort left the tendons standing out in her arms and throat, sweat pouring down her face, mixing with the blood that was dripping out of her nose.

Gideon, though, Gideon was rigid in her grip, mouth opened wide and the expression on his face one of shocked betrayal as his twin overrode his thoughts and his power. She sent him spinning down into psi shock with the last of her strength. Gideon fell to the ground first, Samantha less than a second behind him. But while Gideon was unconscious from the massive psionic overload, Samantha wasn't, and her dark blue eyes focused on Quinton's bloody, broken face.

Behind her, a skinny form slid into the control room. Quinton could only stare in shock as the girl approached him, the smile on her face cracked and bleeding, her eyes that signature Serca dark blue. He didn't need to be a telepath to recognize the distorted pressure against his shields as that of a dysfunctional mind.

Lucas, you fucking bastard, he thought muzzily through the pain. *You never said anything about this.*

"Shh, shh," that girl whispered as her fingers touched his forehead, stroking over his hot skin.

With every motion of her fingers, she wiped away the pain.

His brain ceased to acknowledge the agony that existed from his elbows on down in each arm, the sudden absence of it leaving him lightheaded and queasy. The pain in his face faded until it was just a distant ache that was hard to breathe through. Quinton's brown eyes snapped open and he stared up in shock at the smiling teenager who knelt beside him, a psion who could only be an empath after that little show of power.

"Promises to keep, Stryker," she cooed at him. "Promises, promises."

"Wha—?" The word came out messy, garbled. Spitting blood, coughing to get air into his lungs, Quinton tried again, concentrating on what he was saying so that he could be understood, even with a broken face. "What?"

"You aren't the only person Lucas needs," Samantha said as she dragged herself into the nearest seat. "Kristen, get him up."

Instinctively, Quinton jerked away from that crazy empath's touch, wishing for the first time in a long while that he had even a sliver of 'path-oriented power in his genes. The knowing look in Kristen's gleaming dark blue eyes told him that his fear hadn't gone unnoticed. Still, for such a small girl, she had a lot of strength; enough to help Quinton get his feet back underneath him. Once vertical, Quinton shrugged her off, stepping away from her grasping, clinging hands.

"Kristen," Samantha said sharply.

"You're no fun, Sammy-girl," Kristen complained as she stepped over Gideon's still body and back to her sister's side.

"Is he dead?" Quinton asked carefully after a few seconds.

"No." Samantha sounded as if the word hurt her. "I don't have enough strength left in me to kill him."

Maybe she did, maybe she didn't. Maybe her reluctance was due to the nine months they floated together in an artificial womb and the eighteen years since that they had stood side by side beneath Nathan's judging eyes. It didn't matter. This was where her loyalty ended—with Gideon still breathing.

Quinton leaned against the other chair, staring at Lucas's sisters while blood dripped down onto the floor from his fingers and his face. "What are you doing?"

"What you couldn't," Samantha explained as she worked her way through the power plant's control system using access codes instead of a hack. "I stripped everything we'd need to bring this place back online out of the minds of the engineers and scientists before killing them."

"You do it on Lucas's order?"

"It doesn't matter."

"The hell it doesn't. Why isn't he here?"

"Because he and that other telepath are busy holding off what's left of the Strykers and Warhounds that are still on the field. We've got maybe five minutes, if we're lucky, to lock in the codes before the military reaches this place."

"Jin Li went after Threnody."

"I know. They both have their parts to play."

"What do you mean?" Quinton demanded, jerking himself up straight again. "You're not going to try and help her?"

Samantha didn't look away from the vidscreen. "I can bring this plant online, but it's going to take time to generate the amount of electricity Lucas needs to reach where it has to go. Threnody's an electrokinetic. So is Jin Li. There is a derecho storm raging outside. Do the math, Stryker."

Quinton didn't need to. He was already staggering out of the control room on shaky legs, heart pounding in his chest as he raced against time, knowing it was already too late even as the first hint of sound started to come from the machines around him.

The power plant was starting to come online again.

[THIRTY-TWO]

AUGUST 2379
BUFFALO, USA

There was a service door—locked, of course—that she had to fry before she could shove it open. It took all her strength against the crushing weight of the wind to move it. Threnody stood in the doorway, braced against the fury of the storm while acid rain lashed her body.

The transformer and transmission lines weren't housed in a separate building. They were outside, maybe twenty meters from the door and farther than that from the cooling tower. Located in the back, far from where the Strykers and the Warhounds were fighting Lucas and Kerr, they were cold, most of the city running off strained backup generators during the storm. Even if they weren't running at full power, they were still capable of transmuting electricity, of carrying it forward.

"I must be losing my mind," Threnody muttered under her breath as she stepped out into the storm.

Getting soaked wasn't new. The ground between the main building and the tall transmission towers was covered in cement, rain flooding the place. It sloshed over her boots, making it slippery to walk, much less run, as she made her way to the bulky transformer.

After the Border Wars, when many of America's and the rest of the world's electrical grids had been destroyed, rebuilding them had been a top priority for the survivors. They were limited, though, built specifically to support small pockets of survivors and expanding no farther than that. The government had controlled the output of electricity back then and still did now, because controlling the resources that everyone needed kept the population in check.

A wire fence surrounded the transformer block, more for safety than to keep anyone out, but it was still a restricted space. The door was locked, the mechanism easy to fry to gain entrance. Shoving the door open as wide as she could, Threnody stumbled toward her goal.

The transformer block was a three-phase system, with heavy wires pulled taut between the transformer and the transmission tower that they fed into. Even with the light coming from the single spotlight focused on the area inside the fence, it was almost impossible to see where those transmission lines disappeared to in the storm.

Swiping water out of her eyes, blinking against the sting it left behind, Threnody maneuvered her way back around the transformer block to the front, running through her options. Walking around that last corner, she came face-to-face with Jin Li. Threnody jerked back out of instinct, her feet nearly sliding out from beneath her. Jin Li followed her with electricity sparking in long arcs between his fingers.

"Your partner's being torn to pieces by Gideon," Jin Li shouted over the noise of the storm as Threnody twisted around the corner.

"He knew the risks," Threnody yelled back. "We all did."

"Those risks are gonna get you dead, girl."

Jin Li lunged forward, aiming his fist at her face. Threnody ducked, twisting her body against his attack and the wind. Her hand hit the ground for balance as she lashed out with a sharp kick to Jin Li's knee that he avoided by jumping out of reach. Threnody hauled herself back to a standing position, sliding her feet farther apart for balance as she tapped into her power.

Blue electricity wrapped around her fists, a match for the power that sparked around Jin Li's. He grinned at her, face eerily lit by the lightning exploding through the sky above them. Threnody could feel the charge in the air, could feel it in her skin all the way down to her bones. Her body practically hummed with the power that the derecho storm was generating.

Jin Li moved over the slick surface of the ground, one hand stabbing forward. Electricity danced through the air between them, crackling against Threnody's power, over her skin. She returned the gesture with a wide arc of electricity that cut through his attack and slammed into him.

Blue sparks lit up the air around them, tiny Vesuvius flares that would have blinded anyone who didn't have their power.

It wasn't often that electrokinetics fought like this, electricity cutting through the air from body to body like lightning did from sky to earth, cloud to cloud. Their power wasn't meant to function like that; they needed a conduit to keep the electricity flowing. The storm above had charged the very air they breathed enough to be that bridge.

This wasn't like Johannesburg. It wasn't even like the Slums. Threnody knew what she was fighting for this time and she couldn't afford to lose. That desperation drove her forward, forcing her inside Jin Li's defenses to take the blows he gave her and pound her own against his body. They used their fists, feet, and knees, the crackling burn of their power, but when it came right down to it, Jin Li was a Class II and she wasn't. He would always have the upper hand, and Threnody still wasn't fully recovered from everything she'd gone through over the past few months.

His foot caught the edge of her knee in a hard kick, knocking her legs out from under her. Threnody grunted as she fell, pain stabbing up her left thigh. Jin Li pinned her to the ground, his weight heavy on her chest, but not as heavy as the hands around her throat. Threnody wrapped her own hands around his wrists, choking against the pressure of his fingers and the bright sparks of his power.

"Lucas was never worth shit," Jin Li said around gritted teeth, electricity crawling over his face in sharp lines that had no pattern. "You chose the wrong side, Stryker. All that's left for you to do is die."

Black spots ate into her vision, the brightness fading. She couldn't breathe, lungs burning beneath her ribs and her heart beating so fast that she could feel its speed. Threnody stared up past Jin Li's determined face, at the swirling blackness of the storm, and thought about everyone in the underground hangars, waiting to launch in scavenged shuttles. About the people who would be left behind when the government chose only those they considered worthy to be human enough to leave this world. She thought about Lucas and Aisling, and wondered how that little girl had died, if she had died like this, with the life choked out of her as the world went to hell.

No, Threnody thought as lightning cut through the sky.

She was a Stryker, a psion. A Class III electrokinetic. Threnody Corwin at your fucking service. But more than that, at the most basic level, she was a living, breathing *battery* with a brain. It's what her power was, it's how her body functioned, charged from the inside out.

She let Jin Li's wrist go, lifting one hand past his head for the sky above them. Electricity sparked dully at her fingertips, the world narrowing to tunnel vision that was all black clouds and white lightning. She could feel the charge in her nerve endings, the way it set her hair standing on end. The smell of ozone as the world got suddenly brighter, a blinding whiteness that exploded through her, running down her arm into her body, through Jin Li's hands, and straight into him.

Jin Li screamed when the bolt of lightning hit them, propelled backward from the harsh shock of a near system overload. Threnody forced herself off the ground. Electricity was jumping between them, flowing over the water-soaked ground and across the metal fence, the transformers, *everything,* flinging back through her and him in a loop that would kill them both soon enough. She wrapped her burning, bleeding hands over Jin Li's shoulders and pushed the momentarily stunned man backward with all her strength until he hit the side of the transformer.

His brown eyes had a blue-white sheen over them when they focused on her. He spoke, but Threnody didn't hear what he said. She doubted he heard her either.

"You're never getting off this planet," she promised.

Threnody kept her eyes wide-open, the world becoming a flash image in her brain as she sucked up every last bit of electric power into her body and channeled it through Jin Li's, forcing it farther into the transformer behind him. The smell of burning flesh reached her nose; her nerves never noticed the damage. Threnody held on, driving the electricity farther, down coils and wires, through conductors, and into the transmission lines, up into the towers that sparked and popped beneath the sudden heavy load.

The power had no place to go except out.

Threnody pried her fingers off Jin Li long seconds later, the man still connected to the transformer by way of burned and melting flesh, his body still jerking from the electricity that was running through him, killing him by quick degrees. Threnody left all the skin of her fingers and palms on his shoulders, blackened strips peeling off as she collapsed to the ground.

Lying there, in the hot water beneath the storm, with acid rain pelting her body and her heart beating jaggedly in her chest, Threnody let the world fade away.

The electricity she had called down out of the sky still burned through the transformer, funneled with precision through the transmission lines as it scattered to the substations that existed throughout Buffalo. It only took seconds for that power to reach through kilometers of power lines and feed a city starved for energy.

That night, Buffalo lit up as if it were on fire for the first time in decades, in centuries, a brightly glowing sprawl that burned defiantly beneath the storm.

PART EIGHT
DELIVERANCE

SESSI`ON DATE: **2128.07.13**
LOCATION: **Institute of Psionics Research**
CLEARANCE ID: **Dr. Amy Bennett**
SUBJECT: **2581**
FILE NUMBER: **638**

"We know you have the answers," the doctor says as she picks up a white card from the deck on the table. One side is blank, the other side holds a shape viewable only by the doctor.

"They aren't your answers. Purple star," Aisling says as the EEG and supporting machines click and whine, spikes reading across the screen. She is kneeling on the chair, attention elsewhere, yellow dress twisted around her legs.

The doctor places the card down and marks something in her notes before picking up another. "Your track record for being right is un-matched."

"With the cards? Orange square."

Another card gets set aside. "With where the bombs fall."

"They're not done falling. I've told you that. This is reeducation on a worldwide level. This is how we start over. Everyone will say the same thing eventually."

"By killing ourselves?" The expression on the doctor's face is angry, but the grief in her voice is what makes the girl finally glance at her. The look in Aisling's bleached-out violet eyes is startlingly adult.

"You kill us without regret. You're killing me."

"Aisling, we're not . . . we're not *killing* you. You've just been a little sick, that's all. We're treating you for it."

"No, you're not," the girl whispers, shoulders slumping. "You can't fix me and I can't see the world how you want me to."

For once, in a long, long while, the machines are quiet.

[THIRTY-THREE]

AUGUST 2379
BUFFALO, USA

The lights in the hangar snapped on with a startling, loud hum, blinding everyone who had been sitting in the flight decks of the shuttles. Jason leaned forward, jerked out of the middle another diagnostic test, and stared at the hangar.

"Fuck, they did it," Jason said as he cut the diagnostics short. He started to upload the destination coordinates that Lucas had given him hours ago into the corresponding shuttles through the hive connection in the computer.

Beside him, Matron opened an uplink on her terminal even as she started to kick the shuttle into full flight readiness. "Alpha shuttle to Beta and all others, do you copy, over?"

She got a multitude of responses, all calling in their status as she strapped into her flight harness. When all thirty-five shuttles came back with positive identification, Matron said, "Do you have power at the launch sites, over?"

More affirmatives.

"Then get the hell into the air, out." Matron cut the uplink and turned her head to look at Jason. "You ready?"

"Already powering up the launch silo," Jason said, his hands flying over the controls in front of him.

Outside the confines of the shuttles, the control terminals to the side of the launchpad were picking up Jason's signals. Computers switched out of power-save mode into full activation as Jason plugged in the commands remotely. Above them, in that wide, round launch silo, lights came on in a continuous line. The blast doors at the top of that long open space responded to the orders currently driving its system and began to open. A hole appeared high above, quickly getting larger, allowing rain and mud to drop down onto the shuttles below.

In Alpha shuttle, Jason was trying to contact Lucas or Kerr telepathically, but no one was responding on the shared psi link. Swearing, Jason shook his head. "They're not answering my call."

"They dead?" Matron asked.

"No. I'd have felt the psi link sever if that was the case. Hurts like a bitch when it happens."

"We can't wait here. Not for much longer." Matron switched to an uplink with the other two shuttles in the hangar with them. "Grady, Torrance, get the hell out of here. We're holding for the main cargo, out."

Jason ground his teeth and dropped his head into his hands. *Lucas, Kerr, I need a response, damn it.*

The roar of the first shuttle activating its vertical-takeoff-and-landing (VTOL) function nearly drowned out Jason's thoughts and the faint, telepathic voice that finally crawled through the psi link.

We need a pickup, Lucas said, mental voice strained and distant, almost fractured. *At power plant two. Teleportation isn't possible.*

Understood.

Jason opened his eyes in time to see the first shuttle launching out of the silo and the second already lifting into the air. "They need a pickup."

"Fuck," Matron swore as she stabbed a finger at Jason. "Blow the charges."

Jason picked up the remote detonator from the control panel and unlocked the device. He gripped it tightly as the second shuttle cleared the launch silo, and then it was their turn. Matron was a scavenger, born and bred, part of a people who possessed any number of skills in order to survive. That she could pilot a shuttle wasn't surprising; he just hoped she was good at it. Matron activated the VTOL, and Jason felt the shuttle shake as it lifted into the air. It rose higher and faster through the launch silo, the storm rushing down to meet them.

They cleared the blast doors and Jason pressed his thumb down hard on the detonator's red button. It sent out a limited-range signal, picked up by the receivers far below. The charge coursed through the C-4, and the resulting explosions rocked the stormy air, buffeting the shuttle with shocking intensity. Despite the wind and the rain, the fire they left behind wasn't going to go out anytime soon.

Matron was already pulling away, banking hard to the left, struggling to keep the shuttle steady in the face of turbulent winds. When she spoke, she sounded almost in awe. "Holy mother of God."

Below them, every street filled with light, was the city of Buffalo. The sprawl stretched from Lake Erie all the way to the east, where it faded into emptiness. The city towers were like burning fingers to the north, a misguided crowning glory.

"Never saw it like this before," Matron murmured, her sharp eyes studying the shuttle's instruments as well as the view.

"Never going to again," Jason said as he plotted a course and uploaded the vector onto Matron's hologrid for her to see.

On their radar, they were picking up thirty-five other bogeys—shuttles scattered around the southern edge of the city—and about a hundred more coming out of Toronto.

"Fuck." Jason leaned closer to the vidscreen and everything that was showing up. "Matron, the military scrambled their jets earlier than expected."

"Shit," Matron said as she accessed the uplink again, getting a chatter of voices coming from all the shuttles. "Crew, this is your boss. We're detouring for the main cargo. Get the fuck out of this airspace. We've got incoming, out."

She kept the connection open, the chatter filling the flight deck to replace the sound of their breathing. Jason was focused on his half of the controls, and Matron was struggling to fly the shuttle through the derecho, forced lower than she would have liked by heavy downdrafts and the thick cloud cover that made it almost impossible to see. The shuttle cut through the storm.

"Never fucking doing him a favor again," Matron decided as she held tight to the stick with both hands and felt the drag of the shuttle in her arms.

The storm wreaked havoc on their instrumentation, giving them hope that it was interfering with the military's as well. They couldn't be sure, and the military had better stealth capabilities than Matron and her scavengers had been able to salvage from the deserted cities of America. What the military didn't have sitting in the cockpits of those jets were psions.

The storm dragged them off course for a precious few minutes. Matron struggled to guide them back in the proper direction. They were almost to their destination when a red warning line filled the bottom of every active vidscreen.

"They've got a lock on us," Jason snapped.

"I see it, I see it!" Matron said, one eye on the red warning cutting across her controls and another on the sky outside the shuttle. She yanked hard on the stick, maneuvering the shuttle into a sharp dive out of the clouds to clear, if rough, skies below.

They were uncomfortably close to the ground, flying over tenements and near-empty streets. A heat-seeking missile, locked onto them, came streaking out of the storm clouds. Jason saw it, on the screen and in the air, and he reached out with his telekinesis, struggling to wrap his power around the fast-moving weapon. He finally caught hold of it. Anchoring his power to that long, dangerous missile, Jason wrenched it around onto a new trajectory.

The military jet that dove out of the clouds could pull all the evasive maneuvers it wanted. That missile was backed by living human thought, not a computer, and Jason sent it straight into the belly of the jet as it rolled. He let go at the very last second so his power didn't block the explosion.

The jet fell in fiery pieces to the city below. Jason didn't have time to worry about the damage the debris would cause. Five more jets were dropping out of the clouds and coming straight at them, requiring his attention, firing a volley of missiles that he didn't have time to grab for independently. Jason erected a wide telekinetic shield between them and the missiles, watching as they exploded in midair. A headache blossomed in the back of his head, but he ignored it.

Some of the jets managed to bank fast enough to get out of the way.

Some of them didn't, their technology incapable of identifying a telekinetic shield. Most crashed at full throttle into Jason's shields. Jason was thrown forward against his flight harness, a physical reaction to the sudden mental agony ripping through his mind. He dropped his shields, gasping for air as his entire head throbbed from the impact of jets against his power.

"You still with me, Jason?" Matron snapped at him, her harsh voice cutting through the painful ringing in his ears.

"Yeah," he ground out, forcing his eyes open. Jason scanned the sky and the shuttle's instrumentation, searching out those last few jets.

They popped back up on radar, coming from behind. Jason focused on the rearview camera feed to guide his telekinesis. It hurt, but he ground his teeth against the pain as he telekinetically ripped the wings right off the fighter jets. They fell to earth, no longer a problem.

Matron let out a breath and guided their shuttle ever lower as the jets disappeared from the radar. So did several of the dots that were identified as transport shuttles, caught in the cross fire of enemy missiles. She tried not to watch the numbers dwindle.

"There," Matron said. "Down below. *Finally.*"

Jason opened his eyes, squinting through the brightness as he realized that the open space Matron was aiming for surrounded a large power plant with steam blowing out of the single cooling tower. Bodies were scattered on the ground, some wearing uniforms that Jason recognized all too easily. Matron landed the shuttle close to the broken doors, the vertical landing sending hard vibrations through the shuttle. Jason wrapped a telekinetic shield around the shuttle even as he undid the straps of his flight harness.

"Stay here," he ordered tiredly as he steeled himself for a teleport. Jason arrived near the first set of doors by the security walls and erected a telekinetic shield around himself for protection as he quickly scanned the area.

He didn't know if those lying on the ground were dead or alive and couldn't care. Moving forward, Jason climbed over the downed doors. He was halfway to the power plant's main entrance when someone exited the building. Kerr was a familiar and welcoming sight. Jason was damned glad to see his partner walking on his own two feet, but he could have done without the person that Kerr was helping outside.

Samantha Serca had one arm slung over Kerr's shoulder, limping along beside the other telepath. Jason wrapped a telekinetic shield around the pair as he hurried as fast as he could through the wind to reach them.

"*You're* who Lucas needed?" Jason asked in a disbelieving voice.

Samantha's face was covered in blood from the nose down, her dark blue eyes half-lidded and full of pain. "Fuck you," she slurred.

"The others are inside," Kerr said, jerking his head back the way they'd come, expression strained. "The shuttle?"

"Out front. Hold on."

Jason wrapped his power around them, pictured the shuttle's cargo bay in his mind, and teleported the pair inside the safety of the shuttle. He continued forward, using his power to wrench the second set of blast doors open wider, despite the throbbing in his skull. He swallowed thickly in fear once he got a good look at the group huddled just inside the power plant.

Quinton's arms were a mess, broken to fleshy pulp, white bone sticking out of his skin. His face wasn't much better, but he didn't seem to notice, kneeling as he was beside where Lucas was sitting with Threnody's mostly burned body in his arms. Standing over them was someone Jason had never even known existed. The girl smiled at him, the rictus look pulling at the skin of her face.

"Calvary has arrived," she announced cheerfully, throwing her arms up into the air victoriously.

"Shut up, Kris," Lucas said as he dragged open his eyes.

Jason stared in shock at the girl's gleaming dark blue eyes, the eerie resemblance she had to Lucas. "Holy shit," he breathed. "There's *four* of you fucking Serca kids?"

Lucas glared at him. "Get us to the shuttle, Jason."

He didn't need to be told twice.

Jason teleported them into the shuttle's cargo bay, where Kerr had already strapped Samantha into one of the seats, the girl fully unconscious now.

"Your sister's mind is a broken mess, Lucas," Kerr said, not looking up from where he was administering a sedative to Samantha, the hypospray pulled from their first-aid supplies, along with a portable IV that he strapped to her arm.

Lucas shrugged minutely. "She'll live. She's used to it."

"Matron, get us the fuck out of here," Jason yelled through the open hatch. "What the hell *happened,* Lucas?"

"Kris, help Quinton strap into a seat. Kerr, you've got another patient," Lucas ordered even as he telekinetically hauled a supply trunk over to his side and began to dig through it. "Threnody's alive, but not for much longer."

"I'm not leaving her side," Quinton said.

"I don't need you yet," Lucas said bluntly. "And you're useless to her right now, so stop arguing. Let Kerr see to your arms and face."

Quinton wouldn't move, so Kristen did it for him. The empath touched his arm above the elbow and altered the emotional blocks she'd implanted in his mind, just enough to remind him of the agony his body was keeping from his brain. Quinton's knees buckled and the only reason why he didn't collapse face-first to the deck was because Jason caught him in time.

"Fucking hell," Jason said as he hauled Quinton over to the nearest seat, refusing to let that crazy empath within reach of either of them.

Quinton tried to fight him, but the pain blocks were gone and there was no moving if a telekinetic didn't want you to move. Jason strapped him down and left him to Kerr's tender mercies even as Matron took them into the air again. Jason telekinetically anchored himself to the deck so that he didn't go slamming into the side of the shuttle. He kept Kerr upright as well. Lucas wasn't moving, neither was Kristen, the pair of them anchored around Threnody's too still body. But he could see her chest moving, albeit out of rhythm and far, far too slowly.

"What happened?" Jason asked again.

"She jump-started the electrical grid before the power plant came online," Lucas said without looking up from whatever he was doing. "She was the only one who could."

Because she was the only electrokinetic they had in their group. Jason swallowed, not sure how she could still be *alive* after that stunt. So much of Threnody's skin was bubbled up red and black, following the lines of her damaged nervous system beneath her uniform like burned circuitry.

"I'm keeping her alive, but just barely," Lucas said even as he ripped the sterile plastic off a med-kit item and withdrew a hypospray full of viscous gray matter. "Her mind wants to shut down."

"Is it my turn?" Kristen asked, tugging on the sleeve of Lucas's shirt. "Is it?"

The shuttle gave another violent shake as Matron guided them back into the storm, everyone in the cargo bay held steady by telekinetic anchors. Lucas looked at where Jason was standing over them and held up the hypospray for him to see.

"You're the only one that can save her," Lucas said, dark blue eyes bloodshot in a too pale face, blood dripping out of his nose, trickling from his ears.

"I'm not a medic," Jason said.

"Shut up and listen to me. You're a microtelekinetic behind those shields of yours. At *minimum,* a Class I psion. Your power has the potential to work on the atomic level. This hypospray holds a regulated amount of nanites that I stole sixteen months ago. We don't have a biotank on this shuttle, which means you're going to have to be the driving force behind getting this stuff to work on Threnody."

Jason stared at him. "I don't understand."

"You will soon enough. Kris?"

Lucas's sister perked up. *"Finally."*

The empath reached for Jason, but he shoved her away telekinetically. Kristen stuck her tongue out at him. "Don't touch me," he said hoarsely. "Lucas—what the *hell?*"

Lucas reached out with his own shaky telekinesis, dragging Jason close enough for him to look the other man straight in the eye.

"Listen to me, you fucking selfish piece of shit," Lucas snarled. "Threnody still has a part to play. If she dies here, then it was all for nothing. Everything I've given up and risked—it's all worth *nothing* if she dies, do you understand? You're no one's messiah, Jason. You're just a weapon, and I'm taking the safety switch off of you. You're the only one who can save her, and Kris is the only one who can break through your shields. We don't have *time* for this bullshit!"

Behind them, Quinton said, "Jason. *Please.*"

In the end, it didn't come down to Lucas ordering him or Quinton begging him. It came down to Jason owing them all as much as they owed him. Loyalty could be bought and it could be sold, but the only kind that mattered was the sort gained by way of blood.

Kristen's hands, when she touched him, were cold.

Her mind, as it entered his, was not.

"You taste so good," she whispered into his ear as her empathic power started to eat through Jason's thick natal shields.

Jason screamed with the first bite she took out of his defenses and didn't stop for a long, long time.

[THIRTY-FOUR]

AUGUST 2379

LONDON, UNITED KINGDOM

The last cartel drug lord—mindwiped to within a synapse of a new personality—was escorted out of Nathan's office in a city tower of Brasília. Nathan leaned back in the chair, closing his eyes against the pain of too many psi surgeries in too short a time. Promises were easily broken and wiped away, but it had taken more effort than he would have liked. He'd had to hunt through old memories and thoughts for every last person who could possibly have been involved in holding oil stolen from the government for the Warhounds. The cartels had been useful, and still were, but Nathan had never intended to give them berths on the *Ark*.

Removing every last shred of detail about the Serca Syndicate had taken a toll on him. Coming off the delicate psi surgery he had performed on Elion, adding in all the ones he'd done in Brasília, Nathan knew he had probably lost another year or two of life. Not exactly what he wanted, but so long as he lived to see Mars, these instances when he relied on himself and not his children would continue to happen.

Nathan opened his eyes and got to his feet, the night sky outside the windows dark. The door to the office opened again and Dalia walked in, still in her identity as an executive assistant.

"The shuttle is ready," she told him, hands clasped behind her back.

"We're done here," Nathan said.

They took the human way to the landing docks that lined the length of the city tower, walking out of the Serca Syndicate branch with a group of Warhounds that doubled as bodyguards to human eyes. Nathan didn't bother to hide his departure, even if he had hidden the arrival and departure of the cartel lords. He was known as a hands-on CEO, which meant surprise visits were inflicted on his subordinants.

When they came to the docking area, the computer guided them down the walkway to the correct shuttle, where their pilot was waiting. Teleportation would have been quicker; however, it wasn't an option at the moment. Nathan hated the veneer of humanity he had to keep up at all times, to pretend to be something he wasn't, but the survival of his company required it.

It also required that he have a successor, a position that never seemed to stay filled.

Sir, a telepathic voice said sometime later into his mind when they were halfway across the Atlantic Ocean, heading for London. He recognized Victoria's psi signature immediately. *We have a problem.*

What now?

The report was dumped straight into his public mind, the woman's tension making her thoughts sharp-edged. Nathan jerked up straight in his seat as he realized what had happened.

"Sir?" Dalia asked.

Nathan ignored her, teleporting straight out of the shuttle and into the tense atmosphere of the Warhounds' command center at the top of a city tower, ignoring the warning twinge in his mind from the effort. Nathan had been receiving field reports over the past few hours, but the emergency evacuation was just starting. The wounded coming off the field required Victoria's specialized skills in the arrival room used for teleportation. That's where Nathan found her working on his son. Victoria looked up at Nathan from where she was kneeling on the floor, both hands cupped over Gideon's temples.

"They found him in the power plant," Victoria said as medics worked to stabilize Gideon's vitals, a hover-gurney waiting close by to transport him to medical.

Retrieval teams were bringing back the living and the dead. Nathan's gaze swept the large arrival room with cold precision. Everything must have gone straight to hell and worse in Buffalo in a short time, otherwise he would have been informed earlier of the problem. Nathan cataloged the dead, his eyes coming to rest at last on a charred husk of a human-shaped body, the only thing identifiable about it.

Victoria noticed where he was staring. "Jin Li," she said quietly, looking away. "A nurse ID'd him through a biometrics scan using dental records. There wasn't enough viable tissue left for the process."

This was not how Nathan thought he would lose his best soldier.

His rage coated every thought that crossed his mind as he stepped closer to his one remaining son. Nathan wasn't gentle as he slid his mind past Victoria's and into Gideon's, into those of all the Warhounds that had returned to headquarters. He wanted—*required*—answers.

Samantha and Kristen were not in any of the returning groups. Warhound coming back knew where they were and reported such to Nathan's demands. Only when Nathan pried open Gideon's damaged mind did he find the answers he was missing.

She did this to me, she did this to me was the repeating, wounded mantra that spun through Gideon's thoughts, a memory of Samantha's betrayal of the Syndicate, of her twin, the most prominent thing in his mind.

Nathan did not take the betrayal well.

As Nathan retreated out of the mind of the only child left to him, he felt the mental grid bend in a way it never before had, a precursor to something terrible. He instantly raised his shields, as did every psion in the Warhound ranks. Everyone felt the novalike explosion that ripped through the mental grid. Such power was in that blast, a psionic strength that Nathan had never before encountered, that it scorched across every psion's mind the world over. A person he hadn't known existed—and somehow Lucas *must* have known.

You deceiving little bastard, Nathan thought, something that resembled disgusted awe coursing through his mind as he reached out with his telepathy, struggling to follow that stranger's mind back to its core. *You knew this power existed, didn't you, Lucas?*

The mind winked out on the mental grid before he could reach it, sucked back into a hole that was impossible to find, no matter how hard he searched. Nathan eventually drew back his power, raising all his formidable mental shields once again. He doubted that unknown psion was dead. Lucas took after Nathan too much, whether he liked to admit it or not, and Lucas never took a risk unless he knew he would win. Losing had never been an option for Nathan's eldest child.

Nathan was only now beginning to realize that.

[THIRTY-FIVE]

AUGUST 2379

CANADIAN SHIELD, CANADA

The world opened up in layers, bright filaments of energy, atoms, the connectivity of a living system that nearly broke him.

Jason found it almost impossible to breathe as Kristen ate through his shields with a ferocity that no one else could have matched. She was insane, with a power that operated through murder, and she almost killed him during that psi surgery monitored by Lucas as Matron flew them through the stormy night sky. Kristen tore down every last piece of that mental block, pulling Jason's mind apart to create a hole for all the power he hadn't known existed to come pouring out.

Every single synapse in Jason's brain turned *on* at once when that power connected with the rest of his mind, the overload having no place else to go except down the bond, the psi link that tied him to Kerr. A bridge that Lucas desperately kept blocked with what was left of his telepathic strength while Kerr screamed at him, *Get out of the fucking way.*

It can't be you, Lucas said in a strained mental voice. *It can't be you, Kerr. It has to be Quinton.*

Jason's the only family I've got, Kerr yelled, his Scottish accent getting deeper with every telepathic word he slammed into Lucas's mind. *I'm not going to abandon him!*

You will, eventually. Just not yet.

Enough with your cryptic bullshit, *Lucas! You're* killing *him!*

No. You are. Lucas pulled at the other telepath through the last shreds of the merge that existed between them, gaining just a little bit of mental traction. *You don't need him anymore. Not like this. And he can't need you. Let it go, Kerr. Let* him *go.*

Fuck you if you think—

You'll kill them both if you don't break the bond and let me attach it to Quinton's mind. You'll kill us all. I can't break it, not right now, but I can keep him from bleeding into you, and then we're all fucked. This is how it's supposed to be, so let it fucking be.

Kerr was silent for a heartbeat, his mind a ball of tension and agony, a swirl of emotion that leaked through his shields into Lucas's ragged thoughts.

Blame me for it when he wakes up, Lucas said.

Oh, I will, Kerr said in a quiet, deadly voice. *Fucking count on it.*

It won't make you feel better.

Fuck you, Lucas. Fuck you.

Carefully, unflinchingly, Kerr severed the bond that had linked him for so long to his partner, to his brother, to the only family the Strykers had ever allowed him to have beneath the shadow of the government. The link had saved his life, his mind, his *sanity,* for so many years. That he had lived this long was a testament to Jason's strength. That it felt as if he were cutting off his own arm told Kerr how much he had grown to rely on the telekinetic, a reliance he would never regret and would always, always miss.

Kerr broke the bond on his side, unable to get past Lucas and into

Jason's mind. It left a gaping, raw hole in his mind where Jason had once resided, the ragged ends of the bond unraveling too fast for him to keep hold of. Left him feeling empty and alone, completely bereft.

Let me, Lucas said. *Just—hold on.*

He was holding back an immense amount of power. Kerr could feel that, could feel the surge in Jason's mind that was burning through the layers of telepathic shields that Lucas had placed around the telekinetic's mind, the protective casings simply being eaten away. Kristen was somewhere inside that mess, steadily taking down Jason's shields, the only one who could do it and survive the overload. Lucas was right, they were running out of time, but that didn't make the transfer any easier.

Why me? Quinton demanded to know as Lucas pulled the pyrokinetic into the psi surgery.

Does it matter? Lucas said tiredly. *He needs another mind, Quinton. He's carrying too much power for one person to contain and live with. Your power is kinetic-based, a better match than Kerr ever could be.*

If it had been anyone else lying in Lucas's arms, Quinton would have refused. And he could have, he knew that. Lucas was worn too thin, carrying too much, to be able to fight on a dozen different fronts right now. But his refusal would kill Threnody, would kill Jason, and that wasn't something Quinton could ever willingly allow and be able to live with himself afterward.

Quinton dropped all of his shields. He had no other choice. Lucas entered his mind, going down deep to the very bottom where the channels that his power stemmed from were located. There, Lucas anchored the bond to Quinton's mind with Kerr's help, tying him to Jason more permanently than the Stryker psi surgeons had been able to tie Jason to Kerr. It hurt, as if Lucas were digging out pieces of who Quinton was and discarding them all, carving out space in his mind to make room for someone else in a place that should have only held him.

Ready? Lucas asked.

No.

It didn't matter.

Lucas removed the block, dragging Kristen out of Jason's mind as she tore apart the last barrier. He threw up a mental shield around them both, around all of them, as Jason's mind exploded.

No thoughts. Just power. A white-hot burn that turned the world inside out and fought for space, for room, for the body that housed it to breathe. It ricocheted down the bond, straight into Quinton's mind, burning through the synapses in his skull and changing everything that he was into whatever Jason needed him to be in order to survive.

An anchor. A shield.

A victim.

Quinton screamed, the sound brief. His eyes rolled up into his skull and he passed out where he sat strapped into his seat. On the deck of the shuttle, Jason lay sprawled beside Lucas and Threnody, bleeding out of his ears and nose. The world was so much *clearer* than it had ever been before as awareness returned in slow, painful increments.

Lucas gripped the hypospray in his hand and injected Threnody with nanites, his mind in hers, forcing her to keep her heart beating, to keep her lungs moving.

You know how to do this, Jason, Lucas said. *Aisling said you would. It's all instinct at this point. It always is.*

Jason turned his head, his power filling the shuttle like a heavy, un-wanted pressure. He closed his eyes, his mind in pieces but still being guided by Lucas's implacable will.

Deeper.

The walls of the shuttle. The burned skin of Threnody's body.

Deeper.

The charred lines of her muscles. The hot flow of her blood.

Deeper.

The nanites that swam there, with their ability to coax cells toward the regeneration of the human body, waiting for their orders.

Deeper.

The feel of his microtelekinesis pulling at Threnody's DNA.

[THIRTY-SIX]

The order came at 0600 hours, on a weekday. It came through the usual channels, and Ciari took the uplink in her office, a twenty-second demand that Erik delivered in a quiet, emotionless voice at odds with the furious expression on his face.

"We require the OIC of the Strykers Syndicate to present herself before the World Court to explain the actions taken in Buffalo."

No more and no less, but the threat was there; the anger and the hate.

The world press was already reporting on the fighting that had taken place in Buffalo, streaming eyewitness accounts of what had happened in the bunkers and aboveground. The most downloaded image from that stormy night was a holopic taken by a military jet, of the sprawl that made up the city burning like a star, running on full power for the first time in generations.

Not the sort of thing the World Court needed to be dealing with when they were so close to the launch.

Pirate streams were already cutting into main media downloads, impossible to ignore. The government was having a difficult time containing everything. Ciari could feel the quiet shift of a city's emotions moving from fear into something much more difficult to deal with—suspicion. Resentment. A mob mentality, when it encompassed the majority of a population, couldn't be ignored.

Ciari dressed with care that morning, in her best uniform, not a hair out of place. Appearances were everything, and she had to look the part she played down to the shine on her boots. She walked with measured strides to Jael's lab two floors below, where the CMO was busy dealing with the wounded Strykers under her care who had survived the field operation in Buffalo. She didn't take kindly to being interrupted.

"I need to speak with you," Ciari said. "Privately."

Jael, having heard about Ciari's summons from Keiko, kept her attention on the datapad in her hands and the Stryker on an exam table. "It can wait."

"No, it can't."

Jael arched a dark eyebrow at the steely tone of Ciari's voice before she sighed and ordered a nurse to take care of her patient. Then she silently led Ciari to an empty exam room, which was harder than it sounded, since most of the rooms were occupied. She watched as Ciari went to stand beside the exam table, showing something Jael might have called regret if it had been anyone else.

"There's something I need you to do for me," Ciari said. "And we have very little time to do it."

"What's going on?"

"I'm pregnant."

In the years after that she survived, Jael would point to that moment, to those words, as the start of it all, of the beginning of the end.

[THIRTY-SEVEN]

AUGUST 2379

ARCTIC CIRCLE

Lucas," Matron said over the comm system, sounding tired, voice raspy and dry. "You should see this."

He blinked open eyes more red than blue, exhaustion, pain, and stress carving deep lines into his face. Blood was dried in streaks over the lower half of his face, his mouth, his throat. Dark, brown-red stains that flaked off as he moved, hands fumbling with the straps of his flight harness, the portable IV and tubing strapped to his left arm catching a bit on the edge of his seat. Everyone except Matron was hooked up to one of them, the IV fluids barely enough to keep them all stabilized. His head ached in a way it never had before, body weakened due to mental damage.

Lucas hit the audio on the control panel of his seat and said, "On my way," out loud instead of telepathically. His mind was so badly strained, teetering between the edge of psi shock and something dangerously deeper, that *thinking* hurt. A psi link was out of the question.

He spared a glance for the people around him as he levered himself to his feet. His sisters, slumped together in a sprawl two seats away from him, tied down by individual harnesses and strong support restraints. Threnody, who was strapped down across a row of flight seats in the center of the cargo bay, hooked up to a portable IV they had secured to the seatback near her hip and a trauma kit to monitor her vitals. The nanites in her veins were still struggling to fix damaged organs, to turn burnt flesh into new, pieces of her skin sloughing off in slow, slow increments.

Quinton, sitting on the opposite side of the cargo bay, his arms and face slowly becoming whole again courtesy of the nanites Lucas had injected him with and Jason's power. Kerr had set Quinton's broken bones as much as he'd been able to. Jason was seated next to Quinton, one hand wrapped around Quinton's wrist, face so white that Lucas could see the veins beneath his skin, power like an inferno behind the new secondary mental shields his mind had created. Kerr sat on Jason's other side, with the ravages of his fight and his loss pressed deep into his body, still unconscious.

All of them a mess. All of them half-dead, it seemed.

Lucas stumbled his way to the hatch, unable to stand up straight, and pressed his hand against the control panel to open it. The flight deck was marginally warmer than the cargo bay. Lucas took the navigator's seat, collapsing into it with little grace.

"Got a total," Matron said, not looking at him as she passed over a hypospray. "Roll call puts us at nine."

Lucas took the hypospray and shot himself full of painkillers. It was a momentary relief that wouldn't numb him long enough to be useful. Closing his eyes, he scratched at the dried blood on his face. Nine shuttles out of thirty-six had survived the launch out of Buffalo and the derecho that was still blowing its way toward the Atlantic. Nine shuttles, which was more than he'd thought they'd actually come away with.

"Take a look at that."

It took effort to open his eyes again, to focus his blurry, tired vision on what Matron wanted him to see. The surviving shuttles were flying in a jagged line over the Arctic Ocean, almost too low to be safe as they struggled to stay beneath whatever security measures the government had up here. Which would be enough, but not too much, because the World Court couldn't afford to draw attention to what they hoarded.

On the horizon, in the constant daylight of an Arctic summer, a black dot could be seen, growing larger with every kilometer they put behind them.

Spitsbergen.

The Svalbard Global Seed and Gene Bank.

Matron's voice came out softly, barely stronger than a whisper. "Your orders?"

"Get us down without them noticing us," Lucas said, curling his hands over the edge of the seat, light from the midnight sun biting into his dark blue eyes. "We've got a world to steal."

PART NINE
PROLOGUE

SESSION DATE: **2128.10.02**
LOCATION: **Institute of Psionics Research**
CLEARANCE ID: **Dr. Amy Bennett**
SUBJECT: **2581**
FILE NUMBER: **921**

She sits listlessly in the chair, a tired, wilted shadow of herself. The wires that connect her to machines are a heavy weight she has long since given up fighting against.

"Aisling," the doctor says, desperation and fear coloring her voice as she leans over the table, body shaking ever so slightly. "Please. You have to help us."

The girl turns her head slowly, looking at the camera. She blinks, the bruises beneath her bleached-out violet eyes darker than her irises. "Are you listening? I can see it, Matthew. It's going to be okay."

The door to the white room slides open. Two more attendants in lab coats rush into the room, mouths open in half-formed screams that the camera is barely able to pick up through the static that cuts across the screen.

"It's going to be—"